By L T Shearer

The Cat Who Caught a Killer
The Cat Who Solved Three Murders
The Cat Who Cracked a Cold Case
The Cat and the Christmas Kidnapper
The Cat and the Halloween Murder

The Cat and the Halloween Murder

L T SHEARER

The Cat and the Halloween Murder

MACMILLAN

First published 2026 by Macmillan
an imprint of Pan Macmillan
The Smithson, 6 Briset Street, London EC1M 5NR
EU representative: Macmillan Publishers Ireland Ltd, 1st Floor,
The Liffey Trust Centre, 117–126 Sheriff Street Upper,
Dublin 1 D01 YC43
Associated companies throughout the world

ISBN 978-1-0350-7632-1 HB
ISBN 978-1-0350-7633-8 TPB

1 3 5 7 9 8 6 4 2

A CIP catalogue record for this book is available from the British Library.

Typeset by Palimpsest Book Production Ltd, Falkirk, Stirlingshire
Printed and bound in the UK using 100% Renewable Electricity
by CPI Group (UK) Ltd

MIX
Paper | Supporting
responsible forestry
FSC
www.fsc.org
FSC® C116313

The Cat and the Halloween Murder

1

'Are we nearly there yet?' said Conrad, in a sing-song voice that suggested he was joking. He was standing on the roof of the canal boat, staring ahead as the wind ruffled his black, white and brown fur.

'Very nearly,' replied Lulu. She pulled the throttle back to slow the engine. There were half a dozen canal boats moored ahead of them, and there was nothing a boater hated more than being tossed around by the wake of a speeding vessel. Not that a canal boat could actually go fast – the top speed of *The Lark* was about four miles an hour on a good day.

Conrad sniffed the air. 'I think it might rain,' he said.

'I do hope not,' said Lulu. She had long since grown used to the fact that Conrad could talk. When he had walked into her life and onto her narrowboat in Little Venice, she had almost fainted when he first spoke to her. But now it seemed the most natural thing in the world, although she was the only one that he spoke to. Anyone else would merely get a meow or a purr. Conrad was her secret, and hers alone.

Conrad turned to look at her, and she smiled. He really was a good-looking cat. His eyes were the vibrant green of emeralds kissed by the sun, and his mouth usually formed a sly smile, as if something was amusing him. The left side of his head was brown and white, the right mainly black, and there was an uneven white patch around his mouth and nose. His lithe body and tail were thick stripes of brown and black and his rear legs had white socks.

'We're not going to see any Shakespeare while we're here, are we?' he said.

'I don't think so. There's nothing planned.'

'That's a relief. When you first said you wanted to visit your goddaughter in Stratford-upon-Avon, my big worry was that you would make me sit through one of his plays.'

'I take it you're not a fan of the Bard?'

'Oh no, his plays are fine. It's just that Shakespeare was always more of a dog man – "let slip the dogs of war", and all that.'

'No mentions of cats, then?'

'He mentions them, but often as an insult. So in *All's Well That Ends Well*, Bertram says: "I could endure anything before but a cat, and now he's a cat to me." That's not nice, is it? And in *A Midsummer Night's Dream*, Lysander says: "Hang off, thou cat, thou burr! Vile thing . . ." But the worst, I think, is in *Hamlet*, when Hamlet himself says: "The cat will mew, the dog will have his day." So the dog is a hero and the cat just meows.'

'I don't know, Conrad. It sounds as if you might be reading too much into it.'

'I much prefer T. S. Eliot. Now, he was a writer who appreciated cats.'

'Next you're going to tell me that you're a big fan of the *Cats* musical.'

'I love it,' said Conrad. 'Andrew Lloyd Webber did a great job of adapting Eliot's *Old Possum's Book of Practical Cats*. I've seen it many times over the years.'

'Conrad, how old are you exactly?'

Conrad smiled. 'Let's just say I still have several of my nine lives to go,' he said. 'How many godchildren do you have?'

'Eight. Four boys and four girls.'

'That's a lot.'

'I think people assume that because I don't have children of my own, I'm a good choice as godmother.'

Lulu increased the throttle as they passed the last of the moored canal boats. Ahead of them was a wooden sign reading BANCROFT BASIN. That was their destination – a canal basin framed by the Bancroft Gardens, a manicured public space for festivals and picnics, and behind it the imposing building that was the Royal Shakespeare Theatre. Lulu smiled to herself. Conrad's dislike of Shakespeare would be tested to the full during his visit to Stratford-upon-Avon; the Bard's presence was everywhere.

Lulu knew that the basin was a historical landmark – it had been built in the early nineteenth century, marking the terminus of the Stratford-upon-Avon Canal and its connection to the River Avon. It would have played a crucial role in the canal system during the industrial revolution, but those days were long gone, and the working narrowboats had been replaced by tourists and liveaboards. Watching over the basin was a huge statue of Shakespeare, deep in thought and holding a pen and scroll.

Conrad sighed when he saw the statue. 'He really is everywhere,' he groaned.

'He's Stratford-upon-Avon's most famous son. And he is generally regarded as the greatest writer in the history of the English language.'

Conrad snorted but didn't say anything.

'That statue was built in Paris,' Lulu said. 'It took twelve years and was finished in 1888. The sculptor was Lord Ronald Gower, and he used Bath and York stone and bronze fittings and figures. It's actually called the Gower Monument by most people.'

'Wonderful,' said Conrad, his voice loaded with sarcasm. 'But you are starting to sound a little bit like a tour guide.'

Lulu ignored the jibe. 'He put four of his most famous characters on the small plinths that surround the main one – Lady Macbeth, Hamlet, Prince Hal and Falstaff.'

'You've obviously been here before.'

'Several times. Stratford-upon-Avon is one of my favourite places, and I do enjoy spending time with Celia and her husband. They're a lovely couple.'

'How did you come to be Celia's godmother?'

'Her mother was a good friend – Roseanne, but everyone called her Rosie. She was a social worker in London, which is where I met her. Then she married and gave up work to raise her family. She had two daughters, and Celia is the older.'

'Where is Rosie now?'

Lulu grimaced. 'She died of cancer when Celia had just finished university. Celia came to stay with me for a few months after it happened. It was a tough time for her.'

'What about her father?'

'Ah, yes. He left when the younger daughter, Charlotte, went to university. He divorced Rosie for no apparent reason, just claimed that he wasn't happy.'

'Did he know she was sick? That would be awful.'

'She didn't know she had cancer until after he'd left. In fact, she never even told him. She said she didn't want him coming back out of sympathy.'

'I can understand that,' said Conrad.

'Anyway, he met a Vietnamese lady online and now he lives in Saigon, or whatever they call it these days.'

'Ho Chi Minh City,' said Conrad.

'Thank you.'

'You're welcome. And what brought Celia to Stratford-upon-Avon?'

'Her husband, Brian. She met him at university. Brian was studying English Literature and Celia did a BA in Theatre Management. Brian became a teacher and Celia worked for several West End theatres; then they moved here about eight years ago to be near his parents. Now she works for the Royal Shakespeare Theatre and Brian does online teaching – when he isn't writing his novel.'

'Oh, he's a writer?'

'He writes. But he hasn't had anything published yet. It's a tough business.'

'Shakespeare did all right out of it.'

'I suppose he did. But back in Shakespeare's day there was no YouTube, Facebook, Netflix or TikTok. There were fewer things vying for people's attention, so they would flock to see Shakespeare's plays.'

Lulu slowed the engine again as they neared the entrance to the basin, then turned smoothly into it. There were plenty of free berths. In the summer months the basin would be packed to the gills, but now it was the end of October and only the hardiest tourists were taking to the water.

She guided *The Lark* into a berth and cut the engine. Then she grabbed the centre line and jumped onto the jetty, pulling the boat closer and tying it up. She followed up with the fore and aft lines, then jumped back onto the rear deck.

'I do wish I could help,' said Conrad. 'But no opposable thumbs.'

'Which is why you can't play the piano, of course.'

'No, I can't play the piano because I'm tone deaf. It was me who put the cat in caterwauling.'

'That's funny,' said Lulu. She looked at her watch. 'Right, I have time for a quick shower before we head off to see Celia and Brian.'

'Do they live far from here?'

'Not far at all. Stratford-upon-Avon is quite a small town – just thirty thousand or so people.'

'Will we be eating?'

'Oh yes, Celia is cooking. And I told her that I have a plus one who is very partial to sea bass.'

'Purr-fect,' said Conrad. 'See what I did there?'

'A play on words,' said Lulu. 'Very clever. Shakespeare would have been proud of you.'

She headed down the steps into the saloon. Conrad padded after her. They had been on the move for almost five hours, and Lulu definitely needed a shower and a change of clothes. Conrad jumped up onto the sofa and began grooming himself.

'You cats have it so easy sometimes,' Lulu said. 'A few licks and you're good to go. Me, I need to shower, put on make-up, decide what to wear . . .'

'There are definitely some advantages to being a cat,' agreed Conrad. 'Though the lack of opposable thumbs does hold us back when it comes to world domination.'

Lulu chuckled as she headed towards the shower room.

2

Celia Brownlow and her husband lived in a pretty terraced house just a ten-minute walk from the basin. Lulu had changed into a blue and white striped Karen Millen dress, but it was a cold evening, so she was wearing her sheepskin jacket over it. Conrad was curled round her shoulders, his nose close to her left ear, his tail draped over her right collar-bone. As always, she marvelled at how little he weighed – she barely felt him at all.

'Are those zombies?' said Conrad.

Coming towards them as they walked along Celia's street were four figures, moving slowly and unsteadily. They were wearing ragged clothes and appeared to have blood smeared across their faces.

'Yes, I rather think they are.'

'Is that normal in Stratford-upon-Avon?'

Lulu laughed. 'It's Halloween, Conrad. Didn't you notice all the houses with pumpkins and skeletons in the windows?'

'I just thought that was the way people decorated their houses here.'

Lulu stopped and turned to face the houses on the other side of the road. One of them had a pumpkin lantern in the window and a HAPPY HALLOWEEN banner above the door. The house next to it had a full-size plastic skeleton hanging on the front door and fake cobwebs across the windows.

'You thought the houses were like this all year round?'

'I have to admit I wasn't really paying attention,' said Conrad.

The zombies reached them. The two tall ones were clearly Mum and Dad, shepherding their young son and daughter, who both carried plastic buckets half-filled with chocolates and sweets. They all had grey and white make-up and streaks of red around their mouths. They were wearing what looked like pyjamas that had been ripped and torn.

'I love your outfits,' said Lulu.

'Thank you,' said the mum. 'I love your cat.'

'Is it a real cat?' said the little boy.

'Oh yes,' said Lulu.

'Meow,' said Conrad, as if to confirm what she had said.

Both children laughed. 'Have a great evening,' said the father, and then all four resumed walking unsteadily along the pavement, moaning and groaning.

'They call it trick-or-treating, don't they?' said Conrad, as the zombie family ambled away.

'They do, yes.'

'So that would be demanding money with menaces, wouldn't it?'

Lulu chuckled. 'I suppose it could be seen that way. But really it's just so children can get some free sweets and chocolates.'

'And we all know how good sweets and chocolates are for the teeth of growing children.'

Lulu laughed out loud. 'Well, somebody got out of the wrong side of bed this morning.'

'Do I sound grumpy?'

'Yes, Conrad, you do.'

'I shall try to look on the bright side.'

'And you do have sea bass to look forward to.'

Conrad purred. 'There is that.'

They reached Celia's house. It was a fairly modern brick building with two large white-trimmed bay windows on the first floor and smaller white-framed windows below them. The front door was also white with a small portico above it. Lulu pressed the doorbell and after a few seconds Celia opened the door. She was wearing a tight-fitting blue dress in a flower pattern and her chestnut hair fell in loose curls around her shoulders. Her face broke into a smile. 'Lulu, so lovely to see you.' She stepped forward to kiss Lulu on both cheeks, then jumped back as she noticed Conrad. 'Oh my goodness me, there's a cat on your shoulders.'

'This is Conrad, my plus one,' said Lulu.

'Of course it is,' said Celia. 'I just didn't expect to see him riding on your shoulders. I suppose I thought you'd have him on a lead.'

'Oh no, Conrad would never wear a collar,' said Lulu. 'Collars imply ownership, and no one owns Conrad.'

'Did he tell you that?' laughed Celia.

'Actually, he did,' said Lulu.

'That's so funny,' said Celia. 'Come in, come in.' She stepped aside and Lulu walked through into the hallway. 'Brian is in the sitting room.' Celia gestured at a door to the right. 'Through there. I'll get some wine. Is rosé okay?'

'Perfect,' said Lulu. She went into the sitting room as Celia headed for the kitchen. There were two leather sofas either side of a Victorian fireplace that surrounded an electric coal-effect fire. Above the fireplace was a flat-screen television showing a wildlife documentary with the sound off.

Brian was sitting on one of the sofas reading a magazine. He was wearing a grey crew-neck jumper that looked as if it might be cashmere and dark green herringbone trousers. He was barefoot, but there was a pair of slippers next to the sofa.

Brian tossed his magazine onto the coffee table and stood up. 'Welcome, welcome,' he said. 'Let me take your coat.'

Conrad jumped down from Lulu's shoulders and sprang up onto an armchair by the door.

'Now that is a well-trained cat,' said Brian, helping Lulu off with her coat.

'I think he just uses his initiative.'

Brian took the coat out into the hall to hang it up. Lulu sat on one of the sofas. 'So you came up on a longboat, Celia tells me,' said Brian as he came back into the room.

Lulu laughed. 'It was the Vikings who used longboats,' she said. 'Mine is a narrowboat. But yes, I'm moored in the Bancroft Basin.'

'And how long did it take to get here from London? A couple of days?'

Lulu laughed again. 'Fifteen.'

Brian's jaw dropped. 'Fifteen days? But it's a two-hour drive.'

'Of course it is. At sixty miles an hour. But a narrowboat travels at three miles an hour. And that's before you start dealing with the locks. There's about a hundred and seventy locks between here and London, and each one takes me ten minutes or so. So the locks alone take more than twenty-four hours.'

Brian shook his head. 'That's amazing. I can't imagine taking fifteen days to travel, what, a hundred miles?'

'It does give you a better sense of distance,' said Lulu. 'You appreciate just how far apart places are. And it's the travelling that makes it such fun – the people you meet, the sights you see.'

Celia came back with a bottle of wine and three glasses. She popped the cork, filled the glasses and gave one to Lulu and one to her husband. They clinked glasses. 'Welcome back to Stratford-upon-Avon,' said Celia.

'And happy birthday!' said Lulu. 'Or rather, happy day before your birthday. What plans do you have to celebrate?'

'Brian has arranged a party at my favourite restaurant tomorrow. He says we need to make a splash because you're only forty once. I told him I was planning to stay thirty-nine for the next five years.' She smiled and sipped her wine.

'And we have a surprise for you tonight,' said Brian. 'There's a midnight performance of *Macbeth* in an old church nearby. Well, it starts at ten and should finish at midnight.'

'So, Shakespeare by night,' said Lulu. She looked over at Conrad, who was still on the armchair. His eyes were closed, but his tail twitched. 'How lovely.'

'One of my friends is in it,' said Celia. 'Actually, she's playing the part of Lady Macbeth. Amy Jenner, she's a teacher at one of the local primary schools.'

'It's one of my favourite plays,' said Lulu. She smiled as Conrad's tail twitched again.

'And there's a Halloween twist,' said Brian. 'The audience will be in fancy dress.'

'Oh – I don't have fancy dress,' said Lulu. 'Space is at a premium on a canal boat.'

'It's all sorted. I have witches' outfits for us both. And

what's great is that one of the witches in *Macbeth* has a cat as a familiar.'

'Really?'

'Yes. A cat called Greymalkin.'

Lulu flashed Conrad a sly look. 'Greymalkin – what a wonderful name for a cat.' Conrad's tail twitched, twice.

'And Brian will be going as Romeo.'

Brian smiled at Lulu. 'You are going to love my codpiece.'

She laughed. 'I'm sure I will.'

'Right,' said Celia. 'Let's get dinner out of the way, and then we can try on our outfits.'

3

Dinner was delicious. Celia was a terrific cook at the best of times, but tonight she had excelled herself. The starter was a tasty beef satay with Thai peanut sauce. Conrad tried some – without the sauce – and loved it. The main course was a traditional coq au vin with sides of new potatoes and broccoli, and the dessert was a light and creamy crème brûlée that melted in Lulu's mouth. Celia had boiled the sea bass for Conrad, and he bolted it down.

After finishing the meal and a bottle of very good red wine that had been the perfect accompaniment to the chicken, Lulu really felt like sleeping. But Celia was clearly keen to see the *Macbeth* performance, so she drank two cups of coffee, hoping the caffeine would perk her up.

Celia fetched their matching witch outfits and they went into the sitting room to try them on as Brian went upstairs for his Romeo costume. There were long black cloaks that were actually quite warm, which meant Lulu wouldn't need to wear her sheepskin jacket, and a wide-brimmed conical black hat with fake grey hair hanging from the inside.

Lulu put on the hat and arranged the hair, then checked herself in the mirror. She burst out laughing. 'I look as if I'm a hundred years old,' she said.

'Do you think we should add witchy make-up?' asked Celia.

'I think this is probably enough,' said Lulu. 'Did you buy them, or are they rentals?'

'Oh, I've had them for a while, but we hired Brian's costume.'

'And it fits like a glove,' said Brian, appearing in the doorway. He was wearing a velvet doublet with gold trim, brocade breeches and a large, padded codpiece. Cream tights, leather boots and a feathered cap completed the look. He grinned and gave them a theatrical bow. 'I am at your service, ladies,' he said.

Both women laughed. 'That's amazing,' said Lulu. 'It looks made to measure.'

'Especially the codpiece,' laughed Celia. 'Now, I have just one thing to finish off my costume.' She headed to the kitchen and returned with a witch's broom, a long smooth handle with a bundle of twigs attached with a leather strap. She grinned as she held it up. 'I'm ready for my game of Quidditch,' she said.

'Brilliant,' said Lulu.

'I only have the one broomstick, but I think Conrad as your familiar is all you need,' said Celia.

Lulu smiled at Conrad. He was sitting on one of the sofas, watching them with what she was sure was a look of disdain. 'My Greymalkin,' she said.

Celia looked at her watch. 'We'd best be going,' she said. 'I have tickets, but seating is first come, first served.'

Lulu scooped up Conrad and let him make himself comfortable on her shoulders. 'Every witch needs a familiar,' she said. He made a soft growling sound and she stroked him under the chin. 'Only joking,' she murmured.

They left the house, and Brian set the alarm and locked the doors. There were still trick-or-treaters around, although now they were mainly teenagers. They passed one group of four who had all dressed up as the serial killer from the *Halloween* films, with white masks, dark blue overalls and what were hopefully plastic machetes. Lulu remembered what Conrad had said about demanding money with menaces. She had to admit that if these scary figures appeared on her doorstep, she would probably give them anything they wanted.

'Hello, Mrs Brownlow,' said one of the figures, waving his machete.

Celia frowned at him and he raised his mask. He was a young teenager with pale blond eyebrows and a cheeky smile. 'Oh, hello Alex. That's a pretty gruesome costume. Jason, right?'

Alex pulled his mask down. 'No, Jason was in the *Friday the 13th* films. We're Michael Myers from the *Halloween* series.' He waved his machete and made a ghostly wailing noise.

'Say hi to your mum, Alex.'

'I will do, Mrs Brownlow.'

The boys walked away, laughing.

'I suppose it's the one night of the year when you can walk around like that,' said Brian.

'You probably wouldn't get away with it in London,' said Lulu. 'There'd be armed response vehicles everywhere and it could end very badly.'

She looked around. There was a group of what looked like vampires on the other side of the road: long capes, white faces and fangs. A girl vampire waved, and Lulu waved back.

'It's such a nice town,' said Lulu. 'I can see why you enjoy living here. It's certainly a slower pace of life than London.'

'It's not all sweetness and light,' said Celia. 'There's a growing homelessness problem here, shoplifting is on the increase and you often smell cannabis when you're walking through the city centre.'

'That sounds more like London,' said Lulu.

'And last week one of the doctors at our local medical centre killed himself.'

'Oh no, that's terrible.'

'It came as a shock to us all. I saw him several times last year when my blood sugar levels went a bit crazy, and he was so nice and helpful. Dr Mackenzie.'

'Lovely man,' said Brian.

'Did he leave a note?' asked Lulu.

'He did,' said Brian. 'Apparently he had money problems and other issues. The note wasn't made public, but the police said there were no suspicious circumstances.'

'Doctors deal with a lot of pain and unhappiness, and that can take its toll,' said Lulu.

'There's the church,' said Brian. Ahead of them was a weathered stone building with a tall steeple. Ivy obscured much of the stonework, trimmed back just enough to frame the arched stained-glass windows, which were dirty but unbroken. The heavy wooden front door was dark with age. The church stood at the junction of two roads, surrounded by a tidy churchyard edged with lavender and yew trees. A low stone wall encrusted with moss ran around the graveyard. Set into the wall was a roofed lychgate, and next to it was a large sign announcing that the Stratford Players were performing *Macbeth* at 10 p.m. and that tickets were still available. Taped to the top of the sign was a handwritten note: 'THE PART OF MACBETH WILL NOW BE PLAYED BY MR EDGAR LAKE.'

'Is that significant?' asked Lulu. 'Is he well known?'

'No, it looks as if there has been a change,' said Celia. 'A local priest was supposed to be Macbeth. The Reverend Troy Harper.'

'Is this his church?'

'Oh no, this church has been closed for years. Well, closed as a church, anyway. It's now used as a community space. The Reverend Harper's church is a few minutes away. St Mary's.'

They walked along the path between moss-covered graves and crosses, their feet crunching on the gravel.

A dozen or so people, all in fancy dress, were lined up in front of the main entrance, where a middle-aged lady in a pirate costume was checking tickets. Eventually they reached the front of the line, and Celia showed her mobile phone to the pirate.

'What's a pirate's favourite letter?' Brian asked the woman as she checked their e-tickets.

'That would be RRRR,' she said.

'I think you'll find it's the C,' said Brian. They all chuckled as the pirate ushered them inside.

There were ten rows of pews in the nave, and another few dozen wooden chairs had been brought in and placed at the sides. Where the pulpit and altar had once been was a stage with black curtains drawn across it. There was a large gold theatrical mask on each side of the curtains, with STRATFORD PLAYERS across the top in gold letters.

The first four rows were full but there was space in the fifth, so Brian led the way. Almost everyone had turned up in fancy dress, and many had stuck with a Shakespearean theme – there were several Antonys and Cleopatras, quite a few men in togas and laurel wreaths, and, it had to be said, at least a dozen other witches. There were non-Shakespearean costumes, too, including a very impressive Darth Vader and a family who had come as masked *Squid Game* guards, complete with plastic guns. Lulu shook her head at the thought of what would happen if masked figures were seen waving guns in London, even ones that were clearly toys.

Celia and Brian filed into the fifth row and sat down. Lulu took the aisle pew. She lifted Conrad off her shoulders and placed him on her lap. He curled up and was soon asleep. The nave gradually filled up, and as the clock drew close to 10 p.m. there were very few seats available.

Celia leaned closer to Lulu. 'I wonder if we should take off our hats,' she said. 'I think we may be blocking the view of people behind us.'

Lulu looked over her shoulder. 'I think you're right,' she said. They both took off their black hats and stashed them under the seats.

'There's a good crowd,' said Brian, looking around.

'They're a popular group,' said Celia.

'Have you seen them before?' asked Lulu.

Celia nodded. 'I come to all their performances. They do good farces and comedies and often do Shakespeare, but this is the first time I've seen them do *Macbeth*. I'm really looking forward to it.'

'I'm surprised they haven't asked you to help them, with your background in theatrical management.'

Celia laughed. 'Oh Lulu, that really would be a busman's holiday. The last thing I'd want after a hard day at the RST would be to get involved in amateur dramatics.'

The curtains parted and a man appeared. He was in his

sixties, grey haired, and he wore chain mail over a dark woollen tunic with a thick leather belt from which hung a ceremonial sword.

'That's the director,' whispered Celia.

The audience went quiet as the man pulled back his shoulders and raised his chin. 'For anyone who doesn't recognize me in costume, I am Henry Richards, director and producer of tonight's performance,' he said, his voice booming out around the church. 'And due to circumstances beyond my control, I will be playing the part of Banquo. So please be gentle with me.' He smiled and did a half-bow, and there was a ripple of quiet applause. 'The reason I am playing Banquo tonight is because Mr Edgar Lake, who was scheduled to play that part, is instead taking the lead role. So, again, please be gentle with him. Tonight's performance should be, if I have got the timings correct, exactly two hours in duration with no intermission, which means we will be ending precisely at midnight – the witching hour. Could I ask you to make sure that your mobile phone devices are switched off or are on silent.' He spread out his arms. 'And now, without further ado, let us get on with the play – because, as the Bard himself said, the play is the thing.' He bowed and disappeared behind the curtains to a smattering of applause.

The curtains stayed closed for a full thirty seconds, then drew back to reveal three witches sitting around a cauldron on a Scottish moor. Lights flickered, and there was a roll of thunder.

Lulu thought the play was surprisingly good, considering it was an amateur production and the understudy was playing Macbeth. He was in his late twenties, tall, with jet-black hair that kept falling over his eyes. He had a moustache and a goatee beard, but they looked fake.

The director made a good job of playing Banquo, Macbeth's friend and ultimately his victim. Lulu knew the play well – she had seen it several times over the years, including a 1994 performance at the Barbican starring Derek Jacobi, so it was well-trodden ground for her. She gently stroked Conrad, letting the words flow over her as the plot unfolded – the prophecy of the witches, then Lady Macbeth urging her husband to kill King Duncan and framing Duncan's guards after Macbeth murdered the king in his sleep. Macbeth, having been crowned king, then ordered the death of his friend Banquo.

'Your friend Amy is very good,' Lulu whispered, and Celia nodded.

The curtains closed and opened again. This was the banquet scene, Lulu knew – Act 3, Scene 4, where Macbeth sees Banquo's ghost. A pivotal scene, showing Macbeth's descent into madness. Macbeth, having seen the ghost sitting in his chair, began talking to him, now and then drinking from a large goblet.

Lady Macbeth was clearly upset by her husband's behaviour. 'You have displaced the mirth, broke the good meeting, with most admired disorder,' she said.

She tried to take his goblet away, but he moved it out of reach and took another swig. 'Can such things be, and overcome us like a summer's cloud, without our special wonder?' he said, then staggered backwards. He coughed, and wine trickled from between his lips. Lady Macbeth looked at him anxiously.

Macbeth coughed again, then gasped. He had more to say,

Lulu knew. It was quite a long speech. The coughing continued. Lulu frowned. Macbeth had never choked like this in any production she'd seen before. Something was wrong. Something was very wrong.

Everyone on stage was looking at Macbeth now. He was swaying, and the goblet slipped from his fingers and tumbled to the floor, wine spilling over his shoes. He put one hand to his chest and his mouth opened wide. Red froth appeared from between his lips. He was trembling now, and both his hands were up against his chest, balled into fists. His head tipped back and Lulu noticed an old scar, more than an inch long, above his left eye.

She looked around, wondering if anyone was going to take charge. The obvious person would be the director, but he seemed frozen in shock, his eyes and mouth wide open.

'I'm going to have to do something,' she whispered to Celia.

'I think you should,' said Celia.

'Definitely,' said Brian.

Macbeth slumped to his knees. His eyes were wide and fearful and his mouth was opening and closing but making no sound. Lulu lifted Conrad, got to her feet and put him down on the chair. She moved away from the pew and walked quickly towards the stage.

Lady Macbeth rushed over as Macbeth fell forward, his face slamming into the floor. She let out a cry and began to sob uncontrollably.

Lulu reached the stage. There was a lighting desk off to the left; a young man in a black polo-neck sweater and black jeans stood in front of the console. Lulu called to him, 'Could you put all the house lights on now, please!' but he didn't seem to hear her, his eyes fixed on what was happening on the stage. 'Lighting guy!' she shouted at the top of her voice. 'Put all the lights on, now!'

This time he heard her and bent over the console. The lights came on, the sudden brightness making Lulu's eyes water. She held her hands above her head. 'Is there a doctor here?' she called to the audience. 'This man needs urgent medical attention.' She looked around; nobody was reacting. 'A doctor?' she repeated. 'Please!'

A woman in the second row started to get up. 'I'm a nurse,' she said. She was in a nun's fancy dress costume, which Lulu found disconcerting, as they were in a church. The man sitting next to her – presumably her husband – was dressed as a vicar.

'Can you see if you can help him?'

The woman nodded. She stood up, made her way to the end of the pew and hurried over to the stage.

Lulu kept her hands in the air. 'Brian, would you call for an ambulance? Tell them we have a man who has collapsed and is having difficulty breathing.'

'Okay, Lulu,' said Brian, already taking out his phone.

'Ladies and gentlemen,' Lulu continued, 'I know this is upsetting, but could I ask you all to please remain seated. And I would be grateful if no one would leave at the moment. Please stay where you are.'

The nurse in the nun's costume had pulled off her wimple. She was rolling Macbeth onto his back and feeling for a pulse in his neck.

Lulu made her way back over to Celia, who was staring at the stage in horror. Brian held out his phone. 'The ambulance is on the way,' he said.

'Well done. Now, can you call again and ask for the police?' She leaned towards him and lowered her voice. 'Tell them we have an emergency and that there is a man unconscious. They'll ask what happened. Just tell them he collapsed and appears to be coughing up blood.'

'What do you think caused it?' asked Brian.

Lulu put her face close to Brian's and lowered her voice. 'It could be poisoning,' she whispered. 'Just phone them, please.'

As Brian made the call, Lulu put a hand on Celia's shoulder. 'Celia?'

Celia looked up at her. 'This is awful,' she said. 'What a nightmare.'

'I need you to do something for me,' said Lulu.

Celia blinked. 'Me?'

'I've asked for people to stay here but I'm sure some people are going to leave, come what may. Can you stand by the door and video anyone who leaves? Be discreet, but make sure you get everyone who goes.' Celia nodded, getting to her feet, and Lulu patted her on the shoulder. 'Thank you.'

As Celia headed for the doorway, Lulu returned to the stage and crouched down a short distance from the nurse, who was performing hands-only CPR on Macbeth.

'How's he doing?' asked Lulu.

'Not good. He barely has a pulse.'

'There's an ambulance on the way. What do you think happened?'

'I really don't know,' the nurse said as she continued to pump on Macbeth's chest. 'I don't think it's a heart attack or a stroke. The blood suggests a burst ulcer, but there's froth, which suggests a lung problem . . . I've never seen anything like it. I'm not sure the compressions alone are helping but I can't risk mouth-to-mouth, not with all that blood.'

'Just do your best,' said Lulu. She glanced back down the nave. People were leaving now. That was to be expected, and there was nothing she could do to force them to stay. She spotted Celia by the door, filming on her phone.

Henry Richards and Celia's friend Amy – Lady Macbeth – stood by the table, clutching each other as they stared in horror at the nurse as she worked on the now unconscious Macbeth. The rest of the cast had gathered at the far end of the stage, where a tall, bearded man in a denim shirt and black jeans had been talking to them. Now he approached Lulu and bent down to speak to her.

'Excuse me – who are you?' he asked.

'I'm Lulu,' she said. 'Lulu Lewis.'

'You seem to have assumed control of the situation.'

'Yes, I'm sorry about that. Obviously something needed to be done quickly. I used to be a police officer.'

'Ah, I see,' he said.

'And you are?'

'John Fleming. I'm the prop master.' He stuck out his hand and Lulu shook it, rising to her feet. 'Thank you for everything you've done so far,' he said. 'People really don't know how to react in a situation like this, do they?'

Lulu took her hand away. 'The police are on their way and I'm sure they'll want to talk to you, and to Mr Richards. And to the rest of the cast. Could you do me a big favour and get them off the stage? Keep them together in the pews just there.' She indicated the left-hand side of the church, close to the lighting console.

'Has he had a stroke or something?'

'We're not sure what it is. But no matter what the cause, the police will need to compile a report.'

'Okay, sure, yes,' he said. He turned away to speak to Richards and Amy, and after a moment they went over to join the rest of the cast.

Time crawled by. Lulu had done everything she could – now they just had to wait for the professionals to arrive. Eventually she heard a siren in the distance: the ambulance.

'Not long now,' she said to the nurse, who nodded.

Lulu headed down the nave. Close to twenty people were still sitting in the pews, but others were filing out. She reached the door and smiled reassuringly at Celia, who was still filming on her phone. Brian had joined her and was also videoing.

A man dressed as Hamlet, holding a gleaming white, grinning skull, stepped aside to allow Lulu out. The siren was louder now and as she walked along the path through the graveyard she saw the vehicle powering down the street towards the church. She raised her hand and waved.

The driver cut the siren, but the blue lights continued to flash as the ambulance came to a halt. The front passenger door opened and a paramedic climbed out. She was short, barely five feet, with spiky red hair and red-framed spectacles, wearing a green jumpsuit and carrying a green nylon medical bag. Lulu's first thought was that the woman looked as if she was in fancy dress. Then she remembered that she was still wearing a witch's outfit and was in no position to cast aspersions.

'The patient's inside,' said Lulu, falling into step with the paramedic. 'He was on stage performing when he began to lose his balance. He coughed and appeared to have trouble breathing.'

The driver's door of the ambulance opened and a male paramedic got out, tall and lanky and wearing a fleece on top of his overalls. He went round to the rear of the vehicle and pulled out a gurney.

'There was bloody froth coming from between his lips. He collapsed and a nurse is administering CPR right now. Don't be put off by the nun's habit she's wearing. She's really a nurse.'

'So you're not actually a witch?'

Lulu smiled. 'Fancy dress.'

'That's what I assumed.'

They reached the church door and the paramedic pushed her way through. 'Does he have any allergies?' she asked.

'Not that I know of. I don't know anything about him. Just his name. Edgar Lake.'

The paramedic hurried down the nave towards the stage. She went up the steps and over to where the nurse was still working on Lake. The nurse stood up and backed away. The paramedic kneeled down, feeling for a pulse in his neck.

The second paramedic appeared in the doorway and people moved apart to let him through with the gurney. He pushed it down to the stage and left it by the steps as he went up to join his colleague.

Lulu returned to her pew, where Conrad was sitting up and looking around. She slipped off her witch's cloak, rolled it up and set it down beside him, then bent to let him jump onto her shoulders.

'What happened to Macbeth?' he whispered.

'I'm not sure,' Lulu said quietly.

'It looks to me like he's been poisoned.'

'Me too.'

'How does he die in the play?'

'Macbeth is beheaded by Macduff in a final battle.'

'So this is off script.'

'Very much so.'

'I think you did a very good job of keeping things in order.'

'Why, thank you.'

Lulu made her way back to the church door, where Celia and Brian were still videoing people who were leaving. 'Thanks for doing this,' she said to them. 'Hopefully the police will be here soon.' A siren wailed in the distance, and she smiled. 'Right on cue.'

4

'How long are we going to stay here?' asked Conrad.

They were back in Lulu's pew, and he was still comfortably wrapped round her shoulders. The paramedics had taken Edgar Lake away on the gurney. They had attached an oxygen mask to his face, but Lulu hadn't been able to see whether he was breathing, and she feared the worst.

Two uniformed constables had turned up just as the paramedics were loading the gurney into the ambulance. They came into the church, where Lulu explained that Celia and Brian had videoed the people who had left. About two dozen audience members had remained behind, along with the cast and crew. The constables took down their names, addresses and phone numbers and finally allowed the audience to leave, as it was now past midnight. Detectives would soon be coming from the force's headquarters in Warwick; they would need to speak to the cast and crew, so Lulu had volunteered to wait. Celia and Brian invited her to come home with them, but she explained that it would be helpful for the detectives to hear from at least one audience member. 'I just want a word with the SIO,' she said. 'I need to tell the detectives that we have videos of the people who left.'

A long time later, a man and a woman appeared in the doorway. The man paused there to talk to a uniformed constable in a high-vis jacket while the woman scribbled in a notebook. Lulu knew straight away that they were detectives. The man was almost certainly the SIO – the senior investigating officer – and the woman was his bag carrier. The bag carrier was usually a detective sergeant, and their main role was to update the decision log, documenting the what, why and when of critical choices that the SIO made during the investigation, including evidence collection, suspect interviews and lines of enquiry. It provided a permanent record of the investigation that could be checked by senior officers at any point.

The man was in his late forties, his hair starting to grey and his forehead lined from too much frowning. He had a square chin, which he jutted up as he listened to whatever the uniform was telling him. His eyes were scanning the interior of the church. He was wearing a dark overcoat over a blue suit. The woman was possibly half his age, with short chestnut-brown hair and square spectacles, wearing a Burberry trench coat with the collar up.

The man's eyes settled on Lulu. The uniform pointed at her and said something, and the man nodded. Lulu assumed that the constable was telling him that she had been responsible for summoning the ambulance and the police. She stood up and headed towards them, figuring that it would be better to speak to them sooner rather than later.

The man's eyes narrowed slightly as Lulu walked up, but he smiled as he waited for her to speak. 'I'm Lulu Lewis,' she said, offering her hand. 'I was the one who called 999. Well, I asked a friend to do it, actually. He's gone home, but I thought I should stay and introduce myself.' Conrad meowed. 'And this is Conrad.'

The man stuck out his hand and shook. 'Pleased to meet you – and Conrad. I'm Detective Inspector Aaron Dunning, senior investigating officer, and this is my assistant, Detective Sergeant Kirsty Whitlock. The constable on the door says he thinks you were in the job before.'

'I didn't tell him that,' said Lulu.

DI Dunning smiled. 'I think he just assumed it from the way you carried yourself.' His smile widened. 'He said you seemed to know what you were doing.'

'I used to be a detective superintendent with the Met, back in the day. I knew we had to preserve the crime scene, and I did try to stop people leaving, but as I had no authority a lot of them just left. My goddaughter, Celia, and her husband, Brian, videoed the people that were leaving, so you should be able to identify them. I'm told that most of the tickets were sold online, so there will be a record of names and addresses. But there were walk-ins, too, who paid cash.'

'And you were here when the incident happened?' said DI Dunning.

Lulu nodded. 'Fifth row.'

'Can you tell me what you saw?'

'It was the third act. There's a scene in a banquet hall where the characters are drinking and arguing. The actor playing Macbeth – Edgar Lake – began to slur his words and cough, and then he lost his balance and fell. He was foaming at the mouth, so something was clearly wrong. A nurse in the audience tried CPR but it wasn't helping. I got the lights turned up and asked Brian to call for an ambulance and for the police. The ambulance was here within five minutes and the constables arrived not long after that. By then, probably three-quarters of the audience had left.'

'And you saw the ambulance taking Lake away?'

'Yes; they were trying to resuscitate him, but it looked like poisoning to me.'

DI Dunning nodded. 'We've now heard that he was pronounced dead at the hospital, I'm afraid,' he said. 'Who was in charge of the performance?'

Lulu pointed over to where the cast and crew were sitting. 'Henry Richards is the director and he was also on stage, playing the part of Banquo. He's the guy over there with the grey hair, wearing chain mail over a dark wool tunic. Sitting next to him, the bearded chap, is John Fleming – he's the prop master, so he would have been responsible for the wine and the goblets. Oh, and there's something else you should know: Edgar Lake wasn't originally supposed to be playing the lead tonight.'

'Yes, I saw the note outside. Do you know who he replaced?'

'I was told that it was a local priest, the Reverend Troy Harper.'

'All right; thank you so much for your help, Mrs Lewis. The constable was right – you clearly do know what you're doing. Can you give DS Whitlock your phone number so that we can contact you about the videos?'

'Of course,' said Lulu.

DI Dunning walked over to the stage while Lulu gave DS Whitlock her phone number.

'Thank you so much, Mrs Lewis,' said DS Whitlock. 'We'll be in touch tomorrow.' She looked over her shoulder at DI Dunning, who was already talking to Henry Richards and John Fleming, then nodded at Lulu. 'Thank you again.' She hurried over to the stage, notebook at the ready.

'Can we go now?' asked Conrad.

'Just a bit longer.'

Conrad sighed. 'You really want to be part of the investigation, don't you?'

'I just want to know if there's anything else they need. Better to answer any questions they have here and now, rather than waiting until tomorrow.'

She settled back into the pew and watched as DI Dunning spoke to the cast and crew. DS Whitlock stood at his side, making notes.

'What do you think he's asking them?' said Conrad after a while.

'What they saw, obviously. And what information they have about the victim. Did he have any enemies, any conflict?'

'So it's definitely foul play?'

'Not definitely, no. But when someone dies in suspicious circumstances, everything has to be considered. It might well prove to be a medical emergency, but the speed at which it happened and the fact that he was drinking from his goblet does suggest that he was poisoned. Until they know for sure what the cause of death is, they have to cover all bases.'

Richards was staring at the floor as he spoke to the inspector, continually shaking his head. Fleming patted him on the back as if comforting him.

Eventually, DI Dunning turned to walk back towards Lulu; DS Whitlock stayed where she was, still talking to the cast and crew and adding to her notes. Lulu assumed she was taking down their contact details.

Lulu stood up as Dunning approached. He nodded to her. 'I've spoken to everyone, but I think we can wait until tomorrow before formally interviewing them. They're all pretty shocked by what happened.'

'Well, yes, it was fairly dramatic. No pun intended.'

'Did you know that the actor who was set to play Macbeth killed himself today? Or rather, yesterday.' He glanced at his watch.

'The priest? Troy Harper?'

Dunning nodded. 'He hanged himself this afternoon.'

'No, I didn't know that.'

'It was Mr Richards who discovered the body. No wonder he's in a state of shock. First he finds the priest hanging from the banister, then Mr Lake dies on stage in front of him. Mr Fleming is also shaken up. I've called a doctor to check them out, and we'll do the interviews tomorrow.'

Lulu looked thoughtful. 'On the way over here, my goddaughter was telling me that one of the local GPs also killed himself recently – just last week. A Dr Mackenzie. He was having financial problems, apparently.'

'Aren't we all?' said DI Dunning. 'It feels as if half of everything I earn these days goes in taxes.'

Lulu nodded. 'Everybody is struggling,' she said. She looked around the church. 'No sign of SOCO?'

'I'm told that they're on their way, but this time of night is always difficult. It could be a while yet. Obviously DS Whitlock and I will stay until they're done, but there's no need to keep you. Where are you staying?'

'Bancroft Basin. I'm on a canal boat. *The Lark*.'

'You sailed up from London?'

'Drove up rather than sailed. But yes, I came up to celebrate my goddaughter's birthday. I was due to head back the day after tomorrow, but I'm more than happy to stick around.'

He smiled. 'I'm sure we'll have had everything we need

from you by then, Mrs Lewis.' He nodded. 'I shall see you tomorrow to get those videos. Thank you for all your help tonight.'

Conrad chuckled as the detective inspector walked away. 'I'm more than happy to stick around,' he said, in a passable imitation of Lulu's voice.

'I was just trying to be helpful,' whispered Lulu.

'You want to be on the case,' he said.

'You're right, of course. I do. Don't you want to get to the bottom of it?'

'Macbeth might simply have had a medical emergency.'

'Do you think so?'

'No. Not really. Remember all the bloody foam coming from his mouth. I definitely think he was poisoned.'

'Yes, Conrad, so do I. That's why the videos of the people leaving are so important. One of them may well be the killer.'

5

Lulu walked back to the canal basin with Conrad on her shoulders. They could see the very first streaks of light in the sky, orange and red. There was no one else around, and only the occasional car drove by. Lulu had left her sheepskin jacket at Celia and Brian's house but didn't want to disturb them, so she had put the witch's cloak back on over her dress to help keep out the cold. She resisted the urge to wear the black hat, carrying it in her left hand instead.

'You know what I don't understand?' said Conrad as they reached the jetty where *The Lark* was moored.

'Quantum physics?' said Lulu.

'Actually, I have a pretty good understanding of quantum physics and thc bchaviour of the universe at the atomic and subatomic scale. And I'm familiar with the work of Max Planck, Werner Heisenberg, Erwin Schrödinger and Albert Einstein.'

'I do know that you have a pretty low opinion of Schrödinger.'

'After what he did to his cat, how could I not?'

'I've explained to you before that it was only a thought experiment. He never actually hurt a cat.' Lulu climbed onto the rear deck of *The Lark* and Conrad jumped off her shoulders and onto the roof.

'Anyone who even thinks about hurting a cat deserves to be punished,' said Conrad. 'And I would happily do the punishing.'

Lulu unlocked the hatch and pulled it back. 'I'm sorry, I interrupted your train of thought.' She went down the steps into the galley.

Conrad padded after her. 'Yes, you did.'

'So what is it that you don't understand? Given that it's not quantum physics.'

'The Reverend Harper killed himself, right? But he's a Catholic, so that's a sin.'

'It is, yes.'

'Is it likely that a Catholic would kill himself? Especially a Catholic priest?'

Lulu put down the hat and took off her cloak, draping it on the sofa. 'It happens,' she said. 'But yes, people with religious leanings are somewhat less likely to kill themselves than people who don't believe in God.'

'That makes sense,' said Conrad. 'If you really believed in God, then you probably wouldn't want to upset him by killing yourself.'

'I remember reading somewhere that suicide rates do vary between different religions. I think Protestants have the highest rate, then Roman Catholics, followed by Jews and then Muslims. So the short answer is that, while it's not especially likely a Catholic would commit suicide, it is definitely possible.'

'Here's what I'm trying to get my head around,' said Conrad. He wrinkled his nose and tilted his head to one side. 'If the Reverend Harper hadn't killed himself, he'd have died during the performance. He would have drunk the poisoned wine on stage, and he would have died instead of Mr Lake.'

'You're assuming that Mr Lake was poisoned.'

'You don't think he was? It looked that way to me.'

'And me, but it doesn't matter what we think, Conrad. We have to let the evidence speak for itself. It could have been a massive heart attack, or a stroke. We have to wait for the post-mortem.'

'I understand. But let's assume for a moment that he was poisoned. Wouldn't that mean that if the Reverend Harper had been on stage, he would have been the one who died? He would have drunk the poison.'

'I suppose so.'

'So maybe he knew that he was going to be murdered and decided that he would rather die by his own hand.'

'That's only a supposition at this point. And as for Mr Lake, we need to wait for the post-mortem, and we need to see what the lab finds in the wine.'

'You think it was in the wine? If it was, why didn't Mr Richards get poisoned? His character Banquo was also drinking, wasn't he?'

'I don't know, Conrad. Again, we need to see what the forensics say.'

'What did you think about Henry Richards?'

'He seems quite straightforward. Clearly he's unsettled by what's happened. Why do you ask?'

Conrad wrinkled his nose. 'His aura worries me.'

'Really? Tell me more.' Conrad had a gift for seeing people's auras and interpreting them, which was why he was generally such a good judge of character.

'His aura has an uneasy shimmer, like sunlight dancing on water just before a storm. The colours are shifting all the time, pale greys and silver tinged with violet – that suggests he's always alert and calculating what he should do next.

And there's a thin, muted blue running through his aura, as if trust and sincerity are being rationed, doled out sparingly, for fear of discovery. And under the surface there are slivers of dark green and brown, which suggests that there are parts of himself he is keeping hidden. It's as if he's wearing a mask.'

'Like an actor playing a part?'

'Exactly,' said Conrad. 'And his whole aura is tight, like a violin string, as if he's always tense, expecting something bad to happen.'

'Well, something bad certainly happened tonight,' said Lulu. 'Now, I'm going to make myself a mug of cocoa before I go to bed. Can I interest you in anything?'

'A bowl of water, please. And do you by any chance have anything snackable?'

Lulu bent down and opened the fridge. 'There's some tuna,' she said.

'Ah, the chicken of the sea,' Conrad said, and smacked his lips. 'Perfect.'

6

Lulu woke just after nine in the morning. She had only managed a few hours' sleep, but she felt refreshed. She always seemed to sleep better on *The Lark* than she ever did on land. She slipped out of bed, taking care not to wake Conrad, who was curled up nose to tail with his eyes firmly closed.

She lit the burner under the kettle, then cleaned her teeth and showered before pulling on a warm pullover, jeans and thick socks. She was pouring boiling water into a mug when Conrad emerged from the bedroom.

'Good morning,' he said.

'Good morning to you,' she replied as he passed her and jumped up onto the sofa.

He sat with his back straight, his eyes burning into hers. 'I had a thought. Last night. While you were sleeping.'

'I suppose that's one of the advantages of being nocturnal,' said Lulu, adding a dash of milk to her tea and putting the carton back into the fridge.

Conrad chuckled. 'You know very well that cats are not nocturnal,' he said. 'We are actually crepuscular, which means that we are most active during dawn and dusk, not in the middle of the night. But I digress. Here's the thought that struck me. What are the odds that there would be two suicides in Stratford-upon-Avon at about the same time?'

'The Reverend Harper and Dr Mackenzie, you mean?'

'Exactly.'

'Well, the number of suicides in the UK runs at about ten for every one hundred thousand people each year. So for every ten thousand of population, you would expect one suicide in a year.' Lulu sipped her tea, thinking. 'The population of Stratford-upon-Avon is about thirty thousand; if you include the surrounding area, I believe it's about 135,000. So, going by the larger number, statistically you would expect about thirteen suicides a year – which is about one a month. Looking at it that way, two doesn't seem so unusual.'

'Except that both of these were in the town – where, statistically, you would expect three over the year.'

'But that's still more than two, so two isn't statistically unusual.' Lulu frowned. 'You think the two suicides may be connected?'

'They're either connected or it's a coincidence,' said Conrad.

'But if they are connected, then we would have a common thread linking two suicides and one murder.' Lulu's frown deepened. 'I can't help but feel that we are over-complicating this.'

'How could we find out if there are any connections between Dr Mackenzie and the Reverend Harper?'

Before Lulu could answer, they heard a man's voice shouting from the jetty. 'Hello! Is there anyone home?'

It was DI Dunning. 'Yes, I'm here!' Lulu called back. She went up the steps and opened the hatch.

DI Dunning was standing on the jetty, wrapped up in an overcoat and with a yellow scarf wound around his neck. 'Permission to come aboard,' he said.

'Permission granted,' said Lulu.

He climbed onto the rear deck. '*The Lark*? Nice name.'

'I bought it off a dentist who always said he bought it as a lark.'

'That's funny.'

'It's unlucky to change a boat's name, so they say. But I do like it.'

She led the inspector down into the galley. He looked around. 'Oh, I thought I heard someone talking,' he said.

'I was on the phone,' Lulu said. 'Can I get you a drink? Tea? Coffee?'

'I thought I heard two voices? A man?'

'You did. Speakerphone. I read an article that said it wasn't healthy to hold a mobile phone to your head, so I always take calls on speakerphone.' She lit the burner under the kettle. 'Tea or coffee?'

'Coffee would be great,' Dunning said. He nodded at Conrad. 'Good morning, Conrad.' Conrad meowed at him and the detective laughed. 'He talks!'

'Yes, he does,' said Lulu.

DI Dunning took a seat on the sofa as Lulu spooned instant coffee into a mug. 'You seem bright-eyed and bushy-tailed,' she said. 'You can't have had much sleep, surely?'

'A couple of hours, but that's par for the course in the early days of a murder investigation. Were you on murder enquiries when you were with the Met?'

'Oh, yes. More than my fair share.'

'Do you miss it?'

'I miss some things, yes. But the late nights and the grief from the top I could have done without. I do miss being part of a close-knit team working towards a common aim. These days, it's just me and Conrad.'

'I'm sure he's a very capable bag carrier,' said DI Dunning.

'Not really,' said Lulu. 'No opposable thumbs, so carrying isn't one of his talents. Though he does have many others.'

DI Dunning laughed. 'So, we were able to get a quick basic analysis from the lab overnight, and Mr Lake was definitely poisoned. Aconite is the technical term, but it's more commonly known as monkshood or wolfsbane. It's a highly toxic plant, and apparently there were traces of it in his goblet.'

The kettle whistled, and Lulu poured boiling water into the mug. 'Milk and sugar?' she asked.

'Milk and three sugars,' he said. He smiled sheepishly when her eyebrows shot up. 'I know, but I've always had a sweet tooth.'

She added milk and sugar, stirred it and handed the mug to him. He sipped and nodded his approval. 'Perfect.'

'I've come across wolfsbane before, believe it or not,' said Lulu. 'Back when I was a detective sergeant in North London, a woman killed her husband with it. Brewed some up and told him it would settle his stomach.'

'Harsh,' said DI Dunning.

'To be fair, he would come home drunk most Friday nights and use her as a punchbag. What about the other goblets on stage? Most of the actors were drinking, or at least pretending to.'

'All the other goblets were fine, and the wine bottle too. The poison was only found in Mr Lake's goblet.' DI Dunning took out a notebook and flipped it open. 'Apparently it "interferes with the normal function of voltage-gated sodium channels in cells" – whatever that means. Anyway, it causes neurological and cardiac dysfunction, often leading to fatal arrhythmias. Symptoms can become obvious within minutes.

That would be salivation, sweating, nausea and vomiting, followed by respiratory paralysis and death.'

'That does sound like what we saw,' said Lulu.

'According to Google, it was used as a poison for arrows in the Middle Ages. It's banned or regulated in many countries because of its toxicity, but it's hard to control – you can just plant seeds and it'll grow. I read that wolfsbane is probably what killed Romeo, although Shakespeare doesn't mention it by name.'

'Do you think there's a Shakespearean connection?'

'Oh, there's definitely that,' said DI Dunning. 'The guy due to play Macbeth kills himself, and a few hours later his understudy dies on stage? Yes, there's a connection.'

'When will the post-mortem be taking place?'

'They're doing it this afternoon.'

'Here in Stratford-upon-Avon?'

'No; the hospital here is quite small. The coroner will be using the mortuary at Warwick Hospital, a twenty-minute drive away.' He drank some coffee. 'You saw Mr Lake drinking from the goblet? During the performance?'

'I did, yes.' Lulu's eyes narrowed thoughtfully. 'So, if the poison wasn't found anywhere else, that seems to confirm Macbeth was definitely the target.'

'The actor playing Macbeth was the target; I think we can assume that. But of course the actor who appeared on stage wasn't the actor who was scheduled to appear, was he? So the big question is, was the poison put in the goblet before or after the Reverend Harper killed himself?'

'What about Harper's suicide? Will you be looking at that?'

'Definitely. There was minimal police involvement because it seemed to be a clear case of suicide. He had hanged himself from the banister, and there were no obvious signs of a struggle. A patrol car attended and waited until a doctor came to confirm death, but they took no further action other than to inform the coroner.'

'Did he leave a note?'

'No note, no. But there was a copy of his will on the hall table. He had clearly left it there to be found. He is leaving everything to his cleaning lady.'

'Well, there's motive,' said Lulu.

'She's barely five feet tall and half his weight,' said DI Dunning.

'She could have had help.'

'Fair point. And we will consider all options. But this morning I spoke to one of the uniforms who attended, and he was quite sure that Harper had taken his own life.'

'So you think Mr Lake could have been the intended victim at the church? There's no connection at all with what happened to the Reverend Harper?'

DI Dunning smiled. 'I'm keeping an open mind, Mrs Lewis. That's one of the reasons I'm here today. I wanted to take a look at the church in daylight, and I've arranged to meet Mr Richards and Mr Fleming. Hopefully they'll be in a better state than they were last night.'

'And what about DS Whitlock? Will she be there?'

'I can't go anywhere without my bag carrier,' he said. 'Whitlock doesn't live far from Stratford-upon-Avon, so I'll meet her there. I thought I could pick up the videos from your friends. And any footage you took.'

'Not a problem. Just let me grab my witch's cloak.' Dunning frowned, and Lulu chuckled. 'I wore it home last night. I need to drop it off at Celia's and pick up my jacket.'

7

There was a cold wind blowing across the basin, so Lulu wrapped herself up in the witch's cloak and plonked the conical hat on her head. She locked up *The Lark* and waved for DI Dunning to get off first. Once he was on the jetty, she bent down so that Conrad could jump onto her shoulders. Then she stepped carefully off the boat.

'I don't think I've ever seen a cat ride around on his owner's shoulders before,' said DI Dunning.

'Oh, I never think of myself as Conrad's owner, more as his companion.'

'I don't suppose you are a *Doctor Who* fan, are you?' he asked as they walked along the jetty.

'I've watched it, of course. Mainly when I was a child. I remember hiding behind the sofa when the Daleks appeared.'

'Oh yes, you'd have seen the first series, right? Back in 1963. In black and white. With William Hartnell as the doctor.'

'I'm not quite that old,' said Lulu. 'The first Doctor I really remember was Jon Pertwee. Why do you ask?'

DI Dunning chuckled. 'It was when you said you were Conrad's companion. Doctor Who always had a companion. And there was a cat that played a major role in *Survival*, the final serial of the twenty-sixth season. It was a black cat that was controlled by a being from another dimension. It was a hunter, but it was also acting as a guide to lead humans to a new world.'

'I don't think I saw that one,' said Lulu.

'Sylvester McCoy was the doctor. It was the last of the classic *Doctor Who* episodes, back in 1989. Then the series went off the air until 2005.'

Lulu chuckled. 'You really are a fan,' she said.

'I got it from my dad. I started watching it with him when Peter Davison was the Doctor, but he had all the episodes on VHS.' Dunning smiled sadly. 'He's got dementia now. Early stages. He's still living at home with Mum, but it's starting to get too much for her. Half the time he doesn't even know who she is. But when we sit down to watch an old episode of *Doctor Who*, he remembers everything. Literally. He sits there mouthing the dialogue, and he's always pointing out the references to other episodes.'

'The mind is an amazing thing,' said Lulu.

'It is. As we're watching *Doctor Who*, it's as if there's nothing wrong with him. Then he'll ask where Bobbie is. Bobbie was our dog when I was a kid. He died thirty years ago. But Dad will go out in the garden and start whistling for him.'

'I'm sorry,' said Lulu. 'It can't be easy for you, or your mum.'

'Yeah,' said DI Dunning. 'It's harder on Mum, I know.' He forced another smile. 'Sorry, I didn't mean to burden you with my problems. I should be focusing on the matter at hand.' He pointed to a grey Vauxhall Vectra. 'I can run us there in my car.'

'Sure,' said Lulu. 'But it isn't far.'

'I'll need the car later,' he said.

Lulu took off her witch's hat and they climbed in. She

gave him directions, and after a couple of minutes they were outside Celia and Brian's house.

Lulu rang the doorbell and Brian answered. He was wearing a pale blue soft flannel shirt and well-worn corduroy trousers. 'Lulu, good morning,' he said. 'You really do like that witch's outfit, don't you?' He frowned a little when he saw the inspector standing behind her.

'This is Detective Inspector Dunning,' said Lulu. 'He's investigating the incident last night. You'd left by the time he arrived. It turns out that Mr Lake was poisoned, and he very sadly didn't survive.'

Brian shook the inspector's hand. 'Terrible business,' he said. 'Please come in, Celia's just made coffee and toast.'

Lulu and DI Dunning stepped into the hall and Brian closed the door. Lulu took off her witch's hat and put it on the hall table, then slipped off the cloak and hung it on the banister. Brian led them to the kitchen, where Celia was buttering toast. 'Ah, the more the merrier,' she said when she saw Lulu.

Lulu introduced Dunning again, and they both sat on stools either side of the large kitchen island. Above their heads hung a set of polished copper pans that looked as if they were more for decoration than actual cooking. Celia set the plate of buttered toast on the island.

'So DI Dunning is here for the videos you took last night,' said Lulu.

'I'll get the phones,' said Brian, and he headed out of the kitchen.

'How do you like your coffee?' Celia asked the inspector.

'Milky with three sugars, please.'

'That's how I used to drink it before my doctor told me I had borderline diabetes,' said Celia.

'I burn it off very quickly,' said the inspector. He picked up a slice of toast and bit into it.

'An SIO is always on the go,' said Lulu.

'SIO?' repeated Celia.

'Senior Investigating Officer. DI Dunning is heading a murder investigation team.'

'Isn't that what you used to do?'

'For a time, yes,' said Lulu. 'And I was putting three sugars in my coffee back then, too.'

'Did you say murder?' said Celia, as Brian walked back into the kitchen with two mobile phones.

'We believe that Mr Lake was poisoned,' said Dunning.

'On stage?'

'Yes, we think so.'

Celia placed mugs of coffee in front of Lulu and the inspector. 'That's such an awful thing to happen.'

'Did you know him?' asked Lulu. 'Mr Lake?'

'Not really. I mean, we've seen him in a few productions, and we met him through Amy, but that's about it. He wasn't even supposed to be playing Macbeth last night, was he?'

'No. The actor who was due to play Macbeth committed suicide a few hours before the performance.'

Brian's jaw dropped. 'Troy? Troy Harper?'

'Yes, the Reverend Troy Harper,' said DI Dunning. 'St Mary's Church. Do you know him?'

'That's our local church,' said Celia. 'Troy's dead?'

DI Dunning nodded. 'That's why he wasn't in the play.'

'We just assumed he must be ill or something,' said Celia. 'Why did nobody say anything?'

'I suppose the director felt that the show had to go on,'

said Lulu. 'If they'd announced his death before the play, people would obviously have been upset.'

'They should have cancelled the performance,' said Celia, looking troubled.

'Well, yes, but then the audience would have been disappointed, and all the hard work the cast and crew had put into it would have been wasted,' said Lulu. 'I can see why Mr Richards wanted it to go ahead.'

'And you say that Troy killed himself?' said Brian.

'Hanged himself,' said Lulu. 'From the banister in the hall.'

'That can't be right,' said Brian. 'He's a Catholic priest! Catholic priests don't take their own lives – it's a mortal sin.'

'Did he leave a note?' asked Celia.

'Just a copy of his will,' said DI Dunning.

'And what about Elsie?' said Brian. 'She must be distraught.'

'Elsie Kwan? His cleaner? Yes, she is quite upset.'

'Elsie is more of a housekeeper than a cleaner,' said Celia. 'She didn't live in, but she cooked and cleaned for him, ran his errands and looked after St Mary's. She did all the flower arrangements in the church and kept his books. He always called her his godsend.'

'She didn't find the body, did she?' asked Brian.

Dunning shook his head. 'No. She'd already left.' He finished his piece of toast and sipped his coffee.

'Poor lady,' said Brian. He held up the phones. 'So how do we do this? Do you have WhatsApp?'

'I do, yes.' The inspector gave Brian his number, and Brian transferred over all the videos he and Celia had taken the previous night.

'Do you think the killer was there? In the audience?' asked Celia.

'In the audience or on the stage,' said DI Dunning. 'I think that's a very strong possibility, yes.'

'You think one of the cast might have done it?' said Brian.

'We're keeping all our options open at the moment,' said the inspector.

'But if he was poisoned on stage, surely the killer must have been there?' said Celia.

'We're looking at that,' said the inspector. 'The poison wasn't in the wine bottle, though; we know that much.'

'That doesn't make sense,' said Brian. 'Edgar drank the wine and then collapsed. It had to have been the wine.'

Dunning shook his head. 'The only place our lab found poison was in his goblet. So someone must have put the poison directly into the goblet. Then the wine was poured in and he drank it.'

Brian shook his head in disgust. 'Who would do something like that?' he said. 'Poison is such a cowardly way of killing, isn't it?'

Celia looked at him. 'What do you mean, darling?'

'Well, it's sneaky, isn't it? If you stab a man or choke him, it's face to face. You have to look at the man you're killing. There's a personal connection. Even using a gun means you have to at least be able to see the person you're killing. But a poisoner can pour their stuff into a cup, or mix it with food, and be miles away when the victim actually consumes it.'

Celia frowned. 'You've obviously given this a lot of thought, darling. Should I be worried?'

Brian chuckled and hugged her. 'Academic interest, that's

all. I read a lot of crime books.' He looked over at Lulu. 'But I'm right, aren't I? Generally it's women who use poison to kill?'

'I think statistically you're right,' said Lulu. 'But there have been many cases of men who have used poison to kill. There's Graham Young, the Teacup Poisoner, who began experimenting with toxic substances as a teenager in the 1960s and went on to kill co-workers and family members with antimony and thallium. Then there's Harold Shipman, a doctor who was convicted of murdering patients – mainly elderly women – by injecting lethal doses of diamorphine.'

Brian looked at the inspector. 'Do you think someone was targeting Edgar, or was it random?'

'That's a very good question,' said DI Dunning. 'We'll obviously be looking at possible motives.' He checked his watch, then drained his mug. 'Right, I'm off to the church.' He looked at Lulu. 'Would you like to come along? You were there on the night, so it would be useful to have your insight.'

'Can I bring Conrad?'

Dunning laughed. 'Of course you can. He was a witness, too.'

8

Lulu and DI Dunning climbed into his Vauxhall Vectra. Conrad sat on Lulu's lap, looking through the side window as they drove towards the church.

'He really does go everywhere with you,' said the inspector.

'He's very well behaved,' said Lulu.

'He is. I don't think I've ever seen a cat with such good manners. Why did you call him Conrad?'

'Because that's his name,' said Lulu.

The inspector chuckled. 'I suppose I did ask for that.'

He found a parking space close to the church and they got out. There were still some Halloween decorations up, but most had been taken down. It was still early, and there weren't many people around. A young man walked towards them with an Alsatian on a lead. The dog spotted Conrad and began to bark. The boy pulled the dog away, apologizing profusely.

There was still police tape cordoning off the church. A uniformed female constable in a high-vis jacket was standing by the front door, her head down, looking at her mobile phone. DS Whitlock climbed out of a blue Ford Fiesta and stood waiting for them.

'I thought it might be useful to have Mrs Lewis with us,' said DI Dunning. 'Seeing as she was there when Mr Lake died.'

'Nice to see you again, Mrs Lewis,' said DS Whitlock. 'And you, Conrad.'

Conrad meowed, and she laughed. 'He knows his name.'

Lulu smiled. 'Yes, he does.'

Whitlock looked at Dunning. 'I've already phoned Mr Richards and Mr Fleming, and they'll both be here—' She glanced down the road. 'In fact, there they are now.'

Lulu and DI Dunning turned and saw the two men walking towards them. Richards looked very different out of costume and with no theatrical make-up. He was wearing a duffel coat with large horn buttons. Fleming had on a parka with a fur-lined hood over his head.

'Thank you for coming, gentlemen,' said DI Dunning.

'I'm really not comfortable going back into the church,' said Richards.

'I understand, and I'll try to make this as painless as possible,' said DI Dunning. 'If at any point you feel that it's getting too much for you, just say, and we'll come out.'

Richards nodded. Then he frowned as he saw Conrad on Lulu's shoulders.

'This is Mrs Lewis. She was at the play last night,' said Dunning.

'Ah, yes. You were the one who shouted at everybody not to leave,' said Richards. 'I did wonder who you were.'

'I was there with my goddaughter, who's a friend of Amy's,' said Lulu. 'When Mr Lake fell ill, I wanted as many people to stay as possible, because it was clear that the police would need to interview them as witnesses.'

'Mrs Lewis used to be a detective superintendent in London,' said DI Dunning.

'Is that so?' Richards clearly didn't care either way.

'Retired now, obviously,' said Lulu. 'It must have been an awful shock when Mr Lake collapsed. It was all so sudden, wasn't it?'

'It was.' Richards looked at DI Dunning. 'Was it a stroke? Or a heart attack? Is he okay?'

'I'm afraid Mr Lake has passed away. It appears that he was poisoned.'

'Poisoned?' repeated Fleming. 'How?'

'Perhaps we could take this inside?' said DI Dunning. 'It'll be warmer, and you can fill us in on where various people were when it happened.'

'Poisoned?' murmured Fleming again. He looked over at Richards. 'Did you know that he was poisoned?'

Before Richards could answer, DI Dunning pushed the church door open and then stepped aside so that Fleming and Richards could go in first. The two men walked in hesitantly; Richards had his arms folded as if he was hugging himself. Lulu followed them, with Dunning and Whitlock bringing up the rear.

Their footsteps echoed in the empty church as they slowly approached the stage. Everything was as it had been the previous night, though the goblets and the bottle of wine had gone.

Richards looked around, shaking his head sorrowfully. 'All that work, all those hours – wasted.'

'I understand that, Mr Richards, but a man has died here,' said Dunning.

Richards nodded. 'Yes, of course. I just meant . . .' He shook his head. 'Never mind.'

DI Dunning climbed the three steps to the stage and looked around. DS Whitlock joined him, her notebook in hand. Lulu stood well out of their way, watching, with Conrad on her shoulders.

DI Dunning stepped towards the table, then turned and beckoned to Richards. 'Mr Richards, could you show me where you were standing during the scene?'

'I'd really rather not,' said Richards.

'It would help me put everything in context,' said the detective inspector.

Richards climbed the steps reluctantly, as if walking to the gallows. He was still hugging himself.

'Where were you during the scene?' Dunning prompted him.

'For part of the scene, I was in Macbeth's chair.'

'Can you sit there now, please?'

Richards went over to the chair. He winced and slowly sat down.

'And where was Macbeth while you were in his seat?'

Richards indicated the middle of the stage. DI Dunning crossed over to the spot he was pointing at. 'Here?'

Richards nodded. 'Yes.'

'Could you talk me through the scene, please?'

'Seriously?'

'I'm not really familiar with Shakespeare's work, I'm afraid. Any of it.'

Richards sighed despondently. 'Fine,' he said. 'The scene takes place at a banquet that Lady Macbeth is hosting for local lords and noblemen. Macbeth has hired assassins to kill Banquo and his son Fleance. One of the assassins arrives at the banquet to inform Macbeth that Banquo is dead, but that Fleance escaped. Macbeth then imagines that he sees Banquo's ghost sitting in his chair. Banquo is invisible to everyone else there. Macbeth is terrified and talks to the ghost, but the guests think he is going mad. Lady Macbeth tries to explain his behaviour by saying that he is having a fit, but eventually she has to send all the guests away.'

'And where was Macbeth's goblet during all of this?'

'In Macbeth's hand. He is drinking throughout the scene, as is Banquo.'

'So when you were sitting in Macbeth's chair, his goblet wasn't with you?'

'No, he was holding it. All the way through the scene he is trying to propose a toast, but Banquo's appearance throws him.'

'And at what point did Mr Lake fall ill?'

'He was a bit strange throughout most of the scene. He was breathing heavily and slurring his words. But it was the second time he was preparing his toast that he fell forward.'

'And had anyone other than Mr Lake touched the goblet?'

Richards shook his head. 'Definitely not.'

'The wine that you were drinking on stage,' said DI Dunning. 'Who supplied it?'

Fleming spoke up. 'That would be Ted Simpson. He's a local wine merchant and a big supporter of the group. He helps us financially, and we use his company logo on all our advertising. But the wine was non-alcoholic. Grape juice, really. We wouldn't want our actors getting drunk on stage, obviously.'

'Plus, I'm teetotal,' said Richards. 'I have been for more than twenty years. I wouldn't have allowed alcohol on the stage.'

'Where can we find Mr Simpson?'

'He'll be at his off-licence in the high street.'

'Was he here last night?' asked DI Dunning.

'Of course,' said Richards. 'With his wife and daughters. Front row.'

'And when did he give you the wine?'

'When he arrived at the church. He was here early to chat with the cast and crew. He brought the non-alcoholic wine and a case of champagne for the whole group to drink after the show. He's always generous like that.'

'And who poured the wine into the goblets?'

'The cast, on stage. They start off with the goblets empty, but as the act goes on they pour in more wine.'

'I saw that,' said Lulu. 'Mr Lake poured wine into his goblet, but I don't know for certain that I saw Mr Richards take any.'

'I'm fairly sure I did,' said Richards, with a glance at DI Dunning. 'I remember pouring wine into my goblet as I leered over at Macbeth.'

DI Dunning looked enquiringly at Lulu. 'Maybe I missed that,' she said. 'But I do remember Lady Macbeth helping herself, and two of the Scottish noblemen.'

'Yes,' said Richards. 'Ross and Lennox.' His eyes widened. 'Oh – I see what you are getting at. The wine bottle couldn't have been poisoned, could it? Not if so many people drank it.'

'Tell me about the goblets,' said DI Dunning. 'When were they put out?'

'At the start of the scene,' said Fleming. 'The previous scene takes place at dusk in a park near the palace, where three murderers hired by Macbeth ambush and kill Banquo. Then the curtain falls and we quickly prepare the banquet scene. A long table is wheeled in and chairs placed around it, then the curtain goes up. The goblets are already in position on the table, along with the food and candlesticks.'

'And the food was real?'

Fleming nodded. 'Mostly, yes. It means the actors can take a bite if they want. It adds realism. I always try to make my productions as real as possible.'

'Does each actor have a specific goblet?' asked DI Dunning.

'They do. The main characters' are slightly different. Macbeth's is the largest and has a more regal look. Banquo's is ghostly, with a cobweb motif. They rehearse using the goblets, so yes, on the night they would each have known which one to use.'

'And you set the goblets out?'

Fleming nodded again. 'I did, yes.'

'Before that, where were they?'

'In one of the prop boxes. I brought them into the church at about nine o'clock yesterday morning.'

'On your own?'

'Good lord, no. There were literally dozens of boxes, because I handle the costumes, too. I have three assistants. Well, actors really, or spear carriers to be more exact. They're all students, happy to help for the sake of experience.'

'And you have, what, a van?'

'Yes. A Mercedes Sprinter, which is just about big enough. We picked the boxes up from the WI hall where we had been rehearsing and took them into the church.'

'The WI?' repeated Dunning.

'The Women's Institute,' Fleming clarified. 'Amy Jenner – she plays Lady Macbeth – is a leading light in the WI, and she arranged for them to let us use their hall to rehearse.'

'And after you had taken the boxes into the church, what then?'

'We set up the dressing area and the make-up area. Those are in the back rooms, out of the way. Then we spent most of the morning setting up the lights and curtains.'

'Seems like you do everything,' Dunning observed.

'Anything not acting related, yes, I suppose I do. We're a small team. But dedicated.'

'We couldn't manage without John,' said Richards.

'We all have our roles, Henry. I'm just happy to play my part.' Fleming smiled faintly at him, and at Dunning. 'Once the curtains and lights are in place, we set up our sets. There are basically four locations in our production – Macbeth's castle in Inverness, the Royal Palace at Forres where Macbeth later holds court, Dunsinane Palace, where he has his final battle and meets his death, and an outdoor setting that we use as Birnam Wood and the opening scene where the witches meet.'

'Eye of toad and wing of bat?' said DS Whitlock. 'I think that's the only Shakespeare I can remember.'

'The original text refers to "eye of newt and toe of frog, wool of bat and tongue of dog",' said Richards. 'The ingredients of the witch's brew. John did an amazing job with the cauldron.'

'Dry ice is the key,' said Fleming. 'Lots of it.'

'And the banquet scene?' said DI Dunning. 'Tell me about that.'

'Yes; the banquet scene is in the main hall of Macbeth's Inverness castle. So we have wall coverings and antlers and a bear's head, a brazier with fake fire in it, and the table with food and candlesticks.'

'And the goblets.'

'Goblets, plates, bowls. Everything you would expect on a banqueting table.'

'And what time would the goblets have been put on the table?'

Fleming wrinkled his nose. 'Two o'clock? Half past two, maybe. We don't work to a schedule, we just do what needs to be done.'

'And do I have this right, you set up the table and then it's just left there ready to be wheeled onto the stage when it's needed?'

Fleming nodded. 'That's pretty much it, yes.'

'Could anyone have gone near the table between the setting up and the start of the play?'

'Absolutely anybody,' said Fleming. 'In fact, there was quite a bit of nibbling going on.'

'Nibbling?' echoed Whitlock.

'The food. People would keep taking food. So there were always people at the table.'

'Have I got this right?' said Richards. 'You think someone put poison into Macbeth's goblet?'

'We're considering a range of possibilities at the moment,' said Dunning.

'Because if that's what you're suggesting, that means it was a member of the group that killed Edgar.'

'Are you saying that there were no strangers in the church prior to the curtain going up?'

Richards frowned and rubbed his chin. 'I can't remember any strangers being there.' He looked at Fleming. 'What about you?'

'I only remember my team being here in the morning. And the electrician was here.'

'Electrician?' said Dunning.

'There's no power here, so we have to run a cable in from next door to run the lights. We used a local firm. He was here when we arrived, and he left at about four o'clock in the afternoon once we had the lights up and running.'

'What was his name?'

'Jimmy. I don't know his family name, but his company is called Bright Sparks.'

'And by local you mean Stratford-upon-Avon?'

Fleming nodded, and DS Whitlock scribbled in her notebook. 'But other than Jimmy, there were no other strangers in the church.' He and Richards both shook their heads.

There was a brief pause, and Richards began to get to his feet, but DI Dunning held up a hand. 'I've a few more questions for you, Mr Richards, if you don't mind. And you, Mr Fleming.'

Richards and Fleming exchanged a look, but then they both shrugged. 'No problem,' said Richards.

DI Dunning pulled out a chair and sat down. 'Of course, two men died yesterday,' he said. 'Mr Lake and the Reverend Troy Harper.'

'But Troy's death was a suicide, wasn't it?' said Fleming, with another glance at Richards.

'We're waiting for the results of the post-mortem. But yes, it certainly did seem that way. Mr Richards, do you recall what time it was when you discovered the Reverend Harper's body?'

'It was yesterday evening, about four hours before the show was due to start.'

'So, about six o'clock? The play started at ten, correct?'

'Yes. Six o'clock, that sounds about right. I rang the

emergency number as soon as I found him – they must have a record of the call? That would give you a more exact time.'

'Did you go round to the rectory?'

'I did,' said Richards. 'Troy hadn't turned up at the church and he wasn't answering his phone, so I walked over and knocked on the door. There was no answer, so I went round to the side of the house and looked in through a window.' He shuddered. 'I saw him hanging from the banister.'

'And you phoned the police immediately?' asked DI Dunning.

Richards nodded, looking upset. 'I decided that there was no need for an ambulance. Troy was clearly dead.'

'And you waited there for the police to arrive?'

'I knew they'd take their time,' said Richards. 'The Stratford-upon-Avon police station's front desk has limited opening hours due to staffing issues, so it shuts at five p.m. every day, two p.m. on Sundays.'

'It's ridiculous,' said Fleming. 'It's not as if criminals stop work at five, is it?'

'I came back to the church,' said Richards. 'I explained to Edgar that something had happened and asked him if he thought he could take the lead. He jumped at it.'

'You didn't consider cancelling the performance?'

Richards shrugged. 'The show must go on, right? I know that sounds harsh, but we had sold tickets, and everyone had worked so hard to put the play together. And Edgar knew the part backwards. In fact, he had been pushing to play the lead when we first announced we would be doing the Scottish Play.'

'The Scottish Play?' Whitlock said.

'That's what we call it,' Richards explained. 'It's considered bad luck to say the name of the play inside a theatre, so we say "the Scottish Play" instead.'

'It was certainly bad luck for Mr Lake,' said DS Whitlock. DI Dunning shot her a warning look.

'Mr Lake was happy to step into the role of Macbeth?' asked DI Dunning.

'He really did jump at it,' said Fleming. 'He was like the cat that got the cream.'

'I know the part of Banquo well enough to step in,' said Richards. 'Which is what I did. So Edgar took the role of Macbeth, and I played Banquo.'

'You did a bang-up job, Henry,' said Fleming. 'Especially at such short notice.'

'I did my best,' said Richards. 'It's not a huge part, and the dialogue isn't too difficult.'

DI Dunning raised a hand to recapture their attention. 'After you came back here to talk to Mr Lake about taking on the role of Macbeth, did you go back to the rectory?'

Richards nodded. 'I got back just as the police arrived. I took them to the window and showed them the body, and they broke down the door. It was too late. Troy had clearly been dead for a while, but they insisted on calling an ambulance. I didn't understand why, frankly. An undertaker would have been more appropriate.'

'There's a procedure that has to be followed in the event of a suicide,' said Dunning. 'Did you tell anyone else that he was dead?'

Richards looked uncomfortable. 'I was in a quandary about that,' he said. 'I mean, we had to tell everyone that Edgar would be standing in, but I didn't want to upset everyone. I especially didn't want everyone knowing that poor Troy had killed himself.' He managed an ironic smile. 'That would have taken the gloss off the evening somewhat. Though as it turned out, of course, things went from bad to worse.'

'Who did you tell?'

'Well, I told Edgar. And Amy was there when I explained what had happened, but I asked them not to broadcast it. And I told John.' He indicated Fleming, who nodded.

'Anyone else?'

Richards screwed up his face as he tried to remember. Eventually he relaxed. 'Just Edgar, John and Amy. I mean, we told everybody that Edgar would be stepping up as Macbeth, but they were only told that Troy was unavailable.'

'And when the police arrived at the rectory, did you go inside with them?'

'I did, yes. They said to wait outside, but Troy was my friend – I wanted to be there.'

'And I'm told that you found the will?'

'I did. On the hall table. There was an envelope with "To be opened in the event of my death", and as soon as I saw what it was, I gave it to the police.'

'Really, you shouldn't have touched it,' said DI Dunning. 'We'll have to take your fingerprints for comparison purposes. And you didn't see a note?'

'No, there was no note.'

'Which is strange, because usually when somebody takes their own life by hanging, they do leave a note,' said Lulu. Everyone turned to look at her. 'That's been my experience, anyway,' she said.

'There was no note,' Richards said emphatically. 'Just the will.'

DI Dunning turned back to him with a polite smile. 'Okay. Mr Richards, what I'd like you to do is to go back into the rectory with me and talk me through what happened there. Are you able to do that?'

Richards shrugged. 'I suppose so.'

DI Dunning nodded. He was still smiling, but his eyes were hard, Lulu noticed. 'Excellent,' he said. 'We really do appreciate your assistance.'

9

DI Dunning walked out of the church with Lulu. Conrad was on her shoulders, his tail curled around her neck. Richards and Fleming followed with DS Whitlock.

In the churchyard a black crow sat high on a leaning stone cross, feathers ruffled by the wind, watching them like a thief sizing up an opportunity. As they passed through the lychgate, Dunning thanked Fleming and told him they wouldn't need any more of his time.

As Fleming walked away, a black BMW pulled up behind DS Whitlock's car. The driver's door opened and a woman in police uniform climbed out. She was in her late forties or early fifties, with short dyed blonde hair cut pixie style and wire-framed circular glasses perched on a slightly upturned snub nose. The single crown and a pip on her uniform epaulettes showed that she was a chief superintendent.

'Chief Superintendent Alice Delaney,' whispered DI Dunning. 'I'm not sure why she's here. She's not with the murder investigation teams – she's number two in the local policing section. Reports directly to the Assistant Chief Constable.' He smiled and nodded as Delaney came towards them. 'Hello, ma'am. Can I help you?'

'The ACC asked me to swing by, seeing as how I'm local,' said Chief Superintendent Delaney. 'She's worried that we might have a media circus. Macbeth dying on stage is going to be a big story.'

'We haven't had any media involvement yet,' said DI Dunning.

'It'll come,' said Delaney. She frowned as she saw Conrad sitting on Lulu's shoulders.

'This is Mrs Lewis, formerly a detective superintendent with the Met. She was in the church when Mr Lake died, so I took her back in to see if she remembers anything pertinent.'

Chief Superintendent Delaney offered her hand. 'Nice to meet you, Mrs Lewis.' They shook hands. Delaney had a firm grip and a direct gaze. 'That must have been quite upsetting.'

'It was, yes,' said Lulu. 'For all concerned.'

Delaney released her grip on Lulu's hand. 'And you have a cat on your shoulder.'

'That's Conrad. He's also a witness.'

The chief superintendent nodded. 'Has he given a statement yet?' She chuckled at her own joke. 'Thank you for your assistance, anyway, Mrs Lewis.'

'Please, call me Lulu.'

Delaney didn't respond, turning her attention to DI Dunning. 'How is the investigation going?'

'The lab has confirmed that there was poison in the goblet the victim drank from on stage. We're compiling a list of people who could have added the poison to the goblet. Luckily, Mrs Lewis got her friends to take videos of everyone leaving last night, so we're tracking them down and we'll interview them.'

'I doubt that was luck, DI Dunning,' said Delaney, shooting Lulu a meaningful glance as if to say that casual sexism was still alive and well in the police.

'I didn't have the authority to stop anyone leaving,' said Lulu. 'I did ask, and some members of the audience agreed to stay, but most left.'

'I spoke to the chap in charge, and he said that most of the ticket sales were online, so they have names and addresses that we can cross-check with the videos,' Dunning continued.

'How much do we know about the victim?' asked Delaney.

'His name was Edgar Lake. He wasn't local but had lived in Stratford-upon-Avon for the past year. He was a journalist and ran a Shakespeare-based podcast. He joined the Stratford Players drama group not long after he arrived in town.'

'Family?'

'According to the people we spoke to last night, there's no wife or children, and no significant other. Everyone seems to think he lived alone.'

'How old was he?'

'According to his driving licence, twenty-eight.'

'And he was definitely poisoned?'

'Well, as I say, the lab has confirmed poison in the goblet – wolfsbane. And it was only in his goblet, not in any of the others; nor the bottle. But until we get the results of the post-mortem, we can't be certain that was what killed him.'

'But it looks likely that it was?'

Dunning nodded. 'Very much so.'

'Is it in any way possible that Mr Lake killed himself?'

Dunning frowned. 'Drank his own poison, you mean?'

'Why not? Actors are generally self-centred. If he did decide to kill himself, he might have wanted an audience to witness his final moments.' Delaney shrugged. 'It's just a thought.'

'I'll bear it in mind,' said Dunning. 'But we've finished here for now.'

'All right. Keep me updated on any developments,' said Delaney. 'The ACC wants this tied up as quickly as possible.'

'Sure,' said Dunning, although Lulu sensed that he wasn't exactly comfortable with the idea of the chief superintendent looking over his shoulder.

'Did you know that there was a suicide yesterday, ma'am?' asked DS Whitlock.

The chief superintendent frowned. 'No, I didn't,' she said.

Whitlock glanced at Dunning to check that she hadn't spoken out of turn. He smiled tightly, nodding for her to continue. She turned back to Delaney and explained, 'The actor who was due to play Macbeth, the Reverend Troy Harper, hanged himself yesterday afternoon.'

Chief Superintendent Delaney's hand flew up to cover her mouth. 'Troy Harper? I know him,' she said. 'Oh my God.'

'I'm sorry,' said Dunning. 'It was dealt with by uniforms yesterday and treated as a possible suicide with no suspicious factors. But we have asked for a post-mortem, and it'll be carried out this afternoon.'

'Did he leave a note?'

Dunning shook his head. 'Only a copy of his will. Leaving everything to his cleaner.'

'Elsie?'

'That's her. You know her?'

'I'd sometimes see Troy shopping with Elsie at Rother Street market on a Saturday,' said Chief Superintendent Delaney. 'Troy had no family, or not that I knew of. And he was due to play Macbeth, you say?'

'He was. Mr Lake was due to play another role, but he had understudied Macbeth, so he stepped in at short notice.'

The colour had drained from Delaney's face. 'I can't believe Troy is dead,' she said. 'He was a lovely man.' She shook her head. 'Was he unwell?'

'Not that we know of,' said Dunning. 'I was about to go and take a look around his home with Mr Richards.'

'I'll come with you,' said the chief superintendent.

'Of course,' said Dunning. 'It's not far.'

The chief superintendent locked her car and set off alongside Dunning. DS Whitlock followed with Henry Richards.

'They didn't say we couldn't go with them, did they?' whispered Lulu to Conrad.

'They didn't say we could,' Conrad pointed out. 'And why would they? You're a civilian.'

'Yes, all right, I am. But I was there when Edgar Lake died, and I did help secure the crime scene; so I am already involved, aren't I?'

'Yes, you are. That's what you want to hear, right?'

Lulu smiled. 'Yes, I suppose it is.' She set off after the police team at a safe distance. 'Come on, Conrad, admit it – aren't you the least bit curious?' She chuckled. 'Of course, now you'll remind me what curiosity did to the cat, won't you?'

'And you know we have Shakespeare to thank for that,' he said.

'I did not know that,' said Lulu.

'Well, sort of. The phrase used to be "care killed the cat", because at the time *care* meant worry or grief. Ben Jonson used the phrase in 1598 in his play *Every Man in His Humour*. Then, eight years later, Shakespeare used it in *Much Ado About Nothing*. I think his exact words were, "What, courage, man! What though care killed a cat, thou hast mettle enough in thee to kill care." It wasn't until the nineteenth century that *care* became *curiosity*. But yes, you are quite right; curiosity can have its downside. And not just for cats.'

'You didn't answer my question, though. Don't you want to know what happened? And if Edgar Lake was murdered, don't you want to know why?'

Conrad sighed. 'Of course I do. You know me too well.'

'Right back at you, Conrad. We are birds of a feather.'

'That's an inappropriate metaphor if ever I heard one.'

'No offence was intended.'

'Then none is taken.'

After five minutes of brisk walking, they reached St Mary's Church. It stood at the end of a narrow road, a pale stone building with a squat bell tower topped by a single wooden cross. The rectory was to the right of the church, shielded by a line of yew trees. It was a brick-built house with tall, narrow windows screened by yellowing lace curtains. The garden was enclosed by a low privet hedge and edged with neglected rosebushes. A path of cracked flagstones led to the front door and followed the contours of the building around to the rear garden.

There was a Warwickshire Police patrol car parked outside the rectory. Next to it stood a uniformed constable. He was young – only just into his twenties – and Lulu noted that his uniform and stab vest were at least one size too big for him.

She kept a discreet distance as DI Dunning led Richards over to the constable. 'I'm sure you remember PC Bennett, Mr Richards?' said Dunning. 'He accompanied you into the rectory yesterday evening.'

'I remember,' said Richards.

'Good morning, Mr Richards,' said the constable. He straightened up when he recognized Chief Superintendent Delaney. 'Ma'am,' he said. His eyes darted nervously around as he tried to work out if he was in any sort of trouble.

Sensing his unease, Dunning smiled. 'Chief Superintendent Delaney is here as an observer,' he said.

'You found the body?' asked Delaney.

'I did, ma'am,' said the constable. 'Actually, it was Mr Richards who saw it first, through the window. I gained entrance to the property under Section 17 of PACE, as I reasonably believed immediate action was required to save a life.'

'No one is worried about the lack of a warrant, PC Bennett,' said the chief superintendent with a kindly smile. 'You did the right thing.'

'I have Elsie Kwan in the car, ma'am,' he said. 'She wanted to go inside, but I said she'd have to wait.'

'That's all right. I know Elsie,' said Delaney. She went over to the patrol car and opened the rear passenger door. A small woman got out, dressed in a blue coat and carrying a hemp shopping bag. Her name suggested to Lulu that the woman was probably Chinese. She was in her fifties with tightly permed, glossy dyed black hair, and she wore thick-lensed black-framed glasses. Her cheeks were damp with tears and her eyes were red. She wiped her nose with a large white handkerchief, looking relieved when she recognized the chief superintendent.

'I am so sorry for your loss, Elsie,' said Delaney.

'I need to go inside to clean,' said Elsie.

Delaney looked over at Dunning. The inspector shrugged.

'SOCO have been and gone,' he said. 'There was nothing to suggest that it was anything but a . . .' Elsie put her handkerchief over her face and started to wail, and the inspector left the sentence unfinished.

Delaney put a hand on Elsie's shoulder. 'Could you wait in the car, please, Elsie, until we've had a look around? Then you can go in and clean if you want to.'

Elsie nodded tearfully. She got back into the car, and Delaney gently closed the door before turning back to join the others. As they headed for the front door of the rectory – Lulu and Conrad trailing behind – she said to Dunning, 'And you're saying that Troy Harper left everything to her in his will?'

The inspector nodded. 'He doesn't seem to have any living relatives. And to be honest, there probably wasn't much to leave. The rectory is Church property; he didn't own a car; there isn't much of value in the house. I suppose he may have had money in the bank but that's not likely, not on a priest's salary.'

'But you will check?'

'Yes, of course. We've put in a request to the bank already. Do you know Elsie's background?'

'Hong Kong Chinese. She's been in the UK five or six years, I think. The British Government started issuing passports to Hong Kong citizens after the Chinese started clamping down on democracy there.'

'Husband? Children?'

'I'm really not sure,' said Delaney.

There was police tape across the front door, but it wasn't closed; the door frame was splintered where the constable had kicked it in the previous day.

'Can we make good this damage as soon as possible?' said the chief superintendent.

'It's in hand, ma'am. Hopefully before midday.'

Delaney nodded. 'Excellent. And SOCO have done all they need to?'

'All done and dusted, ma'am,' he said. 'No pun intended.'

Delaney ignored the attempt at humour. 'So it's no longer a crime scene. There are no issues with allowing Elsie in to clean, are there?'

'None at all,' said the inspector.

Delaney turned to the constable. 'Right, constable. Show me exactly what happened when you arrived here yesterday.'

'Mr Richards took me round to the side of the rectory. There is a window there that looks into the hall, and we could see the Reverend Harper hanging from the banister. Then we came to the front door. I rang the bell, but there was no answer. Mr Richards said that the priest lived alone, so I forced the door.'

'So Elsie doesn't live in?' the chief superintendent asked Richards.

Richards shook his head. 'I think Troy felt that his parishioners might frown on that,' he said. 'She usually arrived at eight in the morning to cook his breakfast and left at five.'

'So he killed himself after she left?'

'I assume so,' said Richards.

'Okay,' said the chief superintendent. She looked over at the constable. 'Right, so what then?'

'I went inside.'

'On your own?'

'I asked Mr Richards to wait outside, but he followed me in.'

'I wanted to help,' said Richards. 'Troy was a friend. I'd

been in the rectory many times. We often used to rehearse there.'

Delaney gestured for the constable to open the door, then followed him in. DI Dunning and Richards went in after them, and Lulu and Conrad brought up the rear with DS Whitlock. The hallway was wide, with bare polished floorboards and heavy wooden furniture: a hat stand, a sideboard, a bookcase. Most of the books were on religious or theological subjects, Lulu saw, but there were several volumes of crossword puzzles and sudoku too.

To the left was an open door leading to a sitting room. Lulu could see a battered leather sofa, a matching armchair and a Victorian cast-iron fireplace. Ahead of them was a staircase, and to the right was the window that the constable had looked through.

Lulu heard Conrad sniffing the air. She reached up to stroke his neck, but he dropped down off her shoulders and landed on the floor with a dull thud. He arched his back, stretched, then padded into the sitting room.

PC Bennett walked along the staircase and pointed up. 'He had tied a rope to the banister, then put the noose over his head and lowered himself over. It didn't look to me as if he broke his neck. I'm pretty sure the noose strangled him.'

'So he didn't use a chair or a ladder? He just dropped over the banister?' Delaney's gaze travelled along the wooden banister, which was covered with fingerprint powder.

'Yes, ma'am,' said the constable.

'Did you untie him?' asked Dunning.

'I tried, but I couldn't. So I ran to the kitchen and got a carving knife.' PC Bennett pointed down the hallway. The kitchen door was open. Lulu could see old-fashioned kitchen cabinets and a scuffed oblong pine table with four chairs. 'I cut the rope and he fell to the floor. I checked for a pulse, but he was dead. That's when I called for an ambulance.'

Conrad was walking around the sitting room, sniffing, his tail vertical. Lulu waved at him to come back into the hall, but he ignored her.

The chief superintendent looked at Richards. 'And where were you while PC Bennett was cutting him down?'

Richards pointed at the sideboard. 'I was standing there. That's where I saw the letter. I opened it and saw that it was his will. His last will and testament.'

The chief superintendent frowned. 'You just took it upon yourself to open a private letter?'

'He'd written "To be opened in the event of my death" on the envelope, so he clearly wanted it to be opened.'

'And where is the letter now?'

'I left it on the sideboard,' said Richards.

PC Bennett nodded. 'It was there. I saw it,' he said.

'SOCO took it with them,' said DI Dunning. 'We'll arrange to take Mr Richards' fingerprints for elimination purposes. Maybe he can go back to the station with you when we're done here?'

Delaney shook her head at Richards. 'It would have been far better if you hadn't touched it,' she said.

'I'm really sorry,' said Richards. 'I wasn't thinking straight.'

Conrad reappeared at the door to the sitting room. Lulu bent down so that he could jump onto her shoulders, but he ignored her and turned down the hall towards the kitchen.

The chief superintendent looked around. 'So there's

nothing to suggest that this was anything other than suicide, DI Dunning?'

'It seems straightforward enough,' said DI Dunning. 'But we'll know for sure after the post-mortem this afternoon.'

'I'll tell Elsie that she can get on with her cleaning.'

'That's fine,' said the inspector. 'Though I would have thought it was the last place she'd want to be.'

'Sometimes a routine can help you through the grieving process,' said Lulu.

He met her eyes briefly. 'I guess so.'

Conrad padded back down the hall. This time when Lulu bent down, he jumped up onto her shoulders and settled round her neck.

'That is quite a trick,' said the chief superintendent. 'How long did it take you to teach him to do that?'

'Actually, he taught me,' said Lulu. 'And I was a quick learner.'

10

Lulu watched as Delaney's black BMW pulled away.

'Is it usual for a chief superintendent to get involved in an investigation like this at such an early stage?' she asked DI Dunning.

'Very unusual,' he replied. 'But she is local, and she does – did – know Troy Harper. And I can see her point: an actor dying during a Halloween performance of *Macbeth* could well attract national attention. The sooner we tie everything up, the better.'

'I always hated senior officers looking over my shoulder,' said Lulu.

'I'm not a fan, either,' said the inspector. 'It would be different if she had an investigative background, but she was traffic followed by local policing. She's never been out of uniform.' He realized that DS Whitlock was within earshot and cleared his throat. 'Mind you, any input at this stage is welcome, seeing as we don't really have anything concrete to go on.'

'It seems to me that we still don't know whether Mr Lake was the intended victim, or whether he drank poison that was intended for the Reverend Harper,' said Lulu.

'I can't see anyone wanting to murder a priest, can you?'

Lulu raised an eyebrow. 'That would depend on the priest, wouldn't it? It's the Catholic Church, after all. There are lots of skeletons in lots of closets.'

'I did ask around, and no one has a bad word to say about Harper. He was very well liked in the town. There hasn't been a hint of scandal.'

'Will you be speaking to his doctor? I know you told Delaney you weren't aware of any health problems . . .'

'It's in hand. But if he did have health issues or money trouble, that only makes it more likely that he killed himself. And the fact that he left the will out to be found does suggest that he wanted his affairs tied up.'

'That's true,' said Lulu. 'But the lack of a note still worries me.'

'He may have assumed that the will itself would be enough of a note. But either way, I really can't see that anyone had reason to kill him.'

'What about Edgar Lake?' asked Lulu. 'Would anyone have a motive for wanting him dead?'

'From the little I've found out, I'd say Lake had more enemies than the Reverend Harper.'

Lulu frowned. 'How so?'

'Lake was a journalist. Most of his time seems to have been spent on a podcast about Stratford-upon-Avon and things Shakespearean, and he has quite popular TikTok, Instagram and Facebook profiles. His podcast has about fifty thousand regular listeners around the world, which means he was probably earning a decent living from it.'

'I can't see how a podcast would make him a target.'

'He moved here a year ago. Prior to that, he was an investigative journalist. He worked for the *Observer* in London for a few years on their investigative team and then went freelance, specializing in crime and terrorism. Crime-wise, he turned over several major London gangsters and also did a series of articles exposing corruption in London and Dubai, especially in the defence industry. He wasn't afraid of naming names.'

'So he would have made a lot of enemies,' said Lulu, nodding.

'Definitely. I was thinking that could be why he'd left London and moved to Stratford-upon-Avon. Maybe he was made an offer he couldn't refuse. Or maybe he thought they wouldn't come after him here.' Dunning held up his hands. 'I know – supposition.'

'But would gangsters bother with poison? Wouldn't they be much more likely to shoot him?'

'You'd have thought so. But he wrote about corrupt Russian politicians, and the Russians do like their poisons. And he exposed an Iranian government official who was paying backhanders for access to Number Ten. The Iranian government has used poison to kill off its dissidents in the past.'

'Had he written anything recently that might have put a target on his back?'

'Nothing in the past year; but of course we don't know what he was working on. I've applied for a warrant to search his home, computer and phone.'

'What about the *Macbeth* cast and crew? Did he have any problems with them?'

'None that they talked about.'

Lulu frowned. 'Do you think there was something they weren't saying?'

The inspector shrugged. 'I'm not sure. Just a feeling.'

'Copper's intuition?'

'It's a thing, right?'

'Of course it's a thing. And the more experience you have, the sharper your intuition becomes. So, what was your copper's intuition telling you?'

DI Dunning shook his head. 'Really, I'm probably overthinking it. And of course they were all in shock, seeing what they'd seen.'

'No question of that. I was shocked, and I wasn't on the stage. What's troubling you?'

'It was when I was questioning them about what had happened. None of the actors or the crew seemed to be displaying much emotion. I'm not saying they were ready to dance on his grave, but on the other hand, they didn't seem particularly upset. For instance, when we were in the house just now, you could see that Richards was obviously affected by the priest's death. And the cleaning lady was crying. But at the church the other night, none of the cast or crew showed anywhere near that kind of reaction to Lake's death.'

'You did say they were in shock,' said Lulu.

'I did. And they were. But take Richards, specifically – Harper's death clearly affected him, but I didn't get the feeling that he was upset about Lake. Stunned, yes, at what he'd seen, but there wasn't the sense that he'd lost a friend or someone he liked. And the woman playing Lady Macbeth . . . she was actually smiling. She was almost grinning at times.'

'Really?' Lulu was intrigued. 'I didn't see that. On stage, she was definitely disturbed by what had happened. She looked horrified. Could it have been a nervous grin? People react differently to shocking situations. Did you mention it to her?'

The inspector shook his head. 'I didn't.'

'I should be seeing her tonight at my goddaughter's birthday dinner.'

'Lady Macbeth?'

Lulu nodded. 'Amy Jenner. She's a good friend of Celia's. In fact, that's the main reason we went to see the play. I'm sure she'll be at the restaurant tonight, so I'll talk to her and try to get a feel for what she thought of Lake.'

'Tactfully, I hope?'

Lulu smiled. 'Don't worry. Tact is my middle name.'

'Lulu Tact Lewis? It has a nice ring to it.' Dunning looked at his watch. 'We'd better be going, but I have time to run you back to your boat,' he offered.

'That would be very nice of you,' said Lulu.

As they approached his Vectra and DS Whitlock's Fiesta, Whitlock's phone rang. She took the call, said 'Yes' a few times and then 'Thank you so much,' before ending the call. 'That's the manager of Harper's bank. He's happy to talk to us.'

'Did we get a court order?' asked DI Dunning.

'It's in hand, but the manager says he'll talk to us anyway. Apparently, the bank has had some issues with his account.'

'Right, well, let's strike while the iron is hot,' said the inspector. 'Are you okay to come along, Mrs Lewis, and then I can drop you at *The Lark* afterwards?'

'Of course,' said Lulu. She eased Conrad off her shoulders and climbed into the passenger seat of the Vectra, where Conrad curled into her lap.

It was a short drive to the bank, a red-brick building at the top of the high street. Dunning and Whitlock found parking spaces nearby and they all headed in, passing a sound-activated plastic skeleton that emitted a ghostly wail and rattled. After a couple of minutes' wait they were shown into the manager's office. According to the plate on the door, his name was Roger Ballantine. He looked as if he was probably in his early thirties, with light brown hair that was receding. He wore a dark blue suit with a waistcoat and a light blue tie with what looked like rugby balls on it.

DI Dunning and DS Whitlock showed their warrant cards and introduced themselves. 'And this is Mrs Lulu Lewis, who is assisting us today.'

'I didn't realize that the police had feline units as well as canines,' said Mr Ballantine, nodding at Conrad.

'Conrad is just along for the ride,' said Lulu.

Two high-backed chairs were in front of Ballantine's desk, and there were two more against the wall by the window. 'Perhaps you could pull one of those over?' the bank manager asked DI Dunning. The inspector went over and picked up a chair. He placed it next to the other two, and they all sat down.

Once they were settled, Ballantine said, 'I appreciate that you are in the process of obtaining a court order to see the Reverend Harper's account, but I wanted to have a chat with you first in view of what happened yesterday.'

'His suicide, you mean?' said DI Dunning.

'Yes, that – but I also spoke to him yesterday morning. On the phone. The branch was concerned about some activity on his account, and I asked him to come in for a chat. We arranged an appointment for next Monday.'

'What concerns did you have?' asked DI Dunning.

Ballantine picked up a pen and began toying with it. A sign of nervousness, Lulu realized. That, and the fact that his left leg seemed to be trembling.

'I can't give you specific figures, not until my head office has been served with the court order; but I can talk to you generally, if that's all right with you?'

'Any guidance you can give us will be much appreciated,' said DI Dunning.

'That's what I thought,' said Ballantine. 'The thing is, the Reverend Harper has been making regular cash withdrawals, on the last day of the month. He has been doing that for the past six months. Well, last month was the sixth. The account is almost empty, so he was unable to make a withdrawal this month.'

'How much were these withdrawals?' asked the inspector.

The bank manager shifted uncomfortably in his seat. 'I shouldn't . . .' he said, but then he shook his head. 'I don't suppose it matters; the gentleman is dead now. Three thousand pounds. Every month. The last withdrawal he made took his account down to just one thousand pounds, give or take.'

'Was money being paid into the account?' asked the inspector.

'Some, but nowhere near that amount, so he was running the balance down. From what I understand, priests generally receive a stipend rather than a fixed salary. It's an allowance provided by the Church to support the priest with their ministry and daily living expenses. The amounts do vary, but on average there was about twelve hundred pounds going into his account each month.'

'Did you ask him what he needed the money for?'

'Of course. The first time he asked to withdraw three thousand pounds, the cashier questioned him. It was a red flag because it was way above any withdrawals he had made in the past. He said he was having work done on the rectory and the builder wanted to be paid in cash. That's not unusual, so the withdrawal was approved. The next month he said the same thing, and from then on he wasn't questioned.'

'Do you believe he was paying a builder?' asked DI Dunning.

'I did walk past the rectory three months ago and didn't see any building activity,' said Ballantine. 'But really, there's a limit to what we can do in cases like this. We can issue a Suspicious Activity Report with the UK Financial Intelligence Unit if we suspect illegal activity such as money laundering, fraud or terrorist financing, but we had no evidence that he was involved in anything like that. He was a Catholic priest, for God's sake.'

'So what did you think he was doing with the money?' asked the inspector.

'What I thought would only be an assumption, which is why I asked him in for a meeting,' said Ballantine.

'I understand that, but I'd like to hear your thoughts on what his reasons might have been for taking out three thousand pounds a month.'

Ballantine continued to fiddle with his pen, but his left leg had gone still. 'In my experience, if customers begin making unexpected large cash withdrawals it's because of sex, drugs, alcohol, gambling or extortion. And I have to say, it's the internet that's behind most of it. We had a customer last year who wanted to transfer twenty thousand pounds to a US account because Brad Pitt needed help to pay an unexpected hospital bill.'

'*The* Brad Pitt?' said Lulu.

'Well, she thought it was Brad Pitt the movie star, but we

suspect it was a Nigerian fraudster. She had been talking to him for more than a month. Not talking face to face, but he was chatting to her on Facebook and Messenger. He said that he'd never met anyone like her and that she was a refreshing change from the people he had to hang around with in Los Angeles. He'd started talking about settling down with her in the UK.'

'Unbelievable,' said DI Dunning.

'It happens a lot,' said the manager. 'There are a lot of lonely people around.'

'A lot of lonely, stupid people,' said DI Dunning.

'Stupid maybe, but the bank has a responsibility to take care of its customers,' said Ballantine. 'We managed to convince her eventually that she was dealing with a fraudster, but I felt that she always blamed me for the end of her romance. Not that I think the Reverend Harper had fallen in love with a Hollywood movie star. And I doubt that drugs would be a problem, but you never know.'

'There'll be a post-mortem, and that will show up any drug or alcohol use,' said DI Dunning.

'I would have thought gambling would be the more likely option,' said the manager. 'It's so easy to lose large amounts online these days.'

'Except he wanted cash,' said Lulu. 'If it was online he'd be using a credit or debit card.'

'True,' said the manager. 'But there are plenty of bookmakers in the town. Four or five at the last count.'

'Is it likely that a priest would be popping into a betting shop?' asked Lulu.

The manager raised his hands and shrugged. 'I was just running through the options.'

'Extortion was the last possibility you raised,' said DI Dunning.

'Yes. Extortion or blackmail. I wanted to explain his options to him, and that if he was under any sort of duress we have people within the bank who could offer him help and advice.'

'When you spoke to the Reverend Harper on the phone, how did he sound?' asked the inspector.

'He was quiet. He said he understood my concern and that he would explain everything when he saw me. We probably spoke for less than two minutes. I suggested we meet on Monday; he said fine, and I said how about ten o'clock, and he said he'd be here.'

'And what time would this have been, when you made the call?'

'Between nine and ten in the morning. Closer to half past nine, I think. I'm always in the office at eight – I spend the first hour answering emails, and then I do my phone calls between nine and ten.'

DI Dunning looked over at DS Whitlock, who was diligently taking notes. 'Anything else?' he said.

She shook her head. 'I think we're good, sir.'

Lulu raised a hand. 'Could I ask a question?' she said. 'How long was the Reverend Harper a customer here?'

Ballantine leaned over and tapped on his keyboard, then peered at his screen. 'A few months shy of fifteen years.'

'And was his account transferred from another branch?'

Ballantine looked at his screen again, then shook his head. 'No, the account was opened here. Before my time.'

'And I don't suppose the computer would say if he supplied any banking references?' DI Dunning frowned at her, and she smiled. 'I was just wondering where he worked before coming to Stratford-upon-Avon. It's nothing, really.'

'It's a good question,' said Dunning, nodding. 'What about it, Mr Ballantine? Were references supplied?'

The manager tapped on his keyboard. 'I can't see any references on file,' he said. 'To be honest, as a Catholic priest taking up a post at a local church, it's possible that he wasn't asked to supply references.'

'Thank you,' said Lulu.

Dunning stood up and nodded to Ballantine. 'Thank you for your time,' he said. 'And for being so helpful.'

'If you could possibly keep what I have told you to yourself until the court order is served, you'd be doing me a service,' said the manager. 'I was just worried that in some way I'd been responsible for . . . what happened.'

'I really wouldn't worry about that, Mr Ballantine,' said the inspector. 'I doubt that it was the prospect of a meeting with you that made him do what he did.'

'Did he leave a note? Did he explain why he was doing it?'

'He didn't, I'm afraid,' said Dunning.

The bank manager winced. 'Well, I hope he's at peace now; that's all I can say.'

11

Lulu, DI Dunning and DS Whitlock walked back towards the cars.

'You were wondering what the Reverend Harper did before he came to Stratford-upon-Avon,' Dunning said.

Lulu nodded. 'I don't think he had an alcohol or drugs problem,' she said thoughtfully. 'The rectory didn't look like the home of an alcoholic, and if he had been an addict, I don't see that the Stratford Players would have given him the lead role in a production of *Macbeth*.' She stroked Conrad's neck, and his claws tightened on the shoulders of her sheepskin jacket.

'He could have been a high-functioning alcoholic. Or hidden his drug use,' Dunning suggested.

'True. But it's not likely, is it? So, do we think he has a secret lover?'

'Of course not.'

'You answered that quickly.'

DI Dunning chuckled dryly. 'He was, what, fifty-five? Not great looking, and living on a priest's stipend. I don't see women flocking to his door. Leaving aside the fact that priests are supposed to be celibate.'

'Which, if the bank manager's list is correct, leaves us with extortion or blackmail. And if he had done anything wrong here, it would be known, wouldn't it? It's a small place. Tongues would wag. So it occurred to me that if the money was to pay off an extortionist it would probably be because of something that had happened in the past, before he came here.'

'Ah,' said DI Dunning. 'Yes, that makes sense. Okay, I'll talk to the diocese and see what they know about his previous posting.'

'Of course, the money could be for something completely innocuous,' said Lulu. 'He might have been helping out parishioners who had fallen on hard times.'

'Do you believe that?' asked the inspector.

Lulu paused before answering. 'Not really,' she said. 'I was just trying to give him the benefit of the doubt.'

'As I said, I'll reach out to the diocese.'

'Yes, that's the obvious thing to do, but the Catholic Church does have a track record of sweeping things under the carpet.'

'Let me give it some thought,' said Dunning. 'But our priority at the moment has to be identifying Edgar Lake's killer.' He looked at his watch. 'Can one of us offer you a lift back to your boat? DS Whitlock could drop you at the basin.'

'Oh, no, it's fine. I'm happy to walk. It's such a pretty town, I love soaking up the atmosphere.'

'No problem. And please let me know how you get on at your goddaughter's birthday party tonight.'

'I will. I'll call you if I get anything at all from Amy.'

He nodded. 'Excellent.'

Dunning unlocked the Vectra, and Whitlock headed for her Fiesta with a parting smile to Lulu. Lulu waited until both cars were out of sight before speaking to Conrad.

'All right, spill the beans,' she said.

'What beans?' said Conrad, innocently.

'You know very well what beans. What got you all excited back at the rectory?'

'You didn't notice it? Of course you didn't. Humans have no sense of smell.'

'We do so have a sense of smell. It's just that a cat's nose is more sensitive.'

'Fifteen times as sensitive, if you must know.'

'You clearly smelled something in the sitting room.'

'I did. Yes. Wolfsbane. The poison.'

'No.'

'Yes. And it was in the kitchen.'

'That can't be.'

'My nose doesn't make mistakes.'

'But why would there be poison in the rectory?'

'I'm just telling you what I smelled. And I definitely smelled wolfsbane.'

Lulu shook her head in confusion. 'It doesn't make any sense.'

'It does if someone in the rectory poisoned Mr Lake.'

'But the only people in the rectory were the Reverend Harper and Mrs Kwan. And the Reverend Harper was dead when Mr Lake died, so it couldn't possibly be him.' Lulu shook her head again. 'That can't be right.'

'What can't be right?'

'What possible motive would either of them have for killing Mr Lake? No, there must be some other explanation.' Her eyes widened. 'What if there's wolfsbane in the garden? It grows wild. They could have brushed up against it and taken the pollen inside.'

'Did you see wolfsbane in the garden?'

'No, but I wasn't looking.' Lulu pursed her lips and exhaled. 'We need to have a look around for ourselves.'

'You know wolfsbane is highly toxic to cats,' said Conrad.

'So many plants are,' said Lulu as she started walking back towards the church. 'You've told me before that you can't go near lilies, foxgloves, chrysanthemums, daffodils, tulips . . .'

'It's a very long list. Gardens can be death traps.'

'You're welcome to stay on my shoulders.'

'I shall take you up on that,' said Conrad.

After a few minutes, they reached the rectory. Lulu opened the gate and walked up the path to the front door. There were lots of roses but no wolfsbane. She followed the path around to the right, where more neglected roses grew along the side of the house. There were two rhododendron bushes, one with pink flowers and one with blue. Lulu knew they were on Conrad's list of plants to be avoided, but they couldn't have been the source of the poison that killed Mr Lake.

The back garden was unkempt, with a grass lawn that clearly hadn't been mown for months, surrounded by overgrown flower beds. There were large flowering plants but there were weeds, too, that had clearly been growing for years. In a far corner, Lulu spotted several plants that were considerably taller than her, with single stems shooting up from a base of large, slightly hairy leaves. Halfway up the stems were bell-shaped, pendulous purple flowers that hung downwards as if avoiding the sun. She headed towards them for a closer look.

'Foxgloves,' said Conrad. 'Just as poisonous to cats – and humans – as wolfsbane, but for different reasons. You can get digitalis from foxgloves, which can be used to treat heart conditions. But even a tiny amount of the leaves or flowers can lead to cardiac arrest. They contain cardiac glycosides, whereas wolfsbane contains alkaloids like aconite, which is a potent neurotoxin that can cause sudden death. As we saw during the performance of *Macbeth*.'

'You certainly know your chemistry,' said Lulu.

'It helps to know what's poisonous and what isn't.'

'So the Reverend Harper would have easy access to digitalis, wouldn't he?' said Lulu. She paused in front of the plants. 'I mean, there it is, clear as day.'

'As would his cleaner. In fact, as would anybody who took the time to visit the garden.' Conrad stiffened. 'Uh-oh – she's watching us from one of the upstairs rooms.'

Lulu glanced up and saw Elsie Kwan looking down at them from behind a faded lace curtain. Lulu smiled and waved, but the curtain fell back into place and she couldn't see the cleaner any more.

'Do you think she could see that I was talking to you?' Lulu asked.

'If she could, she probably assumed that you're a crazy cat lady who talks to herself.'

'That's reassuring,' said Lulu.

'Is it?'

Lulu laughed. 'Not really.' She headed around to the front of the house and out through the front gate.

'Could it have been digitalis that you smelled inside the rectory?' she asked as they headed back towards the canal basin.

'It would be like you confusing the smell of an apple with an orange,' said Conrad. 'They are two very different scents.

It was definitely wolfsbane I smelled. In the kitchen and in the front room.'

'But it doesn't make sense, does it? Why would either of them use wolfsbane as a poison when they have such easy access to foxgloves and digitalis?'

'Maybe it means that neither of them is the killer,' said Conrad.

'If that's the case, why does the house smell of wolfsbane?'

'That's a very good question, Lulu. And it's not one that I can answer at the moment. But I shall definitely give it some thought. As the Bard himself said, let me muse awhile.'

'What play is that from?' asked Lulu.

'Ah, I might have made it up,' said Conrad. 'Artistic licence.'

12

Back on board *The Lark*, Lulu made herself a mug of tea and served up some tuna for Conrad. He bolted it down in less than a minute. 'Goodness, you were hungry,' she said.

'We missed breakfast, remember?'

'So we did. I forgot, in all the excitement. Still, we should be in for a treat tonight. Apparently the restaurant we're going to is one of the best in Stratford-upon-Avon.'

'Michelin starred?'

'Well, no. I don't think there are any Michelin-starred restaurants in the town.'

'Makes you wonder why Shakespeare wanted to live here.'

Lulu opened her mouth to reply, but then realized Conrad was joking. She wagged a finger at him. 'You almost had me there. Now, it may not have a Michelin star, but it is definitely cat friendly, and they have some very tasty wild salmon for you.'

Conrad licked his left paw as Lulu sipped her tea. She put down her mug and went to the bedroom. She opened the wardrobe, wondering what she should wear. A dress, she decided – which brought her options down to five, as she had already worn one to Celia's house. She took out two dresses and held them up, then decided she needed a second opinion and stepped back into the saloon. 'What do you think?' she asked.

Conrad stopped licking his paw and put his head on one side as he studied the dresses. 'The blue one,' he said.

Lulu smiled. 'You're right,' she said.

'Of course I'm right,' he said. 'That's why you asked my opinion.'

'I can't argue with that. You do have wonderful taste.'

Conrad sat up. 'I've been thinking about something you said earlier. About how people who take their lives by hanging usually leave a note. '

Lulu nodded. 'It's not a hard and fast rule. But in my experience, the more thought and planning goes into a suicide, the more likely it is that the person will leave a note.'

'I suppose that's logical, isn't it? If it's an impulsive decision, there may not be time to write a note.'

'Exactly. And – well, hanging does take a bit of preparation. In the case of the Reverend Harper he had to get the rope, climb the stairs, tie it to the banister and around his neck, then climb over and drop. All that takes time. And if there was no rush, then he could have sat down to write a letter explaining why he was doing it. Although of course, if there are mental health issues at play, the person might not feel able to write a letter.'

'Mental health issues,' said Conrad. 'Is that what typically makes a person suicidal?'

'Sadly, it's a common trigger. People get depressed, or they suffer from things like anxiety, bipolar disorder, PTSD . . . And it can be so difficult these days to get the correct treatment.'

'What other reasons are there?'

Lulu sighed and sat down beside him. 'Oh, there are so many things that can trigger it. It really depends on the person. Something that seems quite trivial to one person could drive a more vulnerable person to kill themselves. And lots of people have experienced trauma in one form or another. That can have lasting psychological effects, even much later in life. Despair or hopelessness can be triggers, where people feel trapped in situations they think will never improve. Sometimes it's because they have lost a loved one, or even lost a job that was important to them. Loss can be a major trigger. Or loneliness, or ill health.' She forced a smile. 'This conversation has taken a very dark turn.'

'I'm sorry,' Conrad said. 'It's just something that has always fascinated me.'

Lulu raised an eyebrow. 'Fascinated?'

'Maybe that's not the right word. But I find it hard to understand why anyone would choose to end their life, when life is so precious.'

'I do agree with you,' said Lulu. 'After my husband passed away, I was depressed. Distraught. I felt awful, and I cried for days – weeks, even. But no matter how low I was, I never thought of ending my life. The idea didn't even occur to me. And earlier, I had setbacks during my police career that made me depressed and angry; there were very difficult times, but I wouldn't have considered suicide.'

'So maybe it's a personality type?' said Conrad. 'Could it be that some people are more susceptible to killing themselves?'

'What, you mean it's in their DNA? It's genetic?'

'Well, if loss and pain affect people in such different ways – yes, maybe it's down to your genes.'

Lulu picked up her mug of tea. 'I suppose if I were in real physical pain, and if no medicine could provide relief, and if I knew that the pain would never go away, then maybe . . .'

'Really?'

She smiled at the concern in Conrad's voice. 'I'm only speaking hypothetically. But that's the only circumstance where I can really begin to imagine considering it. And even then, I doubt that I would go through with it. What about you?'

'It's not something that cats do,' said Conrad. 'In fact, I don't think any animals other than humans deliberately end their own lives.'

'What about lemmings?'

Conrad chuckled. 'Please don't tell me you bought into that myth.'

'I thought lemmings were renowned for leaping off cliffs.'

'Absolute tosh,' said Conrad. 'Lemmings are small rodents that live in Arctic regions, and their populations go through natural boom and bust cycles, during which they migrate in large groups in search of food. Now, during migration, some might accidentally drown while trying to cross rivers or lakes. But they don't deliberately kill themselves.'

'But I've seen footage of them leaping off cliffs.'

'Fake footage, yes. Done long before faking videos was really a thing. The scenes you will have seen come from a 1958 Disney documentary called *White Wilderness*. Those scenes were staged. The producers forced those poor lemmings off the cliff for dramatic effect.'

'That's terrible!'

'It is. But the myth lives on. And I stand by my premise, that humans are the only animals who take their own lives.'

'Okay. You may well be right.'

'Oh, I'm sure that I am. But now, can we talk about the Reverend Harper? Why do you think he killed himself?'

'Without a note, it's hard to say. But there's no doubt he was having money problems. And extortion is a definite possibility. Or blackmail.'

'There had been no reports of mental illness, though?'

'No, that's true. And a priest is always talking to parishioners, so if he had been really unwell, it would probably have been noticed.'

'He hadn't lost anyone recently. And he wasn't in danger of losing his job.'

'We don't really know that for sure, do we?'

'I'm just saying, it looks as if the extortion or blackmail possibilities are the most likely motives for his suicide.'

Lulu frowned. 'I tend to agree with you. But how does that help us solve the murder of Edgar Lake? The Reverend Harper took his own life, there's no doubt about that. But Mr Lake was definitely murdered. I think that's what we should be concentrating on.'

'I still feel that the two are linked.'

'Feline intuition?'

'It is an accepted fact that cats are both intuitive and empathic,' said Conrad. 'And yes, my gut feeling is that the deaths are in some way connected.'

'But the scenarios are completely different.'

'I didn't say I knew how they are connected, just that they are. I keep coming back to what I said before. If the Reverend Harper hadn't killed himself, would he instead have died on stage after drinking from the poisoned goblet?'

'Well, that would depend on whether he was the person the killer really wanted to kill, or if they intended to kill Mr Lake.'

'Exactly!' said Conrad. 'But only someone who knew that

the Reverend Harper was dead would know that Mr Lake would be playing Macbeth.'

'No, the troupe announced it, remember? They put up a sign saying that Mr Lake would be taking the role. Because of unseen circumstances, they said – but it means that everyone knew.'

'In that case, it also depends on when the poison was put into the goblet,' said Conrad. 'If that was done earlier in the day, then surely the Reverend Harper must have been the target. But if the killer put the poison into the goblet *after* the announcement was made, then he must have wanted to kill Mr Lake.'

Lulu nodded. 'You talk a lot of sense.'

'I am a very sensible cat.'

'Yes, you are. And of course this was all well planned in advance.'

'Why do you say that?'

'Because wolfsbane takes time to prepare. You can't just pop into a chemist and buy it. You have to get the plants and boil them to get the extract. It wasn't a spur-of-the-moment thing.'

'Which, as always, brings us back to motive,' said Conrad. 'If we knew *why*, then we'd have a chance of knowing *who*.'

'But we don't know why, do we?'

'Not yet. We need to start looking. What about going back to talk to everyone involved? Sometimes people remember things after the event, don't they?'

'They do, absolutely. But I'm retired, Conrad. My days of knocking on doors are over. I'm just a civilian now. People don't have to answer my questions.'

'No; but they might, if you ask nicely.'

Lulu laughed. Actually, Conrad was right. It always amazed her how easily people could be persuaded to talk if you smiled sweetly. Many of her former colleagues would put on a game face when they carried out an interrogation, trying to look as menacing as possible. Or they might stay cold and impersonal, aloof even, and let the facts speak for themselves. Lulu's approach was always far less adversarial, and more often than not the 'softly-softly' technique would pay dividends. Not with hardened criminals, of course. They were immune to tactics and would just sit with their heads down and arms folded, saying nothing other than 'no comment'.

'If we could talk to anyone, who would you talk to?' she asked.

'The electrician, the Bright Sparks man. He was there when the table was being set up, wasn't he?'

'Jimmy, surname unknown. Yes, he would be worth talking to. But I'm sure DI Dunning has that in hand.'

'And Amy, Celia's friend. DI Dunning said that she had a strange reaction to Mr Lake's death.'

'He said she was smiling a lot; but sometimes that's how people react to stress. Anyway, as I said to the inspector, she'll be at the birthday party tonight, so I can talk to her then.' Lulu smiled. 'Now you're starting to get interested, aren't you? Before, you were teasing me about wanting to get involved in the investigation, but now you're as keen as I am to find out what happened.'

'It's a puzzle, and I don't like unsolved puzzles,' said Conrad. 'And the biggest puzzle is who was the intended victim. We're no nearer answering that question, are we? Did the killer want to poison the priest and kill Mr Lake by mistake, or was Mr Lake always the intended victim?'

'That's the $64,000 question, isn't it?' She smiled. 'Why is it $64,000, do you know? Why do we say that?'

'It comes from a popular American TV game show from the fifties. The contestants had to answer increasingly difficult questions for cash prizes that doubled each round, starting from $64 and going all the way up to $64,000.'

'So like *Who Wants to Be a Millionaire*?'

'Exactly. In fact $64,000 back then would be worth about half a million pounds these days.' Conrad wrinkled his nose. 'The key to answering our $64,000 question is to find out when the poison was put into Macbeth's goblet.'

'Agreed.'

'Shall we go for a walk?'

Lulu looked at her watch. 'I don't see why not. We have time.'

Conrad wrinkled his nose. 'As Shakespeare said, we have time and grace and means to do good.'

'Is that another made-up quote?'

'It might be.'

'Will you be making up the Bard's quotes all day?' asked Lulu.

'Probably not,' said Conrad.

'Good,' said Lulu.

13

Stratford-upon-Avon's high street ran through the medieval heart of the town. It was lined with timber-framed Tudor buildings with crooked beams and leaded windows that leaned over the pavement. Independent boutiques sat alongside bookshops, antiques shops and branches of familiar high-street chains, many of which still had Halloween decorations in their windows. During the summer months, the street would be thronged with tourists heading to or from Shakespeare's birthplace at Henley Street or strolling down towards the River Avon; the pavements would be packed with street performers and humming with conversation in a dozen languages. But this was early November. There was a cold wind blowing down from the river, and what few tourists there were had wrapped themselves up in warm coats and scarves.

Lulu walked past the half-timbered frontage of the Garrick Inn, which she knew was supposedly the oldest pub in Stratford-upon-Avon. Parts of it dated back to the fourteenth century.

'It's funny to think that Shakespeare could well have nursed an ale in there as he plotted out his latest play,' she murmured.

'It is very old, isn't it?' said Conrad.

'More than six hundred years,' said Lulu. 'Imagine the millions of people who must have passed through those doors in that time.'

'Most of whom are now dead.'

'That's a cheery thought, isn't it?'

'Well, you started it,' said Conrad. 'But I do appreciate your point. It is living history. And yes, the Bard probably did walk down this very street and sit inside to warm his bones.'

'If only the walls could talk, wouldn't that be something?'

'That would be as amazing as if a cat could talk, wouldn't it?'

Lulu chuckled. 'It would indeed.'

The Bright Sparks office was wedged between a cafe with a window full of large carved pumpkins and a witch's broom, and a chemist's. It had leaded dark wood bay windows and a wooden door that looked hundreds of years old. There was a range of small electrical appliances on display and a sign that read ALL ELECTRICAL JOBS UNDERTAKEN. ASK FOR A FREE QUOTE.

'We could ask for something from *Macbeth*,' said Conrad.

'What?'

'They're offering a quote. To be or not to be.'

'That's from *Hamlet*.'

'Yes, I know. I just think it's funny that here in the birthplace of Shakespeare, they're offering free quotes.'

As Lulu pushed open the door, a tiny bell rang above her head. There were shelves of electric appliances to her left – toasters, kettles, hair dryers and air fryers. To the right was a counter displaying smaller items like adapters and batteries. There was a man sitting on a wooden stool studying his smartphone, and he looked up as they walked in. He was short, a little over five feet six, Lulu figured, and totally bald but with thick, bushy black eyebrows and a black goatee.

'Good afternoon,' he said. 'Cold out, isn't it?'

'It is,' said Lulu.

'I do like your scarf,' the man said, then blinked and grinned. 'Blow me down, that's a cat.'

'Yes, his name's Conrad. My constant companion.'

'He's lovely. I'm a cat man myself. We've got four at home. Mum and dad and two kids. The dad is Garfield, he's a ginger. And the mum is Snow, who is pure white. And the weird thing is that the kids are the spitting images of them – a ginger boy and a pure white girl.'

'That's interesting,' said Lulu. 'Genetics is a fascinating science.'

'I had expected the kids to be mixed. Well, you would, wouldn't you?' He peered at Conrad. 'What do you call that colouring? Tortoiseshell?'

'I always think of him as calico.'

'Conrad the calico cat – that has a nice ring to it.' He smiled. 'So how can I help you, Miss . . . ?'

'Lulu,' she said. 'Call me Lulu. This is going to sound a little strange, but I wanted to talk to you about the job you did at the church for the Stratford Players.'

Jimmy frowned in confusion. 'You're not police, are you? I already spoke to them.'

'Oh, did DI Dunning come to see you?'

'DI Dunning? No. It was a lady – Detective Sergeant Whitlock. And she phoned me first thing this morning.'

'Ah, yes, she works with DI Dunning. He's what they call the SIO. The senior investigating officer.'

'And do you work with them?'

'In a way. I was at the church when it happened.'

'It must have been awful. The detective lady said he died on stage.'

'It was quite shocking. One moment he was saying his lines, the next he was struggling to breathe. The ambulance was there fairly quickly, but they weren't able to save him. What was DS Whitlock asking you?'

'She wanted to know who I saw at the church while I was working there.'

'You were there most of the day, weren't you?'

'I got there just before eight thirty, but I had to wait because John Fleming didn't have the key until nine.'

'He's the prop master, right?'

'That's the title he uses, but really he's a jack-of-all-trades. So I had to wait for him and the three Smurfs to get there.'

'Smurfs?'

'His helpers. They're interns, kids so desperate for work experience in the theatre business that they'll work for nothing. For some reason they were all wearing blue that day, so I called them Smurfs.'

'So Mr Fleming let you in?'

'He did. I had just carried my stuff inside when the lighting guy turned up. Finchy. Peter Finch. He's the guy who got me the gig in the first place; I've worked with him before. He has all his own gear but there's no power in the church, so I run it in from a neighbouring building. The owners are theatre buffs and they don't charge, so it's all good. I was doing what I had to do when a woman from the council turned up and started giving us grief about damage to the woodwork. Absolute bollocks. I wasn't doing any drilling. I was using duct tape to hold anything in place that needed holding in place.'

'What was her name?'

'Walcott. Mrs Walcott, she said. I don't think she gave me her first name. She was only there for about ten minutes, and she said she'd come back later that evening to check my work.'

'And did she?'

Jimmy nodded. 'At about four o'clock. She was clearly there to find fault, but she had to admit that I'd done a good job. She left, and then I left not long afterwards. Why are you interested in her comings and goings?'

'What did the detective tell you?'

'Not much. She just asked me questions, and whenever I asked her something she said she couldn't comment on an ongoing investigation. So can you tell me what's happening?'

Lulu's jaw tensed. She wasn't in a position to give out any information on the case. Often the investigation team would hold back specific facts, especially things that only the killer would know. The last thing Lulu wanted to do was tread on DI Dunning's shoes.

'It's early days,' said Lulu.

Jimmy chuckled. 'You sound like the lady detective.'

'Well, that's to be expected,' said Lulu. 'I used to be a detective, down in London.'

'Did you investigate murders?'

'I investigated lots of different crimes.'

'But Edgar Lake was murdered, right? That's why all the questions. If he wasn't murdered, the police wouldn't be interested.'

'It certainly looks that way.'

'And from what I'm told, it happened while he was on stage. He wasn't stabbed with a sword or whatnot, so if it was murder, then it had to have been poison, right?'

Lulu nodded. 'That's the theory the police are working on, yes.'

'So the police were asking me what I'd seen because they think I might have seen the murderer. The poisoner.'

'I suppose so, yes.'

'Why on earth didn't they just say that?'

'Well, in the early stages of an investigation it's all about collecting intelligence. You try not to have a single theory or motive, because then there's a danger that you'll prioritize the facts that fit your theory. An 'intel-first' approach keeps the investigation flexible and open to new ideas. It's like building a jigsaw puzzle. You place as many pieces as possible before deciding what the picture is. If you jump to conclusions too early, you end up forcing pieces into the wrong place.' She shrugged. 'That's how I used to work, anyway.'

The man frowned. 'But the picture is on the box.'

Now it was Lulu's turn to frown. 'What picture?'

'When you do a jigsaw, the picture is on the box. So even before you touch a single piece, you know what the complete picture will look like.'

Lulu wrinkled her nose as she considered what he had said, then realized that he was absolutely right. 'Oh my goodness me, I've been using that analogy for years, and no one has ever corrected me before. A murder investigation is nothing like a jigsaw.'

'I mean, I suppose it would be like trying to do a jigsaw without looking at the box,' said Jimmy. 'But who would do that?'

'Exactly,' said Lulu. 'Well, you live and learn.'

'Hopefully that's true,' said Jimmy. 'Anyway, I was worried that they might think I was the killer.'

'Seriously?'

'Well, I knew Edgar. I did some work for him on his house

last year, just after he moved in. Or rather, not his house – he rents it – but he needed the Wi-Fi boosting, and his landlord sent me to do the job. Nice guy. Very chatty.' He grinned. 'Edgar was always asking questions, too. Like you. He was interested in everything.'

'He was a journalist; that's what they do.'

Jimmy nodded. 'Yeah, he worked for some big London papers. He wrote a lot of crime stories and used to drink with gangsters, he said. But London got a bit hot for him, so he moved here. He did a podcast on Shakespeare. I listen to it sometimes when I'm in the van.'

'Where is the house?'

Jimmy pointed to the right. 'Go past the Garrick Inn and down to Scholars Lane. Turn first right and his house is about halfway down.' He leaned over and tapped on his computer keyboard, then peered at the screen. 'Number twenty-two.'

'Who owns it?'

'Mr Kumar. He owns half a dozen houses around town and gets me to do most of his electrical work.' He frowned. 'You said the police like to gather intelligence. They don't really think I did it, do they?'

'I wouldn't think so,' said Lulu. 'Did the detective ask you if you knew Mr Lake?'

'No, she just wanted to know who I'd seen at the church while I was there. And if I saw anyone go near the banqueting table.'

'And did you? See anybody?'

'Go near the table, you mean? Well, John and the Smurfs, obviously, because they were setting everything up. The guy who runs the group was there, Mr Richards. He was at the table for a while. But he was everywhere, checking up on everything. I think he was giving John a hard time. I saw them arguing once.'

'Anybody else?'

'Not really. I told the lady detective it was very quiet.'

'So you didn't see anyone you didn't recognize?'

Jimmy shook his head. 'Definitely not.'

'It was a long shift for you, wasn't it? You started at nine-ish and finished when? Four o'clock?'

'Just after four. It wasn't too long. I usually do eight-hour days.'

'Without a break?'

'Without a break? No, I popped back for lunch with the missus. She did her fish pie, and there's no way I was going to miss that.'

'How long were you away from the church?'

'Just half an hour. Forty minutes, maybe.'

'Did you tell the detective that?'

Jimmy shrugged. 'She didn't ask. All she was interested in was who I'd seen.' He frowned. 'Is there a problem?'

'I'm sure she got everything she needed,' said Lulu.

'So Edgar was poisoned?'

'All the evidence points to that, yes.'

'Who would want to kill him?'

'That's what we're trying to find out, Jimmy. Anyway, thank you so much for your time.'

'We cat people have to stick together,' said Jimmy.

'We do,' said Lulu. She thanked him again and let herself out of the shop with Conrad nestled around her neck.

'He was nice,' said Conrad.

'Wasn't he? Cat people generally are.'

'That is so true. It's a historical fact that dictators are almost always dog people.'

'Is that so?'

'Hitler, Stalin and Mussolini all kept dogs. And Vladimir Putin is always being photographed with dogs. Now, name me one dictator who likes cats.'

'I can't think of any.'

'There you are,' said Conrad. 'Case proved.' He looked around. 'You're heading for Scholars Lane, aren't you?'

'It wouldn't hurt to take a look at Mr Lake's house, would it?'

'I guess not.'

The wind blowing up from the River Avon seemed to be getting colder, and Lulu thrust her hands into the pockets of her sheepskin jacket. They passed the Garrick Inn and turned onto Scholars Lane. After a few minutes they were standing in front of Edgar Lake's house. It was in a terrace, topped with a red-tiled roof, built from brick on the ground floor and white roughcast render above. There was a tiny front garden dotted with shrubs and a paved path leading up to a front door that had been painted a vivid red, the colour of fresh blood.

'Do you think there's anyone at home?' asked Lulu.

'You want to ring the bell, don't you?'

'Would that be so wrong?'

Conrad chuckled. 'How to answer my question without actually answering my question.'

'The more you know about the victim, the more you know about the killer,' said Lulu.

'I'm sure that's true. But aren't the three top motives always money, revenge or love?'

'I think I'd say jealousy rather than love. But yes, you're right, those three account for the majority of homicides.'

A blue Ford Fiesta drove slowly down the road towards them. 'Isn't that DS Whitlock's car?' asked Conrad.

'It is indeed,' said Lulu. 'And that's DI Dunning in the car behind, if I'm not mistaken.'

'You are not,' said Conrad. DI Dunning was following the Fiesta in his Vauxhall Vectra. 'I shall shut up, then.'

'Probably best,' said Lulu.

'Meow.'

The two cars parked at the roadside and the detectives climbed out. DS Whitlock was the first to spot Lulu and Conrad, and she said something to Dunning and pointed over at them. Lulu smiled and waved, then walked towards them.

DI Dunning was smiling, but his gaze was clearly weighing her up. 'Hello, Mrs Lewis. This is a coincidence. Or is it?'

Lulu returned his smile. 'Conrad and I were out for a stroll and thought we might take a look at Mr Lake's house.'

'Okay,' said Dunning. 'But how did you know where he lived?'

Lulu knew there was no point in lying to the detective. Policemen generally knew when they were being lied to; the ability to read people came with experience, and DI Dunning clearly had plenty of that. Plus, lies had to be told quickly if they stood any chance of being believed, and Lulu had already hesitated. At this point, telling the truth really was the only option. 'I was just at Bright Sparks in the high street, talking to Jimmy.'

DI Dunning looked amused. 'Were you now?'

'We were passing by, and I remembered it being said that he had been at the church on the day of the performance . . .'

'And you thought you might pop in and ask him a few questions?'

Lulu shrugged. 'Once a detective, always a detective. I was there when Mr Lake died; I just feel . . .'

'Involved? Invested?'

'Yes, both. There was nothing I could do to stop him dying, but maybe I can help bring his killer to justice.' She smiled sweetly. 'Is that so wrong?'

Dunning chuckled. 'It's not wrong at all, Mrs Lewis. But I don't have to tell you that murder investigations have to be left to the professionals.' Lulu opened her mouth to speak, but he held up a gloved hand to silence her. 'I know you have a wealth of experience in murder investigations – far more than me – but I'm the SIO, and you are retired.'

'I'm sorry, DI Dunning. I didn't mean to tread on your toes. I absolutely understand that this is your investigation. I just wanted to . . .'

'Help?'

Lulu wasn't happy that the detective had developed the habit of finishing her sentences, but she continued to smile. 'Yes. Help.'

'And was Mr Baxter helpful?'

Lulu frowned. 'Mr Baxter?'

'Jimmy Baxter. The electrician.'

'There you are, see. I didn't even know his name.' She smiled again. Her face was starting to hurt from all the smiling, she realized, and she could see from the look in Dunning's eyes that he wasn't buying her sweet and innocent routine. 'Really, DI Dunning, I'm sorry. You're right, of course. I never liked people butting into my investigations when I was SIO, so I do hear where you're coming from.'

'It's not a problem, Mrs Lewis. To be honest, the way things are going, I could do with your input.'

'No promising lines of enquiry?'

The detective sighed. 'Nothing. Zilch. I mean, the team is covering all the bases, but we're just not getting anywhere. You'd think that with more than a hundred witnesses to a crime we'd have something to go on, but of course watching him drink the poison doesn't tell us who put the poison in the goblet. Or when the poison was added.'

'We do at least know that it wasn't added during the performance. I mean, we saw Macbeth and Lady Macbeth pouring wine, but there was no poison in the bottle, so it had to have already been in the goblet,' said Lulu. 'But you're right, of course. None of the witnesses saw anything that would help identify the killer.'

'And Jimmy Baxter was adamant that no outsiders went near the goblets while he was there, which was most of the morning and the early afternoon. Which means that the poison was added before he arrived or after he left.'

'Except he did take up to three-quarters of an hour for lunch.'

DI Dunning frowned. 'He what?'

'He popped home for lunch with his wife. Fish pie. He was away for between half an hour and forty-five minutes.'

DI Dunning looked across at DS Whitlock, and his jaw tightened. 'I didn't know that.'

DS Whitlock opened her mouth to speak, but the inspector silenced her with a shake of his head.

Lulu realized she might have created trouble for the detective sergeant. 'We were chatting about it being a long day for him because he was having to do it single handed. That's when he said he'd taken a break. I don't think he would have mentioned it otherwise.'

'So during the time he was away, anyone could have entered the property? And any of the people there could have gone over to the table?'

'I'm afraid so.'

DS Whitlock's cheeks had flushed with embarrassment.

DI Dunning grimaced. 'Bugger. But how does you talking to Jimmy Baxter end up with you outside Mr Lake's house?'

'Jimmy did some work on Mr Lake's house when he first moved in. He needed Wi-Fi boosters or something.'

'Ah. So you asked him for the address.'

'I wasn't planning on breaking in, honestly,' said Lulu. 'We just wanted to see where he lived.'

DI Dunning frowned. 'We?'

'Conrad. We talked it over and thought it might be a good idea.'

The inspector laughed and shook his head. 'You do make me laugh, sometimes,' he said. 'Would you like to go inside?'

'Is that a trick question?'

DI Dunning took a set of keys from his coat pocket. 'The search warrant came through. That's why I'm back in Stratford-upon-Avon. We're allowed to go through the house and Lake's personal effects to look for any evidence that anyone might have wanted to do him harm. I'm happy for you to accompany DS Whitlock and myself. An extra pair of eyes, and all that.'

'Two extra pairs,' said Lulu, stroking Conrad's head.

'Even better,' said the inspector. He opened the gate and walked down the path to the front door. He unlocked it and stepped aside to allow Lulu and Whitlock to go inside first.

The interior was surprisingly modern with pale oak floors, minimalist furniture, white walls and recessed LED lights. Dunning looked around. 'Nice,' he said. 'So, I spoke to the landlord, and Edgar Lake has been here almost a year. The rent is paid by direct debit. The landlord comes round twice a year for a property check and says that Mr Lake is – was – the perfect tenant.'

'And he lived here on his own?'

'Apparently.'

'It's very clean and tidy.'

'Maybe he had a cleaner,' said DS Whitlock.

There was a staircase to the left and a living room to the right. A hallway led to the kitchen at the rear of the cottage. Dunning walked into the living room, and Lulu followed him. The floor was the same pale oak as the hall and there were matching blinds across the window. There was a large television on one wall with a low white sofa facing it. By the window was a glass and chrome table set up as a desk, with a high-backed black leather ergonomic chair, two computer monitors and a single keyboard. Beside the desk was a battered old metal filing cabinet.

Lulu nodded at the cabinet. 'That seems out of place,' she said. 'I'm guessing he brought it with him.'

Dunning pulled open the top drawer of the filing cabinet. It was packed with blue and green cardboard files. He took one out and opened it to reveal a thick wad of printed sheets, newspaper and magazine cuttings, and photographs. 'Old school,' said the detective. He flicked through the papers. 'Mickey Green, AKA The Pimpernel. Former armed robber turned drug smuggler.'

'He died in 2020, didn't he?'

'He did, but Mr Lake wrote several stories about him the year before he died. Even tracked him down in Spain.'

'But obviously not a suspect in his murder,' said Lulu.

'Obviously,' said the inspector. 'Green being dead and all.' He slid the file back into the cabinet and closed the drawer. 'But the murderer could well be in one of those files.' He turned to DS Whitlock. 'Can you arrange for the files to be collected and taken to the incident room?'

'Will do, sir.'

Dunning bent over the computer and tapped on the keyboard. He looked at the screen. 'Password protected,' he said. 'That's to be expected, I suppose.' He straightened up. 'We'll need our technical boys to have a look at this, too.'

'Yes, sir.'

'What about his phone?' asked Lulu. 'Are you looking at that?'

'We couldn't find his phone at the church,' said Dunning. 'We went through his clothes. I was hoping we'd find it here.'

'It would be strange if he left it behind, wouldn't it? Who goes out without their phone these days?'

'Yes, that's what I thought. But I didn't want to jump to conclusions. I had a good look around the church and it definitely wasn't there. I had Mr Richards call the number, and the phone was off. Nobody there remembered seeing him use his phone.'

'Like you, I always try not to jump to conclusions, but it looks likely that someone at the church took it.'

The detective smiled. 'And that someone is probably the killer. Great minds think alike. Anyway, I've already put a request in to his phone company for phone data and GPS details. But as always, there's a backlog. I'm still hoping that we'll find it here, though.'

'No harm in hoping,' said Lulu.

The inspector looked over at the sergeant. 'Kirsty, can you do upstairs?'

'Sure,' said DS Whitlock. She put her notebook in her pocket and went up the stairs.

'I know we can do this faster if we work separately, but I think it best if we stay together,' the inspector said to Lulu. 'If you do find anything that ends up in court, your presence might muddy the waters. So perhaps you could use your eyes but not actually touch anything.'

'That makes sense,' said Lulu.

DI Dunning went over to a pale oak sideboard and began opening the drawers.

Lulu went back into the hall and along to the kitchen. It was small, with barely enough room for a circular table and two chairs. The appliances were all Bosch and the oak cabinets were finished to a high standard. There was a window overlooking a lawn the size of a badminton court that was surrounded by a thick privet hedge.

'This is a very nice house, isn't it?' whispered Lulu.

'It's not what I expected,' said Conrad. 'A single guy living alone, you'd have thought there would be more clutter.'

'There's nothing personal here, is there? No pictures, no artwork on the wall, no posters. It's like a show house.'

'Which means what, do you think?'

'I don't know. I suppose he could have had OCD, obsessive compulsive disorder. Or he could have been a neat freak.'

'You're very tidy on *The Lark*.'

'You really have to be on a narrowboat,' said Lulu. 'Space is at a premium.' She opened the fridge freezer.

'Didn't the inspector say not to open anything?'

'I'm not looking for evidence, I'm just trying to get a sense of who he was, and fridges are good for that. You can tell a lot about a person from their fridge.'

'I suppose you can,' said a voice behind her, and she jumped. It was Dunning; he had come into the kitchen without her hearing him.

Lulu closed the door and turned to him with what she hoped was a disarming smile. 'Was I talking to myself again?'

'Yes, you were,' he said.

'I really must stop doing that,' she said. 'It comes from being on the boat on my own for hours on end.'

'And what did the fridge contents tell you?'

'That Lake was possibly vegan. Or vegetarian, anyway. Lots of fruit and veg and tofu, but no meat or eggs. Although there is some milk; so, not vegan. Did you know that vegans won't eat milk or honey?'

'I did. My sister's vegan. Won't shut up about it, truth be told. But Mr Lake wore leather shoes, too, so definitely not vegan. Maybe he just ate healthily.'

'There's wine, and beer. So he drank. I can't get over how tidy the place is.'

'He likes his coffee,' said the inspector, nodding at a Nespresso machine with three stainless steel racks filled with pods.

'Any joy with the phone?'

Dunning shook his head. 'Nope. I was hoping it would be here but, like we said, it would have made more sense for him to take it with him.'

'Hopefully the phone company will be able to help, data-wise. And what about the post-mortems? Were they any help?'

'They confirmed that the Reverend Harper's cause of death was asphyxia due to strangulation, with no drugs or alcohol in his system. The marks on the neck match the rope that he used to make the noose. No other marks on the body, just a bruise on his left leg that probably happened when he climbed over the banister. And no medical issues that might have given him cause to take his own life. He wasn't in perfect health by any means – he had some coronary disease, and he was clearly overweight – but certainly nothing life threatening. Anyway, the pathologist is certain that it was suicide. There'll still be an inquest, of course, but it seems clear enough.

'And Mr Lake. Again, he was in perfect health up until the point he ingested the aconite. The lethal dose is about five milligrams, and there was more than that in his stomach. Death would have occurred from ventricular fibrillation leading to cardiac arrest. Let me read you what the report says. It's quite technical.' Dunning peered at the screen and squinted slightly. Lulu wondered if perhaps he needed reading glasses. 'Toxicological screening detected high concentrations of aconitine in gastric contents and in femoral blood. Gas chromatography-mass spectrometry confirmed the presence of aconitine along with trace amounts of related alkaloids mesaconitine and hypaconitine, consistent with ingestion of *Aconitum napellus*, commonly known as wolfsbane or monkshood. So that's definite. Wolfsbane poisoning.'

'And it was definitely in the wine? It couldn't have entered his system any other way?'

'I suppose it might be possible – but there were traces of aconite in his goblet, so it looks pretty cut and dried.'

'This is going to sound like a very strange question, DI Dunning, but please humour me. Was there any trace of aconite in the Reverend Harper's system?'

DI Dunning's face hardened and his eyes narrowed. 'Why would you ask that, Mrs Lewis?'

'Oh, it was just a thought. We still really don't know who the poison was meant for, do we? If the Reverend Harper had played Macbeth at the performance, well, he would have died on stage, wouldn't he?'

'But that doesn't explain why you would think he had been exposed to aconite.'

Lulu stroked Conrad's neck. There was no way that she could tell the inspector that Conrad had picked up the scent of aconite in the rectory. 'It was just a thought,' she said. 'Probably a stupid question.'

'Not at all a stupid question,' said DI Dunning. 'Because yes, there were traces of aconite in his system. Small traces – not enough to kill him or even make him ill – but he had definitely been exposed to it.'

'Which means what, do you think?'

'That would lead us into supposition again, and I'm reluctant to go down that road.'

'Could the exposure have come from him preparing the poison?'

DI Dunning wrinkled his nose. 'That was my first thought when the pathologist gave me the blood test results.'

'Which would mean that the Reverend Harper prepared the poisoned goblet but then killed himself before Mr Lake drank from it. That would be murder-suicide. It's not so unusual for a murderer to take their own life.'

'No; but I can't think of many cases where they've done

it before their victim dies.' Dunning shrugged. 'I don't know, Mrs Lewis. It's making my head spin, frankly.'

'If it's true, then it means we're not actually hunting a murderer. The murderer is already dead.'

'Yes, but that's complete speculation,' said the inspector. 'It's equally possible that the Reverend Harper prepared the poisoned goblet and intended to drink it himself during the performance. Then, for whatever reason, he changed his mind and decided to hang himself, forgetting that the poisoned goblet was there and that the understudy would be drinking from it.'

'Oh my gosh, yes. That's possible, isn't it? Mr Lake's death was an accident. A horrible accident.'

'Well, not really an accident. The placing of the poison in the goblet was a deliberate act, but yes, it is possible that Mr Lake wasn't the intended target – just in the wrong place at the wrong time. But that would be supposition, of course. And supposition is always best avoided.'

DS Whitlock came down the stairs and into the kitchen. 'No sign of a phone,' she said.

'Did you see anything of a personal nature upstairs?' asked Lulu.

'There's stuff in the bathroom – a razor, toothbrush, comb. And clothes in the wardrobes.'

'What about family photographs?'

'There was a framed picture by the bed.' Whitlock took out her phone and tapped on it, then showed a photograph of a man and woman with a young child. A family portrait. Lulu peered at the photograph. The man certainly wasn't Edgar Lake; he was older and stockier. But the young boy could well have been him as a child.

'Could you send me that picture?' asked Lulu.

'Of course,' said Whitlock.

'Why would you want it?' asked Dunning.

'Only because if Mr Lake was the intended victim – and I do realize that's not yet proven – then we should really know as much about him as possible. People are rarely murdered at random. And poisoning is a very personal way of killing someone. So the more we know about him, the better. Do we have any idea yet who might want him dead?'

'We'll work through his files and look at the stories he wrote over the last few years or so,' said the inspector.

'I did wonder if perhaps a story he had written resulted in someone being sent to prison. Then, if they were released recently, they might have been after revenge.'

Dunning nodded. 'I'll have someone work through Mr Lake's files to draw up a list of suspects.'

'Do you think that maybe he gave up on investigative reporting and moved to Stratford-upon-Avon because someone had threatened him?' said Lulu. 'It does seem quite a change, from crime reporting to hosting a podcast on Shakespeare.'

'I did phone a couple of his ex-bosses, and they both said he wasn't the sort to react to threats. Water off a duck's back. Being threatened comes with the turf and most gangsters know that hurting a journalist will only cause them more grief. They both seemed confused by Lake's decision to give up crime reporting; but then, they both also pointed out that there isn't as much money in it these days. Newspapers aren't as profitable as they used to be, and all newsrooms are cutting back.'

'And how many members of the audience have you ID'd?' asked Lulu.

DI Dunning laughed. 'I'm starting to wonder who is actually the SIO on this investigation.'

'I'm sorry,' said Lulu. 'You're quite right. It's none of my business.'

'No, really. I'm grateful for your input. And you do help to clarify my thoughts on what is becoming a very confusing case. As for your question, I would say we have now identified most of them. By the time we got there, there were still thirty-eight audience members, so we have their names and addresses. The videos your goddaughter and her husband took were very helpful, and we're cross-referencing those with the online ticket purchase data. We've been asking anyone who took videos during the performance to send in what they have, and that's turned up some helpful footage. One of the guys in the incident room is working on a seating plan. People could sit wherever they wanted, but we should be able to work out where everyone was eventually.'

'Excellent,' said Lulu. She looked at her watch. 'I'm going to have to go,' she said. 'As I told you before, it's my goddaughter's birthday party tonight.'

'DS Whitlock can give you a lift,' offered Dunning.

'Oh, I'm fine. I can walk.'

'It's freezing out there, and we're just waiting for SOCO to give this place the once over. No point in both of us hanging about here. Whitlock may as well make herself useful.'

Lulu winced at the implied criticism of the detective sergeant. 'That would be lovely, thank you.'

She followed DS Whitlock outside, and they headed for the car. 'I'm so sorry if I dropped you in it back there,' Lulu said as they walked.

'No, it was my fault. I clearly didn't ask the right questions. The thought that Jimmy might have gone off for lunch didn't occur to me, and he didn't mention it.'

'I'm not in the business of teaching anybody to suck eggs, but it's always best to interview people face to face. If you do it on the phone, you only have the voice to go on. Oftentimes, you need to be able to see someone's expression to get a true read on them.'

'I know; I was stupid. I just had so much to do.' Whitlock unlocked the car.

Lulu took Conrad from her shoulders and sat in the front passenger seat, settling him on her lap before closing the door. The detective sergeant climbed into the driver's seat and started the engine.

'You weren't stupid,' said Lulu. 'And all you wanted to know was who else he had seen at the church. And he told you that. So you achieved your objective. But sometimes when you interview someone it helps to let it be more organic. Just chat and see where the conversation goes. You can't really do that on the phone. The main reason he opened up to me was because he's a cat person too. He has four cats at home, apparently. That gave us something to chat about. But I take your point about being busy. Being a bag carrier is a hard enough job on its own.'

'Were you ever a bag carrier?'

Lulu chuckled. 'Yes, for more years than I care to remember. But I worked with some very good people, and I learned a lot.'

Whitlock smiled thinly. 'I feel as if I am on a very steep learning curve,' she said.

'You'll probably still feel that way on the day you retire,' said Lulu. 'You're always learning, no matter how much experience you have.'

DS Whitlock started the engine and pulled away from the kerb.

'How do you feel the investigation is going?' asked Lulu.

Whitlock thought for a moment before answering. 'We don't seem to have any momentum,' she said. 'Everyone is busy, but we're like hamsters on a wheel. Running like crazy but not getting anywhere.'

'That's a good analogy,' said Lulu. 'More effort doesn't always equate to more results.'

'I mean, we have the crime scene – but there's nothing there to identify the killer. We have more than a hundred eyewitnesses who saw the crime being committed, but again, nobody saw anything that helps us identify the killer. We have a complete timeline – we know exactly when the victim died – but we have absolutely no clue as to motive.' The detective sergeant paused, focusing on the road. Then she went on, 'My worry is that it might be a totally random killing. Edgar Lake could have just been in the wrong place at the wrong time.'

'But the fact that his phone is missing suggests he was targeted, doesn't it?'

'I suppose so, yes.'

'In which case, there may be useful intel on the phone. If the murderer didn't think it was important, he wouldn't have taken it . . .' Lulu shook her head. 'See what I did there? I referred to the murderer as *he* when it could just as easily be a woman.'

'I'll try to push things forward on the phone front.'

'I know it's tough,' said Lulu. 'The mobile phone companies just don't have enough staff to deal with all the police requests they get. These days, phones play a big part in almost every investigation, so they get literally thousands of requests every day. You might want to ask DI Dunning to get a senior officer to push the request. Sometimes that helps.'

DS Whitlock nodded. 'Maybe he could get Chief Superintendent Delaney on the case. She seems to be taking a personal interest. I'll suggest it.'

'It couldn't hurt,' said Lulu.

'It just feels that at the moment, we're not really any further ahead than when we were called in,' said the detective sergeant. 'We don't have a motive, we don't have a suspect; so we don't know if they had the opportunity or the means to commit the crime, and we've no alibis to test. We don't really have anything, do we?'

'That's part of the problem when poison is the murder weapon,' said Lulu. 'The poison can sit for hours or even days before it takes effect. I don't know much about aconite, but in its pure form, it's a crystal. That means it could have been applied to the goblet initially as a liquid, then dried onto the inner surface, and then redissolved when the wine was poured.'

Whitlock nodded slowly. 'So it could have been put in days before the performance.'

'Weeks, even.'

DS Whitlock wrinkled her nose. 'But if it was, then the killer would have expected the Reverend Harper to be the one drinking from the goblet, because he was set to play Macbeth.' She shook her head. 'No; the fact that Mr Lake's phone was taken means he must have been the intended victim.' She glanced quickly at Lulu. 'Right?'

'That's my thinking, yes. Unless, of course, he simply lost

his phone. The GPS tracking will tell us for sure. If the phone was there when he arrived and then disappeared later, I'd say there's a strong chance that the murderer took it.'

'Exactly. And if Mr Lake was always the intended target, then the poison can only have been put into Macbeth's goblet after they knew for sure that the Reverend Harper was dead and that Lake would be playing the role.'

'Again, I can't fault your logic.'

A slow smile spread across the detective sergeant's face. 'But that means Jimmy couldn't have seen the murderer. He had already left by the time anyone knew that the Reverend Harper had died. So what Jimmy saw or didn't see is irrelevant.'

'Assuming that Mr Lake was always the intended victim, then you're right. As I said, I think his phone will be the key to proving that the poison was for him.'

'I feel a bit better knowing that I didn't wreck the investigation, that's all.'

'My dear, there was never any question of that. A murder investigation is a group activity, and everyone plays their part. It's a bit like a play, in fact, with a director and actors and extras and people working behind the scenes. It isn't like you see on television, where a maverick detective with a drink problem or anger management issues or both solves murders with the aid of a plucky sidekick. In the real world, it's a team sport. It's only by working together that the crime is solved.'

'Thank you,' Whitlock said.

They had arrived at the canal basin. The detective sergeant pulled over to the side of the road. 'How long will you be staying in Stratford-upon-Avon?' she asked.

'Originally I'd planned to be here for three days, maybe

four. But now I think I might stay a while longer. That's the great thing about living on a narrowboat – I have everything I need.'

'It'd be good to have you around, Mrs Lewis. I'm learning a lot from you.'

'That's so sweet of you. Thank you. And please, call me Lulu.'

Conrad meowed.

'And Conrad says you should call him Conrad.'

DS Whitlock laughed. 'I love the way he talks.'

'So do I,' said Lulu.

14

Lulu had arranged to drop by Celia's house before the party. She and Conrad arrived at seven o'clock on the dot, just in time for a glass of Prosecco and a chat. Celia was wearing a pretty red dress with a black belt, and Brian was looking much smarter than usual, sporting a grey suit, pink shirt and a tie that matched his wife's dress. They drank their wine in the sitting room, with Conrad curled up at Lulu's feet.

'So how goes the murder investigation?' asked Brian.

'Oh, I'm just an observer,' said Lulu.

'So tell us what you've observed.'

'To be honest, the police aren't much further forward,' said Lulu. 'They know for a fact that Mr Lake was poisoned, but then I think anyone who saw him collapse could have guessed that. The poison was in Macbeth's goblet and not in the wine bottle, so that tells them it was intended for the actor playing Macbeth. But what they still don't know is whether the poisoner thought that would be the Reverend Harper or Mr Lake.'

'So motive is the key, isn't it?' Brian saw Lulu's surprise at his comment, and he laughed. 'I'm sorry. I probably read too many crime novels.'

'No, you're absolutely right. If they could pin down a motive, that would go a long way towards identifying the killer.'

'I can't see anyone wanting to poison a priest, can you?' said Celia.

'You never know,' said Lulu. 'The police have to consider all options.'

'They have to avoid tunnel vision, as they call it,' said Brian, looking at Celia. 'Or confirmation bias. Where investigators focus too narrowly on one suspect or theory, ignoring other possibilities or evidence that doesn't fit. Or where police interpret evidence in a way that supports their chosen suspect. Agatha Christie often has her police suffering from tunnel vision.'

'I met Mr Lake a couple of times,' said Celia.

'Oh, I didn't know that,' said Brian.

'It was last year. Not long after he started his podcast. He came to the theatre to interview our artistic directors, and a few weeks later he was in to do a podcast with the chief executive. I met him both times. And he came along a few times to interview actors – we get a lot of famous faces passing through. But I didn't see him on those occasions. So, twice.'

'What did you think of him?' asked Lulu.

'He was nice enough,' said Celia. She sipped her wine. 'It was just . . .' She left the sentence unfinished.

'Just what?'

'He was one of those people who only smile with their mouth and not their eyes, you know?'

Lulu nodded. 'I know what you mean.'

'So he was polite and soft-spoken, but somehow I felt that it was an act.'

'Well, he was a journalist,' Lulu said, 'and I suppose they do spend a lot of time trying to get people to open up to them. It's the same with the police. Often you really don't like the person you're interviewing, but you have to smile and try to build some sort of connection – otherwise they just clam up.'

'You catch more flies with honey than with vinegar,' said Brian.

'That is certainly true,' said Lulu.

'Actually, the chief executive said it did feel a bit like a police interrogation,' said Celia. 'Not while they were taping the podcast – then Lake was funny and relaxed. A bit like Graham Norton, but without the Irish accent. But when they weren't recording, he was asking some quite personal questions about the chief executive and other members of staff. He seemed particularly interested in the theatre's finances.'

'He used to write quite in-depth investigative pieces for some of the London papers,' said Lulu.

'Which is fine, but he told us he was doing a podcast aimed at Shakespeare enthusiasts, and to be fair he did do that. Everyone was very pleased with the podcasts. So all's well that ends well, I suppose.'

Brian looked at his watch. 'We should be going,' he said. 'Fashionably late is perfectly acceptable for your own birthday party, but we don't want to be *late* late.' He drained his glass. 'We'll walk to the restaurant, if that's okay with you, Lulu? It's only five minutes.'

'I love to walk,' said Lulu as she finished her drink.

'It's probably the same speed as when you travel on your boat,' said Celia.

Lulu laughed. 'That's true. It isn't unusual to be overtaken by joggers.'

They put their coats on and headed out, Lulu scooping Conrad up to put him on her shoulders.

Exactly five minutes later, they arrived at an Italian

restaurant tucked between Tudor facades. Its timber frame was painted cream and its windows glowed amber against the dusk. Inside, the ground floor was a cocoon of warmth and noise, with the clatter of cutlery and the hiss of pans rising from an open kitchen. The air was rich with the scents of garlic, oregano and scorched pizza dough, and it seemed to Lulu that every table was occupied: couples leaning close over candlelight, tourists sipping Chianti, a waiter weaving expertly through the crush with a tray balanced above his head.

'We're upstairs,' said Brian. He waved to a matronly waitress who waved back and blew him a kiss. They went up a winding staircase to a large open-plan room where streamers and helium balloons crowded the beams and a paper banner sagged between two pillars with the message HAPPY BIRTHDAY CELIA. A long table ran almost the length of the room, crowded with guests whose jackets were already slung carelessly over chair-backs. Platters of bruschetta and bowls of olives were passed from hand to hand, corks popped, and somewhere music from a Bluetooth speaker fought to be heard over the laughter.

A man in a dark blue blazer spotted Celia, pointed and shouted, 'The birthday girl is here!' Cheers broke out around the room.

Two chairs had been left in the middle of the table for Brian and Celia, and they were ushered over to them. Lulu looked around and spotted an empty place next to Amy Jenner. She went over and smiled warmly at Amy. 'Is anyone sitting here?' she asked.

'Oh, hello! You're Lulu, Celia's godmother, aren't you? Yes, of course, please do sit.' Amy was wearing a white lace cardigan over a blue and white striped dress, paired with a slim gold watch. 'This is my husband, Alfie.'

Alfie was in his fifties with thick, greying hair and a George Clooney smile. He was wearing a tweed jacket over a white linen shirt. He offered his hand. 'Pleasure,' he said. 'Celia is always talking about you.' He grinned when he spotted Conrad on Lulu's shoulders. 'And you've brought the famous Conrad with you.'

'Oh, yes. Conrad goes everywhere with me,' said Lulu. She gently took Conrad from her shoulders and eased him under her chair. A waiter appeared at her shoulder and asked her if she wanted a drink.

'I would love a glass of Prosecco,' she said, and the waiter nodded and left. 'How are you getting on?' Lulu asked Amy. 'You must have been so shocked by what happened. It was bad enough for us in the fifth row – I can't imagine how it must have been to actually have been on stage.'

Amy nodded. 'At first I thought it was part of his performance. I'd never seen Edgar play Macbeth before, so everything he did was new. Troy had his way, and I was used to that, but Edgar's delivery was very different. So when he started to cough, I thought it must be some way of showing the stress that Macbeth was under. But then, of course, I saw the blood . . . It was awful.' She shuddered, and Lulu nodded sympathetically. Amy managed a smile. 'But it was very impressive, the way that you took control of the situation.'

'Somebody had to,' said Lulu. 'We needed to get an ambulance there as quickly as possible, and as there was a chance that a crime had been committed, we needed to preserve the scene until the police arrived.'

'You sounded very authoritative. Celia tells me that you were a police officer in London?'

'A long time ago, yes. But I've been retired for years.'

'And she says that you live on a canal boat.'

Lulu nodded. 'I do. With Conrad. Our permanent mooring is in Little Venice in London, but we take her all over the canal system.' She leaned over towards Alfie. 'I didn't see you at the play, did I?'

'I had one of my migraines, so I was lying down in a dark room,' he said. 'I was planning to go; I had a ticket, but on the night I just felt so bad that I had to stay at home. In a way, I'm glad I didn't see what happened. But I wish I'd been there to support Amy.'

The waiter returned with Lulu's glass of Prosecco. She thanked him and tasted it. It was perfect – light and clean, with just enough fizz to tickle the tongue without burning the back of the throat. The first sip was crisp, almost like biting into a green apple, followed by a whisper of peach and pear.

'How well did you know Mr Lake?' Lulu asked Amy.

'Edgar? I wouldn't say I knew him at all.'

'I thought he was a funny bugger,' said Alfie, leaning towards Lulu.

'Funny in what way?' asked Lulu.

'Always asking questions,' said Alfie, waving his glass around. 'It was like he was always interviewing you.'

'You met him?'

'A couple of times, after he first joined the drama group. Sometimes I go along to rehearsals with Amy. But I started to avoid him. It was exhausting talking to him.' He took a drink of wine.

'What about you, Amy?'

'I know what Alfie means; Edgar was quite intense. But not unpleasant.'

'He was always weighing you up,' said Alfie. 'He had a policeman's eyes.'

Lulu chuckled. 'A policeman's eyes?'

'You know what I mean. Of course you do; you used to be a police officer. Even when he was standing still, his eyes were working. He didn't linger on anything for long, but you got the feeling he remembered every detail. When his gaze settled on you, it didn't feel invasive, just . . . thorough. As if he was quietly building a file in his head.'

'Am I like that?' asked Lulu.

Alfie smiled. 'You're more subtle, Lulu. But I get the impression that you don't miss much.'

'I like to think I'm observant, yes.'

'Observant – yes. But Edgar was much more aggressive.' Alfie wrinkled his nose. 'No, that's not the right word. He wasn't aggressive. More purposeful.'

Lulu looked at Amy. 'Is that how you felt?'

Amy shrugged. 'I never really gave it much thought. He was just someone I acted with.'

'And was he a good actor?'

Amy nodded. 'I'd say so. He knew his lines and where to stand, and that's half the battle.'

'Oh, darling, you're downplaying your craft. Your acting is so much more than that. You have a gift.'

Amy took Alfie's hand, smiling at him. 'That's so sweet of you to say.'

'It's the truth,' he said.

They heard the clink of a spoon against glass and turned

to see Brian on his feet, calling for quiet. He gave a brief but heartfelt speech about Celia, how much she meant to him, and how successful she had been at her job. He was clearly deeply in love with her, and there were tears in his eyes when he finally sat down to rapturous applause.

Waiters began circulating to take everyone's orders. Amy took a sip of wine and set her glass down before placing a hand on Lulu's arm.

'Lulu . . . I know this is terrible timing, in view of everything that's happened. But could I ask a favour of you?'

Lulu winced. 'I'm afraid I don't really have much in the way of contacts in the Met these days,' she said.

Amy raised her hands. 'Oh no, nothing like that. It's more your canal boat experience that I'm interested in.' She sighed. 'As always, I'm not explaining myself very well. The Reverend Harper was due to give a lunchtime talk at the Women's Institute tomorrow. I've booked the hall and arranged the catering – sandwiches and cakes, nothing special, but it's all booked and paid for. Now the Reverend Harper isn't . . .' She hesitated.

'Available?' said Lulu, helpfully.

'Yes, available,' said Amy, with a wry smile. 'And even though that's awful, I do need to fill the slot, or I'll be disappointing a lot of ladies. Could you possibly come along and talk for an hour? Answer a few questions, that sort of thing?'

'Well . . .'

'You really would be helping me out,' said Amy. 'And the sandwiches are always very tasty.'

'I am a big fan of tasty sandwiches,' Lulu said with a smile.

'So you'll do it?'

'Of course I will,' said Lulu.

15

Lulu got back to *The Lark* just before eleven o'clock. It had been a wonderful night; the food had been absolutely delicious, and they had provided a lovely piece of salmon for Conrad. The wine had flowed like water. Lulu was aware that she was a little tipsy, so she took extra care as she stepped from the jetty onto the rear deck.

'Are you drunk?' asked Conrad. He jumped onto the roof and cocked his head on one side as he looked at her.

'I'm a little merry,' said Lulu.

'What's the difference?'

Lulu smiled. 'Conrad, my old friend, *merry* is a delightful condition – a twinkle in the eye, a readiness to laugh, a little more colour in the cheeks, and perhaps a fondness for reminiscing over harmless stories. But drunkenness dulls the wits and makes a person stumble over their words and often become argumentative. In my experience, crimes are committed more often by drunks than by those who are merely merry.'

Conrad chuckled. 'I don't think I have ever seen you as drunk as this before.'

'I am not drunk,' said Lulu firmly. 'I am merry.' She fumbled with the key that opened the lock on the hatch. Narrowing her eyes, she gazed determinedly at the lock, willing her hand to stop trembling.

'I'd help you with the lock but, sadly, no opposable thumbs.'

Lulu laughed loudly. Too loudly, she realized, and she pressed her lips together as she concentrated on opening the lock. It clicked open at last, and she smiled. 'Easy peasy,' she said. She slid the hatch back and went down the steps. Conrad followed her.

'I think I might have a nice cup of coffee,' said Lulu as she walked unsteadily to the galley.

'That's probably a very good idea,' Conrad agreed.

Lulu lit the burner underneath the kettle, then took off her sheepskin jacket and dropped it onto the sofa. She misjudged it, and the coat fell onto the floor. She giggled, bent down and picked it up, then sat down, hugging the coat to her chest. 'Tonight was fun,' she said.

'It was,' said Conrad, jumping up beside her on the sofa. 'Are you allowed to drive a canal boat while under the influence? Not that I'm suggesting we go anywhere, obviously.'

'Actually, the Railways and Transport Safety Act of 2003 sets an alcohol limit for those in charge of a vessel. It's the same as for motorists – eighty milligrams per hundred millilitres of blood. If you do get caught being drunk in charge of a vessel, it can lead to prosecution, fines and even imprisonment.'

'Good to know,' said Conrad.

'Brian's speech was lovely, wasn't it?'

'It was. He clearly worships Celia.'

'And it was lovely to see that she has so many friends.' Lulu sighed.

'You miss Simon, don't you?'

'Of course I do. Every day. I'll never not miss him.' She frowned and flashed him a sideways look. 'Did you just read my mind?'

'I could follow your train of thought,' said Conrad. 'It

wasn't difficult. You were talking about how much Brian loves Celia, and then you looked a bit sad.'

'I do get sad sometimes.'

'I understand that. You were married a long time.'

'Yes, we were.'

'Do you think one day you might get married again?'

Lulu gave another sigh. 'I don't think so. I'll never meet anyone like Simon again. He was the love of my life.'

'But he'd want you to be happy.'

Lulu smiled. 'Oh, but I am. Most of the time.' She reached over and stroked Conrad's head. 'Especially when you're around.' She frowned. 'You won't ever leave me, will you?'

'I don't intend to,' he said.

'That's good to hear.' Lulu yawned. 'I might pass on the coffee and just go straight to bed.'

'Make sure you drink plenty of water,' said Conrad. 'You need to stay hydrated.'

'I will,' Lulu said. She stood up and turned the burner off. Then she took a bottle of water from the fridge and walked unsteadily to the cabin. Conrad padded after her. Lulu started to undress, but tiredness overcame her. She lay down and was asleep within seconds.

When she awoke, the cabin was flooded with light. Lulu blinked and focused on her wristwatch. It was almost ten o'clock. She lay back and looked up at the ceiling. Her mouth was dry, but she was pleased to discover that she didn't have a headache.

'Welcome back to the land of the living,' said a voice.

'Simon?' She sat up. It was Conrad, of course, sitting on the end of the bed.

'It's just me,' he said.

'Sorry. I was dreaming about Simon.'

'He was very much on your mind last night,' said Conrad.

'Was I drunk?'

'You told me you were merry.'

Lulu chuckled. 'Did I really?' She opened her bottle of water and drank deeply. Her phone rang and she picked it up. It was DI Dunning calling.

'Hello, Inspector. I was just about to call you,' Lulu said.

'Good morning,' he said. 'I was wondering how it went with Amy Jenner last night.'

'I spoke to her at length, and I didn't sense any bad feeling towards Edgar Lake. She was certainly shocked by what she saw. I did have one thought, though – Mr Lake didn't have a file on her by any chance, did he?'

'Ah, well . . . there's a problem there, I'm afraid. The files have gone missing.'

'Missing?'

'Misplaced is what we're hoping. They were in the incident room last night, but this morning they can't be found. And the same goes for Lake's computer.'

'Someone's taken them?' Lulu was suddenly alert.

'At the moment, we are assuming – hoping – that they have just been moved. We've checked the evidence room, and they're not there. We're searching the building as we speak.'

'Has anything like this ever happened before?'

'Well, it's not unknown for evidence to be misfiled, and we have had detectives take files home with them, so we're not overly worried at the moment. It's a big team, and we haven't spoken to everybody yet.'

'Doesn't CCTV help?' asked Lulu.

'There are dozens of cameras in the station, but they are mainly in the custody suites and interview rooms,' said the inspector. 'We do have them in some of the public-facing areas, the reception area and the entrances. But generally we don't have cameras in the back offices, briefing rooms or locker rooms, and we have no footage of the files being removed from the incident room.' He paused for a moment. 'It may be a genuine mistake. It's possible that someone has just relocated them. But at the moment, we have no idea where they are.'

'I do think that the key to solving this lies in those files,' said Lulu. 'It's someone from Lake's past, I'm sure. No one I've spoken to seems to have the depth of feeling to have done him any harm. Some people do seem to have been a little wary of him, but that's all.'

'Wary?' repeated the inspector. 'In what way?'

'I think it's his investigative background more than anything,' said Lulu. 'He was always asking questions.'

'Surely that's what reporters do, isn't it?'

'That's what I said. There was just a feeling that he was being too . . . inquisitive.'

'But that's hardly a motive for murder, is it?'

'Exactly,' said Lulu. 'I think that it's more likely that someone from his past would have a stronger motive to want to harm him.'

'You could well be right,' said DI Dunning.

'What about phone data?' asked Lulu. 'Has the phone company come back to you with any information yet?'

'Not so far, but I'll chase them up today. What about you? What plans do you have?'

'I'm giving a talk to the local WI, of all things.'

'Not about the case, I hope?'

'No, Amy invited me to talk about life on a narrowboat. They'd booked the Reverend Harper to speak, so she needed a replacement at short notice. It'll give me a chance to talk to her again.'

'All right. Do let me know if anything turns up,' said the inspector.

'I will,' said Lulu. 'And good luck finding those files.' She ended the call and looked at Conrad. 'That's interesting,' she said. 'Lake's files have gone missing.'

Conrad frowned. 'I thought DI Dunning had his people going through them?'

'He did. But now they can't be found.'

'How could that possibly happen?' asked Conrad.

'That is a very good question,' said Lulu.

16

The local chapter of the Women's Institute met in a half-timbered hall with a pitched, tiled roof and tall arched windows that let in plenty of natural light. Lulu found Amy waiting for her outside the building, standing in front of a noticeboard with neatly pinned posters advertising community events, craft fairs and seasonal fêtes.

Amy smiled and waved when she saw Lulu, clearly relieved that she had turned up. She was wearing a camel-coloured wool coat that fell just below the knees, with a neat collar and large, plain buttons. 'Thank you so much for this, Lulu. You're a lifesaver.'

'It's a pleasure,' said Lulu. Conrad meowed on her shoulder. 'And Conrad is happy to be here, too.'

Amy laughed and took Lulu through a plain, blue-painted wooden door into a foyer that smelled faintly of polish and tea. Inside, the main hall was rectangular with a polished wooden floor and a slightly raised stage at one end for speakers or performances. A table and two chairs had been placed on the stage and a couple of dozen folding chairs had been arranged in lines facing them. Most of the chairs were occupied by middle-aged women, several of whom Lulu recognized as having been in the audience at Edgar Lake's final performance. A buzz of conversation gradually died away as heads swivelled in their direction.

'I think about an hour should be enough,' said Amy.

'Perhaps you could talk for half an hour and then take questions for another half an hour. Then we'll bring out the sandwiches and cake.'

'Perfect,' said Lulu.

Amy took Lulu up onto the stage, gave her a quick but flattering introduction and sat down. Lulu took Conrad off her shoulders and placed him carefully on the stage, then removed her sheepskin jacket and draped it over the back of the chair. Conrad jumped up onto the chair and sat watching the audience, which prompted a ripple of laughter.

Lulu spent the next half hour describing her life on *The Lark*, and it was clear from the attentive faces of her audience that she was doing a good job. Then it was on to questions, half of which were about life on the canals and half about Conrad. The hour whizzed by and before Lulu knew it, Amy was thanking Lulu and asking if the ladies would please stack the chairs against the wall.

Lulu lifted Conrad back onto her shoulders, then followed Amy down from the stage. Amy led her over to a wall covered with framed photographs. 'This is our Wall of Stars,' she explained with a smile. 'We'll put your photograph here too, once I've printed it.' She took out her phone and stepped back. 'Say cheese!'

Lulu smiled. She reached up and tickled Conrad under the chin, and he also smiled for the camera.

'Lovely,' said Amy.

Lulu turned to look at the thirty-odd framed photographs on the wall, each with a small note saying who the person was and when they had given their talk. She spotted Chief Superintendent Delaney immediately, resplendent in her uniform.

'Oh, I've met her,' said Lulu.

'Yes, Alice gave a very inspiring talk on being a woman in the police. And some very helpful advice on home security. She lives locally, you know.'

Lulu nodded. 'Yes, she mentioned that. I met her yesterday.'

She spotted another familiar face among the photographs – Elsie Kwan. Lulu pointed at the photograph, which showed Mrs Kwan standing behind a table displaying a selection of bottles and jars. 'That's the Reverend Harper's cleaner, isn't it?'

'It is. Elsie. She's a delight. It was Troy who suggested that she give a talk on traditional Chinese medicine – she's quite the expert. She knows all about acupuncture and acupressure, too. I told her that I often had trouble sleeping, and she showed me *Anmian* – that's behind the ear acupressure – and *Yintang*, where you massage between the eyebrows. They're calming points, and a gentle massage there for a couple of minutes has me out like a light.'

'She wasn't at the play, was she?'

'I think she had intended to come along, but after what happened to Troy . . .' Amy shook her head.

Lulu studied the other photographs, reading each name. 'And there's Ted Simpson, the wine merchant . . .'

'Oh, Ted's talk was a hoot. He turned it into a wine tasting, and by the time he'd finished we were all a bit squiffy.'

Lulu frowned at one of the photographs – a middle-aged blonde lady holding a large mixing bowl and spoon. She was smiling professionally, her gleaming white teeth emphasized by bright red lipstick. 'Now, where do I know her from?'

Amy beamed. 'That's Sarah – Sarah Collins. She's a local councillor, but you'll know her from being on the TV. She runs a local restaurant, but she's always appearing on cookery shows.'

Lulu recognized a few more faces: one was a pop singer from the eighties, another the author of a biography of Fleetwood Mac, one of Lulu's favourite bands. And Edgar Lake was there, arms folded as he stared into the camera. He wasn't smiling. It looked almost as if he was angry at whoever was taking the picture.

'What did Mr Lake talk to the group about?' asked Lulu.

'Journalism, mainly. It wasn't long after he had moved to Stratford. To be honest, I think it was just a way for him to meet people quickly. Usually I have to seek out our speakers, but he actually volunteered, and I remember he was very flexible about his dates. His talk was interesting – he's written a lot about gangsters and high-profile criminals, and he told us all about that. But it was quite a short talk, and then he spent almost two hours meeting us all and asking us all sorts of questions.' She smiled. 'It was almost as if he was interviewing us.'

'Maybe he was,' said Lulu. 'I suppose since journalists spend their working lives asking questions, it can be hard to turn it off.'

'Yes . . . I just found it a bit much, that's all.'

'I get the feeling that you didn't like him.'

Amy looked uncomfortable. 'I really don't want to speak ill of the dead.'

'I understand, but you don't have to like everyone you work with,' Lulu reassured her. 'I met plenty of people I didn't get on with during my career. You can't be friends with everybody.'

Amy hesitated. 'He was a bit – stressful to be around,'

she said. 'It almost felt as if he was hiding something from everyone. That the person we saw wasn't the real Edgar Lake. He was projecting an image.'

Lulu nodded, considering this. 'His performance on stage was very polished, wasn't it?' she said.

'Word perfect,' Amy said. 'And I did think that was a little strange. He only had a few hours to prepare, but he was faultless. Henry did really well too as Banquo, especially considering the circumstances, but he still stumbled a few times. I did wonder how Edgar managed to be so good at such short notice.'

'I suppose that's the job of the understudy, isn't it?'

'It is, yes . . . but then, Edgar wasn't officially Troy's understudy. It was just that when Henry said Troy was dead, Edgar said he'd be happy to play Macbeth.'

Lulu turned to examine the framed photographs again. She paused at a picture of a dark-haired woman standing in front of what looked like a garden shed. She stepped towards it for a better look and felt Conrad shifting slightly on her shoulders.

'Brenda Milton,' Lulu read aloud from the note beneath the photograph.

'Ah, yes – Brenda has a health food shop in the high street and runs a podcast about healthy living. She gave us a wonderful talk about running an allotment. There are some in the town, but for years she has been growing food on one of the Pebworth Allotments. They're in the village recreation ground in the middle of Pebworth. She grows all sorts of fruit and vegetables and flowers. In fact, come to think of it, you'd have seen some of her produce at the play. She supplied most of the fruit and flowers on the banqueting table.'

'Sounds fascinating.' Lulu peered at the photograph. Brenda was grinning at the camera, holding a bunch of carrots in one hand and a large cabbage in the other. The small shed behind her was painted yellow, with a flat felt roof, and there was a large blue plastic water barrel beside it.

To the right of the shed was a line of plants, each about five feet tall and spaced out with almost architectural precision. The flowers were hooded and deep violet, each one curved like a small monk's cowl. They clustered near the tops of the stems, facing outwards in neat succession, their dark colour sharp against the green of the leaves.

Lulu recognized them immediately. Wolfsbane.

17

Amy thanked Lulu profusely as they stepped out of the hall. 'The ladies loved it,' she said effusively. 'They were hanging on your every word.'

'They're a nice group. And they did seem genuinely interested.'

'I think because you made it sound such fun,' said Amy.

'And the sandwiches were delightful. As were the cakes. I fear I may have put on a few pounds.'

'We do pride ourselves on providing a good spread,' said Amy. She glanced around. 'Shall I call you a taxi?'

'No, I'm happy to walk.' Lulu reached up and stroked Conrad, who was curled around her neck. 'And Conrad is a fan of fresh air.'

'Thank you again, Lulu. You were a godsend.'

Lulu smiled and headed down the street.

'I wonder if you've persuaded any of them to become canal boat people,' said Conrad when they were out of earshot.

'I like to think that some of them might be tempted to give it a try,' said Lulu. 'So many people these days fly to another country and just sit around a pool, surrounded by people just like them, complaining about the heat and the food. But a week on a narrowboat can be so relaxing. Chugging along at three miles an hour slows you down and really does make you live in the moment.'

'I know about living in the moment,' said Conrad. 'That's

how cats live. Humans are always fretting about the past or worrying about the future, but we cats are fully present in whatever we do.'

'Well, of course, focusing on the present is a survival skill. Attention to our immediate environment is crucial for hunting, avoiding danger, and social interaction. But are you saying you don't worry about the future at all?'

'I take it as it comes,' said Conrad. 'As Doris Day sang, *Que será, será.*'

'That's as good a philosophy as any,' said Lulu.

'Better than most, actually. Though I have to say, we both spotted the wolfsbane at the same time, didn't we?'

'We did, yes.'

'So I suppose we'll be popping over to Pebworth Allotments at some point,' said Conrad.

'Definitely,' said Lulu. 'Although I think we need to visit Mrs Kwan first, don't you?'

'Will she be at the rectory, do you think?'

'I thought we could try,' said Lulu. 'It isn't far.'

They fell silent as a mother approached and passed them, pushing two toddlers in a double buggy. For the rest of their five-minute walk to the rectory the pavements were busy with people, preventing any further conversation.

Eventually they reached the rectory. Lulu stood by the gate and checked out all the windows. No curtains were twitching.

'She might not be here, of course,' said Conrad.

'Ever the optimist,' said Lulu. 'We can but try.' She opened the gate and walked down the path, then rang the doorbell and stepped back. The seconds ticked by. She tried again, and this time they heard footsteps. The door creaked open, just a few inches. There was a security chain in place.

Elsie Kwan peered out, blinking behind her thick-lensed spectacles.

Lulu gave her most encouraging smile. 'Hello, Mrs Kwan, do you remember me? I was here yesterday, with the police.'

Mrs Kwan nodded. 'I remember. The cat lady. And you were in the garden later, talking to yourself.'

Lulu laughed. 'I do that, I'm afraid,' she said.

'Why were you in the garden?'

'I just wanted a look, it's so pretty. I do love cottage gardens, especially ones that look natural.'

'It's a mess,' Mrs Kwan said. 'I keep telling Mr Troy to get a gardener to tidy it up, but . . .' She left the sentence unfinished. 'Too late now, of course.'

'Mrs Kwan, could I possibly come in and ask you a few questions?'

'Will questions bring Mr Troy back?' Mrs Kwan said, folding her arms. 'I don't think so.'

'No; but they could help us understand what happened. I'd be very grateful.'

'Mr Troy killed himself. That's what happened. What else is there to understand?' Mrs Kwan began to close the door.

Lulu took a step forward. 'Please, Mrs Kwan. Just a few minutes.'

Mrs Kwan sighed heavily. After a moment, she took off the security chain. 'I was just making tea,' she said.

'Tea would be lovely,' said Lulu.

Inside, Mrs Kwan led her down the hall to the kitchen. 'Jasmine tea,' she said. 'It improves heart health, boosts the immune system, and promotes relaxation and mental clarity.'

'And it tastes good,' said Lulu.

There was a Formica-topped metal table by the window,

with three mismatched wooden chairs around it. The kitchen was a throwback to the 1950s, with wooden cabinets that had clearly been repainted several times, a large Belfast sink crazed with a network of fine hairline cracks and an ancient gas stove. One of the burners was hissing under an old-fashioned cast-iron kettle with a wooden handle. An old fridge, rusting in places, hummed and vibrated in the corner. Everything was heavily worn but spotless, and the only smells in the air were of flowers and pine.

Conrad dropped down off Lulu's shoulders and landed on one of the chairs. 'The cat goes everywhere with you?' asked Mrs Kwan as she switched off the gas.

'Yes, he's my constant companion.'

Mrs Kwan poured boiling water into a large brown teapot. Immediately the sweet scent of jasmine filled the room. 'Cats have spiritual powers,' she said as she carefully carried the pot over to the table. 'They can ward off evil spirits and bad luck. And they can see things that humans do not.'

'That is certainly true,' said Lulu.

Mrs Kwan placed the teapot on the table, then took two teacups and saucers from a cupboard. She sat down opposite Lulu and poured tea into the cups.

'What will happen to you, Mrs Kwan? Will you be staying on?'

'Perhaps,' said Mrs Kwan. 'Mr Troy hired me, and he was the one who paid me, not the church. But someone from the church came by yesterday. They asked me to continue to clean, at least until they know who will replace Mr Troy.'

'Is that what you want? To stay on?'

'I am not sure. Everything reminds me of Mr Troy. Every time I go into a room, I expect to see him there. And sometimes I can feel him behind me, as if he is watching me.' She shuddered. 'I am a stupid old woman.'

'No, I know exactly what you mean. I had to move out of my house when my husband passed away. There were just too many memories crowding in on me. And like you, I kept expecting to bump into him. I'd be watching TV on the sofa, and I could swear that I'd hear him opening the fridge and taking out a bottle of wine.'

'A ghost,' said Mrs Kwan.

'No, not a ghost. But a presence. Definitely a presence. And in the end I had to move out. I don't mean I was trying to forget him; he's always in my thoughts. But the house just had too many memories.'

Mrs Kwan nodded. 'You must never ignore his spirit.'

'Oh, I don't.'

'Spirits are of Yin, because they belong to the unseen realm. Humans are a mix of Yin and Yang, so there must always be a balance with the spirit world. If the Yin becomes excessive, either through improper rituals or neglecting ancestors, then the spirits can disturb the living.'

'And cats? What about them? Are they Yin or Yang?'

Mrs Kwan smiled over the rim of her cup. 'Oh, cats are filled with Yin qualities. They have a calm, reflective energy. Not like dogs. Dogs are all Yang: active, loud and dominant. Cats have some Yang qualities – playful chasing, bursts of energy and territorial behaviour – but they lean heavily towards Yin.' She sipped her tea. 'Because spirits are Yin and cats are mainly Yin, cats are said to be able to sense spirits and ghosts.'

'I am sure that cats see things differently from us humans,' said Lulu, taking a sip. 'Oh, this is very nice,' she said.

'I have it sent from Hong Kong,' Mrs Kwan said.

'Are your family still there?'

Mrs Kwan shifted uncomfortably in her chair. 'My husband died, but my two children still live there.'

'I'm sorry to hear about your husband,' said Lulu. 'Was he ill?'

Mrs Kwan forced a smile. 'He wasn't, before they put him in prison. But he died a few months afterwards. Pneumonia, they said, and Covid.'

'Why was he in prison, if you don't mind me asking?'

'He was a judge, and because he wouldn't imprison protestors who criticized the Chinese regime, he was himself imprisoned. Hong Kong is a dangerous place for people who express their opinions, and my dear husband was never afraid of doing that. After he died, it was made clear to me that it would be better if I left Hong Kong. My children – my son and my daughter – had somewhat distanced themselves from their father, so they could stay, but I had to leave. I had read some Shakespeare when I was at university, so I decided to come here, to his birthplace.'

'And were you in the legal field in Hong Kong?'

Mrs Kwan shook her head. 'No. I was a doctor.'

Lulu frowned. 'But you are working here as a cleaner. I thought the NHS was desperate for doctors.'

'The NHS only hires medical doctors. But I'm a *zhong yi shi* – a traditional Chinese medicine practitioner. And the qualifications aren't recognized here.'

'So, herbal medicine?'

Mrs Kwan nodded. 'Herbs, minerals, animal products. Whatever is needed to promote good health.'

'How was Mr Troy's health?'

'Considering his age, his health was good. He had a few minor problems, but I was able to offer him some help.'

'Traditional Chinese medicine?'

Mrs Kwan nodded. 'He had an irregular pulse, which sometimes led to palpitations and shortness of breath. The doctors gave him tablets, but the side effects left him tired and gave him nightmares. I was able to help him with Fu Zi, the King of a Hundred Herbs. It is one of the most revered and commonly used medicinal herbs in China.'

'Does it have a Western name?'

'It does,' said Mrs Kwan. '*Aconitum napellus* is the Latin name, but it's also known as . . .'

'Wolfsbane?'

Mrs Kwan's eyes brightened. 'Yes. Wolfsbane, so called because of the old European practice of poisoning wolves with meat scraps laced with aconite roots. It's also called monkshood, because of the shape of the flowers.'

'And the active ingredient is . . . ?'

'Aconite,' said Mrs Kwan. 'Properly processed, it is one of the best treatments for Yang collapse and can be used to treat several autoimmune diseases and even cancer.'

'But it can also be very toxic, can't it?'

'Oh yes, if used incorrectly it can be dangerous. Lethal, even. In traditional Chinese medicine, there can sometimes be a thin line between kill and cure. In its raw form, it is extremely poisonous, but even processed aconite can be toxic.'

'Do you process it yourself from the flowers?'

Mrs Kwan chuckled. 'Oh, no. Definitely not. Aconite is powerful, and even as a well-trained practitioner, I would hesitate to prepare it personally. No, I have it shipped to me from Jiangyou in Sichuan. That's where the best aconite comes from. They take the roots and process them. Fu Zi is the daughter root and Chuan Wu is the mother root. Each has its own properties. For Mr Troy, Fu Zi was the better option.'

'What do the roots look like?'

'They're tubers, like small, dark brown carrots or turnips.'

'And are they shipped as roots?'

'No. The roots are also very poisonous, though not as deadly as the flowers. All the processing takes place in China, and it is then shipped as a powder. The powder has all the health benefits but none of the toxicity.' Mrs Kwan lifted her cup and inhaled the fragrance of her tea. 'You seem very interested in Fu Zi.'

'I'm just fascinated by traditional medicine. It seems that we have so much to learn from herbal remedies.' Lulu sniffed her tea, too. It had a heavenly bouquet, sweet and floral, lightly perfumed with a fresh, green undertone. It made her think of blooming jasmine blossoms on a warm spring day. 'Can I ask you, Mrs Kwan, were you surprised that Mr Troy killed himself?'

Mrs Kwan nodded. 'Yes. Of course. If I had thought he was depressed, I would have given him something to help him. Bupleurum root or albizia bark. But he seemed relaxed and at ease. He was especially happy to be in the play. He loved acting.' She smiled. 'I helped him practise his lines.'

'So nothing happened that might have depressed him?'

Mrs Kwan wrinkled her nose. 'Well . . .'

'You've thought of something?'

'Something or nothing. I'm not sure. But he received a letter that afternoon. He read it in the sitting room and I heard him cursing. He never cursed, never used strong words. That wasn't his style. So I went in to see what he was upset about. He had the letter in his hand, but he said it was nothing and that I wasn't to worry.'

'What time was this?' asked Lulu.

Mrs Kwan frowned as she tried to remember. 'About half past three, I think.'

'What did he do with the letter?'

'I think he threw it into the fire. I light it for him first thing each morning, then I take him a cup of tea with Fu Zi powder, and after he has had his bath, I cook his breakfast.'

'And you're sure he burned the letter?'

'No, I'm not sure. But when I tidied the room later, I didn't see it.'

'And what time did the postman deliver it?'

'Oh, it wasn't the postman. The postman came at about ten o'clock and it was only bills. This letter was pushed through the letterbox, and it didn't have a stamp on it.'

'So it was hand delivered?'

'I expect so, yes.'

'But you didn't see who delivered it?'

Mrs Kwan shook her head. 'No. I just saw it lying in the hall and I gave it to him.' She frowned at Lulu. 'You don't think the letter upset him so much that he killed himself?'

'Oh, I wouldn't be jumping to conclusions like that, Mrs Kwan. Did you tell the police about the letter?'

Mrs Kwan shook her head again. 'The only time I spoke to the police was yesterday morning, when that constable wouldn't let me into the house. Then I spoke to the detectives when you came. I'm just the cleaner, aren't I? Nobody cares about me or my feelings.'

'Oh, I care, Mrs Kwan. Very much.'

Conrad meowed, startling them both.

'And Conrad says he cares about you, too.'

18

'That was interesting, wasn't it?' said Conrad as Lulu closed the garden gate and walked away from the rectory.

'It was, yes.'

'Are you going to tell DI Dunning?'

'About the letter, or about Mrs Kwan giving aconite to the Reverend Harper?'

'Well, both, obviously.'

'Of course. It clears up the mystery of why the priest had aconite in his system.'

'But then it gives us a new mystery – the hand-delivered letter.'

'Indeed.'

'I know we hate jumping to conclusions, but isn't it possible that whatever was in that letter caused the Reverend Harper to take his own life?'

Lulu nodded. 'That does seem to be the logical explanation, yes.'

'So what could have been in the letter?'

'A threat, perhaps. Or bad news.'

Conrad considered this. 'We know his health was generally okay. And from the will, we can assume that he has no immediate family. So I can't see what bad news he could have received. He might have lost his parish, I suppose, but no one seems to have mentioned that; and he must have been close to retiring, anyway . . . What if it was a threat to his life?'

'Why would anyone threaten a priest? And what sort of threat would result in him killing himself? Couldn't he have just gone to the police?'

A man was walking towards them with a golden retriever on a lead. The dog's tail began to swish from side to side when it spotted Conrad, and Lulu moved aside to give them plenty of room to pass. She waited until they were out of earshot before continuing. 'Then, of course, there is the money he was withdrawing from the bank at the end of every month. What if the letter was from a blackmailer?'

'The bank manager said his account was almost in the red.'

'So maybe the letter was saying that if he didn't pay up, his secret would be exposed – whatever it was. If the Reverend Harper knew that he had no money left, then maybe he thought suicide was his only option.' Lulu sighed. 'But this is all conjecture, of course.'

'Will the police investigate, even though the Reverend Harper is dead?'

'If they think that blackmail is involved, yes, definitely. Let me raise it with DI Dunning.'

'I wonder what he could have done that would have left him vulnerable to blackmail?' said Conrad.

'Best we don't go down that route.'

'Too much conjecture again?'

'The Catholic Church has more than its fair share of black sheep among its flock,' said Lulu. 'But yes, at this stage conjecture wouldn't be helpful.'

Lulu's phone rang. She took it out of her pocket and smiled at the screen. 'Speak of the devil,' she said.

'Not literally, I hope,' said Conrad.

'DI Dunning,' Lulu said as she took the call.

'Hello, Mrs Lewis, are you by any chance on the boat?' Dunning asked. 'I was thinking of swinging by later. I have some information to share with you.'

'I'm actually out and about,' said Lulu. 'Not far from the rectory, as it happens. I have some information for you, too.'

'Perfect. I'm with DS Whitlock in Yorks, a cafe in the high street. Why don't you join us, and we can exchange intel over a coffee?'

'Excellent idea,' said Lulu. 'We'll be about ten minutes.'

'We?' said Dunning. Then he chuckled. 'Ah, of course. Conrad.'

Lulu ended the call and headed for the high street. Yorks was located in a timbered seventeenth-century house, its crooked beams dark with age. Inside, the cafe was very modern, with stripped brick walls, raw wooden tables and utilitarian iron chairs that reminded Lulu of a schoolroom. The air smelled of roasted coffee, warm bread and polish, undercut by the faint, acrid tang of damp wood. Light came in through tall street windows, filtered through the leaves of potted plants set as if to soften the severity of brick and iron.

Lulu spotted the detectives at a corner table. DI Dunning stood up when he saw her walk in. DS Whitlock was sitting with her back to the door and she twisted round in her chair, then stood up as well. Lulu smiled at their politeness.

They all sat down, Conrad jumping to the floor and then up onto Lulu's lap. A young waitress with waist-length hair came over, and Lulu asked for a cappuccino. The two detectives already had coffees in front of them, and Dunning had a half-eaten Danish pastry.

'So, do you want to go first?' he asked as the waitress walked away.

'All right,' said Lulu. 'By the way, I gave my talk to the Women's Institute earlier . . .' She saw concern flash across Dunning's face, and she raised a hand. 'As I said before, I wasn't there to talk about the case. I spoke about living on a canal boat. I think it went down rather well.'

'I'm sure it did,' said DI Dunning.

'And while I was there, I discovered that Elsie Kwan had also given a talk there before. About traditional Chinese medicine. She's something of an expert. In Hong Kong she worked as a doctor, but her qualifications aren't recognized here.'

'Okay . . .' said DI Dunning.

'Long story short, she had been giving aconite to the Reverend Harper.'

'Had she now?' Dunning and Whitlock exchanged a glance.

'Yes, but it was purely for medicinal reasons. He was having heart problems, and in the pure form, aconite helps. But the aconite Mrs Kwan uses is a medical formulation that she imports from China. She says it's totally safe.'

'Well, she would, wouldn't she?' said Dunning.

'Oh, I feel sure she was telling the truth,' said Lulu. 'And your lab people could easily test the aconite that she has. But it would explain how it got into the Reverend Harper's system and showed up in your lab tests.'

'It would, yes. I'll certainly look into it. Thank you.'

'But that's not the really interesting thing I got from Elsie. It seems that a letter was hand delivered to the rectory at about half past three on the day that the Reverend Harper died. It was after the postman had called. Harper read the letter, and according to Elsie, it quite upset him. She heard him cursing.'

'Does she have it?'

'She thinks that he burned it. But it could well have been a trigger for his suicide.'

Dunning nodded thoughtfully. 'That would make sense.'

'Now, I did notice a few doorbell cameras on houses close to the rectory,' Lulu continued, 'and at least one council CCTV camera at the road junction there. If we're lucky . . .'

'We might have the killer on camera.'

'Or at least, the person who delivered the letter,' said Lulu. 'Whether or not they are Edgar Lake's killer remains to be seen.'

'It sounds as if you've had a very productive day,' said the inspector.

The waitress returned with Lulu's cappuccino. Lulu waited until she had walked away before continuing. 'There's more,' she said. 'While I was at the WI, I saw a photograph of another previous speaker, a Brenda Milton. Apparently she's a healthy living podcaster, and she has a health food shop in the high street. She gave them a talk about running an allotment, and in the photograph I saw, it was clear she had wolfsbane growing there.'

'Where is this allotment?'

'A place called Pebworth.'

'I know it,' said DS Whitlock. 'There's a group of council allotments there.'

'Well, this Brenda Milton supplied some of the food that was on the banqueting table. She must have been at the church that day, and if she was dressing the table she would have had every opportunity to put wolfsbane into the goblet.'

DI Dunning shook his head in amazement. 'If you carry on like this, Mrs Lewis, you'll be cracking this case on your own.'

'Oh no, solving murders is very much a team game,' said Lulu.

'You've opened up two brand new lines of enquiry right there,' said DI Dunning. 'Well done. Makes my input look quite inconsequential by comparison.'

'I'm all ears.'

'We got location data back from the phone company,' said the inspector. 'The GPS was off, but cell tower pinging shows the phone in the vicinity of the church from four o'clock onwards. But then the phone went off at just after eleven o'clock at night and hasn't been on since.'

'That means the phone went off after Lake died.'

DI Dunning nodded. 'Now, it is possible that the battery simply died and that the phone is still somewhere in the church. But I've had a search team in there, including a sniffer dog, and there's no sign of it. It's a reasonable assumption that someone switched the phone off and took it away.'

'That makes sense. And it would confirm that the killer was there when Mr Lake died. All we have to do now is to identify them from the hundred or so people who were present that night. It's very doable. What about the message and call data?'

'We're still waiting for that. But I have been promised a fast-track.' Dunning popped the last piece of Danish into his mouth and looked at his watch. 'Do you think you could identify the allotment that this Brenda Milton uses?'

Lulu nodded. 'Yes, I think so.'

19

It was a twenty-minute drive from the high street to Pebworth. The allotments were on the edge of the village, in an elevated position that caught plenty of sun throughout the day. DI Dunning had driven, with DS Whitlock in the front passenger seat and Lulu and Conrad sitting in the back. Dunning parked by a metal five-bar gate and they all climbed out. Lulu sniffed the November air. She could smell the sharp tang of bonfire smoke.

Dunning opened the gate and they walked through. In the distance, a man in dark blue overalls and green Wellington boots was prodding a bonfire with a pitchfork.

The allotments were divided into long plots separated by grass paths. There were sheds dotted around, some smartly painted, others patched with scruffy tarpaulin or sheets of corrugated iron. Many had plastic or metal butts to collect rain water to be used during the drier months.

Lulu stood up on tiptoe and shielded her eyes with her hand as she surveyed the allotments, looking for a shed similar to the one she had seen in the photograph. She couldn't spot a match, so she took out her phone. She had taken a snap of the picture of Brenda Milton when Amy wasn't looking. She found the picture and showed it to the two detectives. 'That's what we need to find,' she said. 'It's a yellow shed with a flat roof, next to a blue plastic water barrel.'

They all looked around but couldn't see a yellow shed. They started walking around the outer edge of the allotments, which ran in rough, practical rows. Cabbages pushed their way up through the peaty soil along with potatoes and carrots. There were apple trees and pear trees, and raspberry and blackberry bushes looking wild and scruffy as they prepared for winter dormancy.

They passed another bonfire, this one being tended to by a grey-haired woman wearing dungarees and a wide-brimmed cowboy hat.

'Over there,' said DS Whitlock, pointing off to the right.

Lulu squinted into the distance. She could just make out a yellow shed with a flat roof. 'Yes, I think that's it.'

They walked along the strip of grass that separated two allotments that appeared to be devoted solely to cabbages, then turned right and passed a dilapidated greenhouse that used plastic sheeting instead of glass. As they got closer to the yellow shed Lulu could see the blue water barrel.

Mrs Milton's allotment was neat and tidy, with rows of potatoes, leeks and turnips, a selection of fruit bushes, runner beans growing on A frames built of bamboo, and some very healthy-looking courgettes. Lulu walked over to the line of wolfsbane plants. They were definitely the ones in the photograph, but the colourful blooms had now died and given way to dark brown seed pods.

'It doesn't look dangerous, does it?' said DS Whitlock.

'Oh, the whole plant is quite deadly,' said Lulu.

'I was going to say, doesn't the fact that the flowers have died mean it couldn't be used as a poison?' said Dunning.

'Far from it,' said Lulu. 'The seeds are extremely poisonous, especially when ground into a powder. Just a few of them can be lethal. In fact, every part of the plant is poisonous, including the flowers, the leaves, the pods and the roots.'

The inspector reached out his hand towards one of the plants. 'I'll take a sample back with me,' he said.

Lulu grabbed his wrist. 'Best not to touch it with bare hands,' she said.

DI Dunning's cheeks flushed. 'That was stupid of me, wasn't it?' He pulled a pair of blue latex gloves from his coat pocket and put them on. 'If they're so deadly, why do people grow the damn things?'

'Mainly because of their ornamental appeal,' said Lulu. 'They do look dramatic when they're in full flower. You find them a lot in historic gardens. Also, they are very robust perennials, so they keep coming back year after year. They've been planted here to provide a bit of privacy from the allotment next to hers, I think.'

The inspector finished putting on his gloves and took out an evidence bag. He pulled away a few leaves and put them into the bag, then added three seed pods. As he was sealing the bag, a voice cried out behind them. 'Excuse me, can I help you?' It was the woman in the cowboy hat who had been tending the bonfire. She was holding her garden fork at the ready and Lulu got the impression she would be prepared to use it if necessary.

Whitlock took out her warrant card and showed it to the woman. 'We're with Warwickshire Police, madam,' she said. 'I'm Detective Sergeant Kirsty Whitlock, and this is Detective Inspector Aaron Dunning.'

'So you're finally going to do something about the thefts, are you?' huffed the woman. 'It's about time.' She lowered the fork and nodded towards the yellow shed. 'Did they steal from Brenda? I keep telling her she needs to put a padlock on that door. They'll steal anything that isn't nailed down.'

'Have you seen strangers around much?' asked DI Dunning.

'They tend to come after dark,' said the woman. 'It never used to be like this. I remember when you could leave tools out all day and night and not think twice about it.'

Whitlock nodded sympathetically. 'What have you had stolen?'

'Well, they can't get into my shed because I lock it every night, but I've lost marrows and courgettes. Once they dug up two whole rows of potatoes, my entire crop. I understand that times are hard and that some people are hungry, but I put my sweat and tears into my allotment, and it's so bloody unfair to have all my hard work stolen.' She frowned. 'Why are you on Brenda's allotment?'

Lulu looked over at Dunning, wondering how he was going to answer the question.

He smiled at the woman. 'We're here as part of an ongoing enquiry,' he said. 'But I will definitely speak to the Pebworth Neighbourhood Policing Team on your behalf.'

'We've tried that. Our area is covered by the West Mercia Police's Evesham Safer Neighbourhood Team, and they're about as useful as a chocolate teapot. They sent out one of those plastic coppers. He was no use at all. Looked like a teenager, still wet behind the ears.'

DI Dunning tried not to smile. 'A community support officer?' he said. 'I'll try to get you more help. If nothing else we should be able to get a patrol car to swing by during the night. And we might be able to arrange some CCTV cameras. Leave it with me.'

DS Whitlock took out her notebook and pen. 'If you give me your name and phone number, I'll update you on any progress,' she said to the woman.

The woman gave Whitlock her name – Amanda McKinlay – and her phone number.

'Do you see Mrs Milton here a lot?' Dunning asked her.

Amanda nodded. 'Not every day. She runs a health food shop in Stratford. But most days, sure. Allotments require constant work – there are always jobs that need doing. That's why it's so frustrating when someone just comes in and . . .' She trailed off and stuck the fork into the ground as if she were impaling one of the thieves on its prongs.

'I'll see what I can do,' said Dunning. 'Anyway, we'll leave you to your gardening, or rather allotmenting, or whatever it is you do.'

'One works an allotment,' Amanda McKinlay said.

'Works it is,' said the detective. 'We shall leave you to it.' He and Whitlock began heading back towards the car.

Lulu began to follow them with a parting nod to Amanda, who said, 'I do love your cat.'

Lulu paused, turning back. 'Thank you so much. I love him too.'

'He's a calico, isn't he? But he's a male. Isn't that unusual?'

'Conrad is a very unusual cat.'

Amanda pointed at the line of wolfsbane plants. 'Don't let him touch those plants, they're lethal to cats.'

'And to humans. Do you know why Mrs Milton grows them?'

'She said she likes them. They remind her of the cottage she lived in when she was a child.'

'But she is aware of how dangerous they can be?'

'Only if you touch them with your bare hands. But cats can get sick just brushing against them.' Amanda looked at Lulu for several seconds as if weighing her up. 'You're not with the police, are you?'

'I came here with DI Dunning and DS Whitlock, but no, I'm not officially with the police.'

'Retired?'

Lulu nodded. 'Yes. For some years now.'

'And how are you finding it? Retirement?'

'Oh, I love it. Conrad and I live on a narrowboat and we spend a lot of time just travelling on the canal system. What about you? You're retired?'

Amanda nodded. 'I spent thirty-five years as an NHS administrator. Left two years ago and haven't looked back. There isn't a thing I miss about it.' She wrinkled her nose. 'Those detectives – they were here for a reason, weren't they?'

'I'm sorry; I really can't say anything, as I'm not a police officer. I was just along for the ride.'

'With Conrad.'

'He goes everywhere with me.'

Amanda smiled. 'I'm a dog person. I have two Yorkies, but I have to leave them at home when I come here; they'll dig anything up.' She took a step closer to Lulu and lowered her voice. 'May I tell you something, just between the two of us?'

'Something you don't want the police to know?'

'No, it's not exactly that. It's just that talking to someone who has just shown you their warrant card seems so . . . official.'

'I absolutely understand,' said Lulu, and she meant it.

Most people found it difficult to speak to a police officer, even when they were in plain clothes.

Amanda went on, 'The male one, the inspector . . . He took some seed pods, didn't he?'

'He did, yes.'

'So it's the wolfsbane he's interested in?'

'Yes. But it might be nothing.'

'What's your name?' Amanda asked.

'Lulu. Lulu Lewis.'

'Listen, Lulu, I want to tell you something, something that's been worrying me. But I don't want to make it a big thing.'

'Okay . . .'

'It's just that a few evenings ago, I saw Brenda doing exactly what the inspector was doing. Removing pods from the plants and putting them into a bag.'

'Did she say why?'

'I didn't get the chance to talk to her. She was with a man. I'm afraid I didn't get a good look at him because I was too far away. He had grey hair, I remember that much, and he was wearing a black raincoat with a belt. When I saw them, I called out to Brenda, but I don't think she heard me because they left, walking back to the road. I remember at the time thinking it was strange, but maybe he was a gardener and she was offering him seeds. She does have some very good specimens, so it would make sense to propagate from them.'

'I suppose that's possible, isn't it?'

'Yes, it is. But the inspector wasn't collecting seeds to propagate just now, was he? So maybe what I saw is of some relevance. But I don't want to make an official statement. I don't want to go on the record. As I said, Brenda is an allotment buddy, and what happens on the allotments should really stay on the allotments.'

'Like Vegas?'

Amanda smiled. 'Exactly.'

'And it was a few days ago, you said. Can you remember when, exactly?'

Amanda frowned in concentration, biting her lip. 'Four days ago,' she said.

'And about what time?'

'It was just getting dark, so it would have been about four thirty, maybe five.'

Lulu nodded. 'And other than the grey hair and the raincoat, you can't remember anything about the man?'

'He had his back to me the whole time. But I definitely saw Brenda collecting the pods. I remember thinking to myself that I hoped she was wearing gloves. And then I saw that she was – bright yellow gloves, which I'm guessing were Marigolds.'

'Okay, well, thank you for that. I'll have a quiet word with the inspector, and I'll make sure it stays off the record.'

'You're an angel, Lulu. Thank you. May I interest you in a courgette?'

Lulu laughed. 'Are you serious?'

'Of course. They didn't steal all of them. Come on.'

They walked back to the bonfire and Amanda bent down and plucked two courgettes, each almost a foot long. She gave them to Lulu, who thanked her profusely. 'I'll cook these tonight,' she said.

'Cut them into slices, about the thickness of a pound coin,' said Amanda. 'Season with salt and pepper and fry in olive oil over a medium heat for three to four minutes on one side, then turn them over for another three to four minutes. I always have them with a mixture of sweet chilli sauce and soy sauce.'

'I'll try that,' said Lulu. She thanked Amanda again and walked back to the car.

'She seems nice,' said Conrad when they were out of earshot.

'She's lovely,' said Lulu. 'I think allotment people and canal people have a lot in common. You can't rush an allotment; it takes time to grow crops, and it takes time to travel on a narrowboat. There's no rush, rush, rush. We all have to live in the moment.'

'Which is exactly how cats live.'

'Of course it is,' said Lulu.

20

DI Dunning and DS Whitlock were sitting in the Vauxhall Vectra with the engine running. Lulu climbed into the back and held Conrad on her lap with one hand as she held up the courgettes with the other.

'Cucumbers?' asked DS Whitlock.

'Courgettes,' said Lulu.

'I can never tell the difference,' said DI Dunning.

'They're both gourds, but a different genus,' said Lulu. 'Generally you eat cucumbers raw and cook courgettes. Cucumbers grow on vines, and courgettes grow on a bush-type plant.'

'You seem to know a lot about gardening,' said DI Dunning.

'Oh, I have quite a large garden at my house in Little Venice. I used to do a lot of the gardening myself.'

'I thought you lived on *The Lark*?'

'I do, but I still have the house. I can't bring myself to sell it.' Lulu put the courgettes down beside her, settling herself and Conrad into the seat. 'I've just had a very interesting chat with Amanda.'

'About courgettes?' said DI Dunning.

'About wolfsbane, actually. It seems that four days ago – in the late afternoon – she saw Mrs Milton gathering seed pods from the plants, much as you were doing today.'

DI Dunning twisted around in his seat to look at Lulu. 'She was doing what?'

'Picking seed pods. And wearing Marigold gloves to protect her hands.'

'Amanda McKinlay told you this?' said DS Whitlock. 'Just now?'

'Yes, she did.'

'But why didn't she tell us when we were there?'

Lulu shrugged. 'I'm not sure.'

Whitlock shook her head. 'I don't understand how you do this, Lulu. How do you get people to just open up to you? She had two detectives standing right there in front of her; why didn't she tell us then? It's the same with Jimmy Baxter – telling you that he took time off for lunch, but no mention of that to me.'

'I think having a cat helps. Although Mrs McKinlay is a dog person. She has Yorkies. And there's something else . . .'

Whitlock sighed. 'Of course there is.'

'There was a man with her when she was collecting the pods. A grey-haired man, wearing a black belted raincoat. She didn't get a look at his face.'

Dunning grinned. 'Lulu Lewis, you are worth your weight in gold,' he said. 'If we handle Brenda Milton carefully, hopefully she'll identify the man in the raincoat for us.'

He started the engine and drove off. DS Whitlock folded her arms and sat back in her seat. Lulu was tempted to tell her again that murder investigation was a team sport but decided that it probably wasn't the time.

'Shall we drop you back at the basin?' asked Dunning.

'Sure, yes, that'll be fine,' said Lulu. 'What do you plan to do investigation-wise?'

'I'll get the pods to our lab in Warwick, and then I'm hoping we'll have made some progress on the CCTV near the rectory and on Mr Lake's phone data. And I need to brief the team on Mrs Milton and her mysterious visitor.'

'I'll keep my fingers crossed for you,' said Lulu. 'And what about the missing files?'

'The search is still ongoing,' said Dunning grimly.

It took about twenty minutes to drive to the basin. Lulu climbed out and lifted Conrad onto her shoulders. She thanked the detectives for the lift and waved as the Vectra pulled away.

'What do you think?' Conrad asked.

'About what?' said Lulu as she turned towards *The Lark*.

'Do you think he's a good detective?'

'I think he knows what he's doing, yes. He's following the manual. Why do you ask?'

'He doesn't seem to have your flair.'

Lulu chuckled. 'My flair?'

'It's like you said: he's following the manual. But you seem to be more receptive to what's going on around you. You actually listen to people. That's how you found out that Jimmy Baxter took a lunch break. And you realized that Mrs Kwan was the reason there was aconite in the rectory. And you got Mrs McKinlay to tell you about the man in the raincoat. DI Dunning didn't pick up any of that.'

'I was just lucky, I suppose.'

'You're too modest, Lulu. I bet you were a first-class detective.'

'I did okay.'

'I bet you did. DI Dunning is fortunate to have you on the case.'

'Well, I'm not really on the case. I'm just . . . helping, I suppose.'

'I hope he appreciates you,' said Conrad.

'Oh, so do I,' said Lulu. 'I'd hate him to think that I was interfering.'

'So what's the plan for the rest of the day?'

'Chores on the boat. Then I thought we could take a walk to the shops and buy something for dinner.'

'You know what I'd like?'

'Tuna?'

'I was thinking steak.'

'Oh, yes. Steak would be good. Right, that's decided. Chores and steak. And possibly some wine.'

Conrad chuckled. 'Possibly?' he said. 'There's always wine.'

21

Lulu woke later than usual – probably a result of the two glasses of red wine she had drunk with the sirloin steak she'd cooked for dinner – and it was after nine when she stepped up onto the deck with a cup of coffee and a bacon sandwich, Conrad at her heels. She sat and drank her coffee, wondering what the day held for them. Her plan had been to head up to Birmingham after visiting Celia and Brian, but the murder had changed that. Now she was determined to stay in Stratford-upon-Avon until the mystery had been solved.

'Lulu!' shouted a man's voice in the distance.

Conrad jumped onto the roof and looked in the direction of the call. A man was approaching along the jetty. He had greying hair and was wearing a dark raincoat. He was holding a cigarette, and he waved in their direction.

'Do you think that's allotment man?' asked Conrad.

'I'm not sure . . .' said Lulu, watching as the man made his way along towards *The Lark*. 'Ah, yes. I know him,' she added as he got closer. 'Danny McGrory. McGrory the Story. He's a journalist.' She waved back. 'He's one of the good guys.'

Danny tossed his cigarette into the water and hurried over to *The Lark*, his raincoat flapping behind him. He was in his late forties, with windswept grey hair and piercing blue eyes. Under the coat he wore a dark blue suit, a white shirt and a blue and black striped tie. He always dressed more like a City financier than a journalist, often sporting a red carnation in his buttonhole.

'Lulu!' he called. 'So great to see you. Can I come aboard?'

'Of course you can,' said Lulu, finishing her sandwich and putting her now-empty coffee mug on the roof next to Conrad.

Danny climbed onto the rear deck and hugged her. She hugged him back. 'Danny, what a nice surprise! It's been ages.'

'Five years,' he said. 'Maybe longer. How are you enjoying retirement?'

'I love the peace and quiet. And the slower pace of life. But I'm guessing the fact that you're here isn't a coincidence. You know I've been involved with the Edgar Lake murder investigation.'

'The Macbeth Murder, as we're calling it, yes,' said Danny. 'I spoke to a contact on Warwickshire Police, and he said that a former Met police superintendent was helping them with the investigation. I almost fell off my chair when I heard it was you.'

'But how did you track me down to the basin?'

'They said you had come up on a canal boat, and this is a popular mooring place. I was just walking around hoping I'd spot you.'

'I've always said that you would make a great detective, Danny.'

'You have, yes. In another life, I could well have been a cop. But in this life, I'm happy enough being a reporter. How on earth did you end up as a bargee?'

'It's a long story,' said Lulu. She nodded at *The Lark*. 'Would you like a coffee or tea?'

'I would.'

'Then come inside,' she said. She headed down the steps and Conrad ran after her, his tail up.

'And you have a cat,' said Danny, following them.

'I think it's more a case of him having me,' said Lulu. 'His name is Conrad.'

'He looks magnificent,' said Danny. He stepped down through the hatch and into the cabin. 'Well, this is cosy.'

Lulu lit the burner under the kettle. 'It's got everything we need,' she said.

'How do you get on for water and electricity?'

'There's a tank that holds enough water for several weeks, and there's a battery that's charged by the engine. So, tea or coffee?'

'Coffee would be great,' said Danny. 'So you live aboard her?' Conrad jumped up and sat on the other end of the sofa, watching Danny with interest.

'We do. We have a permanent mooring in Little Venice, but at the moment we're travelling around the canal system. We stopped off here because it was my goddaughter's birthday. We're planning to head up to Birmingham next. And what about you, Danny? I assume this isn't a social visit?'

'Did you see the story I wrote? About the Macbeth Murder?'

'I didn't, sorry. I tend not to buy newspapers these days.'

'It was online, too.'

'I definitely don't get my news online,' said Lulu. 'To be honest, it's always so depressing.'

Danny reached into his raincoat and pulled out a folded newspaper. 'Page five,' he said.

Lulu opened the newspaper. The story was the lead article, with a headline reading, 'Police Probe Theatre Poisoning at Macbeth Performance'. There was a large head-and-shoulders shot of Edgar Lake, and another photograph of the actor Michael Fassbender dressed as Macbeth.

'You see, that's just misleading,' said Lulu, tapping the Fassbender photograph. 'A casual reader might think that a famous actor died.'

'I guess they wanted a photograph of the play, and he was in the 2015 *Macbeth* film. I take your point, but decisions like that are taken by the sub-editors.'

Lulu quickly read through the story. Danny clearly had a good source within Warwickshire Police, as all the details were pretty much accurate. She nodded and gave the paper back to him. 'If you're here for a quote, I can't really help you, Danny. This isn't my investigation; I'm just along for the ride. I was a witness, you see. I was at the theatre when it happened.'

'So I gather,' said Danny. 'It must have been traumatic.'

'It was. And there was nothing anyone could do.'

'I'm told that you took charge?'

'Oh, please don't write that, Danny. All I did was try to help preserve the crime scene and call for a doctor. And I tried to keep people there until the police arrived, but most of them left. Understandably, of course.'

'I'm not here for a quote or an interview, Lulu.' Danny folded the paper up and put it back into his coat pocket. 'After the story was published, something very interesting happened. I received a phone call from the victim's cousin, a lady called Sue Carroll. And she told me that the man who died on stage that night wasn't Edgar Lake.'

Lulu stared at Danny in surprise. She had just opened her mouth to speak when the kettle began to whistle. She switched off the burner and poured hot water into two mugs, then stirred in Gold Blend instant coffee.

'If he wasn't Edgar Lake, then who was he?'

'Well, to be fair, he clearly is Edgar Lake – I mean, I met him a few times in London, and that was his by-line. But his cousin says it wasn't his real name. Or at least, it wasn't the name he was born with.'

Lulu poured milk into Danny's mug. 'Sugar?' she asked.

He shook his head. 'Sweet enough.' Lulu gave him the mug and offered him a box of oatflake and cranberry biscuits. He took one, sniffed it and then bit into it. He nodded his approval. 'Nice.'

'So Edgar Lake changed his name at some point?'

Danny nodded. 'Apparently so.'

'So what was his name before?'

'I don't know. The cousin didn't want to go into details with me on the phone, but she agreed to meet me. I'm on my way to see her and thought you might like to come with me.'

'To be honest, Danny, I think you need to tell the SIO.'

'I will, of course. But I want to talk to Sue first. If the police get involved, I won't be allowed to talk to her.'

'That's a bit naughty of you.'

'Not really. They'll get the information, but I'll get what I need first. Quid pro quo.'

'That's not really what quid pro quo is. But I can see what you mean.'

'I'm more than happy to help the police, Lulu, you know that. But first and foremost I'm a reporter, and the paper pays my wages. So will you come?'

'Come where?'

'Solihull. On the outskirts of Birmingham. It's about twenty miles. I have my car.'

'I assumed you didn't want me to take you there on *The Lark*,' said Lulu. She looked at her watch. 'Okay, yes. Why not. But once you've spoken to her, you really must tell DI Dunning.'

'I will,' Danny said.

They finished their coffees. Lulu put the mugs into the sink and led Danny and Conrad out onto the rear deck. She locked up the hatch.

'Do canal boats get burgled much?' asked Danny.

'It depends,' said Lulu. 'Canal folk are generally good people. Where there are problems is when you moor in a city, just because there's more foot traffic and opportunity. And unattended boats are more vulnerable, obviously.' She put Conrad on her shoulders and stepped onto the jetty.

Danny followed her. He took the opportunity to light a cigarette and smoke it on the way to his car, an almost new white BMW 3 Series.

'Goodness, you're clearly doing well,' said Lulu when she saw the car.

'One of the advantages of being footloose and fancy free,' Danny said.

'You never got married?'

'I've never found a woman who could put up with the hours I work,' he said as he unlocked the car. 'Journalists and coppers work such antisocial hours. And both jobs tend to take over your life. Not many wives would tolerate it.'

Lulu smiled as she realized yet again how lucky she was to have had Simon as her husband. He had never complained about the late-night phone calls, the endless missed meals and social events, the last-minute cancellations, the coming and going at all hours. He had understood that it was part of the job, and he had always been supportive. She climbed into the passenger seat, placed Conrad on her lap, and closed the door.

It was a forty-five-minute drive to Solihull, during which Lulu and Danny chatted about what they both considered to be the good old days. While Lulu had been a detective inspector, a chief inspector and then a superintendent, Danny had worked as a member of the Insight team, the investigative unit of the *Sunday Times* newspaper. He had later transferred to *The Times*, and he had never once betrayed Lulu's trust. Conrad rested in Lulu's lap. His eyes were closed, but Lulu was sure he was listening.

Eventually Danny parked outside a tired-looking 1930s semi-detached, pebble-dashed in a shade of grey that had long since dulled with soot and grime. The small front garden had been paved over to make space for a car, though an old oil stain suggested one hadn't been there in years. A low, leaning wooden fence separated it from the neighbouring property, its paint peeling to reveal bare wood. The windows were uPVC replacements, double glazed but already smeared with condensation between the panes. A satellite dish clung precariously to the brickwork, cables trailing like vines down the wall. The front door was uPVC too, white once, now yellowing at the edges, with a cheap Yale lock and a dent where it looked as if someone had once tried to kick it in.

The street itself was lined with near-identical houses, some tarted up with fresh driveways and coloured doors, others looking worse for wear. At one end was a row of equally tired shops, most with their shutters down, and a boarded-up pub stood on the corner, graffiti scrawled across the brickwork. Two young men in hoodies were standing outside the pub, and Lulu would have bet money that they were dealing drugs.

'Right, she's expecting us,' said Danny. 'At least, she's expecting me. Her name is Sue Carroll. Her mother and Edgar's mother were sisters, apparently.'

They climbed out of the car and Lulu placed Conrad onto her shoulders. She followed Danny to the front door, where he pressed the bell. The door opened after a few seconds to reveal a woman in her early thirties with dyed blonde hair tied back in a ponytail. She was wearing an oversized grey sweatshirt, black leggings and white trainers. She frowned when she saw Lulu and Danny on her doorstep, and Danny quickly introduced himself.

'I was just about to go to the gym,' said Sue.

'We won't take up too much of your time,' said Danny. 'This is Mrs Lewis. She was there when your cousin . . . passed away.'

'I'm sorry for your loss,' said Lulu.

'Oh, it was no great loss, not really,' said Sue. 'I haven't seen Eddie for going on twelve years.' She looked at her watch, a black Apple model. 'I suppose you should come in.'

She opened the door, and Danny and Lulu stepped into the hall. To their right were two reception rooms that had been knocked into one, and Sue waved them through. There was a blue plastic sofa and matching armchair which had been draped with soft grey fleece throws and scatter cushions in cheerful floral prints. A small coffee table sat in front of the sofa with a few coasters stacked neatly in the centre beside a scented candle. A vase of artificial flowers, clearly chosen for their colour rather than realism, added a splash of brightness. Against the far wall stood a medium-sized TV on a simple black unit, along the top of which a small string of fairy lights had been carefully draped. In the corner, a small bookcase held a mixture of paperbacks, framed photographs and a few ceramic ornaments.

'Please sit down,' Sue said, waving them to the sofa. 'Can I get you a drink? Tea or coffee?'

'We're fine,' said Danny, sitting on the sofa.

Lulu dropped down next to him, and for the first time Sue spotted Conrad. 'Oh my goodness, what a lovely cat,' she said. 'He's splendid, isn't he?'

'He is,' said Lulu. 'His name is Conrad.'

'I thought calico cats were always female?' said Sue.

'Conrad is a very unusual cat, in many ways.'

'I love cats, but my husband is allergic,' said Sue, sitting down on the armchair. 'Or rather, he says he's allergic, but actually I think he just doesn't like cats. I wish I'd known that before I married him . . .' She took a deep breath and seemed to gather herself. 'So, you're here about Eddie?'

'On the phone, you mentioned that wasn't his name?' said Danny, taking out a notepad and pen.

'Eddie was short for Edward, not Edgar. And his father's family name was Gastrell, which is what caused all the problems in the first place. So Eddie was Eddie Gastrell, and definitely not Edgar Lake.'

Lulu took out her phone and pulled up the photograph she had taken from Lake's bedroom. She stood up and showed it to Sue. 'Would this be Eddie's family?'

Sue squinted at the screen and nodded. 'That's right. That's Eddie with Frank and his mother, Alison. Alison was my mother's sister. So Eddie and I are – were – first cousins.'

Lulu sat down again and showed the photograph to Danny.

'You said his name caused problems,' said Lulu. 'What do you mean by that?'

'It's a long story, and to be honest it's a stupid one. But it wrecked Eddie's life.' Sue gave a sad smile. 'And maybe it ended it.'

'Please explain what you mean,' said Lulu. 'I'm getting very confused.'

Sue took a deep breath, as if to steady herself before continuing. 'The Reverend Francis Gastrell lived in Stratford-upon-Avon in the eighteenth century. In 1756, he bought New Place, which was where Shakespeare had lived during the final years of his life. The Reverend Francis became very unpopular with the townsfolk – partly because he was always arguing about local taxes, and partly because he refused to allow visitors to the house. You have to remember that back then, Shakespeare was as popular as someone like J. K. Rowling or Stephen King today. In fact, Francis got so annoyed with the sightseers that he chopped down a mulberry tree that Shakespeare was supposed to have planted. And three years later, he demolished the entire house. Out of spite. That made him the most hated man in Stratford-upon-Avon, and shortly afterwards he left in disgrace.'

'He sounds like a horrible little man,' said Lulu.

'He was, by all accounts,' said Sue. 'It's said that the people of the town hated him so much, they passed a by-law prohibiting anyone with the name Gastrell from taking up residence there again.'

Danny wrote rapidly in his notebook.

'I think that may just be folklore,' Sue continued. 'But it doesn't matter whether the by-law exists or not; what matters is that anyone with that family name is guaranteed to have a tough time.'

'And Eddie was Eddie Gastrell,' said Lulu.

'Frank was from Leicester. He married Alison, my aunt. She was working there as a waitress, but she'd always talked about moving back to Stratford-upon-Avon. Frank was a baker by trade and had always wanted to open his own shop. He worked hard for a few years, saving every penny he could, and then they moved to Stratford-upon-Avon and opened a shop in the high street. Gastrell's Bakery. Alison had been quite young when she left the town to work in Leicester, so she wasn't aware of the Gastrell story. But as soon as the sign went up, they had problems.'

'What sort of problems?' asked Danny.

'Small things at first. Snide comments. The occasional bit of graffiti on the window. But basically people just avoided the shop. Hardly anyone went in. During the tourist season they did okay, because tourists weren't aware of the whole Gastrell thing, but during the quiet months he barely sold a loaf. He tried to get a business loan, but the manager told him to his face that he wasn't prepared to help anyone called Gastrell. It sounds funny, doesn't it, but it wasn't a joke. People seriously hated him because of his name.'

'That is terrible,' said Lulu.

'And Eddie got the worst of it,' said Sue. 'I'm sure you know how cruel kids can be. Name-calling. Refusing to sit next to him. It never stopped.'

'He told you about this?' asked Danny.

'Generally he didn't talk about it. But one Christmas when he was about nine, he opened up to us. I remember him bursting into tears. He didn't have any friends, and he said his teachers were no help. In fact, some of them actually joined in the teasing.'

Lulu shook her head sadly. She could only imagine what the poor boy had gone through.

'They put him in hospital once, the kids. They were chasing him and throwing stones at him. He had a nasty cut over his eye, and he had to have stitches.'

Lulu nodded. 'I saw the scar.'

'He begged his father to move the family back to Leicester, but Frank had invested everything in the shop, and the family lived in the flat above it. Frank did his best, but the bakery made no money and he soon ran through their savings.' She looked at her watch. 'I need a drink,' she said. 'I've changed my mind about going to the gym, and I'm declaring it wine o'clock.' She stood up and headed for the kitchen. 'What about you, Lulu? You have the look of a wine drinker.'

Lulu chuckled, not sure if she should be offended or not. But Sue was right; she did enjoy the occasional glass. Normally not this early in the day – but then, joining Sue might encourage her to share more details. 'As you say, it is wine o'clock.'

'What about you, Danny?'

'I'm driving, so maybe I could take you up on that coffee,' he said.

Sue disappeared into the kitchen at the rear of the house. 'Did you know any of this?' Lulu asked Danny.

'Nope,' he said. 'I've always known him as Edgar Lake. I never met anyone who called him Eddie or Edward.'

'How long did you know him?'

'I suppose eight years in total, but I lost touch with him a year ago.'

'Which is when he moved to Stratford. Would you say you were friends?'

'I wouldn't say that, exactly. I'd see him at press conferences and crime scenes, but he was never really part of the press pack.'

'More of a lone wolf.'

Sue returned with a tray bearing coffee for Danny, a bottle of Pinot Grigio and two glasses. She set it down on the coffee table. 'It's screw top, I'm afraid,' she said.

'Oh, don't apologize,' said Lulu. 'In fact, I prefer screw tops to cork. The wine doesn't go off and there's no faffing around with corkscrews.'

Sue poured wine into the glasses, passed them both their drinks and dropped back into her armchair. She took a sip of wine, and then a gulp. 'So, Frank was locked into a loss-making business and Eddie was being bullied at school. It all put the marriage under strain, because Frank blamed Alison for not warning him about his surname being an issue in the community. But she couldn't have warned him, of course, because she didn't know. Eddie said they were always fighting. He wanted to run away, but he had nowhere to go.'

'Poor kid,' said Lulu, sipping her wine. It was light, crisp and very easy to drink, with hints of pear, apple and a touch of lemon. It went down smoothly, leaving a dry finish.

'It went from bad to worse. Eddie was suspended from school, and he developed asthma, which the doctors blamed on all the stress he was under. And then one day, Frank just upped and left. Didn't even pack a bag. He just got into his van and drove away, and he was never heard from again. To this day, I don't think anyone knows whether he's alive or dead.'

'And they never found the van?'

'The van, they found. In Birmingham about a month later. The police couldn't tell if it had been stolen or if Frank had abandoned it.' Sue leaned towards Lulu. 'Can someone really just disappear?'

'People do vanish, yes. Sometimes because something bad has happened to them; sometimes because they just want to leave their old life behind.'

Sue nodded slowly. 'I think he's dead,' she said. 'I don't think he could have walked away from Eddie like that. I think it all just got too much for him, and he killed himself.'

'Is that what Eddie thought?'

'He was sure his father was dead, yes.' Sue sighed and drank more wine. 'The bank took the bakery and the flat from them, and Eddie and his mother had to move out. No one lifted a finger to help them. The curse of the Gastrells. She went back to Leicester and started waitressing again. Eddie would have been nine when they left town. Life wasn't much better for him, but at least his name was no longer an issue. Alison was never the same, though. She had all sorts of health issues, mental and physical, and she died when Eddie was seventeen.'

'How did she die?'

'She killed herself.' Sue's voice was sad now. 'It was absolutely terrible for Eddie. He found her body.'

'Oh, how awful,' Lulu said.

'Alison's funeral was the last time I saw him. It would

have been about twelve years ago. My mum took me, and I had a long chat with Eddie. He was a complete mess. He was still so young, and his school was trying to persuade him to join the army – said it would make a man of him.'

'And did he do it?'

'I don't know. I was heading off to uni; we lost touch. I tried to find him on social media a few times, but I kept drawing a blank – no wonder, if he'd changed his name. Do they have any idea who did this to him?'

'The investigation is ongoing,' said Lulu.

Sue drained her wine and refilled it after offering the bottle to Lulu, who shook her head; her glass was still half full.

'I just don't understand why Eddie would go back to Stratford-upon-Avon,' Sue said quietly. 'He hated the place and he hated the people. I remember him saying that if he could press a button and drop a bomb on the town, he'd do it without a second thought.' She shook her head in confusion. 'And in the paper it said he died on stage while he was performing *Macbeth*?'

Lulu nodded. 'I was there.'

'But Eddie hated Shakespeare, too. He couldn't stand anything to do with the man or his work. Which is just what you'd expect, after everything he'd been through. Why would he want to appear in a Shakespeare play? It doesn't make any sense.'

'It was actually quite a good performance,' said Lulu. 'And he'd been in the group for a while. Apparently he'd been in a few of their productions.'

'Well, all I can tell you is that when I knew him, he was absolutely clear that he hated Shakespeare, hated Stratford-upon-Avon, and hated all the people who lived there. I was so confused when I read the story in the paper. And why did he change his name?'

'Don't you think it was just that he wanted to distance himself from the whole Gastrell thing?'

'I get that. But why not use his mother's maiden name, Nicholson? He could easily have used Eddie Nicholson. In fact, why change Eddie, anyway? His first name was never the problem; it was Gastrell that got people's backs up. He could have just used Eddie Lake.' Sue was looking flushed. She drank more wine. 'Will there be a funeral?'

'I expect so. But not until the case has been resolved.'

'It's just, I'd like to go if I could. And I'm sure my mum would.'

'We have your number, Sue, so as soon as I know when the funeral is, I'll let you know.'

'You were there when it happened?'

Lulu nodded. 'I was.'

'Was it really bad?'

Images of that night in the church flitted through Lulu's memory. Yes, it had been bad – really bad – but there was nothing to be gained by telling Sue the gory details.

'They said he was poisoned? That's what it said in the paper.'

'That's what the police think, yes. It was quite quick,' Lulu said gently. 'The ambulance was there within minutes, but there was nothing they could do.'

Tears welled up in Sue's eyes. 'Poor Eddie,' she said. 'Do you think they'll catch who did it?'

'I hope so,' said Lulu. She took out her phone and brought up DI Dunning's phone number. 'This is the detective in charge of the investigation,' she said, showing it to Sue. 'His name is Aaron Dunning, and he's a detective inspector. I'm sure he wouldn't mind talking to you, if you'd like to hear more.'

Sue picked up her phone and copied Dunning's name and number into her phone's contacts. 'Thank you,' she said.

'No, thank you for your time,' said Lulu. She put away her phone, finished her wine and looked over at Danny. 'Is there anything else you need?' she asked.

'I think we're good,' said Danny.

Lulu and Danny stood up. Lulu scooped up Conrad and placed him on her shoulders.

'Again, we're sorry for your loss,' said Lulu.

'I just hope that Eddie finds peace now,' said Sue. She gulped down the rest of her wine, then showed them out of the sitting room into the hall and stepped forward to open the front door. Her eyes were brimming with tears, but there was nothing Lulu could say that seemed likely to make her feel any better.

Sue closed the door, and Lulu and Danny walked back to his car.

'That went well,' said Danny.

'Story-wise or investigation-wise?' asked Lulu.

'Well, it certainly gives me a story, but I'm thinking I might sit on it until they've caught the killer. It's really just background at the moment. And – can you send me that photograph you showed her, the one of Lake's family?'

'Of course.'

'Where did you get it from?'

'It was by his bed. It clearly meant a lot to him.'

'How close are the cops to having a prime suspect?'

'Oh, Danny, you'll have to talk to DI Dunning about that.'

Danny grinned. 'Come on, Lulu, we go back a long way.'

She laughed. 'We do, yes.'

'And you're a civilian now.'

'That's true.'

'So give me something. I need to file something, or my boss will be spitting feathers.'

They reached the car and climbed in. Conrad sat on Lulu's lap and curled up, nose to tail.

'There was something missing from your story,' she said to Danny.

'I'm listening.'

'You reported that Edgar Lake died on stage performing Macbeth, but you didn't mention what had happened earlier in the day that led to him playing the part.'

Danny frowned. 'Okay . . .'

'Edgar Lake was supposed to be playing the part of Banquo, but the actor set to play Macbeth killed himself earlier that same day. He hanged himself. Edgar stepped up to play Macbeth at short notice, and his place as Banquo was taken by the show's director.'

'And who was the actor who was supposed to play Macbeth?'

'A Catholic priest. The Reverend Troy Harper.'

'Yeah, that works as a story. The director is Henry Richards?'

Lulu nodded. 'That's right.'

'I've got his number. I spoke to him, but he didn't mention the suicide.'

'It was Henry who found the body,' said Lulu. 'He probably didn't want to talk about it.'

'I'll give him another call,' said Danny.

'And do you know what the poison was?'

'I was going to check with the coroner.'

'I can save you the phone call,' said Lulu. 'It was wolfsbane. That's quite a nice angle, because it's always assumed that was the poison used by Romeo.'

'Thank you, I can definitely use that. Now, where can I drop you?'

'The basin will be fine,' said Lulu. She stroked Conrad, and he purred. 'Actually, I've just had a thought. Why don't we pay a visit to the local library?'

'To check out this whole Gastrell thing?' Danny grinned. 'Sounds like a plan.'

22

The Stratford-upon-Avon Library was on Henley Street, close to Shakespeare's birthplace. It was a striking timber-framed building dating back several centuries. With its black beams, whitewashed plaster and leaded windows, the exterior blended seamlessly into the neighbouring Tudor houses. From the street, it had the appearance of an old coaching inn or merchant's house, its gabled frontage leaning slightly with age; but as they drew closer, they saw a sign: STRATFORD-UPON-AVON LIBRARY & INFORMATION CENTRE. Someone's carved pumpkin was sitting on a windowsill, its candle long dead, its grin collapsing in on itself.

'I like the way they blend the new with the old,' said Danny. 'Though it does have the feel of a theme park in places. Shakespeare Land. Bardworld, maybe?'

'The town is built on tourism, so I suppose they have to embrace it,' said Lulu. She rubbed Conrad's neck, and his claws dug ever so softly into her shoulder.

'Does Conrad go everywhere with you?' asked Danny.

'Pretty much,' said Lulu. 'To be honest, I'd be lost without him.'

Conrad meowed, and Danny laughed. 'It's as if he understands every word.'

'Oh, he does,' said Lulu.

They went inside. Heavy wooden beams ran across the ceilings and uneven stone floors hinted at the building's medieval origins, but the space itself had been adapted to suit modern needs. Shelves of books and DVDs and a row of computers sat comfortably against the historic backdrop. Whoever had repurposed the building had retained its large brick-and-tile fireplace, complete with a pot hanger and a carved vine-trail frieze that must have been hundreds of years old.

Lulu spotted a librarian behind a counter – a balding man in his fifties, wearing a dark green cardigan and brown corduroy trousers. He had reading glasses attached to a fine chain around his neck, and they were perched on the end of his nose as he studied a computer monitor. He looked up and smiled as Lulu and Danny approached, his smile widening when he spotted Conrad. 'Oh, a calico,' he said. 'I do love calicos.'

'His name is Conrad,' said Lulu.

'Conrad the calico cat,' said the man. 'I love it.'

There was a small badge pinned to his cardigan confirming that he was a librarian and bearing his name – Oliver.

'Oliver, we'd like some information on Stratford-upon-Avon,' said Lulu.

'Then you're in exactly the right place,' said Oliver. 'How can I help you?' He took off his glasses and let them hang on their chain.

'We've heard that anyone with the Gastrell family name was banned from the town because of the man who demolished Shakespeare's house.'

Oliver grinned. 'Are you a Gastrell, by any chance?'

'Oh, no, I'm a Lewis. Lulu Lewis. But if I was a Gastrell, would I be in danger of being run out of town?'

Oliver chuckled and shook his head. 'No. We're a peace-loving people; nothing like that would happen. But it is an interesting story.'

'Was the Reverend Francis Gastrell really run out of town? Is that part true?'

'Well, yes, tempers were high at the time because of what he did. The phrase "sent to Coventry" was often used, but I believe he and his family actually went to Lichfield, about twenty miles away. It was never a legal punishment, more what you'd call community-driven exile. Over the years, of course, the story was embellished, and a popular version now is that the Gastrell name was cursed and banned from the town. But that's simply not true.'

'So people called Gastrell are welcome to visit?' asked Danny.

Oliver chuckled. 'You know, we get letters and emails pretty regularly from people asking that very question, especially Americans. It isn't a common surname, far from it, and anyone who searches for it online will find the story. I always tell them that so long as they behave themselves, they'll be welcomed. And there is most definitely no by-law banning them from the town.'

'You're from Stratford, are you, Oliver?' asked Lulu.

'I am, born and bred,' he said. 'There isn't anywhere in the world I'd rather be.'

'So do you remember when there was a Gastrell Bakery in the high street?'

'Oh, now you're going back a while,' said Oliver. He wrinkled his nose. 'Fifteen years ago? Maybe longer? It was on the other side of the road to the Garrick Inn, I think.' He rubbed his chin thoughtfully.

'Do you remember what happened? Did that Mr Gastrell have problems?'

'You know, now that I think of it, yes – there were issues. I remember seeing something in the *Herald*.'

'The *Herald*?' repeated Danny.

'The *Stratford Herald*, the local paper,' said Oliver. He came around the counter and went over to a shelf filled with large red-bound books with gilt writing on the spines. He ran his finger along the volumes and then pulled one out and brought it back to the counter.

'I think this might have been the year . . .' he said. He opened the cover to reveal bound copies of the *Stratford Herald*. 'It's a weekly newspaper, published every Thursday. Devoted to local news, but it also covers Solihull, Warwick and Banbury.' He took a small rubber thimble from his pocket, put it on the middle finger of his right hand and used it to flick through the papers. He was about halfway through the volume when he stopped and tapped a photograph in the middle of the page. 'There you are,' he said. 'The shop was vandalized. It happened a few times, I think.'

He turned the volume around so that they could see the photograph. It was a Tudor building and the ground-floor windows looked in on shelves filled with loaves of bread and cakes. In black lettering above the window were the words GASTRELL BAKERY, and a sign in the window proclaimed 'Freshly Baked Every Day'.

Somebody had sprayed 'SHAKESPEARE KILLER' across the window in red paint.

'Shakespeare killer?' said Danny. 'That doesn't make sense, does it?'

'It was probably young people,' said Oliver. 'Vandalism and common sense don't usually go hand in hand.'

Lulu took out her phone and nodded at the paper. 'Do you mind?' she asked.

'Go ahead,' said Oliver.

Lulu took a photograph of the article. 'Do you know what happened to the shop?' she asked.

'It closed eventually,' said Oliver. 'I think there's an antiques shop there now.'

'So was the baker run out of town?' asked Danny.

'There was repeated vandalism, I do remember that.' Oliver frowned and rubbed his chin again. 'I know the bakery shut after a few years, but I really don't know the reasons why.'

'The vandalism can't have helped the business, can it?' said Danny.

'True. True.' Oliver looked curiously at them. 'Why are you so interested in the bakery?'

'It was just a story we'd heard from a friend,' said Lulu. 'She was sure that there was a by-law banning Gastrells from the town.'

'Well, that's definitely not true,' said Oliver. He closed the volume.

'I'll be sure to tell her. And thank you so much for your time and help.'

'It's a pleasure,' said Oliver. 'You have a wonderful day.'

23

'It doesn't make any sense, does it?' said Danny as they walked out of the library. 'Why would Eddie come back to Stratford-upon-Avon after everything that happened? Okay, I get that the family probably wasn't run out of town by a mob of pitchfork-wielding locals; but he can't have had many favourable memories of his time here.'

'Why do you think he changed his name?' asked Lulu.

'Presumably to distance himself from his past,' said Danny.

'But why choose Lake in particular? As Sue said, why not just use his mother's maiden name, Nicholson? And why change Eddie to Edgar?'

'Good questions, Lulu. And I'm afraid I have no answers. Look, do you think that it's at all possible that Eddie was killed because of his name?'

'That someone found out that he was a Gastrell and murdered him because of that? I don't think so. As Oliver said, there's no real animosity between the townsfolk and the Gastrells, it's just a story for the tourists.'

'That's what he said, right enough. But what if he was just trying to paint the town in the best possible light? Maybe he was giving us a watered-down version of the facts.'

Lulu pointed down towards the high street. 'Why don't we take a look at the shop? It's only a few minutes away.'

Danny nodded. 'Sure.' He took out a pack of cigarettes and held them up. 'Do you mind?'

'Of course not.'

Danny used a fluorescent pink disposable lighter to light a cigarette. He smiled at the look of surprise on her face. 'People are always taking my lighters,' he said. 'No one steals a pink one.' He blew smoke up towards the grey clouds. 'Didn't you used to smoke?'

'It was hard not to on an MIT,' Lulu said. 'Murder investigations were always fuelled by nicotine and caffeine.'

'And curry,' said Danny.

'Oh, definitely curry,' said Lulu. 'Though I think these days it's probably avocado smoothies and quinoa.'

They reached the high street and headed south. The Garrick Inn was to their right, so they crossed the road. Lulu took out her phone and studied the photograph she'd taken in the library, then looked down the street. 'I think that's it,' she said, pointing.

Danny looked at her phone, then at the line of shops. 'I think you're right.'

They walked past a gift shop where a shopkeeper was peeling paper bats from the windows, the tape leaving ghostly outlines behind. As they got closer they could see that the bakery had indeed been refashioned as an antiques shop. There was a black metal sign hanging over the front door. Lulu's breath caught in her throat, and her eyes widened as she stared at the sign. 'That can't be,' she said.

Danny frowned. 'Can't be what?'

Lulu pointed at the sign. It read, HENRY RICHARDS ANTIQUES – EST. 2013.

'Henry Richards?' said Danny. 'But that's . . .'

'Exactly,' Lulu said. She stopped walking. 'And that can't be a coincidence, can it?'

'Well . . . coincidences do happen, don't they?'

'They do. Of course they do. But this . . .' Lulu shrugged. 'I'm getting goosebumps, Danny.'

'So the man who was on stage when Eddie died now owns the shop which used to belong to Eddie's father. Eddie must have known that, right?'

'How could he not?'

'And Eddie hated Shakespeare; that's what his cousin said. Why would he have wanted to appear in a play being produced by the man who stole his father's shop?'

'We don't know that Henry Richards *stole* the shop, do we?'

'Maybe not, but that's probably how Eddie would have seen it. I need a drink, Lulu.'

'Yes, I rather think I do, too.'

'Let's have a quick one in the Garrick while we plan our strategy.'

Lulu nodded. 'Let's.'

They walked across the road and into the Garrick Inn. The front bar was tiny, with polished wood and leaded windows looking out onto the street. The timber beams were low and dark, giving the rooms a cosy, intimate atmosphere. The walls were decorated with old pictures and other reminders of the inn's long history, and narrow passageways led into other rooms – some snug, others more open for dining. Dark wooden tables, polished smooth from long use, were scattered through the rooms, some small and round for intimate gatherings, others larger and rectangular to suit diners.

'You find us a seat, and I'll get the drinks,' said Danny. 'I could do with a whisky; I think I need it.' He grimaced. 'Except I'm driving, so it'll be a cappuccino.'

'I'll have a cappuccino, too,' said Lulu. 'I think I'm going to need a clear head.'

She walked down a narrow hallway to a small, low-ceilinged room with a square dark oak table flanked by straight-backed wooden chairs and a cushioned bench by the window. She sat on the bench. Conrad jumped down next to her.

'I see dead people,' he said in a spooky voice.

'You do not.'

Conrad chuckled. 'Just joking,' he said. 'But you can easily imagine Shakespeare sitting here and working on his latest play.'

'You can, can't you?'

Before Conrad could answer, Danny appeared with their coffees. Conrad jumped down onto the dark uneven floor-boards and made himself comfortable under Lulu's legs.

Danny sat down, passed Lulu her coffee, and raised his cup. 'Cheers.'

'Cheers.' They clinked their cups, and both drank. Lulu took a deep breath and let it out with a sigh. 'My mind is in a whirl, Danny,' she said. 'I just don't know what to say.'

'It's one for the books,' he said.

'Maybe we should pass on what we've learned to DI Dunning and let him work it out.'

'If we do that, I won't be able to get near Henry. And if they charge him, then we can't publish anything until the trial.'

'Well, we're not sure that Henry is the killer, are we? In fact, in terms of motive, wouldn't you have expected Eddie to have killed Henry? Eddie would have been the one with the grudge.'

'Maybe Eddie did try to poison Henry but there was a mix-up, and he ended up drinking his own poison.'

Lulu laughed. 'Seriously?'

'Okay; what if Henry switched the goblets, and Eddie drank his own poison?'

Lulu gathered her thoughts. 'Eddie had the Macbeth goblet, and Henry had the Banquo goblet. They couldn't have mixed them up. And we have to assume that Henry didn't know that Eddie was the son of the baker. If he had recognized Eddie, surely he would have been wary of him.'

'Is it actually possible that Henry didn't recognize Eddie?'

Lulu nodded. 'Of course. He was only a young boy when he left Stratford-upon-Avon, wasn't he? And in his late twenties by the time he came back. And we don't know that Henry actually knew the Gastrells. If Henry had recognized Eddie, would he really have wanted him in his drama group?'

'We definitely need to talk to Henry,' said Danny.

'We can't tell him what we know.'

'No, of course not. But we could talk to him about what happened. Get a read on how he felt about Eddie.'

'You can't call him Eddie, not while you're talking to Henry. He died as Edgar Lake, remember.'

'Sure, yes, of course. But we can talk about how they first met, the plays they've done together, what it was like working with him . . .'

'But at some point we'll have to tell DI Dunning what we know.'

Danny waved his coffee cup in the air. 'Of course. Absolutely. But let's at least have a chat with Henry first. I've already spoken to him on the phone, so it would be perfectly natural for me to drop by now that I'm here.' He drained his cup. 'Ready?'

Lulu finished her coffee, too. 'As ready as I'll ever be,' she said.

Conrad meowed.

'I'm guessing that means Conrad is also ready,' said Danny.

'It does,' said Lulu.

24

Lulu and Danny walked slowly along the pavement towards the antiques shop. Conrad was back on Lulu's shoulders and his tail was twitching.

'Maybe you should do the talking, Lulu,' said Danny. 'Seeing as how you've met him.'

'Happy to take the lead,' said Lulu. She pushed open the door.

A buzzer sounded off in the distance as they stepped inside. The shop was surprisingly bright, its leaded windows allowing in shafts of daylight that danced across rows of glass-fronted cabinets. Dust drifted through the sunbeams, catching on the polished surfaces of silver tea sets and brass candlesticks. Every corner was packed with antiques: there were porcelain figures arranged in careful tableaux, gilt-framed mirrors propped against the walls, and shelves of leather-bound books whose spines gleamed with faded gold leaf.

The air smelled faintly of beeswax polish and lavender. Conrad sniffed, and his claws flexed on Lulu's shoulders.

In the middle of the room, under an elaborate chandelier, was a large circular table cluttered with curiosities – old opera glasses, ivory-handled canes, cameo brooches and a scattering of coins that had clearly passed through many hands. A tall grandfather clock dominated the far end of the shop, its pendulum swinging steadily, while in front of the door lay a Persian rug, richly coloured though a little threadbare. The walls were lined with framed pictures, watercolours and oils, a mixture of portraits and landscapes.

Henry Richards appeared from a back room. He was wearing a worn tweed jacket over a cream shirt and a wool waistcoat. On his wrist was a simple gold watch, and his dark trousers met polished brown leather shoes, a little scuffed from years of use. A pink silk scarf hung loosely around his neck. He had a professional smile on his face, but it hardened a little when he saw Lulu.

Lulu greeted him with what she hoped was a disarming smile. 'Henry, it's Lulu Lewis, from the church.'

He nodded curtly. 'Of course, I'm hardly likely to forget, not after the way you took charge that night. Once a police officer, always a police officer, right? So what brings you to my humble shop?'

Conrad jumped down from Lulu's shoulders and landed with a dull thud on the carpet. He walked under a display case and disappeared from view.

'I really wanted to introduce you to an old friend of mine – Danny McGrory. You spoke on the phone, and he was hoping to meet you in person.'

'Ah, the journalist,' said Richards.

Danny held out his hand. 'Good to put a face to the name,' he said, smiling pleasantly.

Richards looked at the hand for several seconds, then finally extended his own and gave Danny a limp handshake.

'Your shop is simply fabulous,' said Lulu, looking around. 'There are so many fascinating things here.'

'Thank you,' said Richards. 'Are you looking for anything in particular?'

'Really, I just wanted to make sure that you were okay,' said Lulu. 'What happened that night was so awful, wasn't it?'

'It was, yes.' Henry looked at his watch as if seeking an excuse to get her out of the shop.

'Had you known Edgar for long?' asked Lulu. She saw Conrad disappear through the door at the rear of the shop, his tail held high.

'About a year.'

'Oh – so, since he first moved to Stratford?'

Richards nodded. 'He came into the shop and saw a poster about my amateur dramatics group. We got talking, and I suggested he come along for an audition. He did and he was surprisingly good, so he began acting with us.'

'He was good, wasn't he?' said Lulu. 'Especially considering he was only the understudy. He knew all the lines, word perfect.'

'He was always prepared,' said Richards.

'You were good, too, as Banquo. That can't have been easy, stepping in at such short notice.'

'I've played the part before, so it wasn't too much of a stretch,' said Richards, but he was clearly pleased by the compliment.

'Yes, but you'd had such a stressful day,' said Lulu. She looked at Danny. 'It was Mr Richards who discovered the body of the Reverend Harper, who was supposed to be playing Macbeth.'

'That must have been terrible,' said Danny. 'He hanged himself, didn't he?'

Richards nodded. 'It was a shock.'

'So he hadn't been depressed or anything?'

'Not that I know of,' said Richards.

'You were good friends?'

'Friends, yes. I'm not sure that I'd say we were good friends. But Troy had been part of the drama group for almost ten years.'

'And when did you first come to Stratford, Henry?' asked Danny.

The man's eyes narrowed a little.

'It's such an amazing town,' added Danny, trying to make it less of an interrogation.

'Twelve or thirteen years ago.'

'So you opened the shop as soon as you got here?' said Lulu. 'I noticed that the sign says you've been here since 2013.'

'I decided that I wanted to open an antiques shop, and I looked at several properties.'

'This is perfect because you're so close to the Garrick Inn,' said Lulu. 'You must have so many tourists passing the shop.'

'That's what I thought,' said Richards. He looked at his watch again.

'Do you know what was here before?' asked Lulu.

'It was a bakery. But everything had been stripped out, so it was easy enough to move in.' Richards smiled at them stiffly. 'I don't want to appear inhospitable, but I do have several business phone calls to make.'

'Oh, not a problem,' said Lulu. 'As I said, we just wanted to check that you were okay.'

Richards nodded at Danny. 'You're from London, aren't you?'

'I am, yes.'

'On the phone, you said you worked for *The Times*?'

'I do, yes.'

'Why is *The Times* so interested in what happened here?'

'It's a news story, Mr Richards. It always is when someone dies under mysterious circumstances. Our readers want to know what happened.'

'I don't see that a man's death should be exploited for the public's amusement.' Richards shuddered.

'Henry, do you have any idea who might have wanted to hurt Edgar?' asked Lulu.

Richards shrugged. 'I don't think he had any enemies,' he said.

'Would you say that you were his friend?'

'That's a strange question to ask.'

'Not really. I mean, you obviously interacted through the drama group, but did you see each other socially?'

'We'd go to the pub sometimes. But we met mainly with the group as a whole. He was always very keen to learn.'

'Was he a good actor?'

'I'd say so. Not good enough to be a professional, but he knew his lines and could reach inside himself to express real, believable emotions.'

'Did he tell you much about his past? His background?'

'Not really, no. He was quite a private person in that respect.'

'So you didn't really know him all that well?' said Lulu.

'I suppose not.' He smiled. 'As Hamlet says, "God has given you one face, and you make yourself another." Is anyone really what they seem to be?'

Lulu nodded. 'That's very true. And didn't Hamlet also say that one may smile, and smile, and still be a villain?'

The man's eyes hardened and his smile vanished for a second, but then it returned and he looked at his watch. 'I'm afraid I must go and make those calls.'

'Absolutely,' said Lulu. 'Thank you so much for your time.' She looked around. 'Now, where has Conrad gone?'

'Conrad?' repeated Richards.

'My cat. He was here a minute ago.'

Conrad appeared from under a display case. He arched his back, his tail vertical, and stretched.

'Ah – there you are,' said Lulu, scooping him up and putting him on her shoulders.

'It was a pleasure to meet you,' Danny said to Richards, and turned and pulled the door open. Lulu went out first and Danny followed, closing the door behind him.

'I got the feeling that he didn't know Edgar Lake was actually Eddie Gastrell,' said Lulu.

'If he did, he did a bloody good job of hiding it,' said Danny.

'He is an actor, after all,' said Lulu. 'But if he didn't know who Edgar Lake really was, he doesn't have a motive, does he?'

'You think he'd want to kill him if he found out that he was a Gastrell? That wouldn't make any sense. It's certainly not a motive.' Danny grinned. 'His facade did crack a little when you made that reference to smiling villains,' he said.

'I couldn't resist it,' said Lulu.

'I nearly laughed out loud,' said Danny.

They began walking towards Danny's car. 'So we know now that Richards took over the shop from Frank Gastrell,' said Danny. 'Eddie must have known that, too. The sign alone is a giveaway.'

'Yet he walks in and starts discussing the drama group. What's that about?'

'He was trying to get close to Richards,' said Danny. 'And he succeeded.'

'But with what aim in mind? The only thing that makes sense is that he was playing some sort of long con – but if it was revenge he was after, how does *he* end up dead?'

'Maybe Richards discovered what was happening and got his defence in first.' Danny took out his pack of cigarettes and lit one.

'That would mean that he knew who Edgar really was. Okay. Assume that he had the motive, and he definitely had the opportunity; but did he have the means?'

'The poison?' Danny blew smoke up at the leaden sky. 'That's a good point. Could he have access to wolfsbane?'

'It would be nice to know if he has a belted black raincoat,' mused Lulu.

'Why do you say that?'

'Just a thought,' said Lulu. 'We need to talk to DI Dunning now.'

'Do we really have to?'

'We have information vital to his investigation,' said Lulu. 'Withholding it wouldn't necessarily be a crime, but it would certainly make his job a lot more difficult.'

'Do we know where he is?'

Lulu took out her mobile phone. 'I'll call him.'

25

Warwickshire Police Headquarters was based at Woodcote House in Leek Wootton, a cutely named village tucked away between Warwick and Kenilworth. Woodcote was a former gentleman's residence dating from the 1860s, built from red brick with stone dressings, steep gabled roofs, tall chimneys and the large sash windows typical of the period. The grounds were landscaped, giving the building an even more secluded feel. It certainly wasn't an institution that welcomed the public.

'This seems to be the future of policing, doesn't it?' Danny observed as they followed the curving driveway to the Victorian country house. 'Shut down as many city stations as possible, and move management as far as you can from the communities they serve.'

'I'm afraid so,' said Lulu.

'You're based in Little Venice; when was the last time you saw a bobby walking a beat?'

'Covid,' she replied. 'Mask checks, and making sure there was only one person per bench in the parks.'

'Exactly,' said Danny. 'I live in Battersea, and you never see a policeman walking along the street. When you do see them, they're in a patrol car flashing by with the blues and twos on.' He waved his hand at the impressive property ahead of them. 'How does this kind of thing make the community feel safe? How do the people in there stay in touch with the people they're supposed to be serving? It's madness.'

'It's supposedly more efficient, and cheaper,' said Lulu. 'But you're right. A successful police force stays in touch with the people it serves. Bobbies on the beat were a vital source of intelligence back in the day. They were like Father Christmas – they knew exactly who was naughty and who was nice.'

Danny laughed. 'Those days are long gone,' he said. 'I'm too young to remember *Dixon of Dock Green*, but I was brought up on *The Bill*. Back then, you trusted the police – you knew that if you were in trouble, they'd help. These days it seems they're more likely to charge you with saying hurty things on social media.'

Danny drove slowly round to the back of Woodcote House, where there was a huge car park crowded with marked and unmarked vehicles. Next to it was a radio mast twice the height of the building. Danny parked and they walked back to the front, then climbed a flight of stone steps to the main entrance. Conrad, as usual, was riding on Lulu's shoulders.

A massive reception desk dominated the hall, with a discreet security arch beyond. To the left, a set of heavy double doors opened onto what had once been the drawing room and was now a conference suite; inside, Lulu glimpsed a long table littered with files, laptops and the inevitable half-drunk mugs of tea and coffee. On the opposite side of the hall, the former library had been converted into a briefing room. Its doors stood open, revealing walls covered in maps, photographs and timelines of current investigations.

Lulu approached the reception desk, which was occupied

by a middle-aged man in a grey suit. He looked up from his computer monitor, meeting her smile with a frown that suggested he resented being disturbed. Lulu explained who she was and that she was there to see DI Dunning, and the man directed her to a seating area where a number of grey armchairs had been arranged haphazardly around circular coffee tables.

'Someone will be along shortly,' he said.

Lulu wasn't sure when exactly the man put in a call to Dunning, but it was a full thirty minutes before DS Whitlock appeared from a corridor. She apologized profusely for keeping them waiting. Lulu introduced her to Danny, and they both followed Whitlock through a rabbit warren of corridors that eventually connected with a newly built annex. Whitlock took them up in a lift to the second floor and along a modern corridor with grey carpet tiles, flanked by pine doors. Many of the doors were open, presumably to aid with ventilation, and they could see detectives bent over paperwork and civilian staff fielding phone calls. The air was filled with a steady hum of printers and low voices.

At the end of the corridor were double pine doors. DS Whitlock pushed them open to reveal an incident room filled with desks, computer terminals and whiteboards filled with photographs and printouts. There were more than a dozen detectives working at computers and making calls, and half as many civilian support workers.

'The DI is through here,' said Whitlock, nodding towards a door to her left. Through an inset glass panel they could see Dunning on the phone. He had taken off his jacket, rolled up his sleeves and loosened his tie. Lulu smiled in sympathy, recognizing the signs of an SIO under pressure.

DS Whitlock tapped on the door and opened it. The inspector waved her in. There were two wooden chairs facing his desk. Lulu and Danny sat down. DS Whitlock closed the door and stood with her back to it, arms folded.

DI Dunning finished his call and replaced the receiver. He smiled at Lulu. 'This is a nice surprise,' he said.

'I'm sorry to drop by unannounced, but there's something we need to share with you.' She gestured at Danny. 'This is Danny McGrory. He works for *The Times*.'

The inspector's eyes hardened. 'I can't make any comment on the case, Mr McGrory,' he said. 'You'll need to talk to our press office.'

'It's Danny. And Mrs Lewis seems pretty certain you'll want to hear what I have to say.'

Lulu nodded. 'Danny has information that will help with your investigation. Trust me, you do need to hear this.'

Dunning leaned back in his chair. 'Okay,' he said, but Lulu could hear the doubt in his voice.

Danny smiled. He began to explain about the phone call from Sue Carroll and how he had driven to Solihull to talk to her. The inspector's jaw gradually dropped as Danny went on to describe the problems Frank Gastrell had faced when he opened his bakery in the town, and the fact that his son, Eddie Gastrell, had changed his name when he moved to London. But it was when Danny talked about Henry Richards buying the former Gastrell Bakery that the inspector really looked shocked. He looked over at DS Whitlock, who was also staring open-mouthed at Danny.

Eventually, Danny finished talking. He looked at Lulu, who nodded her support: yes, he had covered everything.

DI Dunning leaned forward over his desk. 'Wow,' he said.

'It took me some time to get my head around it,' said Danny.

'It definitely complicates things,' said Lulu.

The inspector smiled thinly. 'You don't know the half of it, Mrs Lewis,' he said.

Lulu frowned, not sure what he meant.

DI Dunning sighed. 'Kirsty, could you ask Andrea to join us, please?'

'Yes, sir,' said DS Whitlock, and she hurried out of the room.

The inspector fixed his gaze on Danny. 'I'm going to share some information with you, Mr McGrory, because I think we're going to need your help.'

'Danny,' said the journalist again, amiably. 'You can call me Danny.'

'Okay, Danny. But what I am about to tell you has got to stay between us. It absolutely must not appear in your paper.' Dunning looked at Lulu, too, making certain they both understood that he was serious. 'It has to stay within these four walls.'

'I understand,' said Lulu, intrigued by the inspector's manner.

'But I will be able to publish the information at some point?' said Danny.

'After the trial, yes.'

'And after the trial, I'll have the information exclusively?'

'I can't say at this point how much will come out at the trial. But what I can tell you is that I won't talk to any other media, and I'll let you have any photographs and so on that you may need. Do I have your word that nothing you hear today will be published before the trial?'

Danny nodded. 'Okay. Yes. Sure.'

The door opened and Whitlock reappeared, accompanied by a young woman in a dark blue trouser suit. She had long chestnut hair and oblong-framed spectacles, and she wore a police lanyard around her neck and carried a clipboard.

'DC Brumen, come in,' said the inspector. 'This is Lulu Lewis, formerly a superintendent with the Met. She was at the church when Mr Lake died. And this is Danny McGrory, a journalist. He has just supplied us with some very useful information, which I shall go through with you later. But in the meantime, I want you to bring us up to speed on what you've found out about Mr Richards.'

'Everything, sir?'

DI Dunning nodded. 'Everything.'

DC Brumen was standing with Whitlock, her back to the door. She took a deep breath as if steadying herself before speaking. 'All right. Mr Henry Richards is the director and producer of the Stratford Players, and it was Mr Richards who discovered the body of the actor due to play Macbeth – the Reverend Harper. While inside the rectory with the police, Mr Richards picked up an envelope containing a will that the Reverend Harper had left in full view. We therefore needed to take fingerprints and DNA from Mr Richards for elimination purposes. In the event, the only fingerprints on both the envelope and the will itself were those of Mr Richards and the Reverend Harper. Now, at that point the fingerprints taken from Mr Richards should have been deleted from our system, but they were inadvertently submitted to IDENT1.' She hesitated, looking at the inspector. 'Do I need to explain what IDENT1 is?'

'Might be best,' said DI Dunning.

DC Brumen smiled at Danny. 'Basically, IDENT1 is a database that holds all the fingerprint records from people taken into custody and from crime scenes across the country. It forms part of the UK's biometric infrastructure, alongside the National DNA Database, and is run on behalf of the Home Office through what we call HOB – Home Office Biometrics. Long story short, we got a match. But it wasn't a match to a Henry Richards. The fingerprints belonged to a Mr Benjamin Lloyd.'

Lulu's jaw dropped. This was probably the last thing she had expected to hear.

'Back in the noughties, Mr Lloyd had served a two-year prison sentence for embezzlement. Prior to that, he was an accountant, but following his imprisonment he was expelled from the Institute of Chartered Accountants in England and Wales and his practising certificate was withdrawn. From that point on, he was unable to work as a chartered accountant.'

Danny looked as if he was about to ask a question, but DI Dunning lifted a hand to silence him. 'You're going to need to hear this in one go,' he said.

'One year out of prison, Lloyd started working for the Kincaid crime family in Newcastle,' continued DC Brumen. 'The Kincaid organized crime group was involved in drugs, extortion, prostitution, bare-knuckle fighting, organized shoplifting. If it was a criminal activity, the Kincaids would have their fingers in it. The patriarch was Reg Kincaid, and he had five sons and a daughter. Their base was in Newcastle, but their criminal activities were all over – from Scotland all the way down to Birmingham. Lloyd helped them keep track of their cash flow and launder their dirty money. Under

Lloyd's guidance they invested in property in Dubai, beach resorts in Costa Rica, and wind farms and woodland in the UK. Before long they trusted him completely and he was privy to all their business interests, legal and illegal.

'Unfortunately, Lloyd then found himself being investigated by the NCA's UK Financial Intelligence Unit, and his only way out was to give evidence against the Kincaids – which he did. The NCA used him undercover for close to three months, during which time they gathered evidence on all of the family's criminal activities. Lloyd was so helpful that when the Kincaids were eventually arrested and charged, they all pleaded guilty. Lloyd didn't even have to appear in court, although the Kincaids would have been in no doubt as to who had turned them over. Reg and his oldest son, Jason, pleaded guilty to murder and conspiracy to murder and got life with a minimum of thirty years. The rest of the brothers were sent down for between twenty and thirty years, and the daughter – Jenny – got fifteen years. Jenny and four of the brothers are out now. Reg and Jason will be doing the full thirty, obviously. It was one of the most successful Proceeds of Crime operations ever mounted by the NCA. They recouped more than a hundred million pounds of assets, and the NCA was then able to pass on intel to the DEA that helped them bring down one of the biggest Mexican cartels.'

There was a short pause as Danny and Lulu absorbed this information.

'I remember the Kincaids being sent down,' said Danny slowly. 'But there wasn't a lot of detail.' He grinned. 'I do remember the mugshots. They weren't happy.'

'They pleaded guilty to everything, so the prosecution

didn't have to produce much in the way of evidence. They had no choice. And from their point of view, at least by pleading guilty they got slightly reduced sentences.'

'So I'm guessing Lloyd ended up in the witness protection programme? And he became Henry Richards?' said Lulu.

'That's what you would have expected – but no, actually,' Brumen said. 'I spoke at length to one of the NCA guys who was on the case, and it turns out Lloyd refused to go into witness protection. He said he didn't trust the Northumbria Police or the NCA, and that he would rather go it alone. He would change his own name by deed poll and move overseas. He said he would be safer if the police weren't keeping tabs on him.'

'He had a point, didn't he?' said Lulu. 'When you're under a police witness protection scheme, you're not actually off the grid; you're just on a different one. You haven't actually disappeared – you've just moved.'

Brumen nodded. 'True, although in Lloyd's case it was the NCA who were offering to look after him. But he refused point blank. My contact in the NCA said that they figured Lloyd had managed to get his hands on a big chunk of Kincaid money, predominantly crypto.'

'Smart boy,' said Danny.

'If that's true, the last thing he'd want is for the NCA to be constantly looking over his shoulder,' said Lulu. 'But wasn't he taking a huge risk coming back to the UK?'

'Well, Stratford-upon-Avon is a fairly sleepy town with little in the way of organized crime activity,' said DC Brumen. 'And it's doubtful that any of the Kincaid clan would sign up for a Shakespeare tour. But he's also undergone quite a change in appearance.'

She pulled a photograph from her clipboard and placed it on the desk. 'This is what he looked like back then.'

It was Henry Richards, but a much younger version: bearded, and wearing thick black-framed spectacles. He was thin and lanky and had a prominent Adam's apple. 'He has switched to contact lenses and lost the beard. The hair is longer and greyer now, and he's put on almost fifty pounds. And I suspect that he's had some plastic surgery. His chin is wider, his nose is thinner and his ears appear to have been pinned back. He's filled his teeth with veneers. That and the fact that fifteen years have passed probably means there's almost no chance of him being recognized.'

Lulu studied the photograph. It was definitely the man now going by the name Henry Richards, but she could only see the likeness because it had been pointed out to her. DC Brumen was right; there would be almost no chance of anybody from his past recognizing him.

'So how do you deal with this?' she asked the inspector.

'Do we think this is a coincidence?' said Danny. 'Henry Richards isn't Henry Richards, and Edgar Lake isn't Edgar Lake. And Henry Richards is on stage when Edgar Lake is poisoned.'

'If it isn't a coincidence, what is it?' said DI Dunning.

DC Brumen was frowning in confusion. 'Edgar Lake isn't Edgar Lake?' she said.

'It's complicated,' said the inspector. 'Can you gather everyone outside for a briefing in fifteen minutes? I'll explain everything then.'

DC Brumen nodded, still frowning. 'Will do, sir.'

'This is just crazy, isn't it?' said DI Dunning as she left the room.

'My head is still spinning,' said Lulu. 'The thing is, we have no idea whether the name changes are significant. We spoke to Mr Richards, and I didn't get the feeling that he knew that Edgar Lake used to live in the building that now houses his antiques shop. But Edgar Lake, AKA Eddie Gastrell, could only have approached Richards because he was living in his former home. Prior to arriving in Stratford-upon-Avon, he had no interest in acting or Shakespeare. His cousin told us that much.'

'Is it possible that Lake knew who Richards really was?' said the inspector. 'He was a crime reporter in London, after all.'

'It's possible; but Edgar concentrated on the south, really. I don't remember him doing much up north,' said Danny. 'Also, this business with Lloyd and the Kincaids was well before his time. He would have just been a kid when it happened.'

'Have you had any joy with Lake's missing files and computer?' asked Lulu.

DI Dunning shifted uncomfortably in his seat. He glanced at Danny. 'This is not to be mentioned outside this room,' he said.

'Understood,' said Danny.

'We had Lake's files and computer, and somehow they have managed to go walkabout,' said Dunning. 'We're now as sure as we can be that they're not on the premises . . . which means that someone has taken them.'

'So someone in the building is trying to hamper the investigation?' said Danny.

'It looks that way, yes.'

'So there's a bent cop involved?' Danny pressed.

Dunning held up his hands. 'That's not a given. Far from it,' he said. 'There are hundreds of staff here, and many of them are civilian workers. Plus, people are coming and going all the time.'

'Yes, but even so . . .'

'I don't think we should be jumping to conclusions,' said the inspector firmly. 'It's much more likely that the files and computer have been misplaced. I'm sure they'll turn up. Is it possible that Edgar Lake ever wrote about Benjamin Lloyd and the Kincaid family? I understand he was far too young to have covered the original case. But I wonder if he ever wrote about it at any point.'

'I'll run some checks,' said Danny. 'But I do know most of his stories weren't by-lined. A lot of the time he was freelance. He'd do most of the legwork, and a staff journalist would polish it to the paper's style. More often than not the staffer would be given the credit.'

'He couldn't have been happy about that,' said DI Dunning. 'Seeing someone else's by-line on his work?'

'I didn't know him well at all,' said Danny. 'But he never seemed concerned about the fame or the credit. With him, it was all about the work.' He wrinkled his nose. 'Are you thinking he was getting close to Richards in order to write a story about his betrayal of the Kincaids?'

Dunning shook his head slowly. 'I don't really have a theory at all at the moment.'

'Because that wouldn't make any sense. He met Richards almost as soon as he arrived in the town. And he then spent almost a year in his drama group. If he was planning to write a story about him, he'd have done it straight away. He had all the information he needed.'

DI Dunning nodded. 'I hear you,' he said.

'Have you received the data from Mr Lake's mobile phone yet?' asked Lulu. 'It would be interesting to see any text messages between the two of them.'

'I'm told it's in hand,' said the inspector. 'I'm not sure why it's taking so long.'

'Also, I did wonder about the Reverend Harper's phone,' said Lulu. 'It might be interesting to see who he spoke with in the days running up to his suicide.' She saw the inspector's jaw tighten and quickly held up a hand. 'I'm sorry. I'm not trying to teach anyone how to suck eggs.'

Dunning smiled and shook his head. 'It's okay. At this stage, I'm grateful for any help we can get.' He stood up and held out his hand to Danny. 'Thanks for coming in, and for your intel.'

They shook hands, and Danny said, 'I'll stay in touch.' He fished out his wallet and gave the inspector his business card. 'And I'd appreciate a call the moment I can use what you've given mc.'

The inspector took the card. 'Scout's honour,' he said.

'Your word as a DI is good enough for me,' said Danny.

26

Lulu climbed out of Danny's BMW and placed Conrad on her shoulders. Danny had parked on the road next to Bancroft Basin. They had spent the entire twenty-minute drive from Woodcote House trying to work out what Edgar Lake had been up to, but to no avail.

'This has been a fascinating day,' Lulu said. 'Thank you.'

'No, thank you,' said Danny. 'I doubt that DI Dunning would have agreed to see me if it wasn't for you. Tell me, do you think I can trust him? I'd hate to miss out on a scoop and find out that the rest of Fleet Street has beaten me to the punch.'

'He did say "Scout's honour". That has to count for something.'

'He seems okay, right?'

'I barely know him, Danny. But I do get the impression that he's a man of his word. And your intel on Lake – or rather, Gastrell – definitely helps him.'

'You never let me down, Lulu. Not once.'

'To be fair, it was easier for police and journalists to help each other back then. We could meet up for a drink or a curry, and no one would bat an eyelid.'

'Yeah, but that all changed after the phone hacking scandal and the Leveson Inquiry. Now officers have to record all contacts with the media, and off-the-record chats are not supposed to happen casually. If they do, the cop has to declare the relationship, and any sharing of information without authorization could breach the code of ethics or the Official Secrets Act. No one wants to even risk being accused of misconduct in public office, so pretty much all invites for a drink are now rejected out of hand.' Danny sighed. 'I miss the way it was.'

'Are you driving back to London now?'

'I'm afraid so. The days of the paper paying for overnights are long gone,' he said. 'But to be honest, my work here is done. I'll file the piece about the wolfsbane and the priest's suicide, but as we agreed with DI Dunning, I'll hang on to the Gastrell and Lloyd background until after the trial.'

'You think that Richards-slash-Lloyd is the killer?'

'I think he's the prime suspect. And even if it turns out not to be him, I can still use the background. If there is a breakthrough, I can be back here in about two hours.'

Lulu couldn't help but smile. It would take her more than two weeks to get back to Little Venice on *The Lark*.

'And you'll try to find out if Lake ever wrote about Lloyd?'

'Of course.'

She said goodbye and closed the car door, then watched as Danny drove away.

'Alone at last,' sighed Conrad.

'It has been a busy day,' said Lulu. 'I'm looking forward to a relaxing evening, just you and me. What do you think about Danny?'

'He's a very nice guy. Very straightforward. I like his aura.'

'Tell me more.'

'Lots of green; the reassuring green of a well-tended garden. It's wrapped around him, almost like a cloak. Then there is a soft, truthful blue running through it. He's a man who speaks plainly and keeps his word. And then at the edges is a faint golden glow that almost shimmers, which suggests a quiet pride in his diligence and a sense of purpose.'

'I never cease to be amazed at the way you can do that,' said Lulu.

'It goes some way to making up for the lack of opposable thumbs,' said Conrad. 'There are a couple of things you should know.'

'I'm listening.'

'The first thing is that there's no trace of aconite or wolfsbane in the flat above the antiques shop.'

'He could have cleaned up after himself.'

'My nose is pretty sensitive, Lulu. You know it is. Even if he'd scrubbed the flat clean, I'd have picked it up. I can categorically say that there has never been wolfsbane in that flat.'

'Well, that's good to know,' said Lulu. 'And what's the second thing?'

'I wanted to ask you if you have worked out yet why Eddie Gastrell became Edgar Lake.'

'Have you?'

Conrad chuckled. 'I asked first.'

Lulu began walking along the jetty, thinking. A cold breeze blew across the water, but she had her sheepskin coat buttoned up, and Conrad kept her neck warm.

After a few moments, Conrad said, 'You really don't see it?'

'I'm afraid I don't, no.'

'I always knew that my knowledge of the Bard would come in useful one day. He didn't choose the name Edgar

Lake by accident. It was a message. A proclamation of what was to come, if you saw the signs.'

'And you clearly have seen those signs.' Lulu reached up to stroke him. 'Please enlighten me, Conrad, the suspense is killing me.'

Conrad nodded. 'Edgar is a character in *King Lear*, and Edgar is all about justice and order, though he isn't afraid of using questionable methods to get what he wants. He believes in divine justice, that sin will always be punished.'

'And Lake? There's no one called Lake in Shakespeare's work so far as I can remember.'

'No, there isn't . . .' Lulu thought for a minute. 'The only connection I can see is that Lake in Spanish – and Italian – is Lago, and there is an Iago, in *Othello*. One of Shakespeare's greatest villains. It's really the equivalent of James, but Iago looks a bit like Lago, I suppose. Iago is a master manipulator, deceiving those around him to get what he wants. He nudges his enemies to make choices that end up destroying their lives.'

'Ah yes, of course.'

'Clearly, Eddie Gastrell wanted revenge on the people who wronged his father, and he decided to take the name Edgar Lake to carry out that revenge. It's a bit of a stretch, name-wise, but Eddie probably thought he was being clever.'

'The revenge thing didn't work out very well for him, did it?'

'The best laid plans of mice and men.'

'Rabbie Burns,' said Lulu. 'I'm guessing you're not a fan. I mean, he wrote a poem to a mouse, didn't he?'

'He did. And seriously, what sort of plans do mice make? If they're so good at making plans, why do so many die in mousetraps?'

'That's a very good question,' said Lulu. 'So Eddie Gastrell must have had a long-term plan, because according to Danny, he was using the name Edgar Lake long before he moved to Stratford-upon-Avon. According to Danny, that was the name he was using in London. All those years ago, he must already have been planning his revenge. But I keep coming back to the question – what was that intended revenge? Did he kill himself on stage? Was that his plan all along, to die in public view in the town that he hated? But it doesn't seem very likely; and without a note it makes no sense, does it?'

Conrad sighed. 'Lulu, I'm afraid at the moment none of this makes any sense.'

'And why wait a year? What has he been doing for the past twelve months? He had every reason to hate Henry Richards, but he cosied up to the man and even joined his theatre group . . .' Lulu reached for the keys to the hatch, shaking her head. 'My mind keeps going round in circles. It's making me dizzy.'

'Maybe you should sleep on it.'

Lulu smiled. 'Now that sounds like a very good idea.'

27

Lulu woke at just after eight o'clock. She showered and changed into jeans, a denim shirt and a warm pullover. She wasn't a huge fan of make-up but applied just enough blusher, mascara and lipstick to be presentable.

'Breakfast?' she asked Conrad as she went back to the galley.

'What did you have in mind?'

'I was thinking a bacon sandwich.'

'I'll pass,' said Conrad. 'Bacon is very fatty and salty, which can upset a cat's stomach, lead to pancreatitis, or cause long-term heart and kidney issues.'

'But it tastes so good,' said Lulu.

'Things that are bad for you usually do,' said Conrad.

'In that case, may I interest you in some tuna?'

'Tuna would be good,' said Conrad.

Lulu used a match to light one of the burners and placed a frying pan on the flames. She popped in two slices of back bacon, and while it cooked she opened a can of tuna and put several pieces on a saucer. She set the saucer down on the sofa next to Conrad, then finished frying the bacon and made a mug of tea. She put the bacon between two slices of white bread with a fair amount of tomato ketchup and sat down next to Conrad to eat her sandwich and drink her tea.

'What are your plans for today?' asked Conrad.

'I'm not sure.'

'So we're not heading back to London?'

'Don't you want to see how the investigation ends?'

'I can see that you do,' said Conrad. 'But do you think the police are even close to finding the killer? They don't even appear to have a motive yet.'

'That's why we should stay,' said Lulu.

'Because they need our help?'

'Exactly.'

'Okay, so if you were the senior investigating officer, what would you be doing?'

'I'd be focusing on the phone data, for sure. I'd be going through Edgar Lake's phone records and seeing who he was in contact with. And I'd be doing the same with Henry Richards. Not having Lake's computer makes life difficult, doesn't it?'

'DI Dunning seems very relaxed about the loss of the files and the computer.'

'I don't think he wants to admit how big a problem it is. Also, if they were taken from the incident room, then it's his responsibility.'

'It has to be a police officer who took them, doesn't it?'

'Maybe not – as he pointed out, there are plenty of civilians in the building. The question is, why were they taken?'

'Presumably because there's information on the computer or in the files that could identify the killer.'

Lulu drank some tea. 'That makes sense, yes. But if the killer knew that there was information that could identify them, why not break into Lake's house and take them? Why wait until they were in the incident room?'

'You're assuming that it was the killer who took the files and the computer.'

Lulu frowned. 'Who else would have a reason to take them?'

'Think it through,' said Conrad. 'If the killer killed Mr Lake knowing that there was incriminating evidence on Lake's computer or in his files, wouldn't he – or she – take care of the evidence as soon as they had carried out the killing? Why would they wait until the police had the evidence before taking it?'

Lulu's frown deepened. 'They could have placed the poison in the goblet, then broken into the house and taken the computer and files while Mr Lake was on the stage. In fact, it would have been far easier for the killer to have murdered Mr Lake in his house and taken the stuff then.'

'Exactly,' said Conrad. 'Shall I tell you what I think?'

'Please do.'

'I don't think the killer took the computer and the files. I think the killer wanted Mr Lake dead, and that was all. But someone else realized that his death meant the police would be examining Mr Lake's files and his computer, and they had reasons of their own not to want that to happen. So they had to steal them. Now, the big question is why they had to take the evidence from the incident room and not from his house.'

'And do you have an answer to that question?'

Conrad wrinkled his nose. 'It's sort of obvious, isn't it? It has to be someone working in Woodcote House.'

'So you're saying that we need to look for a police officer or a civilian worker who was featured in Mr Lake's files?'

'It seems logical, doesn't it?'

Lulu nodded. 'It does. Yes.' She finished her sandwich and tea, then washed the plate, saucer and her mug.

'Right, let's go,' she said, pulling on her sheepskin jacket and a pair of red woollen gloves.

'Go where?' asked Conrad.

'In my experience, when an investigation starts to flag, the best way of regaining momentum is to return to the scene of the crime.'

Lulu went out onto the rear deck. Conrad jumped smoothly onto the roof and then up onto her shoulders. She locked the hatch and stepped carefully onto the jetty.

There was a young couple standing together on the rear deck of their narrowboat, *Pot Luck*, and the sweet aroma of cannabis wafted over. The man waved a joint in the air.

'Good morning,' he shouted.

'Good morning to you,' called Lulu.

'We love your cat!' shouted the girl, and she giggled.

'Thank you,' Lulu replied.

'It's a bit early to be under the influence, wouldn't you say?' muttered Conrad as they walked away.

'They're young and full of the joys of spring,' said Lulu.

'It's November.'

'It's just an expression,' said Lulu. 'Anyway, cats have their catnip and humans have their cannabis. Both are naturally occurring plant chemicals that affect the nervous system.'

'I've never seen the attraction in catnip,' said Conrad. 'I get high on life. I don't need chemical stimulation.'

'Good to know,' said Lulu.

She left the basin and walked through the streets to the church. The police tape had been removed and there was no longer a uniformed officer standing guard. The poster advertising the *Macbeth* performance had also gone. Lulu walked up the path to the front door and opened it.

'There's someone inside,' said Conrad quietly.

'Who?' said Lulu.

'I have sensitive hearing, Lulu, not X-ray vision.'

Lulu chuckled. 'My mistake,' she said. She stepped into the church.

John Fleming was standing on the stage, unscrewing a panel of scenery which was being held in place by two teenage boys. He looked over his shoulder and smiled at Lulu.

'Are you here to help?' he said. 'I'm short-handed. One of my helpers is off sick.'

'I was just passing, but I'm happy to offer a hand,' Lulu said. She bent down so that Conrad could jump to the floor. 'What can I do?'

Fleming gestured at a stack of cardboard boxes at the side of the stage. 'If you could wrap each prop in bubble wrap and put them in a box, that'd be a big help.'

'Of course,' said Lulu. She grabbed a black rubbish bag and went over to the table. There were bowls of raspberries and strawberries that were starting to go mouldy, as well as several bunches of bananas and two melons. She tipped the fruit into the bag.

'Mrs Milton didn't grow these on her allotment, did she?' Lulu asked.

Fleming chuckled. 'No, not with the weather we get in Stratford-upon-Avon. They're from a local supermarket. Ted Simpson brought them when he delivered the wine. He persuaded the supermarket to donate them, though I think they were past their sell-by date.'

'When did Mr Simpson deliver the wine?' asked Lulu.

Fleming looked over his shoulder, frowning. 'That's a strange question to ask,' he said.

'I know, I'm sorry. I can't stop thinking like a detective.'

'That's right, you said you were in the police. But you're retired now, surely.'

'I was. And I am. But old habits die hard.'

Fleming turned away from the scenery. 'You're not investigating Edgar's death, are you?'

'Not exactly, no. It's just that I was here when it happened.'

'Do the police have any idea who did it?'

Lulu shrugged. 'Investigations are ongoing,' she said.

'Why were you asking about Ted and the wine? I thought the police had already said that the poison was in Edgar's goblet and not in the bottle.'

'That's true. I was really wondering who else was here when he dropped the wine off.'

'Well, I was here. And my three interns.'

'What about Jimmy the electrician?'

'Jimmy was definitely there. He was there all day.' Fleming frowned. 'Seriously, do you think Ted might have had something to do with it?'

'I think we're considering all options at the moment,' said Lulu. 'Have you spoken to the police again since I last saw you?'

'Yes,' said Fleming. 'Two more detectives came to my house yesterday. But there wasn't much more I could tell them.'

'Did they ask you who might have wanted to hurt Mr Lake?'

'They did, but I couldn't think of anyone.'

'Did you like him?'

Fleming shrugged. 'I didn't like him or dislike him. I didn't really know him.'

'Had he been in quite a few productions?'

'Every single one since he arrived in Stratford-upon-Avon last year.'

'But you didn't have much to do with him?'

'Not really. I'm in charge of the scenery and the props; I don't have much to do with the actors. To be honest, when they're not listening I refer to them as the moveable props.'

Lulu laughed. 'I'm sure they don't appreciate that.'

'Which is why I make sure that they're not listening.'

Conrad jumped up onto the banqueting table and began sniffing at the plates and cutlery. All the goblets and glasses had been removed, presumably by the forensics team.

Lulu placed the bag of fruit on the floor and picked up a sheet of bubble wrap. 'How long have you lived in Stratford-upon-Avon?'

'Ten years now.'

'It seems like a nice place.'

'It'd be perfect if not for the tourists.'

'This isn't a full-time job for you, is it?'

Fleming chuckled. 'Money would have to change hands for this to be a job,' he said. 'No, I do it for the love. I just love the theatre. I don't have what it takes to be an actor, I know that. And I don't have the organizational skills to be a director.' He waved his screwdriver at the set. 'But this allows me to be creative and to be part of it.'

Lulu wrapped a plate in bubble wrap and placed it carefully in a cardboard box.

'So what is your daytime job?'

Fleming looked curiously at her. 'Are you interrogating me? Am I a suspect?'

Lulu laughed. 'Of course not. I'm just making conversation.'

'It feels more like a cross-examination.'

Lulu opened her mouth to reply but was interrupted by the door opening and the appearance of DI Dunning and DS Whitlock. Dunning frowned when he saw Lulu standing on the stage.

'What on earth are you doing here, Mrs Lewis?' he said.

'I was just passing by and offered to help with the clear-up,' said Lulu. 'It's no longer a crime scene, is it?'

'No, the forensics team have finished here,' said the inspector as he walked towards the stage with DS Whitlock on his heels. He gestured at Fleming. 'Mr Fleming, I need you to hand over Mr Lake's phone,' he said.

'His phone? I don't have his phone. Why would you think I have his phone?'

Lulu couldn't help but smile. Fleming's protestations were just about the worst acting job she had ever seen. She could see why he was the group's prop master and didn't appear on the stage. Her smile faded as she considered the implications of what the inspector was saying. Why did he think Fleming had the dead man's phone?

'If you lie to us, you will only get yourself into more trouble,' said DI Dunning. 'If you have the phone now, you need to give it to me. If you refuse, we will search you, and if we do not find the phone on you we will go to your house. We have a search warrant and we will take up your floorboards, we will knock holes in your walls and we will rip apart your ceilings. Is that what you want?'

'Are you stupid? I've just told you, I don't have his phone. Why would I have his phone? That's a ridiculous suggestion.'

Again Lulu could see that the man was lying, and lying badly. He was saying the words without conviction, as if he knew that he wasn't going to be believed.

Dunning sighed. 'Mr Fleming, the phone company has alerted us that Mr Lake's mobile was activated an hour ago. It was on for ten minutes. And according to the GPS data, the phone was at your house.'

Fleming grinned savagely. He pointed the screwdriver and stabbed it towards DI Dunning in time with his words. 'Look, I know you're lying. If I did have his phone and if I did switch it on, I wouldn't have his PIN number, would I? So I couldn't possibly use his phone, which means it couldn't have logged onto the network.' He sneered at the two detectives. 'So you're bluffing.'

Dunning smiled coldly. 'We don't bluff, Mr Fleming. That's not how we work. For your information, even without a PIN code, when you power on a mobile phone it will still register with the nearest cell tower. As soon as you turn the phone on, the cellular modem powers up and looks for a signal. This happens before the operating system is fully loaded and before you enter the PIN. We know for a fact, an absolute fact, that Mr Lake's phone was switched on at your property this morning. That means either you or your wife switched it on. As you are denying that it was you, can we assume that it was your wife who did it?'

'Of course not,' snapped Fleming.

'Because we can always take her in for questioning, if that's what you'd prefer.'

Fleming's eyes blazed with anger, but then the fight seemed to drain out of him. 'I didn't kill him,' he whispered.

'Mr Fleming,' said DS Whitlock, 'before you say anything else, I have to tell you that you do not have to say anything, but it may harm your defence if you do not mention when questioned something which you later rely on in court.

Anything you do say may be given in evidence. Do you understand your rights as I have explained them to you?'

'Of course,' said Mr Fleming. 'I'm not stupid.'

'Where is the phone?' asked DI Dunning. 'Is it here?'

Fleming shook his head. 'No.'

'Is it at your home?'

Fleming didn't answer for a moment. He appeared to be close to tears. 'Yes,' he whispered at last.

28

DI Dunning motioned for Lulu to join him as he and DS Whitlock took Fleming out of the church. 'It would be useful to have your input, seeing as how you were on the scene that night,' he whispered as DS Whitlock put Fleming in the back of the Vauxhall Vectra.

'Not a problem,' said Lulu. Conrad was perched on her shoulders, and he dug his claws into her sheepskin jacket.

'The plan is to take him home, get the phone and then take him to Woodcote House for questioning.'

'Do you think he killed Lake?'

'Let's see how the questioning goes.'

DS Whitlock sat in the back with Fleming, so Lulu climbed into the front passenger seat. It took less than five minutes to drive to Fleming's house. It was midway in a long row of terraced homes set back slightly from the pavement, the red-brick frontage softened by years of weathering. A bay window on the ground floor projected just enough to break the line of the terrace, with matching sash windows above. A small wrought-iron gate marked the entrance from the street. The gate opened onto a short path leading through a narrow front garden bordered by low brick walls to a front door painted a pale blue.

DI Dunning parked close to the house and switched off the engine. He twisted round in his seat to address Fleming.

'DS Whitlock will go with you into the house to get the phone. Please don't make our lives difficult.'

Fleming stared at Dunning in horror. 'I didn't kill him,' he said.

'I didn't say that you did,' said Dunning.

Fleming lowered his voice. 'My wife is inside.'

'All the more reason to handle this as smoothly as possible. Just get the phone, and then we can talk.'

DS Whitlock opened the car door and climbed out, then held it open for Fleming. He got out slowly and deliberately, as if hoping that DI Dunning might change his mind and tell him to get back in. Whitlock opened the gate for him and walked with him down the short path to the front door. Fleming was reaching for his key when the door was opened by a woman in her late thirties, her permed hair framing an almost circular face with small eyes and thin lips. It was clearly Mrs Fleming. She said something, and Fleming shook his head. Then he and Whitlock disappeared inside.

'I don't think he's your killer,' said Lulu.

'Copper's hunch?'

'I can't see him using poison, for a start. But it's not that. It's all the work he put into the production. The actors only have to learn their lines and rehearse; Fleming does all the scenery and the props. It's a huge amount of work. By killing Edgar Lake on stage, all that effort went to waste. Would he do that? Wouldn't he at least wait until after the play had finished?'

'You think that would make a difference?'

'People are basically selfish,' said Lulu. 'They tend to act in their own best interests.'

'I get that,' said DI Dunning. 'But there's no doubt that he took Lake's phone.'

'Then we need to find out why he took it, obviously.'

The Flemings and DS Whitlock appeared at the door. Mrs Fleming was saying something, and her husband was shaking his head. Then Whitlock spoke to the woman and led Fleming back down the path and towards the car. She opened the door for Fleming, and he climbed in.

'My wife is not happy,' he said. 'She wants to know how long you'll be holding me.'

'At the moment we're not holding you, Mr Fleming,' said Dunning. 'You're not under arrest. You're simply helping us with our enquiries. Now, where is Mr Lake's phone?'

'Your sergeant has it,' said Fleming.

Whitlock had taken her seat beside him. She pulled the car door shut and held up an iPhone in a plastic evidence bag to show Dunning.

'Well done,' said Dunning. He started the engine, put the car in gear and drove away from the kerb.

Fleming said nothing during the drive to Woodcote House. He sat in the back, staring out of the window, his arms folded. Once they reached the police headquarters, Whitlock took him away to an interview room.

DI Dunning took Lulu aside. 'I'm happy enough for you to watch the interview, Mrs Lewis – in fact, I'd appreciate your input. But best you watch from a monitoring room.'

'That's fine with me,' said Lulu. Years ago, senior officers had often watched interviews being conducted from behind a one-way mirror. These days most interviews were video-recorded, and it was a simple matter to pipe a feed into another room.

The inspector showed her to a monitoring room. It was a narrow, windowless chamber with white walls that had yellowed slightly under years of strip lighting. On a table stood two monitors and a single speaker. There were four wooden chairs facing the table, plain and utilitarian, the sort that encouraged alertness rather than comfort. A shelf above the monitors held a scatter of ring binders and case files, their spines marked with neat numbers in black pen. Two mugs had been left on the table, one ringed with dried coffee at the lip, another resting on a paper coaster covered in scrawled notes.

'It's not very salubrious,' he said. 'Sorry about that. Would you like a coffee or a water?'

'We're fine,' said Lulu. She sat down, and Conrad jumped down off her shoulders and onto the chair next to her.

DI Dunning switched on the monitors, then tapped on a keyboard. The two screens came alive. One showed Fleming sitting on a wooden chair, his elbows on a table, his head in his hands. The other showed DS Whitlock sitting on the other side of the table, her notebook in front of her.

'Right, there you go,' said Dunning. 'I'll be back after the interview.' He left the room.

Conrad's ears twitched. 'Why do you think Mr Fleming took the phone if he didn't kill Edgar Lake?'

'There must have been something on the phone that Mr Fleming didn't want the police to see,' said Lulu. 'So the moment that he realized Edgar Lake was dead, he grabbed it.' She smiled. 'But that's supposition, of course.'

'Of course,' said Conrad.

'What about Mr Fleming's aura?' said Lulu. 'How did it look to you?'

Conrad wrinkled his nose. 'It's muted, as if there's a veil over it. All the colours are soft, washed-out blues and gentle greys, which suggests someone who is reserved. Careful. But there's a flicker of green that shows unease. He's not a violent man – the aura doesn't flare or bristle. It folds in on itself, as if he's hiding a secret.'

'That is such a gift you have,' said Lulu.

'It does come in useful,' said Conrad.

Lulu looked at the right-hand screen, where DI Dunning had entered the interview room and taken a seat next to DS Whitlock.

Dunning adjusted the cuffs of his suit and nodded at Fleming. 'This interview will take place while you are under caution, Mr Fleming. I need to remind you once more that you do not have to say anything, but it may harm your defence if you do not mention when questioned something which you later rely on in court. Anything you do say may be given in evidence.'

'What are you charging me with?'

'At the moment you are not charged with anything. But you need to be aware of your rights while you are being questioned.'

'You think I killed Edgar.'

'Why would we think that?'

'Because I had his phone.'

'So tell me, why did you have Mr Lake's phone?'

'I was taking care of it.'

'Did he ask you to take care of it?'

Fleming shook his head.

'Because you took it after he was dead?' said Dunning.

'Yes . . . but not because of what you think.'

'And what do I think?' asked Dunning.

'You think I killed him and took his phone to – I don't know, protect myself, maybe.'

'Protect yourself from what?'

'From being arrested.'

'Then you tell me the truth, Mr Fleming. Why did you take Mr Lake's phone?'

Fleming lowered his eyes and stared at the table. 'I can't tell you,' he whispered.

'Try.'

Fleming shook his head. 'I can't.'

'But you can see how you taking the phone does suggest that you were involved with his murder.'

'I didn't kill him. I was happy enough to see him die, but I didn't kill him.'

'Why do you say that, Mr Fleming? Why did you want him dead?'

'Because he was a bastard, that's why. A blackmailing bastard who deserved what he got.'

Lulu's jaw dropped, and she looked at Conrad. His mouth was also open in surprise. They both looked back at the screens.

Fleming had folded his arms defensively. 'I did not kill Edgar Lake,' he said quietly. 'But whoever did deserves a medal.'

'Was Edgar Lake blackmailing you?'

Fleming flinched as if he had been stung, but he didn't reply.

'Was Edgar Lake blackmailing you?' the inspector repeated.

'I didn't kill him.'

'That's not what I'm asking you. Was Mr Lake blackmailing you?'

'Yes,' said Fleming, his voice a soft whisper.

'How much did you pay him?'

'Three thousand pounds. Every month.'

'Cash?'

Fleming shook his head. 'Through PayPal. I paid the money to an email address.'

'What was that email address?'

Fleming shook his head again. 'I can't tell you,' he whispered.

'You have to.'

Fleming began to sob, and tears rolled down his cheeks.

DS Whitlock took a pack of tissues from her pocket and passed them over the table to Fleming. He took one out and dabbed at his eyes.

'I need to know the email address tied to the PayPal account.'

'Twistedsister2610 at gmail dot com.'

Dunning repeated the address to confirm it, and Whitlock wrote it down in her notebook.

'And what is the significance of the numbers in that address?'

'It's the date that my sister died,' said Fleming quietly.

'I need to ask you why Mr Lake was blackmailing you,' said Dunning. 'What did he have on you?'

'He knows – he knew – about my sister and me.'

'What about your sister and you?'

Fleming sobbed again.

'You need to tell me, Mr Fleming,' pressed the inspector.

'I got a letter, sent to my house. From someone who said they knew about my sister and me when we were teenagers.'

'Knew what?'

Fleming sighed. 'We were going through a lot. Our mum had died, and our dad was a drunk. We . . . got close. We needed each other. We knew it was illegal, but . . .' He dabbed his eyes with the tissue. 'The letter said that they had a diary of my sister's that detailed everything that had happened. And that if I didn't pay, he'd go to the newspapers with the diary.'

'So you paid him?'

Fleming nodded. 'I sent him three thousand pounds that month and three thousand pounds every month afterwards.'

'For how many months?'

'Six.'

'And when did you learn the identity of the man who was blackmailing you?' asked DI Dunning.

'Two days before the play. I got an anonymous letter saying that it was Edgar Lake who was behind the blackmail.'

'And you believed the letter?'

Fleming frowned. 'Why wouldn't I?'

'Did the letter suggest that you do anything?'

His frown deepened. 'Like what?'

'Did the writer of the letter suggest that you should kill Mr Lake?'

'No, of course not!'

'So why do you think you were sent the letter?'

'Someone wanted me to know, I suppose.'

'And once you knew it was Edgar Lake who was blackmailing you, how did you feel?'

Fleming seemed at a loss. 'I don't know.'

'You were angry?'

'Of course.'

'And you felt betrayed? By a man you thought was your friend?'

'Yes.'

'So you wanted revenge?'

'Yes. No – I mean, yes, but I didn't even think about killing him.'

'What did you think about?'

Fleming sighed. 'I thought about going to the police. I was trying to work out what would happen to me if the diary was made public. If I went to the police – to you – would my life end up being in a worse position? Would I lose my job? Would my wife . . .' He shrugged. 'I was going round and round in my mind, and I couldn't see a solution. And then he died. He died there on the stage in front of me, gasping for breath and bleeding from his mouth. The one thought that was going through my mind was that my ordeal was over. Hopefully my secret would die with him. Then I thought about his phone. I figured the police would be sure to look at it and that there might be something on there that could be linked to me.'

'But you said he blackmailed you with letters?'

'Yes, but in the first letter there were photographs of Jane's diary and pages from it. I thought that he might have used his phone to take the photographs. So I slipped back to the changing room and grabbed his phone. I switched it off and put it in my pocket and went back into the church.'

'And you switched it on today?'

'It was driving me crazy, not knowing whether the photographs were on the phone. But of course I couldn't open it. He'd set it up with facial recognition. So I switched it off again. I didn't realize you'd be able to trace it so quickly.' He gritted his teeth. 'You'll be able to examine the phone, won't you?'

'We're doing it as we speak,' said DI Dunning. He leaned towards Fleming. 'Mr Fleming, what did you do with the letter you were sent that told you about Mr Lake?'

'I flushed it down the toilet,' Fleming said. 'I couldn't risk my wife seeing it.'

'Was it typed? Printed? Handwritten?'

'Printed, I think. All in capital letters.'

'And obviously it wasn't signed?'

'Whoever sent it had put "A FRIEND" at the end.'

'And you have no idea who sent it?'

Fleming shook his head. His eyes widened. 'You need to find who sent the letter, don't you? They must be the killer?'

'We'll see.'

'Can I go now?' asked Fleming.

'I'm afraid not,' said the inspector.

'But you know I didn't kill Edgar Lake. If anything, I'm the victim here.'

'We need to check Mr Lake's phone first.'

'You can't just keep me here,' said Fleming. 'I have rights.'

'And those rights have been explained to you,' said DI Dunning. 'By law, we can question someone for up to twenty-four hours without charge. That time is meant for gathering evidence and testing accounts. If we need longer, we must apply to a magistrate for an extension. It's not a punishment, Mr Fleming, it's just a procedure. We will also need to send a forensics team to your house.'

'My house? Why?'

'Because by telling us that Edgar Lake was blackmailing you, you have given us a motive for his murder. We need to check your house for wolfsbane, the poison that was used to kill Mr Lake.'

'My wife is going to hit the roof,' said Fleming.

'We will try to cause as little disruption as possible,' said the inspector.

Fleming sagged in his seat, put his hands over his face and sobbed.

29

DI Dunning approached the table with two steaming mugs of coffee and a plate bearing a single Danish pastry. He set one of the mugs before Lulu, then lowered himself into the chair opposite.

The Woodcote House canteen was tucked away at the back of the building, looking out over the gardens. Outside, autumn leaves drifted past the windows. Around them, uniformed officers, plainclothes detectives and office staff chatted over plates of hot food, the hum of conversation giving the room a homely buzz.

'Are you sure you don't want anything to eat?' asked the inspector.

'No, thank you, I'm fine,' said Lulu. She tried her drink. It was surprisingly good. Most police coffee was weak and insipid, but this was strong and full of flavour. Conrad was on the chair next to her, apparently dozing, but his ears were twitching. She knew that he was awake and listening.

'Your interview went very well, I thought,' she said.

'I was just relieved that he didn't ask for a solicitor and go the "no comment" route,' said the inspector.

'Which is in his favour,' said Lulu. 'That's not the way a guilty suspect behaves, is it?'

'True,' said the inspector. 'But he does have a motive, and he definitely had opportunity. He was the one who set up the banqueting table.' He sipped his coffee. 'We're checking on that email address he gave us, but that will take time.'

'He did look like a man who was being blackmailed, I thought.' Lulu winced. 'It's such a pity we don't have Mr Lake's files. Tell me, how do you think they got the filing cabinet out of the building without being seen on CCTV?'

'Oh, we didn't have the cabinet itself, just the files. The warrant covered files, computers and phones but didn't cover furniture. So the files in his house were transferred to bags to be taken to the incident room. There were about forty in all, some of them quite thick. We've checked CCTV at all the entrances and exits from the time the items were last seen, but there are hundreds of people working here, and many of them left carrying something – a holdall, or a carrier bag, or a large briefcase.'

'But that quantity of files would have needed a pretty large bag, wouldn't they?'

The inspector nodded his agreement. 'They would have fitted into a decent-sized holdall. But whoever took them could have made several trips. So we were looking for a person with a large bag, or someone who made multiple trips with something smaller. We came up with almost fifty possibles using those criteria.'

'And have you spoken to them? Asked them what they were taking out of the building?'

The inspector shifted uncomfortably in his seat. 'We would run into problems with the Police Federation and the union representing the civilian workers,' he said. 'We can't just question people at random, there'd be an uproar.'

As he took a bite of his Danish, the canteen door opened and DS Whitlock appeared with DC Brumen on her heels.

They spotted Dunning and Lulu and hurried over to their table. Whitlock was out of breath with excitement.

'I've passed Lake's phone to the digital forensics team,' she said. 'They say it'll take time to access the data on it, and they can't guarantee that they'll be successful. They suggest we apply to the phone company for the provider records, which of course we've already done. But the good news is that the phone company have now provided the details that we asked for earlier.' She nodded at DC Brumen. 'Andrea here has all the details.'

DI Dunning grinned. 'Finally some good news.' He waved at the empty chairs. 'Please, sit.'

Conrad stood up and stepped gently onto Lulu's lap, and DC Brumen took his place. She placed a wad of papers on the table.

'The phone has been in use for just three weeks,' she said. 'At least, the SIM card has; we don't know how long Mr Lake was in possession of the actual phone. It's on a SIM-only deal, so it's basically a burner. There are six numbers stored in the address book, all with initials attached, not names. Most of the messages sent were through WhatsApp, which as you know is encrypted, but messages for the past week hadn't been deleted, so we can see them. Most of the messages were to and from someone who is working here, at Woodcote House.'

'Really?' said DI Dunning, leaning across the table.

DC Brumen nodded. 'Mr Lake was asking for information on a man by the name of James Thompson. He gives the man's address and is clearly looking for a PNC check, but he doesn't use those words. The person he's messaging says they are in WH, which I assume means Woodcote House, but that they are in meetings and cannot get to a computer. Mr Lake tells them to do it as soon as possible.'

'Let me see,' said the inspector, and Brumen slid a sheet of paper across the table. He picked it up and read it. 'This is good,' he said. 'This is obviously his police contact. The contact is clearly used to providing him with information from the Police National Computer.'

'Do you see the initials of the contact?' said Brumen quietly.

'Sure, yes. AD. So we're looking for someone with the initials AD.' Realization dawned. 'Wait a minute. Those are my initials.'

'Yes,' said Brumen. 'I had noticed that.'

The inspector sat back in his chair. 'That's pretty weird, isn't it? Does that mean I have to investigate myself?'

'Of course not,' said Lulu. 'You do realize that there is another officer in the building with the same initials, don't you?'

The inspector's eyes widened. 'Of course,' he said.

30

DI Dunning left Lulu in the canteen with Conrad and headed out with DS Whitlock and DC Brumen. Conrad jumped back onto the chair next to Lulu and looked around to reassure himself that no one was listening.

'Well, that was a surprise,' he said.

'Wasn't it?' said Lulu.

'Everybody suddenly got very busy, didn't they?'

'She is in the building, so I assume it won't be long before she hears that the police now have Mr Lake's phone and that Mr Fleming is being questioned. Hopefully she still has the files and computer in her possession. But if she has, she'll be getting rid of them in double-quick time.'

'How quickly can they get a warrant?' asked Conrad.

'For a search like this? Minutes, literally. They just have to apply to a magistrate, and if he – or she – is satisfied there are reasonable grounds and the application is in the correct form, a warrant will be issued on the spot.'

'And then what will happen?'

'If they do find the files and computer, she will immediately be questioned, and then I would expect charges to follow very quickly. The WhatsApp messages alone would probably be enough to convict her.'

'Not of murder, surely?'

'Oh, no, I don't think anyone thinks that she killed Edgar Lake. And if she did, she'd hardly leave his phone to be stolen. No, the theft of the files and the computer is separate from the murder. Well, separate but connected, I should say.'

'So we're no closer to knowing who the killer is?'

'I wouldn't say that,' said Lulu. 'The net is definitely closing.'

'And what do we do now?'

'As the inspector said, we wait.'

'The suspense is killing me.'

Lulu smiled. 'Me too.'

The seconds ticked by. A minute passed. And another. Lulu fetched herself a cup of coffee and a tuna sandwich. She shared the sandwich with Conrad. Then she bought herself a chocolate muffin, which she didn't offer to share. Conrad had taught her that chocolate contained theobromine, which cats cannot metabolize effectively, and that even a small amount could make them ill.

Three hours passed before DS Whitlock returned, and she was clearly excited.

'It's done,' she said. 'DI Dunning and a team went to her house, and they found the files and the computer. We've contacted her service provider for her phone records and marked it as urgent. And DI Dunning is taking her to the interrogation room now. He's asked me to take you to the observation room. If you want to watch the interrogation, that is?'

'Oh my gosh, yes,' said Lulu. 'I wouldn't want to miss it.' She scooped up Conrad, placed him on her shoulders, and followed the detective sergeant out of the canteen.

Whitlock took Lulu back to the room where she had watched Mr Fleming being interrogated. The detective sergeant bent over the keyboard, and after a few seconds the two monitors kicked into life. The video feed appeared to be coming from the same interview room as before, but this time it was Chief Superintendent Delaney sitting at the table, her arms folded.

DI Dunning was sitting opposite her. He had taken off his jacket, rolled up his sleeves and loosened his tie. There was a mug of tea or coffee in front of him.

'Right, I'll leave you to it,' said DS Whitlock. 'Wish me luck.'

'Break a leg,' said Lulu.

Whitlock frowned. 'What?'

'It's what you say to actors as they are about to go on stage,' said Lulu. 'It's considered unlucky to wish them luck.'

'Right,' said Whitlock. 'Okay.' She was still frowning as she slipped out of the room.

'I think you confused her,' said Conrad.

'Yes, I rather think that I did,' said Lulu.

She sat down on one of the chairs. Conrad jumped up onto the other. They watched the screens.

DI Dunning was drinking from his mug on the left-hand screen. On the other, Chief Superintendent Delaney was staring at the wall. After about a minute, Whitlock opened the door to the interview room and sat down next to Dunning. She took out her notebook and pen and looked expectantly at him. He nodded at her, then put down his mug and addressed the chief superintendent.

'As you are being interviewed under caution, you have the right to free legal advice. You may be represented by your solicitor and/or a Police Federation rep,' he said.

'I waive that right,' said Delaney. 'I am happy to talk to you without legal representation.'

Dunning smiled thinly. 'To be honest, chief superintendent,

I would prefer you to be legally represented. I wouldn't want this interview to be in any way invalidated down the line because it was felt that you didn't receive the correct legal advice.'

'I am comfortable handling this myself,' said Delaney. 'I've probably been involved in more interviews of this nature than you have.'

'Nevertheless, I am going to ask a duty solicitor to sit in with you. You don't have to talk to him, but he will be there if there are any legal points that require clarification.'

Delaney folded her arms, her expression neutral. 'Fine,' she said.

DI Dunning nodded at DS Whitlock, who stood up and left the room. She returned a few moments later, accompanied by a balding, portly man. He was wearing a tweed jacket with leather patches on the elbows and carrying a bulging black nylon holdall.

'I'm sure you know Mr Gilbert,' said DI Dunning.

Delaney gave the solicitor a tight smile. 'Good afternoon, Nigel.'

The solicitor nodded. 'Good afternoon, Alice.' He sat down, pulled a yellow legal notepad from his holdall and put the holdall on the floor. He interlinked his fingers as he looked at Dunning. 'I would appreciate it if you would allow me to talk to my client in private,' he said.

Delaney held up a hand. 'It's all right, Nigel. I have a pretty good idea of how this is going to go down.'

'Are you sure?'

The chief superintendent nodded. 'I'm sure.'

'If at any time you want to speak in private, just say.'

'I will,' she said. 'How's Jenny, by the way?'

'On the mend,' said the solicitor. 'Thank you for asking.'

'Give her my best.'

'I will.'

Chief Superintendent Delaney looked at DI Dunning. 'Okay, let's do this.'

The solicitor took a Parker pen from his jacket and placed it on his yellow legal notepad.

'Just to remind you that you are still under caution,' said DI Dunning.

'Of course.'

'We have recovered a number of items from your home. Items which appear to have been taken from Warwickshire Police Headquarters without permission. Specifically, a number of files pertaining to the investigation of the murder of Edgar Lake.'

'Okay.'

'Can you confirm that you took the files home?'

'As you know, I am attached to the investigation, and I took the files home to read.'

'We found the files hidden behind the water tank in the attic of your house.'

Delaney shrugged. 'I do some of my best work in the attic,' she said. 'It's my quiet place.'

'We also found a laptop belonging to Mr Lake up there.'

'I wanted to take a look at the files on his computer.'

'In the attic?'

'As I said, it's my quiet place.'

'I put it to you, Chief Superintendent Delaney, that you removed the files and the laptop from the incident room in order to hinder the investigation into the murder of Edgar Lake.'

Delaney shrugged and said nothing.

'You do know Mr Lake, don't you?'

'I did. Past tense. He's dead now.'

'When did you first meet him?'

'About eighteen months ago.'

'And where was this?'

'London.'

'Specifically, where?'

'At New Scotland Yard. I was there for a press conference, and Mr Lake was one of the journalists. He spoke to me after the press conference and we exchanged cards.'

'And why were you at New Scotland Yard?'

In the observation room, Conrad looked at Lulu. 'The inspector knows the answers to all these questions, doesn't he?'

Lulu smiled. 'That's the only way to conduct an interview,' she said. 'You have your evidence, and you give the suspect the opportunity to explain. And if you know what the facts are, you can immediately tell when they lie. And the more they lie, the more trouble they're in. What you don't want to do is to be asking them for information, because you have no way of knowing if they are telling the truth.'

Delaney was still considering how best to answer DI Dunning's question. 'I spent six months in London on attachment to the Metropolitan Police and the National Crime Agency. Warwickshire Police were fast-tracking me and thought that attachments to the Met and the NCA would advance my professional abilities and form relationships that might be useful in future.'

'So you spent three months with the Met and three months with the NCA?'

'I did, yes.'

'And was it useful? Did you improve your professional skills and build relationships?'

'I did.'

'Is there any one particular relationship that you think we should talk about?' said DI Dunning.

'You're the one conducting this interview, inspector.'

'Very well. What can you tell me about the relationship you formed with Commander Jeremy Tanner?'

Delaney's expression hardened. She took a deep breath, exhaling slowly as she maintained steady eye contact with the inspector.

'We were lovers,' she said eventually.

Conrad's jaw dropped, and he turned to look at Lulu. 'Wow,' he said. 'I did not see that coming.'

31

The solicitor was making notes on his legal pad as Chief Superintendent Delaney sat back in her chair. DI Dunning was taking it slowly, as if he had all the time in the world.

'Commander Tanner is married?'

'Yes,' said the chief superintendent.

'And you are married?'

'Yes. I am.'

'But not to each other?'

Delaney's lips tightened. 'No. Not to each other.'

'So you had an affair with Commander Tanner?'

'*Affair* is probably too grand a term for what we had,' she said. 'We had sex on several occasions. We had dinner. We spent a weekend in Paris.'

'That sounds like an affair to me,' said DI Dunning.

'I'm not proud of what we did. At the time it seemed – exciting. We were both working so hard and it provided a sort of . . . release. With hindsight, of course, it was a huge mistake.'

'Why do you think that?'

'Because it left me wide open to being blackmailed by Edgar Lake.'

'Did you know that she was being blackmailed?' Conrad asked Lulu.

'I suspected as much. Yes.'

'Why didn't you tell me?'

'Because I wasn't sure. Now, shush, let's listen to what she has to say.' They looked back at the screens.

'Tell me about the blackmail,' said DI Dunning.

'He was waiting for me outside NCA HQ in Tinworth Street. I was walking to my car and he said he needed to talk to me. I said no, as a police officer I wasn't allowed to meet with journalists outside of the office. Then he showed me compromising photographs of myself and Commander Tanner.'

'Compromising in what way?'

'We were embracing. Kissing. It was outside my hotel. We were on the way in. Lake and I got into my car, and he showed me more photographs. And he'd managed to get hold of text messages that we'd exchanged. And photographs that we'd sent each other.' She held up her hands. 'I know, I know – looking back, I can't believe how stupid we were. But it is what it is.'

'And you say that Mr Lake blackmailed you?'

'Oh, he was very clever about it. The words *blackmail* and *extortion* were never mentioned. He said he was working on a story about my relationship with Jeremy. He said he hadn't approached any newspapers with the story – he just needed some extra quotes, from my husband and from Jeremy's wife. But when the story was done he was sure he'd be able to sell it for big bucks. And I believed him. He had the contacts. But he said there was a way that I could keep the story out of the papers.'

'If you paid him? If you bought the story from him.'

'That's what he was offering. But he didn't want money.

He wanted my help with other stories that he was writing. I explained that I would soon be going back to Warwickshire and he said that was fine, he was planning on relocating. He said he would be living in Stratford-upon-Avon and that he would need help with stories he was planning to write, and with his podcast.'

'What specifically did he want from you?'

'At that point he wasn't talking about specifics. He just wanted me to agree to help him.'

'And you did?'

She shrugged. 'I didn't have a choice. My career and my marriage would be over if I hadn't said yes.'

'So you agreed that you would be his source when you got back to Warwickshire?'

'I did, yes.'

'And what about Commander Tanner?'

'What about him?'

'Did Mr Lake want anything from him?'

'He said he wasn't going to mention it to Commander Tanner and that I shouldn't either. This was to be between the two of us. He gave me the photographs and he left.'

DI Dunning frowned. 'He gave you the photographs?'

'He had copies, obviously. I think he wanted me to have a reminder of what he had on me.' She shrugged. 'Not that it matters. I destroyed them.'

'And when did you next hear from Mr Lake?'

'About three months later. I was back working in Woodcote House. I drove home and he was outside my house, waiting for me. I said he shouldn't go anywhere near my home. He said it wasn't a problem because it was Rick's snooker night.'

'Rick?'

'My husband. And it was. Rick was out. Lake said he wanted me to invite him into the house, which I did. Don't get me wrong, he wasn't putting sexual pressure on me, he just wanted to show that he had power over me. He said he wanted me to check out Henry Richards, the antiques dealer. He said he was sure there was something fishy about the guy, and he wanted me to run a PNC check on him. I said I would.'

'Even though you knew that you were committing Misconduct in Public Office, and committing offences under the 2018 Data Protection Act and the 1990 Computer Misuse Act.'

The solicitor leaned towards Chief Superintendent Delaney. 'Now might be the time to start saying "no comment", Alice,' he said.

'I think that ship has sailed, Nigel,' Delaney said. She looked at the inspector and nodded. 'In answer to your question, yes, I knew exactly what offences I was committing. But as I said earlier, my career and my marriage were on the line, and I was prepared to do whatever I had to do to keep them. And it's not as if I was helping a gangster or a drug lord. He was a journalist, and a respected one.'

'So you ran a PNC check for him?'

'I did, and got nothing. I told him that and he accepted it.'

'And when did he next ask you to do something for him?'

'About a month later. He asked me to look into a lecturer at Warwick University. The guy's name was John Fleming. Lake had heard there had been allegations of him having an incestuous relationship with his sister when they were in their teens. I checked for him and yes, the police had investigated, but charges hadn't been filed.'

'And would that be the same John Fleming who serves as prop master for the drama group?'

'Yes.'

'And he asked you to do something else on the Fleming case?'

'You've read the file, so I'm assuming you know.'

'I need you to describe what happened for the tape, chief superintendent.'

Delaney sighed. 'There was a diary kept by the sister, detailing their relationship in some detail. It was held as evidence even though there was never any court case. Lake asked me to obtain the diary for him. I did.'

'So you stole evidence and gave it to him?' said DI Dunning.

'Again, I would advise a "no comment" here,' said the solicitor.

Delaney ignored him. 'Yes, I took the diary and gave it to him. To be honest, I didn't see it as too big a thing. There was never going to be a court case, and the evidence would have been destroyed at some point anyway.'

'And what did Lake say he wanted to do with the diary?'

'He said he planned to write a story about the relationship. It ended badly. The sister killed herself a year after the police investigation.'

'You didn't consider the possibility that Mr Lake might use the diary to blackmail Mr Fleming?'

The chief superintendent shrugged. 'Not really.'

'Now tell me about Amy Jenner.'

Conrad looked across at Lulu. 'That's Lady Macbeth,' he said.

'Yes, Celia's friend.'

'This is turning into quite the interview, isn't it?'

'Yes, it is.'

'Amy Jenner is a local primary school teacher,' said the chief superintendent. 'But Lake had discovered that in her twenties she worked as an escort for an agency in London. Edgar had screenshots of the website and he wanted to see if anyone at the agency had been charged with controlling women for prostitution. They had, and I was able to give him dates and details. Amy didn't have a criminal record, but it was clear that the agency she worked for was a front for a prostitution ring.'

'And again, that never appeared in print.'

'I certainly never saw a story about her,' said the chief superintendent.

'Were all the people that Mr Lake asked you to look into connected to the drama group?' asked DI Dunning.

The chief superintendent shook her head. 'No. There was a magistrate he wanted me to look at. Jonathan Fairfax-Pym. Lake was sure that Fairfax-Pym had early onset dementia and wanted me to get his medical records.'

'And did you?'

'I did, yes. And there was a doctor who works at the Warwick Hospital. Dr Sandeep Gupta. Lake was sure that the man was using his own brother's identity, and that his brother was still working in Delhi. He wanted me to check Dr Gupta's Home Office details.'

'And did you?'

'Yes. Turns out that Lake was right. It was his brother, and he didn't have any medical qualifications.'

'Well, that would have been one heck of a story,' said DI Dunning. 'Was it ever published?'

'I don't think so.'

'And is Dr Gupta still working at Warwick Hospital?'

'I don't know.'

DI Dunning sat back in his chair. 'You seriously expect us to believe that Mr Lake was using the information as research for articles he was writing?'

'Yes.'

'Articles that we both know have never seen the light of day.'

The chief superintendent shrugged.

'Isn't it far more likely that Mr Lake was acquiring information that he could use for the purposes of blackmail?'

The solicitor shook his head. 'I really must protest. Chief Superintendent Delaney has no way of knowing what Mr Lake was or wasn't going to do with the information. She's not a mind reader.' He looked across at her. 'Alice, I really would advise you to continue to answer all questions with "no comment" and nothing else.'

'It's okay, Nigel,' she said. 'I know how this works.'

'Who else?' asked Dunning.

'A few months after I gave him the diary, he wanted me to look into the background of a local councillor, Sarah Collins. She was about to marry a well-known businessman who runs an art gallery that showcases local artists. Lake had heard that she had given birth to a child when she was fifteen and that the child had been put up for adoption. At the time she was a drug addict. Everything he had heard turned out to be true, and I was able to give him more details.'

'And again, you didn't see this as a possible blackmail issue?'

'Again, I would advise on a "no comment" here,' said the solicitor.

The chief superintendent ignored him. 'It didn't occur to me.'

'You realize that we have seen the files you hid behind the water tank in your attic?'

'You've made that crystal clear.'

'None of the information you shared ever made it into print. Or onto TV. Or even the internet.'

'I got the feeling that he was a perfectionist when it came to his work. He was just using me for research purposes.'

'You really can't be that naive,' said DI Dunning.

The chief superintendent shrugged but didn't say anything.

DI Dunning leaned towards her. 'Tell me about the Reverend Troy Harper. What did Lake want to know about him?'

'Lake had uncovered allegations of child molestation when Harper was a teenager in Ireland. According to Lake, Harper had changed his name before he entered the priesthood, and he wanted me to confirm that.'

'And did you?'

'Yes, but it took a while.'

'And when did you give the information to Lake?'

'About six months ago, I suppose.'

'Which is about the time that the Reverend Harper began withdrawing three thousand pounds a month from his bank in cash.'

'I didn't know that. Again, how could I possibly know that?'

'But you can see how it could well be that Lake was using the information you gave him to blackmail people.'

'Alice, would you please consider saying "no comment"'

to at least a few of these allegations?' said the solicitor. 'You're doing yourself no favours here.'

Chief Superintendent Delaney ignored him. 'If he was using the information for the purposes of blackmail, I had no knowledge of that.'

'Not that it makes any difference, of course,' said DI Dunning. 'It's the fact that you committed the offences that matters, not what Lake was doing with the information you gave him.'

The solicitor tapped his pen on his pad. 'Inspector, if you have no further questions for Chief Superintendent Delaney, then I suggest that we draw this interview to a close.'

'Oh, I have more questions for the chief superintendent,' said Dunning. He smiled at Chief Superintendent Delaney. 'What was the last job you did for Lake?'

'I wasn't doing jobs for him,' snapped the chief superintendent. 'That implies I was being paid. I was never paid for the information I gave him. I helped him for one reason and one reason only – if I hadn't, he would have ruined my career and my life.'

Conrad snorted. 'That didn't work out so well for her, did it?'

'No, it didn't,' said Lulu. 'Her life is never going to be the same again.'

'She's going to go to prison, isn't she?'

'I'm afraid she is.'

DI Dunning leaned towards the chief superintendent. 'So, the last job you did for him? Before he was killed.'

The chief superintendent sighed. 'Lake came back to me

about Henry Richards, the antiques dealer. He gave me a glass and asked me to check the fingerprints on it. I told him that Richards wasn't on the PNC, but he insisted. I had the prints taken, ran them through IDENT1 and got a hit. It turns out that Henry Richards wasn't really Henry Richards. He was the former accountant of a Newcastle crime family. He had changed his identity and his appearance and was lying low in Stratford-upon-Avon.' She sat back in her chair. 'Can I have some water, please?'

'Perhaps we should take a break?' said the solicitor. 'Half an hour?'

'No, I want to keep going,' said Chief Superintendent Delaney. 'I just need some water.'

'I'll get it,' said DS Whitlock, getting to her feet. 'Still or sparkling?'

'Still, please,' said the chief superintendent.

Whitlock left the room.

'What did Lake intend to do with the information you gave him about Henry Richards?' asked DI Dunning.

'He didn't say. It was never that sort of relationship. He asked me for intel, and I gave it to him.'

'But again, you never saw that he had used that information in a story?'

'No, I didn't.'

'And that was the last time you gave Lake any help?'

Chief Superintendent Delaney nodded. 'I didn't hear from him again.'

'And now he's dead.'

'Yes. Yes, he is.'

'You inserted yourself into the investigation at a very early stage, didn't you?'

'I live locally. It's a high-profile case. You would expect me to get involved, for my local knowledge if nothing else.'

'And the fact that you had a relationship with the deceased.'

'I wouldn't describe it as a relationship, as such.'

'Well, I would, Chief Superintendent Delaney. He was your blackmailer and you were his victim.'

Delaney smiled coldly. 'I'm glad you appreciate that I am a victim in this scenario,' she said.

The door opened, and DS Whitlock returned with a bottle of water and a plastic cup. She gave them to Delaney and sat down again.

'This is about to get very interesting,' said Lulu.

'You wish you were in there, don't you?' said Conrad.

'I do,' said Lulu, nodding. 'Oh gosh, I do.'

32

Chief Superintendent Delaney unscrewed the cap from the bottle and poured some water into her cup. She took a long drink, never taking her eyes off DI Dunning.

'Why did you take Mr Lake's files and computer from the incident room?' asked the inspector.

The chief superintendent lowered her cup to the table but kept hold of it. 'Because the evidence I had given to him is in the files and on his hard drive. I was worried that it might be traced back to me. But you know that already. You've seen the files.'

'Why didn't you destroy them?'

'That's easier said than done. But that was my intention.'

'You must have been relieved when you heard that Lake was dead?'

'I can't lie. Yes. It was a weight lifted off my shoulders. Of course, I didn't know then that I would end up in here.'

'Did you send a letter to John Fleming telling him that Edgar Lake was blackmailing him?'

Delaney didn't reply. She linked her fingers on the table as she stared at DI Dunning.

'We know he received a letter signed, "A Friend". Are you that friend?'

Delaney said nothing.

'Was it you who sent the letter?'

'No comment,' she said at last.

'Why did you want Mr Fleming to know the identity of his blackmailer?'

'No comment.'

The solicitor smiled, obviously happy that Chief Superintendent Delaney was finally taking his advice.

'Would you like to deny that you sent a letter to Mr Fleming identifying Edgar Lake as his blackmailer?'

'No comment.'

'If you didn't send a letter to Mr Fleming saying that Edgar Lake was blackmailing him, then now is your opportunity to say so.'

'No comment,' repeated the chief superintendent.

'In that case, I am bringing this interview to a close,' said DI Dunning. He stood up and said, 'To be continued.' Then he walked out of the interview room.

Conrad turned to look at Lulu. 'That took a dramatic turn,' he said.

'Once a suspect starts saying "no comment", there isn't much you can do,' said Lulu.

'But initially she seemed happy enough to talk.'

'She already knew that DI Dunning had the computer and the files, so talking about them didn't make her situation any worse. But the fact that he knew about the letter she sent to Mr Fleming caught her by surprise. Now she's wondering what else he knows.'

'Why does that matter? The letter?'

'It's not that letter that matters. But if she sent any other letters – if she told other people that Edgar Lake was blackmailing them – one of them might well have murdered Lake. And if they did, that would make Delaney an accessory. That's why she stopped talking to the inspector.'

Before Conrad could reply, the door opened. DI Dunning was grinning, and Lulu could see that he was pleased with himself.

'She's not denying anything,' he said.

'She knows what you have on her,' said Lulu. 'Have you had a look at Lake's files?'

'There are a lot of them, and they're all very detailed. But I flicked through and got the highlights.'

'She spoke about a Dr Gupta. Did you happen to see a file on a Dr Mackenzie? He was the GP in Stratford-upon-Avon who killed himself recently. My goddaughter knew him – I think I mentioned this to you the other day.'

DI Dunning rubbed the back of his neck, nodding. 'Yes, actually, there was a file on a Robert Mackenzie. Lake has a file on him alleging that he was taking kickbacks from pharmaceutical companies and suppliers at his previous practice in Croydon, South London. He was never charged – the practice didn't want the bad publicity. He paid back what he owed and moved to Stratford-upon-Avon.'

'Lake must have been blackmailing him, too. Is it possible that Chief Superintendent Delaney wouldn't be aware of his suicide?'

'Unlikely. She's local. She'd be aware of all deaths on her patch.'

'Might be worth raising it with her in your next interview.'

'I will.'

'And I notice that you didn't ask her whether she'd made contact with Henry Richards. If she tipped off Fleming, then there is every likelihood that she also tipped Richards off about Lake being his blackmailer.'

Dunning nodded. 'There's a problem there, of course. As yet we have no proof that she did contact him. If I raise it in an interview and she denies it, I'm on a sticky wicket. If I don't confront her denial with evidence, then she knows I don't have any, and that gives her an advantage.'

'So you don't plan on raising it until you have evidence?'

'She's a chief superintendent; she knows exactly how this works. We have her bang to rights on the misconduct issue. She can't explain Lake's files and computer in her attic. She's going to go down for that, no question. But the more serious charge is obviously conspiracy to murder, and for that to stick we need to show that she contacted somebody and suggested that they kill Lake. Now, Fleming insisted that she didn't ask him to kill Lake, and I believe that. He's an academic. But there's a good chance that she encouraged Richards to do the dirty deed. That's going to be a lot harder to prove, and again, she knows it. The way things stand at the moment, the minute I mention it she'll know that we don't have any evidence and she'll stick to "no comment", and that'll be the end of it. I'm hoping that there'll be phone data showing she contacted Richards.'

'But she knows how easily the police can track and trace phone calls and messages,' said Lulu. 'She's more likely to have gone old school. Much less chance of a letter being traced, especially if she's careful with her prints and her DNA, which obviously she would be. Don't forget she sent an anonymous letter to Fleming.'

DI Dunning was silent for a few moments, thinking. 'I really don't want her to get away with this,' he said.

'Neither do I. But this case is all about the evidence, and at this point we don't really have enough.' Lulu smiled. 'By "we", I mean you, of course.'

'I consider you part of the team, Mrs Lewis,' said the inspector.

'So what next? What's your game plan?'

'We'll let her sweat for a while. Under PACE we can keep her for twenty-four hours without charging her and then get an extension if needed. But obviously we can charge her with misconduct whenever we want. We have her work phone, but there's every chance she had a burner, so we're back in the house now. And we're getting a warrant for her car.'

'And you're convinced that Richards is the killer?'

DI Dunning grimaced. 'I would say that he's the most likely suspect at the moment. Because of his background, plus he has the best motive. If the Kincaids find out where he is, he's a dead man. That's worth killing for.'

'I suppose so.'

'You don't seem convinced.'

'I'm just not sure that Henry Richards would have used poison. But let's see what the evidence says.'

'Now that we have Lake's files back, we're working through them. We'll start contacting his victims and see if anyone else was tipped off that Lake was their blackmailer. So we could well end up with more suspects.'

'And what about Lake's computer?'

'Our tech boys are working on it now. I'm told it's easier to crack a computer than a phone, so let's see what they come up with. Delaney has given us the PIN code for her office phone, but the fact that she gave it up without a fight suggests there's nothing on it of interest. That's why we're upping the search for a burner.'

'I think I might head off,' said Lulu. 'You obviously don't need me.'

'You have been invaluable, Mrs Lewis. It has been a pleasure working with you. And Conrad.'

'The pleasure has been all mine,' said Lulu.

'Let me arrange a car to take you back to your boat,' Dunning offered.

'No, I'm fine calling a taxi. Your people have much more important things to do.'

33

Lulu climbed out of the taxi, holding Conrad with her left arm as she closed the door. She scooped him onto her shoulders as she watched the taxi drive away.

Conrad looked around. They were standing in front of a school a short distance from the River Avon, framed by neat playing fields and tall plane trees that rustled in the wind. The main building was a red-brick Victorian structure with high arched windows, decorative stone lintels and a bell tower that probably used to call pupils to class. A newer wing, built in pale sandstone and glass, extended behind the older block.

'I'm guessing this is where Amy Jenner works?' said Conrad.

'You really ought to be a detective,' said Lulu, walking towards the school entrance. A discarded Halloween clown mask stared up from the gutter, its grin distorted by the damp.

'And why, pray tell, do you want to speak to Amy?'

'Because the police are going to be talking to her soon, and I just wanted to prepare her. I think the bad news is better coming from me, don't you?'

'You like her, don't you?'

'I do. And I don't think she deserves what happened to her. She may have made some bad choices, but she didn't hurt anyone.'

Lulu pushed open a set of double doors and walked into the school's reception area, where the air was slightly warmer and smelled faintly of polish and photocopier toner. A low counter stretched across the space, behind which a middle-aged man, balding with thick-lensed spectacles, sat in front of a computer with papers neatly stacked at his elbow.

He looked up and smiled politely. 'Can I help you?'

'I'd like to speak to Amy Jenner, please.'

The man glanced at a clock on the wall. 'At about this time of day, Amy usually goes to the cafe across the road for a coffee.' He winked conspiratorially. 'At least, she says she goes for the coffee. Between you and me, I think she has a crafty cigarette or two.'

Lulu thanked him and went back outside. She left the school grounds, crossed the road and headed towards a little row of shops, walking past a hairdresser's, a fish and chip shop and a bookmaker's. At the end of the row was a cafe with a sign in the shape of a kettle hanging above the door.

'That's Amy there, isn't it?' said Conrad.

There was a woman sitting at a table outside the cafe, huddled up in a parka with the hood down, a mug in front of her and a cigarette in her hand.

'It is indeed,' said Lulu. She drew closer to the cafe and waved when Amy looked up.

'Lulu?' said Amy. 'What a pleasant surprise!' She held up the cigarette. 'I'm just getting my nicotine and caffeine levels up.'

'It's not really a surprise,' said Lulu, sitting down. 'I was actually hoping to have a word with you.' Conrad dropped to the pavement and went under Lulu's chair.

Amy frowned. 'Has something happened?'

'Amy, there's no easy way to say this. The police know that you were being blackmailed and will want to talk to you about it.'

The colour drained from Amy's face and her cigarette began to tremble. 'That's ridiculous,' she said. 'Why would anyone want to blackmail me?' Her voice was level and steady, a tribute to her acting skills, but the cigarette was still trembling. She put it into the ashtray and folded her arms. 'You must have the wrong person.'

'I'm sorry to be the bearer of bad news, but I wanted to talk to you before the police so that you have a chance to prepare yourself. They know about the agency you worked for in London, they have screenshots of the agency's website, and they know that the agency was a front for a prostitution ring.'

Tears welled up in Amy's eyes.

'The good news is that the blackmail is over. You don't have to pay any more.'

'I can't give evidence in court, if that's what they want. That's not going to happen.'

Lulu smiled sympathetically. 'They won't need you to go to court. Don't worry about that,' she said. 'Amy, there's something I need to ask you. Do you know who has been blackmailing you?'

Amy shook her head fiercely. 'No. I just get threatening text messages.'

'How have you been paying?'

'Bank transfers into a Starling account. Several accounts, actually. It kept changing.'

'And no one got in touch with you recently to tell you who the blackmailer was?'

Amy shook her head again. 'I wish they had done. I'd have happily killed whoever it was. Are you sure the police won't ask me to give evidence?'

'There's no need,' said Lulu. 'He's dead.'

'Who was it? Do I know them?'

'I can tell you, Amy, but please don't tell the police that I spoke to you. Okay?'

'Okay.'

Lulu took a deep breath. 'It was Edgar Lake.'

Amy's hand flew up to cover her mouth. 'No.'

'Yes, I'm afraid so.'

'That's unbelievable.'

'There's no doubt. The police found files with all the details of the people he was blackmailing.'

'So it wasn't just me?'

'No, there were many others involved.'

Amy picked up her cigarette, took a long drag and blew smoke up at the sky. A frown slowly spread across her face. 'Oh my goodness, someone he was blackmailing poisoned him.' Her eyes widened. 'That's why you asked me if I knew? You thought I might have killed him.'

'No, of course not. I didn't think that at all.'

'If I had known, maybe I would have,' said Amy quietly. 'But I didn't.'

'I believe you,' said Lulu. 'And I'm sure the police will, too.'

34

'She's not happy, is she?' said Conrad as Lulu walked away from the cafe.

'Understandably,' said Lulu. She had her hands in the pockets of her sheepskin jacket and Conrad was riding on her shoulders. 'If the school finds out what she did in her past, there could be repercussions. And she's married, of course. I doubt that she's told her husband.'

'Do you think she'll be able to keep her secret under wraps?'

'I don't see why not,' said Lulu. 'It's the murder that the police are interested in. With Edgar Lake dead, there's no blackmail case to be pursued.'

'I worry about Danny McGrory,' said Conrad. 'What if he gets to see the files?'

'I think DI Dunning will make sure that doesn't happen.'

Conrad looked around. 'Where are we going? This isn't the way to the basin.'

'I think that DI Dunning is getting tunnel vision on Henry Richards. So I want to speak to Mrs Milton about the man who took the wolfsbane seeds from her allotment.' Lulu pointed down the road. 'There we are,' she said.

Ahead of them was the shop she was looking for. It had a narrow frontage, just two windows across, with its upper storeys still bearing the traditional half-timbered pattern in black and white. The beams were sagging slightly, a reminder of their age, while the plaster in between was freshened up with cream paint, giving a sense of careful upkeep. A hanging sign jutted out above the pavement, a painted green board with a stylized leaf swinging gently from the wind blowing down the high street. The name of the shop was on the sign: THE HOLISTIC HUB. There was a sandwich board outside on the pavement with the words 'Locally Sourced Honey' written on it in green chalk, along with a cartoon of a bee flying above a jar of honey.

A small bell gave a polite tinkle as Lulu pushed open the door and stepped inside. She paused for a moment; the brightness of the place was dazzling after the November sunshine. The shop seemed almost new, with shelves of pale wood and long counters gleaming as though polished that very morning. There were rows of jars and packets neatly aligned, their labels printed in clear, modern lettering. Glass-fronted fridges were humming softly, each one arranged with bottles of different coloured juices.

A woman wearing a white coat was standing behind the counter. Her dark hair was clipped back, and her bright red lipstick matched the varnish on her nails. Lulu recognized her from the photograph she'd seen on the wall of the Women's Institute building: Brenda Milton.

Mrs Milton looked up and smiled. 'Good afternoon,' she said. 'How can I help you today?' She spotted Conrad on Lulu's shoulders. 'Oh, what a lovely cat!' she exclaimed.

'Mrs Milton?'

'Yes?' said the woman with a hint of trepidation in her voice.

'I'm Lulu Lewis. I gave a talk at the WI recently, following in your footsteps.'

'You were at *Macbeth* when Edgar Lake died, weren't

you? I remember you telling everybody to stay until the police arrived.'

'I didn't see you there,' said Lulu.

'I was at the back with my daughter. Once Edgar had collapsed and it was clear things were really serious, I whisked her away.' Mrs Milton smiled uncomfortably. 'I know we should have done as you said, but she's only fifteen, and I didn't want her to stay there.'

'I quite understand,' said Lulu. 'Did you know Edgar quite well?'

'Not well, but I knew him, yes. I supply any fruit or vegetables needed for Henry's plays, so I get to meet all the actors and crew.'

'It was a terrible business,' said Lulu. She was finding it difficult to get a read on Brenda Milton, who had a professionally warm manner that probably came from years of dealing with difficult customers. But Lulu wasn't picking up any negativity towards Edgar Lake. 'Have the police spoken to you about what happened?'

'No, why?'

'I think that they've been trying to talk with everyone who was in the church when Mr Lake collapsed.'

'That was a lot of people.'

'Yes,' said Lulu. 'It was.'

'You were sitting near the front, weren't you?'

'The fifth row.'

'Did you see anything?'

'I saw him collapse, of course,' Lulu said. 'But I didn't see anything suspicious.'

'They think he was poisoned, don't they?' said Mrs Milton.

'Yes. With wolfsbane.'

'Wolfsbane? Really?'

Lulu nodded. 'Yes, that's what the tests have shown. You have wolfsbane growing on your allotment, don't you?'

'I do, yes.' Brenda Milton frowned. 'How do you know that?'

'I was out at Pebworth Allotments with the police. Just looking around.'

'Why were the police looking around the allotments?'

'They were looking for wolfsbane.'

Mrs Milton's frown deepened. 'Why would they go all the way out to Pebworth to look for wolfsbane? Half the gardens in Stratford-upon-Avon have wolfsbane in them.'

'They found some in your allotment.'

'It's been there for years. The old chap who used to work the allotment planted it as a windbreak.' Mrs Milton frowned. 'Now wait a minute, the police don't think that I . . . ?' She shook her head. 'Oh, that's ridiculous.'

'I think they're considering all possibilities at the moment,' said Lulu.

'But what reason could I possibly have for wanting to hurt Edgar?'

Lulu looked into Mrs Milton's eyes. It seemed to be a genuine question – the woman was clearly bemused by the suggestion. Lulu believed her.

'Again, I think they regard everybody at the church as a potential suspect. Even me,' she said with a wry smile.

'But you didn't kill him, did you?'

'Of course not,' said Lulu.

'And neither did I. I've a good mind to call them up and read them the riot act.'

'I'm fairly sure you'll hear from them before long, Mrs

Milton. You see, while we were there, a lady from one of the other allotments mentioned that she'd seen you giving wolfsbane seed pods to a man.'

'What? Who said that?'

'A woman in a cowboy hat.'

'Oh, Annie bloody Oakley. She's always pushing her nose in where it isn't wanted. Allotment owners are a close-knit bunch – we always keep an eye out for each other – but Annie Oakley is just a nosey parker.'

'I thought her name was Amanda? Amanda McKinlay?'

'Annie Oakley is her nickname, because of the stupid hat she always wears. So what did she say, exactly?'

'She said that she saw you with a grey-haired man in a belted black raincoat, and that you gave him some seed pods from the wolfsbane plants.'

'What was she doing spying on me like that?'

'She just said that she saw you with the man, and when she tried to talk to you, you left.' Lulu smiled. 'Can I ask you something, Mrs Milton?'

'I suppose so, yes.' Brenda Milton's voice had turned frosty, as if she wasn't happy about being questioned, but she still had a professional half-smile on her face.

'The man you gave the seeds to wasn't Henry Richards, by any chance?'

Mrs Milton's jaw dropped. 'Why on earth would I be giving seed pods to Henry? He doesn't have a garden. He lives above his shop, and he doesn't even have a window box.' She shook her head contemptuously. 'Ridiculous.'

'It's just that Annie – er, Amanda – said the man had grey hair, and so does Henry.'

'Half the population of Stratford-upon-Avon has grey

hair,' said Mrs Milton. 'Wait; are you now telling me that the police think Henry might have poisoned Edgar?'

'As I said, they are considering all possibilities.'

'But Henry and Edgar have worked together for almost a year. I'm not saying they're bosom buddies, but they spend hours together rehearsing. And you must have seen how shocked Henry was when Edgar keeled over. He definitely wasn't expecting it. None of us were.' Mrs Milton frowned again. 'So the police think that there was wolfsbane in the wine?'

'Not necessarily in the wine. More likely it was in the goblet that Edgar drank from.'

'But that was Macbeth's goblet. And Edgar wasn't supposed to be playing Macbeth. That was all at short notice because Troy . . .' She left the sentence unfinished, apparently unable to find the right words for the Reverend Harper's suicide.

'If you don't mind me asking, who was the man who visited your allotment for the wolfsbane seed pods?' asked Lulu.

'A chap who got in touch with me through the allotment Facebook page. I'd posted pictures of my plants when they were in full bloom, and he asked for some seeds. It's not an unusual request.'

'Was he someone you already knew?'

'No, but he is a regular contributor to the page and is always respectful. His name's Ron and he lives in Milcote, which is on my route from here to the allotments. So I picked him up and drove him over. Lovely man, and very knowledgeable. He has his very own Victorian walled garden and wanted to grow some wolfsbane from seed. And yes, he was wearing a black raincoat – it had been threatening to rain all day.' Mrs Milton was starting to sound exasperated.

'I'm sorry – I can see that I've upset you,' said Lulu.

'I hate it that someone might think I had anything to do with poor Edgar's death, that's all.'

'You were in the church during the day, getting ready for the performance?'

'I was there in the early evening. Henry would usually have helped to set up the scenery and dress the sets, but after what happened to Troy, he was stepping up to play the part of Banquo so that Edgar could play Macbeth. That meant Henry had to do some last-minute revising, so John Fleming and his team did most of the set-dressing. I had to wait until they'd prepared the banqueting table before I could put my fruit and veg on it.'

'And you saw the goblets?'

'I think so, yes. Everything was in position. I just had to put my produce in the bowls that John provided.'

'And who else was there while you were?'

'John was there, of course, and his team. Three of them. I don't know their names. Finchy, the lighting guy. And I think Finchy had a young girl helping him. I don't know her name either. Henry was there, but he was sitting in a pew going over the script. I imagine he was still a bit shaken up about everything that had happened. And the cleaning lady was there, sweeping up.'

'What about Jimmy Baxter? The electrician?'

'I didn't see him. The cast were all there, most of them in the back trying on their costumes.'

'And did you see anyone at the banqueting table?'

'John and his team were back and forth. Oh yes, at one point Henry went over and checked his goblet. Actually, now I think about it, he took it away to wash it. Edgar had been using it during rehearsals, so I suppose he wanted to make sure it was clean.'

'And there were no strangers in the church? Nobody who shouldn't have been there?'

'I don't remember seeing any strangers, no. But I was there to work. And not for very long, because I had to go home and cook tea for my family.'

'Was it just you and your daughter who went to see the play?'

Mrs Milton winced. 'My husband hates Shakespeare. And I mean that he hates it. Despises everything the man wrote. He says he can never understand a word that's being said. He's always asking why Shakespeare didn't just write in plain English. I've tried explaining to him, but actually I think he just likes winding me up. Anyway, he stayed at home watching Netflix. In view of what happened, he probably had the right idea.'

Mrs Milton's gaze shifted past Lulu, her eyes narrowing as she saw something in the road outside. Lulu turned to look.

Two police patrol cars had parked outside. One of them was a BMW X5 with white bodywork, high-visibility blue and yellow Battenberg markings, and emergency lighting on the roof. The yellow discs in the windows showed that it was an armed response vehicle.

'I wonder what's happening,' said Mrs Milton.

'I'm sure it's nothing,' said Lulu, though clearly it was something. 'I'm so sorry to have bothered you. I just wanted to put my mind at rest about Mr Richards. He seems like such a nice man.'

'He is,' said Mrs Milton. 'He's a real gentleman.'

35

Lulu thanked Mrs Milton and left the shop. There were three officers sitting in the X5 and they looked as if they were awaiting instructions. She glanced up and down the high street. DI Dunning's Vauxhall Vectra was parked close to the Garrick Inn.

She walked towards it. When she was about twenty feet away, the doors opened and DI Dunning and DS Whitlock climbed out. The inspector's eyebrows shot up when he saw Lulu.

'You're not following me, are you?' he said.

'I was in a shop down the road and I saw all the excitement.'

'Well, there's no excitement yet. We're just planning for any eventuality.'

'You're here for Henry Richards?'

'I think we have to have a word with him, yes. We found a burner phone during the search of Chief Superintendent Delaney's house, and the tech boys have finally recovered the WhatsApp messages she deleted. She had several conversations with Richards in the days prior to Lake's death.'

'Suggesting that Richards kill Lake?'

'Not in so many words. But she made contact with him a number of times, so we need Richards to tell us what she said.'

Lulu gestured at the ARV. 'And you think he might be armed.'

'He worked with some very heavy characters in Newcastle.'

'Best to be prepared, obviously,' said Lulu. 'But before you go in, you should know that Henry Richards wasn't the grey-haired man in the belted raincoat getting the seed pods at the allotments we went to. Turns out that was just a keen gardener who met Brenda Milton on a Facebook page. She agreed to give him some seed pods for his garden.'

'And you know this how?'

'I've just been in Mrs Milton's shop.'

'Passing by?'

'Well, I didn't think it would do any harm. I was surprised that you hadn't already been in touch to ask her about the wolfsbane on her allotment and the man who took the seeds.'

'We had that down for this morning, but then all the Richards stuff kicked off. To be honest, if Richards is our man, the allotment is probably a red herring.'

'And I wanted to put feelers out to see how she felt about Edgar Lake,' Lulu added.

'And?'

'She genuinely seemed to like him. And I didn't get the impression that she was being blackmailed.'

'She wasn't one of the names that Chief Superintendent Delaney mentioned.' Dunning wrinkled his nose. 'So what are you saying – you don't think that Richards is the killer?'

'Oh, he had motive, that's for sure. And he had the opportunity. There's no doubt about that. It's just that if he was the one who poisoned Edgar Lake, he didn't get the poison from Mrs Milton's allotment.'

'I've been told that wolfsbane grows everywhere,' said the inspector.

'That's true. It grows wild, and it's also in a lot of gardens.'

'Once we're inside his house we'll get a forensics team in and they can look for traces of the poison.'

'May I hang around?'

'Sure, but the firearms officers will be going in first. The shop is open and there's someone in there, but we're not a hundred per cent sure that it's him. We're not going to seal off the street. We'll keep any drama to a minimum, and the firearms officers will go in with handguns rather than carbines. It should all be over very quickly. Why don't you stay with DS Whitlock?'

The detective sergeant smiled. 'I'll take care of you, Lulu,' she said. 'And Conrad.'

DI Dunning nodded and walked over to the ARV. The front passenger window wound down and the inspector bent down to talk to a female sergeant who had a police baseball cap covering her ginger hair. They talked for less than a minute. Then the three firearms officers climbed out of their vehicle. They all had holstered guns on their thighs along with incapacitant spray canisters and Tasers.

DI Dunning waved over two uniformed constables in high-vis jackets and briefed them, then nodded at the firearms officers.

Lulu reached up and patted Conrad as the firearms officers headed into the shop, drawing their handguns as they crossed the threshold. There were no frantic shouts or barked commands, and after a few seconds DI Dunning and the two constables disappeared inside. Lulu's heart was racing. The police knew what they were doing, and they trained for situations just like this, but that didn't make it any less dangerous. Conrad purred as if trying to comfort her, and she patted him again.

The seconds ticked by, and Lulu realized that she was holding her breath. She made a conscious effort to breathe.

'I hate the waiting,' said DS Whitlock.

'Me too,' said Lulu. 'But I really don't think that Henry Richards is the sort to get involved in a shootout.'

'I hope you're right.'

Lulu could feel her back tensing up; she wiggled her toes, trying to keep her circulation going. She sighed with relief when she saw DI Dunning reappear at the shop door. He waved them over. Lulu and DS Whitlock hurried along the pavement.

'He's not here,' said the inspector. 'There's a young man in the shop who says Richards called him in this morning. It was supposed to be his day off, but Richards told him he had to meet a client in Nuneaton.'

'Did he take a bag with him?' asked Lulu. 'Has he gone for good?'

'The guy didn't see him. He opened up the shop with his own key at nine o'clock and Richards had already left. The armed cops are doing a sweep of the upstairs flat, but it looks as if the bird has flown. As soon as they give the all clear, we'll go inside and take a look around.'

'Okay,' said Lulu.

DI Dunning took out a pack of cigarettes and lit one. He blew smoke up into the leaden sky, taking care that it didn't go near Lulu or DS Whitlock. He was halfway through the cigarette when the armed police reappeared. Dunning went over to talk to the sergeant. He came back after a couple of minutes and dropped his cigarette into the gutter. 'Good to go,' he said.

He took them into the shop as the armed officers climbed into their BMW and drove away. One of the uniformed constables was standing by the door, the other was next to a young man in a grey suit. He had slicked-back reddish hair and freckles across his nose and cheeks.

'This is Mr Jenkins,' Dunning said to Lulu. 'He helps Mr Richards out in the shop.'

'What am I supposed to do?' said the young man. 'Do I have to close the shop?'

'To customers, yes,' said DI Dunning. 'We have a forensics team on the way. But after they've gone, you can open the shop again. Did Mr Richards say when he'd be back?'

Mr Jenkins shook his head. 'He just said he was going to Nuneaton.'

'Does he have a car?'

The young man nodded. 'Yes. A Tesla.'

'How very environmentally conscious of him,' said DI Dunning. 'I don't suppose you have the registration number?'

'No, sorry,' Jenkins said. Then he hesitated. 'Actually, yes. I took a selfie in front of it a while back.' He took out his mobile phone and scrolled through the pictures on it, then held it out so that the inspector could see the screen.

The inspector nodded and gestured to DS Whitlock to make a note of it. 'Let's get that run through ANPR,' he said.

Lulu knew what a valuable tool Automatic Number Plate Recognition was for any police investigation. Static and mobile cameras automatically read vehicle number plates and compared the number against databases such as the Police National Computer, insurance, MOT and tax records. It could instantly flag vehicles that were stolen, uninsured, untaxed or linked to crime. Having the number of the Tesla meant that the police should be able to follow its journey from Stratford-upon-Avon to wherever it ended up.

'Mrs Lewis, why not come and check out the flat with me?' said DI Dunning. He looked over at DS Whitlock. 'Can you wait here for SOCO, Kirsty? Make sure they know we're looking for wolfsbane.'

'Will do, sir,' said DS Whitlock.

Lulu followed DI Dunning up the stairs. There was a large landing off which led five doors. He pointed at them one by one. 'Main bedroom, second bedroom, sitting room, kitchen and bathroom,' he said. 'Pretty spacious. Bit like the TARDIS. Looks quite small on the outside but lots of space on the inside.'

'But it doesn't travel through time, does it?'

'I shouldn't think so,' said the inspector.

'Good to know.'

The inspector opened the door to the main bedroom. A built-in wardrobe with mirrored floor-to-ceiling sliding doors stretched across one entire wall, reflecting light and making the room appear larger and brighter. One of the doors had been pulled back to reveal a large safe, almost three feet high. The safe door was wide open. It was empty except for a large white envelope.

'I assume that's a sign,' Dunning said. 'It's his way of telling us that he's gone for good and left nothing of value behind.' He bent down and took out the envelope. 'This is addressed to you. It's sealed, so I can't open it, obviously.'

'Obviously,' said Lulu. A sealed letter was private correspondence and protected by law. A police officer could not simply open a sealed letter out of curiosity or because they suspected something. Opening or interfering with post addressed to someone else was illegal under the 2000 Postal Services Act and also breached Article 8 of the 1998 Human Rights Act. If DI Dunning wanted to open the letter he would need a warrant or a court order, either under the 2016 Investigatory Powers Act or the 1984 Police and Criminal Evidence Act, and either would take time.

DI Dunning held the letter out to Lulu. 'Would you mind?'

'Of course not,' she said. She took the envelope, opened it and slid out the letter inside. She unfolded it, scanned it quickly and then read it out to the inspector.

Dear Mrs Lewis,

If you are reading this, you will know that I have already left town. I am sure that the police are going to be on my trail and I will have to deal with that. I can protest my innocence as much as I want, but they won't believe me. That's why I am writing to you. You seem like a decent sort. I spoke to some people in London who came across you, and they all had good things to say about you.

I need you to know that I did not kill Edgar Lake. I had every reason to do so, but I didn't. Killing Edgar wouldn't have changed my position one iota; I have nothing to gain by his death. Yes, he was blackmailing me, and because of that I was preparing to leave town to start a new life. But that was all.

At first I didn't know who the blackmailer was. Clearly it was someone who knew who I had been in my previous life – Ben Lloyd, the former accountant of the Kincaid family in Newcastle. But the fact that anyone has been able to find that out means the Kincaid family could just as easily locate me, so I have no choice but to run. Killing Edgar wouldn't have made escaping any easier. The opposite, in fact.

My plan was to put off my departure until the performance of the Scottish Play was done and dusted. I had put so much work into it, and I do love the play. Even when I was told that my blackmailer was Edgar Lake, I still wanted to go ahead with it. If I'd wanted to kill him, why would I poison him on stage? Wouldn't it have made more sense to kill him at his home? I know where he lives; I could have just gone there and stabbed him. But that's not the type of person I am, Mrs Lewis. I worked for gangsters, yes, I put my hand up to that, but I'm not a gangster myself. And I'm certainly not a killer.

I need you to believe that, and then perhaps you can explain it to the police. I know they tend to get tunnel vision, but they should be looking elsewhere. If they focus all their attention on me, there is every chance that they will let the real killer escape.

With very best wishes,

Henry Richards (for the next few hours, at least)

Lulu refolded the letter. 'Well, that seems pretty clear, doesn't it?'

DI Dunning held out his hand. Now that Lulu had opened the envelope, the letter was fair game. She gave it to him. 'I believe what he says,' she added.

'I don't. He has to be angry with Edgar Lake. First of all for blackmailing him, and second of all for destroying the life he had built here. I take your point that he didn't get wolfsbane from the allotment, but there are plenty of other places he could have got it from.'

'But as he says in the letter, why would he use poison in

the first place? A knife would be easier and quicker. And guns are available if you know where to look. I believe him when he says that he isn't a killer.'

'Let's see what the forensics team says. If we find traces of wolfsbane on his clothes or in his kitchen, we'll know better.'

Lulu smiled. She knew that there was no trace of wolfsbane to find in the flat, but she could hardly tell the inspector that Conrad had given her that information. 'Are you looking for anyone else? Because it's true what he says in the letter – if you remain fixated on him, you run the risk of missing the real killer.'

'Enquiries are still continuing, obviously. But having been told that Edgar Lake was blackmailing him, he does become the prime suspect.'

'*A* prime suspect,' said Lulu. 'We don't know who else Chief Superintendent Delaney told. We know about Fleming, and we know about Richards, but for all we know she could have gone through all of Lake's other files too and told each of the victims who he was. Any one of them could be the killer.'

'It's interesting that Richards didn't mention who told him that Lake was blackmailing him,' said DI Dunning. 'It has to have been Delaney.'

'Yes; but did Richards know that? Or did she tell him anonymously? You see, you're assuming that Chief Superintendent Delaney told Richards that Lake was blackmailing him so that Richards would kill him. But what if she told several of the victims, and she told them anonymously? Maybe all she wanted was for them to go to the police. After all, if she could put him behind bars then he would no longer be a threat to her.'

'That's a nice theory, Mrs Lewis, except for one thing. If we had arrested Lake, he'd have told us everything about Chief Superintendent Delaney. He'd have taken her down with him.'

Lulu nodded thoughtfully. He was right, of course. Getting Lake arrested wouldn't have fixed Delaney's problem – it would have made it worse. The only way of saving her career and her marriage would have been to have Lake killed. But had Richards done as she wanted? Lulu didn't think so. And she was equally convinced that John Fleming hadn't killed Lake. Lulu was sure he didn't have it in him.

'What do you think he meant when he said he would be Henry Richards "for the next few hours"?' asked Dunning.

'It sounds as if he has a new identity all planned,' said Lulu.

'We'll put out an alert to all ports and airports,' said Dunning.

'There are plenty of ways of leaving the country without showing a passport,' said Lulu. 'Especially when you have money.'

Dunning nodded. 'You're right, of course. But we'll go through the motions.'

'Also, he called Mr Jenkins this morning – but I suppose he may already have been out of the country by then,' said Lulu. 'He could well have started his run yesterday.'

'We'll have a better idea once we get the ANPR data,' Dunning said. 'Right, I'm going to have a look round before forensics get here. Just in case he forgot something.'

'Good luck with that,' said Lulu.

DS Whitlock had her phone to her ear when Lulu went back down into the shop. Mr Jenkins was standing behind the counter, looking down at the screen of his phone and tapping with his thumbs. The two constables were now standing outside the shop, their arms folded.

DS Whitlock finished her call. 'Well, that's interesting,' she said.

'What's that?' asked Lulu.

'We have footage from a camera doorbell in a house opposite the rectory. Edgar Lake visited the rectory at three o'clock in the afternoon on the day of the *Macbeth* performance. He was holding an envelope when he approached the property. You can't actually see him putting it through the letterbox, but you can see him walking away without it a minute or so later.'

'That's got to be the letter Elsie Kwan told me about. So presumably Lake threatened the Reverend Harper, which is what led to his suicide. And he burned the letter so we didn't find it.'

DS Whitlock put her phone away. 'That's not the really interesting thing,' she said. 'The video footage also shows Mrs Kwan leaving the rectory at five o'clock.'

'That's the time she usually finished work, isn't it?'

'Exactly. But then it shows her returning thirty minutes later. Again, we can't see her going inside, but after ten minutes we can see her leaving again.'

Lulu frowned. 'But surely the Reverend Harper killed himself not long after she left at five.'

'That's right.'

Lulu's frown deepened. 'So Mrs Kwan must have seen what had happened? She would have seen the body the moment she opened the front door. Why didn't she call the police?'

'We don't have footage of her actually entering the rectory.

She may have just gone up to the door, perhaps posted something through the letterbox . . . Obviously we'll have to go back and talk to her.'

'Where does she live?' asked Lulu.

DS Whitlock produced her notebook and flicked through its pages. 'Windsor Road. Number twenty-eight.'

Lulu took out her mobile phone and opened the Google Maps app. She tapped in Mrs Kwan's address, then the address of the rectory. The app showed her the route between the two places.

'It's a fifteen-minute walk,' she said. 'So Mrs Kwan must have walked home, realized she had forgotten something and gone back to the rectory.'

DS Whitlock nodded. 'That makes sense. We'll talk to her once we're done here.' A white van pulled up outside the shop. 'That's the forensics team,' she said.

'I'll leave you to it,' said Lulu.

36

A cold wind blew down the high street as Lulu walked away from the antiques shop. She thrust her hands deep into the pockets of her sheepskin jacket.

'You don't think that Henry Richards killed Mr Lake, do you?' Conrad asked in a low voice.

'I think what he said in the letter makes sense,' said Lulu. 'First of all, he's not a gangster – he's just an accountant who got mixed up with the wrong people. And second of all, why kill Lake during the performance? The timing makes no sense. The only reason Richards stayed in Stratford-upon-Avon after his cover was blown was because he wanted to finish the play. If he'd wanted to kill Lake, he could have done it after the play had finished. And as he said, why would he go to the trouble of using poison? He's a big man – he could have used a knife or the proverbial blunt object.'

'And there's no smell of wolfsbane in his flat. Not a whiff.'

A couple walking a dog came towards them, so Conrad stayed quiet for a while.

'Why do you think Mrs Kwan went back to the rectory that evening?' he asked eventually.

'I think we should probably ask her ourselves,' said Lulu.

Conrad looked around. 'We're not going back to *The Lark*, are we?'

Lulu smiled. 'No, we're not.'

They walked in silence. Lulu was holding her mobile

phone, but she barely had to glance at the screen; it was a simple route with just a couple of turns.

Elsie Kwan's cottage was relatively new, built from pale Cotswold stone rather than timber and thatch, with a modern slate roof. The windows were double glazed but in a traditional sash design, their frames painted in a dark red that matched the front door. In the summer the garden was probably a riot of colour, but this was November, and beds that once blazed with roses and foxgloves were now filled with skeletal seed heads. Either side of the path to the front door were clumps of hardy lavender clinging onto their silvery foliage, while ornamental grasses swayed in the breeze, their feathery plumes catching the weak autumn light. A few late-blooming chrysanthemums added splashes of russet and gold.

Lulu stood at the gate as she surveyed the garden. She froze when she saw the clump of wolfsbane plants in the far corner. The jagged leaves had curled with the cold and most of the hooded purple flowers had withered, but a handful remained, their colour darkening towards black.

'Wolfsbane,' whispered Conrad.

'Yes,' said Lulu. She opened the gate, went through onto the path, then closed it behind her and headed across the grass towards the wolfsbane plants. She peered at the stalks. There were half a dozen bare places where seed pods had been cut away, leaving small scars and stubs.

Lulu and Conrad both jumped as the front door was thrown open.

'Who are you?' snapped Mrs Kwan. 'What are you doing in my garden?' She frowned as Lulu turned to face her. 'Oh, it's you.'

'I'm sorry to startle you, Mrs Kwan. We were just admiring your garden.'

Mrs Kwan glanced around the garden, frowning. 'We?' She was wearing a knitted thigh-length red cardigan over a caramel-coloured sweater, with thick grey wool trousers that were tucked into fur-lined slippers.

'Sorry,' said Lulu. She reached up to pat Conrad on the head. 'I meant Conrad, of course.'

Mrs Kwan opened the door wider. 'I suppose you had better come in,' she said. She ushered Lulu into the hall and closed the door.

'This way,' she said, walking into a sitting room. There was a sofa draped with a maroon throw with gold dragons on it and a low mahogany coffee table on which stood a selection of novels in both English and Chinese. Against one wall, a dark wooden cabinet displayed a carefully chosen collection of objects: jade figurines, a pair of carved wooden lions, a framed calligraphy scroll, a few family photographs in silver frames. A leafy plant – perhaps a bonsai ficus, Lulu thought, looking at the glossy leaves – stood in the corner, its green a vivid contrast to the neutral walls. Under the coffee table was a patterned rug, muted reds and golds woven through it, and a single armchair was angled towards the sofa, a knitted cushion on its seat.

'Please, sit,' said Mrs Kwan, waving at the sofa. Lulu sat. The door was still open and she could see the stairs in the hallway. Mrs Kwan sat on the armchair and interlinked her fingers. 'Why did you come here, Mrs Lewis?'

'Actually, we were just passing,' Lulu replied. Conrad jumped down from her shoulders, landing on the floor without a sound.

'Passing through my garden?'

'I do love country gardens, and you have some wonderful plants.' Conrad was walking around the room, sniffing, his tail erect.

Mrs Kwan wrinkled her nose. 'You were looking for something, weren't you?'

'Now, what could I possibly be looking for in your garden?'

Mrs Kwan tilted her head to one side like an inquisitive bird. 'Wolfsbane,' she said quietly.

Conrad slipped out through the sitting-room door. Mrs Kwan didn't notice him go.

'I did notice that you had some very attractive wolfsbane plants, yes. They are so dramatic, aren't they? So tall.'

Lulu saw Conrad pad silently up the stairs, his tail still upright. His determined expression suggested he knew where he was going.

'You were asking a lot of questions about wolfsbane when you were at the rectory,' said Mrs Kwan.

'Well, we know that it was the poison used to kill Mr Lake, so a lot of people are interested in wolfsbane at the moment. And you were very helpful, explaining about the aconite that you use.'

'The aconite I use is not a poison, it's a medicine.'

'Exactly. I do understand.'

'But now you are wondering if the plants in my garden are poisonous.'

'Well . . .'

'They are, Mrs Lewis. The flowers, the leaves, the roots, all are quite deadly.'

'It is surprising that people grow them in their gardens, considering how dangerous they are.'

'Because they are beautiful,' said Mrs Kwan. 'There are many flowering plants that look lovely but can be deadly to human beings. Oleander, for instance, has lovely pink, white or red blossoms which are quite deadly – even smoke from burning the plant can cause a fatal heart arrhythmia. Lily of the valley has delicate, sweet-smelling flowers that are often used in wedding bouquets – but they can trigger heart failure.'

Lulu nodded. Conrad had warned her that lilies were poisonous for cats, too.

'Hydrangeas can release cyanide if eaten, and rhododendron leaves and flowers are quite poisonous,' Mrs Kwan continued.

Lulu smiled. 'So gardens can be deadly.'

Mrs Kwan looked at Lulu, her face impassive. 'Yes, they can.'

A kettle whistled in the kitchen. 'I am making tea,' she said. 'Would you like some?'

'That would be lovely,' said Lulu.

Mrs Kwan left the room and headed to the kitchen.

Conrad came down the stairs and into the sitting room. He jumped up onto a chair and up again onto the table. 'Where is Mrs Kwan?' he asked quietly.

'Making tea,' Lulu murmured.

Conrad's eyes widened. 'You're going to drink tea with a poisoner?'

'We don't know for certain that she poisoned Mr Lake. Let's give her the benefit of the doubt for now.'

'You weren't upstairs with me.'

'No, that's true, I wasn't. What did you see?'

'There's a framed photograph of the Reverend Harper by her bed.'

'She clearly thought a lot of him.'

'I think she loved him.'

'I think you're probably right,' said Lulu. 'But that doesn't make her a poisoner.'

'There was a letter by the bed, too. A letter written by the Reverend Harper shortly before he hanged himself.'

'Seriously?'

'Lulu, would I joke about something like that? What sort of cat would I be?'

'I'm sorry. Of course you wouldn't. What did the letter say?'

'He said that he had run out of money, and that Mr Lake was continuing to blackmail him. He apologized for everything that he had done in the past and said he had begged God for forgiveness. And he apologized to Mrs Kwan for the mess.'

They heard footsteps in the hall. Conrad jumped down onto the chair as Mrs Kwan appeared in the doorway holding a tray.

'I thought I heard voices,' she said.

Lulu held up her phone. 'Sorry. I had to take a call.'

Mrs Kwan set the tray down on the coffee table, pushing the books aside. On the tray was a red teapot with gold dragons on the sides, and two small matching bowls. 'This is goji berry and chrysanthemum tea. *Gǒuqǐ júhuā chá*, in my language.' She sat down opposite Lulu. 'The goji berries add natural sweetness and nourish the liver and eyes, and the chrysanthemum has a soothing, calming effect and lowers blood pressure.'

She slowly poured tea into the two bowls.

'It smells lovely,' said Lulu. Mrs Kwan picked up one of

the bowls and placed it in front of her. Lulu smiled. 'Thank you.'

She inhaled the fragrant steam, her mind in a whirl. They were both drinking from the same teapot, but then, Lake and Richards had been drinking from the same bottle of wine. If there was any poison, Mrs Kwan could easily have put it into the bowl that Lulu was going to drink from.

Mrs Kwan picked up her bowl and sipped her tea, then smacked her lips appreciatively. She looked at Lulu's bowl and raised her eyebrows.

Lulu wasn't sure what to do. Part of her didn't want to appear rude, but another part was definitely worried that there might be poison in the tea. She flashed back to Mr Lake dying on stage – the look of panic in his eyes and the bloody foam on his lips.

She flinched as Conrad jumped onto the coffee table. Mrs Kwan sat back, aghast. Conrad walked slowly towards the bowl in front of Lulu, lowered his head and sniffed. His ears were pointed forward and his tail was parallel to the ground. He sniffed again and then sat down. He nodded almost imperceptibly.

Lulu smiled and picked up her bowl. The tea itself was golden, with delicate petals of chrysanthemum floating on the surface and small ruby-red goji berries sinking slowly to the bottom. The first sip was smooth and slightly cooling on her tongue. The chrysanthemum gave the tea a clean, floral note and there was a sweetness from the goji berries that rounded out the flavour, balancing the floral sharpness with a mellow fruitiness. She drank again, and this time it was slightly sweeter.

'Oh, it's divine,' she said.

'I knew you'd like it,' said Mrs Kwan, and she took another

sip from her bowl before carefully putting it down. 'You know, don't you?'

Conrad jumped onto the seat next to Lulu.

'I think I do, yes,' Lulu said.

'And your cat helped you?'

'Conrad is a very intuitive cat.'

'In my culture, cats are believed to be able to see spirits and ward off negative energies.'

'He is always a very positive presence for me,' said Lulu.

Mrs Kwan sipped her tea again. 'The police know too, don't they?'

'They know that you left the rectory around five on the day that the Reverend Harper died, and then returned half an hour later.'

'I'd forgotten my keys. They were in my purse, and I'd left it in the kitchen. It was only when I got here that I realized I didn't have them.'

'So you went back?'

'I did, yes. I rang the bell, but Mr Troy didn't answer, so I used my key.' She shuddered at the memory. 'He was dead. He must have done it just after I left.'

'And you saw the letter? And the copy of the will?'

She nodded, then frowned. 'How do you know about the letter?'

Lulu ignored the question. 'Why didn't you call the police?'

'There was no point. It was too late.'

'And there was something in the letter that stopped you calling them, wasn't there?'

Mrs Kwan nodded but didn't say anything. She took another drink of tea.

'May I see the letter, Mrs Kwan?'

'You want to see it?'

'Please.'

Mrs Kwan smiled faintly. 'I don't see why not.' She stood up and went out of the room. Lulu watched as she slowly climbed the stairs, looking as if the weight of the world was on her shoulders.

'She did it, didn't she?' said Conrad.

'I think so.'

'I like her.'

'So do I.'

Mrs Kwan came back down the stairs, clutching a sheet of paper. She came slowly back into the sitting room and gave the letter to Lulu.

Lulu read it carefully. It was handwritten in blue ink. The writing was spidery, as if very little pressure had been applied to the paper. The Reverend Harper's signature was at the bottom. She read it out loud.

To whoever finds me – I am so sorry to put you in this position. Please call the police. They will know what to do.

I know I have committed a mortal sin, but I had no choice. I am entrusting myself to God's mercy, acknowledging that only God knows the depths of a person's soul and their struggles at the moment of death.

I have been blackmailed by Edgar Lake for something I did in another life, in another country. I regret what I did, but I have spent the rest of my life trying to make amends. Now my money has all gone and Lake will go public with my sins, so it is better I go now rather than face the hell I would suffer on earth.

He made me pay him on the last day of every month. I had to leave the cash in a bag in a vase on a grave by the gate. But now my bank account is almost empty. Today I placed an empty bag in the vase and hid behind a gravestone. I left a note in the bag saying that I had no money left and begging to be left alone. I didn't have to wait long. And when I saw it was Edgar Lake, I was shocked and horrified. I had always thought he was a friend. He took the bag and left.

Today he delivered a letter to the rectory. He said that my soul belonged to him, and either I would spend the rest of my life paying him or he would expose me.

Part of me wants to go to the church tonight and confront him. But how can I do that? And I can't pay. My money has gone. So this is my only way out.

Please show the police this letter. And tell Elsie that I am so sorry for the mess I will have made. Tell her I will miss her. In another life, who knows? But for me, this life is over.

May God forgive me.

Lulu put the letter down on the table. 'He wanted the letter to be given to the police. Why did you take it?'

Mrs Kwan picked it up and held it to her cheek. 'What do you think the police would have done?'

'Well, they would have investigated the allegations of blackmail for a start.'

'Would that have brought Mr Troy back?'

'No, it wouldn't.'

'And would the police have arrested Mr Lake for killing

Mr Troy? No, because Mr Troy killed himself. So they would never have charged him with murder, would they?'

'I hear what you're saying,' said Lulu.

'Mr Lake killed Mr Troy just as much as if he had plunged a knife into his heart. He made Mr Troy's life a misery, and it was his fault that Mr Troy died.'

'That made you angry?'

'It made me angry and it made me sad.'

'So you decided to kill Mr Lake?'

Mrs Kwan smiled coldly. 'It was a very easy decision to make,' she said. 'I came back here and made the poison from wolfsbane seeds. I pounded them to a paste and watered it down a little so that it was sticky.'

'So you knew the performance would go ahead?'

'I knew Mr Richards wouldn't allow it to be cancelled. He puts so much work into his shows.'

'But how did you know that Mr Lake would be playing Macbeth instead of Mr Troy?'

'I went to the church. I saw the note they'd pinned up saying that Edgar Lake would be playing the role of Macbeth.'

'And later that night you went back to the church?'

Mrs Kwan nodded. 'I had helped clean the building before the stage was erected. I put on my cleaning clothes, and I had a bucket and a brush. Nobody ever looks at the cleaning staff, do they? I kept my head down and brushed away, and then got near the banqueting table. Everything was laid out. I'd been to rehearsals with Mr Troy, so I knew which goblet Macbeth drank out of. I poured the paste into the goblet and coated the inside. It took me a few seconds. Nobody saw. I stayed for a bit longer cleaning and then I went home.'

'You didn't want to stay and see the poison do its work?'

'I knew the police would question everybody who was there. It was better for me to be here, in bed.' She forced a smile. 'The police will come for me, won't they?'

'I'm afraid so, yes.'

'What do you think will happen to me?'

'You have to tell the police everything. You have to explain that you found Mr Troy's body and how that made you feel.'

'Will they understand?'

'They'll understand. But you will have to see how they proceed. There are a number of offences they could charge you with. You will need a good lawyer, Mrs Kwan. Somebody who can argue your case.'

'I'm happy that he's dead.'

'I know you are.'

'At least Mr Troy got justice. He deserved that.'

They both jumped as the doorbell rang.

'That will be them now,' said Lulu.

37

Lulu woke up just after eight when a nearby narrowboat started up its diesel engine. The batteries had to be charged on a regular basis if the boat wasn't cruising, which meant running the engine for two to three hours at a time. Out of courtesy it was best avoided early in the morning or late at night, but with her neighbour already running theirs, Lulu felt no guilt about starting her own.

There were always chores to be done on a narrowboat, so before she showered, she checked the engine oil, coolant, and fuel levels, inspected the alternator and battery connections, looked over the bilge pump and drainage, then swept and mopped the decks and cabin floors. She made sure all the ropes, fenders and mooring lines were secure, checked the hull as best she could, and cleaned all of the windows and hatches. Conrad's contribution was to lie on the roof in a supervisory capacity.

Chores done, Lulu showered and pulled on a polo-neck sweater and jeans before heading to the galley. Conrad was now curled up on the sofa, grooming himself.

'I love watching you work,' he said. 'I could do it all day.'

Lulu was about to reply when there was a shout from the jetty. 'Lulu? Are you there?' It was Danny McGrory.

She headed up the steps to the rear deck. Danny was standing on the jetty, wearing his black raincoat. He had a long red scarf wound around his neck and a bottle of champagne in his hand.

'Time to celebrate,' he said, waving the bottle in the air.

'Come aboard,' Lulu said. 'I'll get the glasses.'

She went down into the galley and took two champagne flutes from an overhead cupboard. Danny followed her and deftly popped the cork. Lulu held out the glasses and he poured champagne into them.

'You cracked the case,' he said. 'Well done you.'

'It was very much a team effort,' said Lulu, with a discreet smile at Conrad in his spot on the sofa.

'That's not what DI Dunning says.' Danny put down the bottle, took one of the glasses from Lulu and clinked it against hers. 'Well done.'

They both sipped their champagne. Lulu picked Conrad up and sat down on the sofa, placing him on her lap. Danny joined them.

'Just the one glass for me,' he said. 'I'm driving back to London this afternoon. When are you leaving?'

'Tomorrow. I'm having dinner with my goddaughter Celia and her husband tonight.'

'So when will you be back in London?'

Lulu grinned. 'A couple of weeks. Give or take.'

Danny shook his head. 'That's amazing.'

'That's canal speed,' said Lulu.

'This was one hell of a story, wasn't it? It started with a Shakespearean death and ended with blackmail, police corruption and a gangland informer on the run.' He sipped his champagne. 'What about Henry Richards, AKA Benjamin Lloyd? In theory he can come back now, right?'

'The police aren't looking for him, that's true,' said Lulu. 'But I'm pretty sure the Kincaid family won't ever give up the hunt.'

'You've got to feel sorry for the guy. Sets up a new life in a backwater town, keeps his head down and minds his own business – but because he buys the old Gastrell bakery, he finds himself being targeted by a blackmailer out for some sort of misguided revenge.'

'It's true, he was very unlucky. Just in the wrong place at the wrong time. If he'd bought literally any other property he'd have been fine.'

'Where do you think he'll go?'

'Not anywhere in the UK. He'll have learned his lesson from the whole fingerprint thing. He can change his name and get more plastic surgery, but he can never change his prints. So he'll have to choose another country. Ireland would fit the bill – the British and Irish police are only allowed to share fingerprint data in specific cases. Ditto anywhere in Europe. To be honest, a lot depends on how much money he stole from the Kincaids. Are you going to write a piece about him?'

'Well, it is a great story,' Danny said. '"Informer on the run from a gangster family is on stage when Macbeth dies for real".'

'That sounds very tabloid.'

Danny chuckled. 'My first Fleet Street staff job was on the *Mirror*,' he said. 'But tabloid or broadsheet, it's a good story.'

'Even though it means his face – his new face – will be splashed all over the papers.'

'He'll be fine,' said Danny. 'He can grow his beard, shave his head, go back to wearing glasses. And if he does have serious money, there are plenty of countries where he can buy himself a new identity.'

'But he'll never be able to stop looking over his shoulder,' said Lulu.

'That's the price you pay for getting involved with organized crime,' said Danny. 'What about Chief Superintendent Delaney?'

'Ex-Chief Superintendent, you mean. She's taken early retirement in the hope that she can lock in her pension.'

'Which would be what? Thirty-five thousand pounds a year?'

'I suppose so.'

'Will she be allowed to do that?'

'I don't know. We'll see.'

'Who says crime doesn't pay?'

Lulu chuckled. 'I'm not sure anyone actually says that these days. She's pleading guilty, so there won't be a trial. Misconduct in Public Office can result in life imprisonment, but realistically she's looking at between five and ten years. If she's lucky and has a sympathetic judge, it could even be as little as two years.'

'Why would a judge have any sympathy for a woman who was blackmailed for cheating on her husband?'

'I suppose a judge might think it was more forgivable that she was forced into it, rather than doing it for financial gain.' Lulu shrugged. 'Either way, she'll be going to prison, and that's never a pleasant prospect for a police officer. At least her husband is standing by her.'

'We'll see how long that lasts once the full story gets out,' said Danny. 'Commander Tanner, the one she was having the affair with, has been tipped as a future commissioner. And his wife is related to the Home Secretary.'

'I think she decided to plead guilty partly so that the whole story *won't* get out,' said Lulu.

'That cat is well and truly out of the bag,' Danny said. He looked over at Conrad. 'Not that I'm in favour of ever putting cats in bags, obviously.'

Conrad meowed.

Danny's jaw dropped. 'Did you see that? It's as if he understands what I'm saying.'

'Well, of course he does,' said Lulu. 'So you'll run the story about the affair?'

'Oh, we have to,' said Danny. 'Tanner's a churchgoing family man, always banging on about Christian values. If there's one thing the British public loves, it's to see a hypocrite exposed.'

'So you'll ruin two families and two careers?'

'Lulu, come on. I'm a reporter – I report on things that happen. I don't make things up. They did what they did, they're both in positions of authority, so they deserve to face the consequences.'

'Maybe you're right.'

'You're sympathetic because they're coppers and you used to be one, too. Once a cop, always a cop.'

'That's certainly true,' said Lulu. 'But where will you get the information to write the story?'

'Already done,' said Danny. 'I was in Woodcote House with DI Dunning this morning and he let me see the file that Lake had on Delaney. He let me take copies of the photographs in the file. He wouldn't let me take the file out of the office, but it was more than enough.'

Lulu pursed her lips.

'What's wrong?' asked Danny.

'You don't see any parallels between that and what Chief Superintendent Delaney did? She shared police information with Mr Lake, and she'll be going to prison. DI Dunning shares police information with you, and you get a front-page story.'

'That's a totally different kettle of fish, Lulu. Delaney used the Police National Computer illegally. I was given the opportunity to read a file that Edgar Lake had put together. And it's not as if the file is going to be used in evidence, because she'll be pleading guilty.'

'I don't know, it just feels a bit . . . unsavoury.'

'That's investigative journalism for you,' said Danny. 'And DI Dunning is just holding up his end of the bargain. He's a good cop.'

'I can't argue with that,' said Lulu. 'What about the Reverend Harper? Did DI Dunning show you that file, too?'

Danny nodded. 'He did. I can't use that information as is; I have to get it all officially confirmed. But that's just a matter of time.' He drank the last of his champagne and set the glass down. 'The one I feel sorry for is the murderer – Mrs Kwan. She seems a very sweet lady, by all accounts.'

'I met her a couple of times, and yes, she had a good heart. She certainly wasn't a bad person. She did what she did out of love for the Reverend Harper. She hated Edgar Lake for what he'd done to her boss, and she wanted revenge. An eye for an eye.'

'But that's not a mitigating factor, is it?'

'In murder cases, it's a double-edged sword,' said Lulu. 'Revenge can be considered a mitigating factor if it shows strong provocation or emotional stress, but it can make the offence more serious if it shows planning and intent. Her defence team will have to show immediate provocation or loss of control, and that's down to timing. Mrs Kwan went straight from discovering the Reverend Harper's body to her cottage to prepare the poison, and then immediately went to the church to put the poison in the goblet that he'd be drinking from. If the judge accepts that it was all while she was under emotional stress, she might well get a lighter sentence.'

'I hope so,' said Danny. 'That Edgar Lake, or rather Eddie Gastrell, was a nasty piece of work.'

'He had mental health issues, Danny. He was bullied as a kid, his dad lost his business, his parents split up, his mother killed herself.'

'And he reacts by hating a whole town? Moves there and starts blackmailing everyone that he can?'

'As I said, mental health issues. That doesn't excuse what he did, but it does explain it. And be honest, it's a good story for your paper.'

'Oh, it's a good story, all right. And I wondered if you'd like to be a part of it?'

Lulu's eyes narrowed. 'How, exactly?'

'Well, you were deeply involved in the investigation. And DI Dunning tells me that you were the one who got Mrs Kwan to confess.'

'Oh, I think she would have confessed anyway at some point. It was never about getting away with murder, it was all about revenge. And she got that.'

'But I'd like to write in my article that you were there – and Conrad, of course.'

'Please don't, Danny.'

'Are you sure?'

Lulu nodded. 'Yes, I'm sure.'

Conrad meowed.

'Conrad is sure, too.'

The Cat Who Caught a Killer

Read on to find out how Lulu and Conrad met in the first book in the series . . .

1

It was a gorgeous summer's day when Conrad walked into the life of Lulu Lewis. The sky was a cloudless blue, birds were singing in the distance and the water of the canal was just starting to turn green from the warm-weather algal bloom.

Lulu was about to go out and cut some fresh mint from the small strip of land on the other side of the towpath. The mooring was hers, courtesy of the Canal and River Trust, but she had squatter's rights on the narrow piece of land between the towpath and the hedge, where she grew a selection of herbs including mint, rosemary, chives and thyme. She had just started experimenting with garlic, but hadn't been having much luck.

As she looked out of the galley window she saw a cat heading her way, walking in the middle of the towpath as if he owned it. Lulu could tell it was a tom, just from the way he strutted along with his tail in the air, but she knew right away that he was special because he was a calico – a mixture of black, white and orangey brown – and most calicos were female.

The cat stopped in his tracks and began sniffing the air, his ears up. The right side of his head was mainly black with a white patch around the nose and mouth, and the left side was brown and white. His eyes were a vibrant green. He seemed to be looking right at Lulu and she felt a slight shiver run down her spine. He started walking again.

Lulu leaned forward over the double gas hob to get a better view. His front legs and chest were white, his body and tail were thick stripes of black and brown, and his rear legs had white socks. He reached the prow of the boat. *The Lark*. She hadn't named it; the boat had been ten years old when she had taken it on. The previous owner, a retired teacher, had owned it from new and had bought it as a lark, he'd said. Lulu had quite liked the name, and anyway it would have been bad luck to change it. It was a traditional narrowboat, painted dark green with black trim and with *THE LARK* in gold capital letters over a painting of the bird.

The cat walked slowly along the towpath. Past the double cabin, past the toilet, and then he drew level with the galley. He stopped and looked up at her, moving his head slightly and sniffing. His tail was upright like an antenna.

'Well, good morning,' whispered Lulu. 'What a handsome boy you are.'

The cat's ears flicked forward as if he had heard her, and he made a soft mewing sound. He wasn't wearing a collar but he looked too well fed and clean to be a stray. He started walking once more and reached the rear of the boat. He stopped again, then jumped smoothly onto the back deck.

Lulu turned away from the window. The cat appeared at the doorway and sat down.

'Welcome aboard,' said Lulu. The cat stared at her for several seconds and then mewed. 'You're welcome to come in,' said Lulu. 'You'll be my first visitor.'

The cat stayed where he was at the top of the four wooden steps that led down into the cabin.

'Well now, Mr Calico Cat, I'll get you something to drink

– let's see if that tempts you to come in.' Lulu bent down and opened the small fridge that was barely big enough to hold a carton of milk and half a dozen bottles of wine and water. She took out the milk and picked up a white saucer from the tiny draining board.

She was just about to pour milk into it when the cat coughed politely. 'Actually, I'm not much of a milk drinker.'

Lulu gaped at the cat in astonishment. 'What?'

'Most cats are lactose intolerant. They don't have the enzyme that digests the lactose in milk. No enzyme, so no digestion, so the lactose just passes through our system. It can be messy. So best avoided.'

'What?' repeated Lulu.

'So maybe pour me a nice, crisp Chardonnay instead.'

'What?'

The saucer slipped between her fingers and seemed to fall in slow motion to the floor, where it shattered. She stared at the cat, her mind whirling as she tried to come to terms with what had just happened.

'Well, that wasn't the reaction I expected,' said the cat.

'What?'

The cat put his head on one side. There was an amused look in his piercing green eyes. 'You do speak English, don't you? You can say something other than "what", or am I wasting my time?'

'What? Yes. Of course. English. What?'

'I think you should pick up the bits of the saucer before someone gets hurt,' said the cat.

'What? Right. Yes. Okay.' Lulu shook her head in bewilderment. She put the milk carton back in the fridge and then went slowly down on one knee and carefully picked up the pieces, placing them in a pedal bin to the side of the fridge. Her knee cracked as she stood up again. 'How did you know I had Chardonnay?' she asked.

'I won't lie, that was a guess. I did see the wine bottles, but it could have just as easily been Pinot Grigio. I didn't really want wine to drink, obviously. It was just a joke, I didn't think you'd go all Greek on me.'

'Greek? What?'

'They smash plates, right? The Greeks. It's what they do.'

'Right, yes, okay. I'm sorry, I'm a bit confused here.'

'I can see that. Could I have some water?'

'Water?'

'Water. H_2O. Tap water is okay. Do these boats have tap water or do they have tanks?'

'I have a mains water supply,' said Lulu. 'It's a residential mooring. Electricity, too.'

'Excellent,' said the cat. He looked expectantly at Lulu.

'So, water?' Lulu said.

'Perfect.'

'I have Evian.'

'Well, that will be a treat,' said the cat.

Lulu opened the fridge again and took out a bottle of Evian. She opened an eye-level cupboard, took out a Wedgwood saucer and poured water into it. She put the saucer at the bottom of the steps, then replaced the bottle of water in the fridge. She went and sat on the sofa as the cat padded down the steps. He sniffed the water cautiously and then began to lap.

Lulu watched as the cat drank, then she sighed. 'This is a dream, right?'

The cat looked up from the saucer. 'Are you asking me, or telling me?'

Lulu pinched her own arm, so hard that she winced.

'What are you doing?' asked the cat.

Lulu shook her head. 'If it's a dream, why can't I wake up?'

The cat finished drinking and jumped gracefully up onto the sofa and sat looking up at her. 'You need to relax.'

'What?'

'Let's not start that whole "what" thing again.' He rubbed his head against her arm. 'I'm real. This isn't a dream. Deal with it.'

'But cats can't talk,' sighed Lulu.

'Says the lady who is talking to one.' He gently headbutted her. 'You can hear the lack of logic in your statement, right? If cats can't talk, then we couldn't be having this conversation, could we?'

'Maybe I'm going crazy.'

'Well, that's a whole different conversation, isn't it?'

'If you can talk – and I'm not discounting that this is all a figment of my imagination – but if I'm not crazy and you are talking to me, then why?'

'Why? I suppose that's a step up from what.'

'I mean, why me? Why are you talking to me?'

'You mean of all the canal boats in Little Venice, why did I jump onto yours?'

'If you like. Yes.'

The cat shrugged. 'You seemed like a nice person. And you have a good aura. Lots of bright yellow and indigo.'

'That's good, is it?'

'It's perfect.' The cat chuckled. 'I suppose I should say purr-fect.'

'So I suppose black is bad? For auras.'

The cat nodded. 'It can mean there is anger that's being held inside. Or it could be that the person is sick. Of course, sometimes it's the anger that causes the sickness. Or the other way around. Dark blood red also points to a lot of anger. We tend to keep away from blood-red auras but with black auras we can sometimes help.'

'We? Who's we?'

'Cats. We see auras. Cat auras and human auras. The auras of all living things, actually.'

'I didn't know that.'

The cat snorted softly. 'Why would you? You're a human.'

Lulu frowned. 'You said you could help people whose auras are black.'

'We can make it easier for them, when they pass.'

'When they die, you mean?'

The cat gave the slightest twitch of its whiskers. 'We prefer to say pass. But, yes, if we see someone with a black aura, we can sit with them and help calm them.'

'That I have heard of,' said Lulu. 'There used to be a cat at a nursing home I visit. She was friendly enough but never got onto anyone's bed. Unless they were dying. Then she would jump up and lie next to them.' Her eyes widened and her hand flew up to cover her mouth. 'Oh, my. Oh no. Is that why you're here?'

The cat's eyes narrowed. 'What? No. Of course not. I told you already, your aura is fine. Better than fine.' The cat purred. 'What do I call you?'

'My name? It's Lulu. And you?'

'Conrad.'

'Conrad? Conrad the Cat? Conrad the Calico Cat?'

'That's my name, don't wear it out.'

'It's unusual.'

Conrad snorted softly. 'Says the lady called Lulu.'

Lulu chuckled. 'My dad gave me the name Lulu. There was a singer, a little Scottish girl, who had the number one song when I was born – "Shout" – and Dad said I was shouting all the time from the moment I was born. Who gave you your name?'

'I chose it myself.'

'Good choice.'

'That's what I thought. It means brave counsel. It's German. Originally.'

'And are you brave?'

'Fearless.'

'And you give good advice?'

'I try.'

Lulu turned to look at him. 'Is that why you're here? To give me advice?'

Conrad squinted at her quizzically. 'You keep looking for a reason as to why I'm here,' he said.

'Because it's strange. It's not every day I get approached by a talking cat.'

'Don't overthink it, Lulu. Sometimes paths just cross, that's all there is to it.'

'But why me, Conrad? Why talk to me?'

'You seem like a nice person.'

Lulu couldn't help but smile. 'Well, thank you,' she said. 'You seem like a nice cat, too.' She sighed. 'I need a drink.'

'A nice crisp Chardonnay?'

Lulu chuckled. 'I was about to make myself a glass of fresh mint tea.'

'That does sound rather good.'

'I think that's what I'm going to do,' she said. She stood up, filled the kettle at the sink and then used a match to light one of the hobs. She put the kettle on the flames and went up the steps to the back deck. Conrad followed her. Lulu stepped carefully off the boat and onto the towpath. She heard a whirring sound off to her right and turned to see a young man in a grey hoodie and tight jeans hurtling towards them on an electric scooter. She stood back, as the man clearly had no intention of slowing. 'Idiot,' she muttered under her breath as the man whizzed by. An increasing number of people were using electric scooters along the towpath and several people had been injured. The main problem was that they were practically silent so you couldn't hear them coming. Lulu smiled. Actually the main problem was that they were driven by morons who cared nothing for their fellow man – or cats.

'Aren't you just so tempted to push them into the canal?' said Conrad from the safety of the deck.

Lulu laughed. 'Definitely,' she said. She looked right and left again and walked over to her tiny vegetable plot. Conrad jumped off the boat and joined her. He sniffed the plants, one by one.

'How long have you lived on the boat?' he asked.

'Just two months.'

'I thought you'd been here for years, you seem so comfortable on her.'

'I am, I love it.' She pointed across the road. 'I used to live down there, on Warrington Crescent.'

Conrad nodded. 'Warrington Crescent is nice.'

'It's lovely, but . . .' She shrugged. 'It doesn't matter.' She bent down and ran her hand through the mint plants, then sniffed her fingers. The aroma took her back to her childhood, when she would pick fresh mint from the garden whenever her mother cooked roast lamb. Half a century vanished in a flash and she was a child again.

'Smells always take you back, don't they?' said Conrad. 'More than any of the other senses. Smell just goes straight to the olfactory cortex in the temporal lobe and triggers memories that you never thought you had.'

Lulu looked across at him. 'Did you just read my mind?'

Conrad chuckled. 'Mind-reading isn't in my skill set,' he said. 'You smelled the mint and then you had a faraway look in your eyes as if you were remembering something.' He tilted his head to one side and blinked. 'Elementary, dear Lulu.'

Lulu picked four stems, one from each mint plant. She took them back to the boat. This time Conrad ran ahead of her and jumped onto the deck first. There was a grace to his movements that reminded her of a cheetah she'd once seen on safari in Botswana, many years ago. He turned to watch her walk to the boat. 'Do you ever take her out, along the canal?' he asked.

'Not yet, but I will do,' she said. She stepped onto the deck. 'The engine has been serviced and there's fuel on board. But so far I'm just enjoying living on her. But one day, I plan to go travelling.' She went down the steps. The kettle was already boiling and Lulu turned off the gas. She washed the mint under the tap, placed it into a glass and poured on the hot water. The minty aroma filled the galley. Lulu took the glass over to the sofa and sat down. Conrad gracefully jumped up and sat next to her. She sniffed at the glass, then held it out for Conrad to smell. He nodded his appreciation. 'Nice,' he said. 'But I prefer catnip.'

'What is it about cats and catnip?' asked Lulu.

'We love it,' said Conrad. 'You know how you like Chardonnay? I guess it's the same. The leaves contain an oil called nepetalactone and it stimulates the pheromone receptors.'

'So you get high?'

'We feel euphoric, yes. Happy.'

'So probably more like cannabis than alcohol.'

'Do you smoke cannabis?'

Lulu shook her head. 'No.'

'I didn't think so. I would have smelled it.'

Lulu sipped her tea and looked at the cat over the top of her glass. A talking cat? It had to be a dream. There was no other explanation. Cats didn't talk. End of. But she was clearly hearing this one speak and the only way that made any sense was if she was asleep. At some point she would wake up and everything would be back to normal. She had been having some strange dreams recently. They were often about her husband and, under the circumstances, that was to be expected, she knew. But the chances of her ever having a conversation with Simon again were on a par with her meeting a talking cat. Dreams were dreams, and that was the end of it.

'Penny for your thoughts?' asked Conrad.

Lulu just laughed and shook her head.

2

Lulu finished her mint tea and washed the glass. Conrad sat on the sofa, grooming himself. She turned to look at him, wondering when exactly the dream would end and she would wake up. It was a detailed dream, no doubt about that – probably the most realistic she had ever had – but there was no way any of this could be real. Cats did not talk. They simply didn't.

Conrad stopped grooming and sat up. 'You look as if you want to say something,' he said.

Lulu looked at her watch. It was a gold Rolex. Simon had bought it for her on their tenth wedding anniversary and she had worn it every day since he'd died. 'I should be going.' She wondered if now was the time for her to wake up.

'I'll come with you,' said Conrad. 'Is that okay?'

'Yes, sure, I guess. But there are quite a few roads to cross. Are you okay with roads?'

'I can ride on your shoulders.'

'What?'

'And we're back to "what" already,' said Conrad. 'I thought we'd moved past that.'

Lulu laughed. 'I'm sorry, it's just that I've never heard of that before.'

'It's quite common,' he said.

'I've heard of parrots on shoulders. Long John Silver and all.'

'Same principle,' said Conrad. 'Sit down. I'll show you.'

Lulu walked over to the sofa and sat down. Conrad arched his back and stretched his legs, then smoothly jumped up onto her shoulders. He wrapped his tail around her neck and sat on her left shoulder. 'This is the side position,' he said. 'It's fairly comfortable but it's slightly less secure.' He moved slowly, until he had wrapped himself around the back of her neck, his head on her right shoulder, his back legs on her left. 'I call this the scarf position,' he said.

'I can see why,' said Lulu. She was surprised at how little he weighed; it was almost identical to wearing a fur scarf. Not that she would wear anything made of fur, of course. Not these days.

'Try standing up,' said Conrad.

She did. He was perfectly balanced and within seconds it felt completely natural. 'I love this,' she said.

'Walk up and down.'

She walked past the shower to the main cabin door, then slowly turned. 'This is amazing,' she said. She walked back through the galley and did a twirl. 'You're so light.'

'Why, thank you.'

'And you feel so warm against my neck. Seriously, we can walk around like this? You won't fall off?'

'Not unless you decide to spin around suddenly,' said Conrad. 'So, where exactly are we going?'

'To see my mother-in-law. She's in a nursing home.'

'Is she sick?'

'Actually she's quite strong. But she has a few issues with her memory, so she has to be in a place where she can be looked after.' She picked up her handbag and walked carefully up the steps, then onto the towpath.

The nursing home was close to Lord's Cricket Ground, just over a mile from the canal. There were two ways to get there: along Warrington Crescent or down Clifton Road. Warrington Crescent was slightly shorter but Lulu tended to go the longer way.

Walking with a cat on her shoulders was a novel experience. She walked slightly slower than normal, but there was never any sense that Conrad was uncomfortable or about to fall off. Most of the time he purred softly in her ear.

She got a lot of smiles from passers-by as she walked, especially from children. She headed down Clifton Road, past Tesco and the Venice Patisserie, and walked by Raoul's Deli, a Maida Vale institution that had long been one of Lulu's favourite food shops. Their duck eggs were out of this world. She smiled to herself. Talking cats were also out of this world.

She stopped at the traffic lights at the top of Clifton Road. A postman pushing a cart of letters and parcels stopped and grinned at the cat. 'Did it take a lot of training to do that?' he asked.

'No, he taught me in a couple of minutes,' said Lulu.

The postman frowned, then opened his mouth to reply, but then the lights changed and Lulu walked across the road, chuckling to herself.

'That was funny,' said Conrad.

'Yes, I thought so,' said Lulu. Their route took them from Maida Vale into St John's Wood. St John's Wood was usually regarded as being slightly more posh than Maida Vale, with its high street chock-a-block with trendy cafes and overpriced delis, and its whitewashed villas with Bentleys and BMWs parked outside. It was where The Beatles had made many of their albums in the Abbey Road recording studio, and where Sir Paul McCartney still lived.

Lulu had always preferred the edgier Maida Vale, where three-quarters of the homes were mansion block flats and houses were owned by the likes of Paul Weller and Ronnie Wood. Earl Spencer used to live there, but he had moved.

It took another five minutes to reach the nursing home, a four-storey block built around a central courtyard with a small lawn and shrubs and rockeries, with benches for the residents to sit on and paved areas where wheelchairs could be parked.

The main reception area was small but functional, with two low sofas and an armchair around a glass coffee table. There were two employees behind a teak counter, a young man in his twenties with blue-framed spectacles and curly hair whom Lulu knew only as Gary, and an older woman in a dark blue suit who was one of the home's duty managers, Mrs Fitzgerald. The area was overseen by two domed CCTV cameras and all visitors had to be signed in and given a stick-on badge.

Mrs Fitzgerald smiled brightly when she saw Lulu, but then her eyes widened in surprise when she saw the cat lying across her shoulders. 'Oh my goodness,' she said. 'Will you look at that?'

Gary peered through his glasses. 'Is it real?'

Lulu laughed. 'Yes, of course it's real. Do you think I'd walk around with a fake cat around my neck?'

Gary's cheeks reddened and he shrugged.

'Is it yours?' asked Mrs Fitzgerald.

'He's sort of adopted me. Is it okay if I take him in to see Emily?'

'Of course. We're animal friendly here. We always have been. Animals have a calming influence. Well, most of them. We had one of our residents who wanted to bring his venomous snake collection with him; we had to draw the line there.'

She handed Lulu a paper badge with the date and LULU LEWIS on it. Lulu stuck it on her jacket. 'Does Conrad need a badge?'

'I think he probably does,' said Mrs Fitzgerald. She wrote CONRAD on another badge and gave it to Lulu, who stuck it onto her shoulder, just below Conrad's head.

There were glass doors to the left and right; Lulu went through the ones on the right. The door slid open electronically and she walked down a corridor and then up a flight of stairs to the first floor. There was a lift but Lulu always preferred to use the stairs.

'These places always smell the same,' said Conrad. 'Pee and disinfectant. I'm told that prisons smell the same.'

'Who told you that?'

'A cat who had been into a prison, obviously,' said Conrad.

They reached the first floor and Lulu walked along another corridor to Emily's room. To the left of the door was a small frame and inside it was a typed card. EMILY LEWIS. The typed card and the frame always worried Lulu. It was nice that everyone would know who was inside, but there was a lack of permanence about it: it would be all too easy to slide out the card and slip in another one.

She knocked quietly on the door and then slowly turned the handle. Emily was sitting in the high-backed armchair next to her bed. Her eyes were closed and they stayed closed as Lulu walked over and stood next to the bed. It was a hospital bed with sides that could be raised. Emily had fallen out of bed four months earlier. Luckily she hadn't broken anything but she had been badly bruised so the home had brought in the special bed for her. The cost – an extra hundred pounds a week – had been added to Emily's monthly bill. That seemed a little steep to Lulu; when she had googled the model she'd found similar beds available online for less than seven hundred pounds.

The staff had dressed Emily, probably after giving her a bath or at least a good wash, and brushed her hair. They usually took her down to the restaurant on the ground floor for breakfast. After breakfast she either returned to her room or went to sit out in the garden. Then she'd have lunch.

The Cat Who Solved Three Murders

Retired police detective Lulu Lewis's life changed for ever when she met a street cat named Conrad. There's something very special about Conrad, but it's a secret she has to keep to herself.

When Lulu takes her narrowboat to Oxford, she is planning nothing more stressful than attending a friend's birthday party. And drinking a few glasses of Chardonnay.

But a brutal murder and a daring art theft mean her plans are shattered – instead, she and Conrad find themselves on the trail of a killer.

A killer who may well strike again . . .

Out now!

The Cat Who Cracked a Cold Case

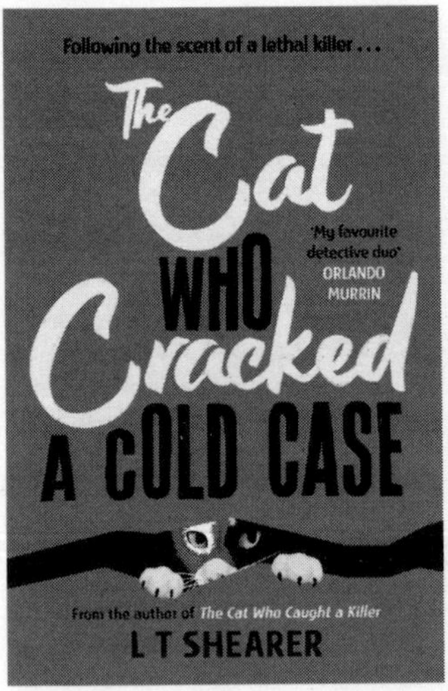

The life of Lulu Lewis, a retired police detective, took an unforgettable turn when Conrad first introduced himself to her. Unforgettable because:
a) Conrad is a special cat;
b) he told her this himself.
Yes, that's right, he can talk.

Visiting an old friend in Manchester, the pair stumble across a chilling news report about a trail of bodies found across the city that echoes a string of cold-case murders from Lulu's past in London.

Joining forces with the local police, the pair must use every ounce of their intuition in order to find a connection between the seemingly random killings – and track down a ruthless murderer . . .

Out now!

The Cat and the Christmas Kidnapper

Join Lulu Lewis, a retired detective with a knack for uncovering secrets, and Conrad, her extraordinary talking cat, as Christmas cheer gives way to festive fear . . .

Hoping for a relaxing festive break, Lulu sets off with Conrad on her canal boat, *The Lark*, to visit friends in the picturesque city of Bath. But when the pair arrive, they learn of a ruthless kidnapping plot that is plaguing parents in the area.

As the kidnappers fuel panic with further demands, the pair must unravel clues faster than Conrad can charm with his witty banter if they are to stand any chance of bringing the criminals to justice in time to save the holidays . . .

Out now!